INVASION ENGLAND 1917

BY

ARTHUR RHODES

Third Millennium Publishing
A Cooperative of Writers and Resources
On the INTERNET at 3mpub.com
http://3mpub.com

ISBN 1-929381-96-4
256 pages

Production Manager – Lennie Adelman

Third Millennium Publishing
1931 East Libra Drive
Tempe, AZ 85283
mccollum@3mpub.com

TABLE OF CONTENTS

CHAPTER 1

4/15/1914

The giant German Zeppelin eased slowly over the tide line of the Scottish coast. The sea flattening through the swell, still bumpy for small boats. Dawn was an hour away and the Zeppelin guided by the stars over the North Sea descended into a damp wet fog, that was hovering over the beach. They were almost blind at sea level.

The captain turned to the commander, Count Zastrov. "Sir, we are here, our navigator tells me exactly at our prescribed destination."

Count Zastrov's scowl indicated he expected nothing less. The captain inadvertently felt a chill, nothing pleased the Count and any communication could result in a criticism or worse. All his captains were afraid of the Count for good reasons. Death was an option for failure.

Zastrov picked up a black folder, opened the door of the cabin, and holding his valuable papers descended down the rope ladder. His heavy black leather outfit shielded him from the dampness and the embers of his cigar, the only light on the beach. His eyes and adjusted to the darkness and the rocky ground, and he could see a cottage set against the cliff. He walked fifty yards to the cottage and stopped when he saw the figure standing in front of him.

The man in a large gray coat spoke first. "Count?"

The Count responded. "Mr. X?"

The man held the door open and Count Zastrov stepped into the warmth of a small room with a coal stove, the smell distinctively a smell of the sea. It was awkward, the Count did not know how to address the stranger. The code signal seemed inadequate for their business.

"I brought the letter," Zastrov said.

Mr. X turned the oil lamp up on the table and took the folder from Count Zastrov.

"The Kaiser signed?" he asked.

"Yes, as you asked."

The Count looked at the man's eyes, they were sad. *I would be sad too if I was about to betray my country*, he thought.

The Englishman spread the letter on the table and read it intently. He recognized the signature.

Now the Count questioned. "If that is alright, do you have something for me?"

Mr. X pulled a brief case from under the table and spread the map on the table next to the letter.

Count Zastrov traced his finger over the map. "This is the entrance to the harbor."

"Yes."

He continued. "The dotted lines are submarine nets and these are barrage balloons."

The answer was barely audible. "Yes."

The Count recognized where battleships and cruisers would be anchored.

Zastrov almost smiled, it was the complete anchorage of the famous English base by the Orkney Islands, at Scapa Flow, Scotland. Even the mine-fields were clear on the map. The Count wanted to leave. He had the information the high command sent him for. He folded the map.

"You have the letter, I have the map, we should part."

The Englishman continued to look grim. He stood up, neither man wanted to shake hands, both felt uncomfortable.

The Count went quickly through the door and walked towards the Zeppelin. Who was the Englishman, a man so powerful he had the plans to Scapa Flow and received a letter from the Kaiser? Zastrov did not know what the letter said, but what could be so valuable that it was worth the plans for the anchorage of the English Northern Fleet. If war was to come the Zeppelins could attack Scapa with these plans and would guarantee great damage. There were blood ties from the Kaiser's family to the royalty in England. Was this man a relative?

Zastrov reached the rope ladder. Better not to speculate. He would forget the Englishman.

He did not look back. The plans he held could mean the destruction of half of the greatest navy in the world. The Zeppelin could not accomplish this alone, but combined with surface vessels and submarines a surprise attack would be devastating. Zastrov thought the English always kept part of the fleet at sea. It would be unusual for the whole Northern Fleet to be at Scapa but his superior

Prince Rupprecht had sent him on this mission. The Prince would have a plan. He always did. The Kaiser was the ruler, but the Prince was in charge of the German military machine and the one who supported the Zeppelins.

As the Zeppelin lifted off the first rays of the sun appeared on the horizon. The ship was quiet the officers and crew glad to be away from the Scottish coast. It was 1914, the sun was coming up but the clouds over Europe were dark. A great war was just over the horizon.

The *New York World* reporter Matty Stevenson walked gingerly into the office of the German leader, the Kaiser. This was the first interview ever by the press, of the powerful man. The Kaiser negative when his staff asked him to speak to the American said, "Why an American, a country of wild Indians and cowboys, not a serious country, besides, what do we care what the press thinks."

The Staff careful to time the request after an army maneuver, accompanied with a successful social event made the best possible argument to their leader.

"Sire, the Krupp Steel Works, think the Americans will be good customers for our steel. We want the world to know we make the best steel. The Americans are not sophisticated, they believe the English propagandist that we are the war-mongers in Europe. The White House is not friendly to us. If the American public and business men could understand what Germany stands for, it would negate some of the English propaganda and create a new market for our steel."

The Kaiser was very proud of German steel, he believed the great guns of Krupp the harbinger of German might. The Kaiser did not understand or respect public opinion. The world was ruled by Kings whose word and wishes moved nations. The staff understood his feelings.

"Sire, your cousin the King of England would not speak to this reporter, we believe he was afraid because his nations positions are weak."

The Kaiser cleared his throat.

"My cousin was afraid? What foolishness. I will see the man, but only for thirty minutes."

The Kaiser had a strong inferiority complex about the English throne. He wouldn't miss an opportunity to show he was superior.

The Americans should learn about Krupp Steel and the German army of many millions of men. The Kaiser assumed once the reporter understood these facts there would be little else to talk about. He had never dealt with the press before.

The Kaiser sat behind a very large desk. The rug insignia was his family coat-of-arms. Stevenson had to stand, his notebook in his hand.

"Your Majesty, are you worried about a war in Europe?"

The first question set the tone. The Kaiser did not expect such a question.

"No, there will be no war in Europe. We are civilized and I will speak to my relatives in England and Russia. We can stop any war."

Stevenson, prepared for a response that supported the divine right of Kings, came back with the ugly reality of a boiling Europe.

"Sir, the Czar of Russia said he will defend Serbia. If Austria puts Serbia in an impossible position, will not Russia fight?"

This was the kind of detail Prince Rupprecht handled and not the concern of the Kaiser.

"The Austrians will clear any policy with us, we are allies."

He was proud of his answer, that should settle that question.

Stevenson said, "An Austrian ultimatum to Serbia caused Sergei Sazanov of Russia to order up a preliminary call of reserves."

The Kaiser hunting on his estates the previous three days was not told of this. He did not answer. Then muttered. "I hadn't heard probably not important."

Stevenson expecting a distant and out of touch monarch was shocked by his lack of knowledge. Was this man really in charge of his country or did he see the arming of all these countries just another war game to be stopped and stared at the referees signal?"

Stevenson a good reporter had obtained the German train schedule in case of war. The schedule called for 550 trains a day to cross the Rhine bridges, and over three million men to be carried to the front on eleven thousand trains. A bridge at Cologne would see a train passed every ten minutes. The organization was staggering, and impressive. Stevenson probed with a question.

"Sir, your train schedule, once it starts, could it be stopped? Can anyone even the leader control it?"

The Kaiser indicated his annoyance with the question.

"Young man, I am the Kaiser, I don't deal in train schedules.

My generals take care of details. Kings have more important concerns."

The Kaiser sought to regain his authority.

"I repeat, Austria does nothing without us, Franz Joseph always views Germany as his senior partner in our relationship. Have you spoken to Emperor Franz Joseph?"

"Sir, I have not, can you use your good offices to introduce me?"

The Kaiser rose to the bait, "If I say he speaks to you, he speaks. Don't you understand Germany is senior."

He was arguing with himself. The Kaiser went from not wanting to talk to reporters to demanding members of his government and Allies to answer questions. Stevenson wondered how the Kaiser's generals would react.

Next Stevenson went to see the Czar of Russia, a far different interview. If the Kaiser was confident, the Czar was worried.

"We are on the brink of war. Austria is using the assassination of the Archduke to crush Serbia, and my government will be forced to react. Austria-Hungary is not formidable, she is a nation of different peoples, different languages and the Emperor is old, but his Ministers ambitious. The problem is Germany will back her up as we and France are united."

Stevenson explained the Kaiser believed he could stop a war.

The Czar shook his head sadly. "The Kaiser and I rule great countries, but once the wheel of mobilization starts can anyone stop it?" he spread his arms helplessly not knowing the answer, but unlike many in power, smart enough to realize he was being carried along by a tide.

"My generals will tell me, we will be defenseless if we don't arm. His generals will say the same thing to the Kaiser, we may not control our destiny."

Stevenson decided to be bold. "Sir, is Serbia worth a world war, a war that will engage millions?"

For twenty minutes the Czar continued to talk, but always returned to the same theme. Years of preparation was more important then any spontaneous quest for peace. The technical cadence of armies not to be disturbed by anyone, King, Kaiser or Czar.

Stevenson thought to himself. "He's just like the Kaiser, he doesn't have any control over the situation.

My God, this whole thing is out of control, the world is hurtling to war, the greatest war in history and some generals at a railroad sidings will start it because he doesn't want some train to the Front to be five minutes late.

All the diplomats, the Kings, the soldiers all were truly waiting for a railroad time table confident they could easily win because they know the overwhelming power their country possesses but very few analyzed the enemies strength.

Stevenson returned to England and met Sir Edward Gray. Gray met with Parliament the day before and said, "No English Army was committed to the Continent." Everyone was talking war when Stevenson met Gray.

"Sir, you told the Parliament British troops may not go to France in case of war. Will England blockade the Continent with its navy?"

"We are committed to the side of France and Russia. King George tried last night to telegraph the Czar and the Kaiser, but we were too late. Hostilities have broken out.

Matty. "So it's decided?"

Gray could not pretend it was good news, but he shared the English strategy.

"We will now send an army under Sir John French to France."

"Sir, the Germans are considered to have the greatest army in the world, and new weapons. They have eighty-seven divisions, and an outstanding General Staff. Can you see a land victory over them?"

Gray knew Stevenson and had great respect for him. "Off the record."

"Sir, if you tell me I will never print anything you say."

"The outcome of the land war with great armies cannot be predicted on the Continent.

We in England have the great Navies, our home fleet is operating out of Scapa Flow.

Our second Southern Fleet is in the Mediterranean. Neither of these Fleets can be challenged though we know Germany has some powerful ships. The war may ebb and flow in France, the political situation in Russia is uncertain, but no German soldier will ever put foot on English soil."

The English Navy would dominate the British contribution to the war. A small army would cross to France to fight the Germans, the Germans and Austria-Hungary faced a two front war. The Germans, the French and English in the west the Russians in the rear. Austria, Hungary would face Russia and Serbia. Both hoped to knock out one opponent quickly and gather to oppose the other.

France began with an attack against the German Center and when that failed moved to protect Belgium and the Channel Ports. If the early plans did not succeed a war beyond the imagination would unfold. Both sides would pursue new Allies, -- Italy, Turkey and others.

Submarine warfare and other new unexpected battlegrounds, the air, Europe was a three dimension battlefield.

CHAPTER 2

The Tiger Soccer Club joined the German Army in Belgium on the second day of the war. The Tigers, eight young men from Stuttgart enlisted together and were assigned to the same squad. Four other members of their team were serving in Russia. The group in Belgium followed the new Corporal, their former captain and goalie Lars Hollweg. Hollweg, tall and thin was quiet, he was a born leader. His second in command was Fredrick who never stopped talking. The Gossip, he would tell secrets, spread rumors and was the perfect squads ear to the Units Headquarters. As they marched along the road Fredrick at Lars' side relayed what he had heard that morning.

"Hear that firing Lars? The French are up ahead, we'll see them later today."

Lars was thinking of food for the Squad, no dinner last night and only coffee for breakfast, the boys were hungry.

Fredrick didn't care, he wanted to talk. "Back at Headquarters they told me Captain Rommel met the French this morning. Has a platoon attached to a farmhouse and they captured twenty-five French soldiers. They all say the captain will be a general some day."

Lars questioned. "He's the short officer?"

"Yes. He's not big, but he's very active and aggressive. First day, and I heard the other officers talking about him, they all admire him. I think everyone wants to perform as well as he did. There is going to be pressure on both the officers and the men. Lars, if we see action we have to do our best."

Lars thought, it might be a long war, but that was an impressing start.

The Lieutenant pulled abreast on his horse, clearly he favored Hollweg as a young man who got jobs done. "Corporal, I have an assignment. Belgian soldiers were sniping at us, we captured four of them. They killed a Private. Our orders are, snipers behind our lines are to be treated as saboteurs. Take your Squad up to that house." He pointed to a house by the road one hundred yards ahead.

"You will execute them"

For a moment Lars froze and realized the Tigers would be a Firing Squad . He felt the pit of his stomach roll. The first action, a Firing Squad.

"Get to that farmhouse, take control of the four prisoners. I'll be with you in ten minutes." The Lieutenant rode off.

With a heavy heart Lars directed his Squad to the farmhouse and took over the four Belgian prisoners. One was a young boy, the second an old man with few teeth, the third a drunk and finally a sad looking Belgian Private, his uniform muddy. Could this be a mistake, Lars thought, this couldn't be the enemy? How could we shoot them?

He told Fredrick their orders. Fredrick responded with the gossip from Headquarters.

"They are saying Belgian civilians are sniping at our troops and we need to teach them a lesson. This group of four maybe innocent, but the Lieutenant needs to show Headquarters he's in the war.

After Rommel's action everyone will be motivated to do their duty."

Lars agreed. He was right. They must obey orders, the army would not excuse a young Corporal on the second day of the war who flinched from a direct order. The gloomy sky mirrored Lars' mood. He told Fredrick to bring Teddy over. Teddy the second oldest was the Tiger whiner. He would upset the others if allowed to voice his opinions. Fredrick looked down as Lars told Teddy what was about to happen.

"Teddy, they want us to shoot these four."

"Shoot them?" Teddy's face was frozen in horror.

"We can't, one is a kid." Lars expected an argument.

"You know from our training to question an order on a battlefield is a court martial offense.

We must obey."

Fredrick continued to stare at the ground. This was Lars decision to handle, so Lars explained. "Headquarters wants to teach the Belgians a lesson."

Fredrick looked at the four prisoners leaning or sitting against the wall. Could they just shoot two, the drunk and the sad looking Private? The kid and the old man were not dangerous. Frederick decided not to volunteer the idea. He didn't want any part of the responsibility or any part of the decision making.

The white washed farmhouse wall was a symbol of the bleak day and bleak mood of the Corporal. *If we have to shoot them, I'm going to miss,* Teddy thought.

Teddy pleaded, "Lars can't you talk to the Lieutenant"

Lars took off his helmet. "I'll ask for a clarification of the order, that's all I can do."

Now Lars got mad. "Teddy, I give you permission to challenge the Lieutenant." His face red, Teddy did not answer. The former Captain of the Tigers decided the discussion was over. No one was going to challenge any orders, it was time to take control. He was responsible.

"Look, we three are the oldest, we have the stripes, the other five will follow us. This is a war zone the Lieutenant saw Captain Rommel attack the enemy. He's not going to permit any wavering by his men."

"The Belgians killed one of our soldiers, and the officer decided these four did it." Lars's back was to the four prisoners.

Teddy looked at the prisoners. "Goddam Lars, its not suppose to be like this."

Lars wanted Frederick to get involved, he's second in command.

"Fredrick, what do you think?"

Fredrick shrank back, he seemed to get smaller. "I don't like it." That was all he would say.

Lars Pulled his jacket tighter. The decision was made.

"Enough discussion, if the Lieutenant gives us an order we're going to obey, we'll shoot the prisoners, you each go tell the others what's going to happen. Tell everyone if they shoot to miss we have to do it again. So lets get this done and get it done the first time."

Lars could see Fredrick and Teddy wanted to be told what to do. By somehow obeying orders they were not guilty.

"After you tell the others tell them to come over to me and you two guard the prisoners."

Lars looked out to the marching column of German soldiers moving to the Front. He wished he was with them. God, he felt bad.

Now the five Privates surrounded Lars. Holtzen the Bull, the best defensive player on the team, a cigarette in his ear would obey orders. The other men respected, and were a little afraid of Holtzen.

Lars would anchor one end of the line, and he would put Holtzen at the other end of the Firing Squad.

Golovin the slim forward, the baby of the group, not yet eighteen.

Bachman the most homesick. He hated the army, and Zimmerman, the gripper, always behaving as if someone had cheated him.

The eighth man was Tuggel. Lars began. "We are going to be given orders to shoot these four. Its not a choice, its an order. I'm in charge, and I don't have a choice, and neither do you."

Four did not answer, they had been told the choices by Fredrick and Teddy. Zimmerman gripped.

"Why us, I'm not volunteering for this?"

Lars decided the issue was settled. "I volunteered you, and the Lieutenant volunteered all eight of us. This is the army and war, we're not back at school. I've told the others, we're all in this, now grow up quick."

Lars boxed in the Squad.

"Holtzen you take the extreme left, I'll stand on the right."

Holtzen settled the issue.

"Lars, I'm on the left, you give the order to fire I will obey."

The Lieutenant rode up on his horse.

"Corporal, line up the prisoners against the farmhouse wall and execute the sentence."

The Lieutenants crisp direction decided the issue.   Lars ordered the men to line up the prisoners. The Squad pushed the prisoners against the wall splashed with slogans in French that attacked the Germans. It didn't make it easier. The old man with the missing teeth was mentally retarded, his head nodded and his lips moved in a conversation with his gods. The drunk leaned against the wall oblivious of his fate. Tears rolled down the cheeks of the young boy who carried water to the soldiers, his Belgian Army hat the only sign he was a combatant. The one soldier a Belgian Private had never fired his gun. None protested, they were told to expect no mercy from the Germans.

Lars could see his men felt sorry for themselves, not the prisoners. He did what for years he had done with this group. He took charge.

"Line up." He ordered. He took a position to the extreme right of the ragged line.

"Ready! He raised his rifle, then turned his head, his stare brought the other rifles to the ready. Teddy was slow, but he obeyed.

"Fire." A ripple of rifle fire and it was done.

The Lieutenant spurred off his horse. The Corporal completed the assignment. His judgment correct, the young man was a leader, the Squad an extension of him. The Lieutenant made a mental note. He would never waste this group in a suicide charge, they would be treated as special, the Corporal trusted to execute important and critical assignments. Until the Lieutenant was killed two years later, this spared the Squad casualties. It started to rain, and the four bodies lying in the mud against the wall were forgotten by all but the youngest, Golovin who said a quick prayer, then hurried after the Lieutenant and the marching columns heading for the Front.

The Squad was quiet as they marched. Holtzen said to Lars. "If they were shooting at us we have to respond, I'd do it again."

Lars realized this was war, he needed the ruthless, toughness of Holtzen and instinctively he guessed the Lieutenant was pleased that a dirty job was well done.

All that day German soldiers shot captured Belgian soldiers and private citizens. The glorious war was over, the dirty mean war started quickly. Next day some Frenchmen were captured but not shot.

The first casualty of the Squad was Zimmerman. Hit in the stomach crossing a small stream, they carried him to an Aid Station, recognizing they were lucky, with only one down. Many other Units suffered far worse.

Holtzen the Bull proved he was the best soldier on the Squad, crawling under the fire of a French machine gun and dispatching it with grenades.

War started in Europe, but mobilization just starting in England. The week after the Germans moved into Belgium volunteers at a London draft Board rioted. The Board announced they did not have uniforms and equipment for the men, and would have to return in two weeks. The rioters were afraid the war would be over before they got a chance to serve. This delusion surfaced all over Europe. The home country strong, the enemy weak, the war over quickly. For nobility, policemen, military, civilians, clergy, and press the war was beginning clean and easy. Within one year many of the mistaken would be dead.

#

After the first week, the Kaiser was stunned when he saw the early casualty figures despite good German success. The Russians caused a German crisis on the Eastern Front when they mobilized faster and at greater strength than expected.

The Germans overran Belgium and Northeast France. Great battles were fought against the Russians. The Germans were the first to realize the power of the defense. A stalemate settled on the Western Front, which zapped the enthusiasm of both sides.

It was a defensive war, barbed wire and massed machine guns with millions of men in trenches. A frontal attack was unlikely to succeed and it guaranteed heavy losses. The German and the English recognized this but the French continued to bleed their Infantry.

Both sides triumphed, heroes, the German Erwin Rommel and Erich Ludendorff. Ludendorff confronted the fortress of Leige, a central citadel in the city surrounded by a circular chain of smaller Forts. He executed his master plan. The Infantry broke into the main Fort, but the outer fortresses refused to surrender. Ludendorff brought up his big Howitzers and shelled, destroying the positions one by one.

The English gunner Thompson alone held off the enemy until his fellow soldiers at Mons were safe. Heroes like Thompson muffled the shock of the many casualties, but officers and men began to realize it was a different war than they were prepared for.

CHAPTER 3

The assembled crews of the Zeppelin stood at attention in the bright sun waiting for Prince Rupprecht. At attention, they stood taller, when the two modern cars were observed driving on the road next to the river Elb, at Nordholz, Germany. Count Zastrov assembled ten crews at dawn in anticipation of the famous Prince's arrival. Rupprecht held a distinction in the Germany Army, not only was he a leader of the Sixth Army, but he was very popular with his men, unusual for such a high ranking officer. A slender man, his thin blonde mustache dominated a hawk like face. He wore few medals, but the braids on his field marshal's headgear conveyed all the authority he needed. The rest of the staff considered the Zeppelins good for scouting, but the Prince held long discussions with the Count and envisioned a different place in the war for the giant ships.

No senior officer had ever visited the base before today. Now the long anticipated review by Rupprecht.

Zastrov required by Rupprecht to submit a plan for heavy bombing, saluted as the Prince descended from his car.

The Prince extended his hand.

"So Zastrov, these are your airships?" They shook hands and Zastrov said.

"Sir, I welcome you to the base. The ships are ready for your inspection."

Rupprecht put him at ease. "Yes, I want to see the ships but first let me speak to your crews."

Zastrov who never thought of the men as anything but an extension of the Zeppelins was not pleased. The review would come first.

Rupprecht recognized Zastrov's professionalism in flying the Great Ships, and also suspected he was not a man that cared for the crews. The Prince was a good manager of men, his generals came in all sizes and shapes, the test was success in battle and the Prince believed that Zastrov would pass that exam even if his methods were heavy handed.

Rupprecht suspected the men had waited a long time and he

deliberately went down the two lines asking many questions and listening intently to the answers.

Finally the Prince and Zastrov inspected the first ships.

"Prince, the Zeppelin is five hundred plus feet long, the engine generates two hundred twenty horse power," said Zastrov

Prince. "The ship is so big she should scare the enemy."

"Sir, we have plans to wage psychological warfare."

"Good, anything that wins the battle. We are stuck on the Western Front, we need a break through."

They climbed into the cabin.

Prince. "The new hull is extra strong, the steel stays give us the capacity to drop three one thousand pound bombs."

Rupprecht was impressed.

"This is a much greater bomb load then you carried before."

"Yes, much greater."

They walked inside the hull, examined the engines, gangways, and climbed up and down ladders. Rupprecht wanted to see everything. He carefully looked at the gas cylinder, oil and fuel tanks and moved quickly down the narrow corridors. In the cabin Rupprecht asked.

"Is this the rudder control?"

"Yes."

"And the new bomb release you told me about?"

The Count puffed up his chest. "Yes, our new electric bomb release is far more accurate than what we used in the past."

The Prince asked. "In your letter you described this as a terror weapon."

"Yes, we plan to line up in a formation of ten, each ship will drop a bomb every two minutes. We have thirty bombs, and in addition the noise you will hear will proceed each drop. Please, hold your ears, it is very loud." Zastrov signaled and a blood stopping horn emitted a sound that would wake the dead. It was a fog horn from a tugboat in the North Sea

"That was a fog horn used in the North Sea, we think it will scare the French."

Rupprecht nodded. "It will."

He questioned. "Can the French guns reach you at ten thousand feet?"

"No, they cannot reach us." Rupprecht looked very serious.

"The Fort you are to attack, has held us for five weeks. I have over one hundred thousand casualties, it is a key position, break the Fort and we open up the whole Front. We open the battle with an artillery duel with the Fort, then your Zeppelins attack and I have picked Storm Troopers to follow up. We need a crack, just a crack, to open up the Fort and it is the beginning!"

After the Prince left Zastrov addressed his crews.

"You have your orders, let no man waiver, Prince Rupprecht and the Kaiser are watching us. My honor is at stake, we attack until the Fort is broken. This is the first combined air ground strike in military history, and I intend to make history. Let no man disappoint me."

One captain had a question. "What if the French surrender?"

The Count answered. "We will continue bombing, and not until we see the Storm Troopers enter the Fort do we stop."

A second question. "Will the French send planes to attack us?"

"We have an escort and the French bullets cannot penetrate our balloon. We also believe that at our height they will have trouble aiming and most bullets will miss us."

This was the Counts greatest moment. All his life he wanted the glory that was just hours away. Not a regular army officer his ambition was greater than a single victory on the Western Front.

He did not invent, build or design the Zeppelin, but it was his drive that maximized the weapon.

The German Army was top heavy with aristocrats, men born to high positions. The Count longed to be accepted in Berlin at the Clubs and social events that recognized the heroes of the German Army. No one must fail him.

The weather was perfect, no clouds. The Fort, an old structure was vulnerable to their bombs. The Prince, a fair man would reward performance. The Count thought only of himself and did not concern himself about the crews. The Prince realized the Count was a selfish prima Donna, but this was a hard war that demanded hard men and that the Count was.

The Prince left a detailed plan for the bombing of the Fort to the Count. The mission was set.

The Key to the defense of the French Forts was the machine gun crews of Captain Renee Sarrall. Despite numerous attempts, the German Infantry couldn't break Sarrall's men. With more then half the original company casualties, the Units of Sarrall stood like a rock. Because of loyalty to the captain. Sarrall was at the critical point in the defense of the Fort for two reasons. He was the best young officer in the French Army, and he was the most outspoken officer against the bleeding of the French Infantry in the trenches, attacking machine guns without support. The generals respected him and disliked him for his protests.

Sarrall spoke to his second in command. "The German artillery is heavy, I expect an attack. Are the men ready?"

"Yes sir, I checked, we have extra ammunition as you ordered."

Sarrall held up his hand. "There go our guns, it will be a hot morning, make sure we have plenty of water. I will inspect all the gun crews in half an hour."

Captain Sarrall was always with the men when a German attack was expected.

At the Fort, the artillery of both sides pounded at each other. After a two hour artillery duel, the giant Zeppelins lined up for the bombing runs. The terrible sound of the horn proceeded the dropping of the first bombs. The initial three bombs destroyed the roof of the middle Fort. Only one Zeppelin did not drop its bombs on the first run.

As Count Zastrov lined up his ships for a second run a mighty fire began to spread with billowing smoke and exploding flames that signaled they hit the ammunition dump. French soldiers began to leave the Fort to flee the flames. Hundreds, then thousands were leaving the Fort and running to the rear.

Captain Sarrell's men carried the wounded captain from the Front lines, bleeding from the mouth. He had a head wound. The captain awoke and protested, then he passed out.

The Count seeing the French fleeing yelled. "Bomb the roads, they have to use the roads, slaughter them all."

Two roads away from the Fort were clogged with men running. The Zeppelins descended to five thousand feet and the bombs and the horn spread terror. It was a route, and before the Storm Troopers could enter the burning Fort men trapped inside began to surrender.

When Zastrov returned to his base a telegram from the Prince announced the victory and summoned Zastrov to come to the Headquarters for a strategy meeting.

Zastrov's staff knew better then to expect he would be happy.

The commander who did not drop his bombs was ordered to Zastrov's Zeppelin, which took off just after he arrived.

For ten minutes Zastrov yelled at the poor man.

"You failed me, Kutler."

"Sir, we were having trouble with the electric switch."

"That was to be checked before you took off. I told you no one should fail me, because I would take it personally."

"Sir, please give me another chance."

Zastrov stood up and motioned the door to the cabin be opened. Zastrov was working himself up, getting madder and madder. He motioned to two crew members to stand the captain next to the open door. They were six thousand feet above the earth.

Zastrov teased the captain. "If I break you that's not much punishment. The crews must know we fight for the Fatherland, failure results in death. Any of the Storm Troopers would have been shot today if they failed their mission."

The man was trembling, Zastrov had him thrown out of the open door.

CHAPTER 4

The German armies and the Tiger Soccer Team moved through Belgium with the German general staff reporting great victories. The French Army retreated along the coast, but the French generals continued to send their Infantry against German machine guns with disastrous results. French enthusiasm was not enough, audacity and spirit, no substitute for firepower. The Germans again claimed victory, but the Chief of Staff asked where were the long lines of prisoners. The French were retreating but not leaving behind field guns or showing signs they were defeated. The French finally made a stand at the Marne River. The Marne joined the Seine not far from Paris, and several other rivers joined the Marne. These waterways disorganized the German advance.

The French and the English struck and the German advance halted. With the German Army frustrated, they caught the French disease, no reconnaissance, little artillery preparation or support, and soldiers sacrificed for the leaders incompetence. The battle of the Marne lasted four days and marked the last chance for the Germans to end the war quickly. Over a million Germans and one million French faced each other. Attack and counter attack, the battle ebbed and flowed, Paris was saved. Later it would be seen as a missed opportunity for the Germans, they should have occupied the Channel ports during the initial advance, but the right wing was not strong enough. Their plans for a short war thwarted.

The Tiger Soccer Team Army Squad did not spend time on great strategy evaluations. Every day was the same to them, for thirty three days it was marching and fighting, carrying heavy packs of weapons and ammunition. The young men considered themselves strong but the found it difficult to keep up with the older veterans.

The veterans experience carried them over the hard days and long nights. The strain on the German rail system added to the troops misery. From the railroad to where ammunition was brought was further and further away from the forward units. In addition, to the long lines of marching Infantry were lines of lorries, vans and horse drawn transports.

The Tigers, sitting in an old apple orchard by the side of the road were exhausted. Like the team the Squad had its leaders. Lars Hollweg was calm and steady, just the way he played soccer. He directed the Squad, never rattled, always sure never asking the impossible. Corporal Fredrick was the conduit to the outside world, he brought the mail usually carried the orders from the Lieutenant to Lars and controlled the Units gossip.

Holtzen the Bull defender was the bravest member of the Squad. Always moving forward, his greatest talent was to flatten himself against the ground and still wiggle forward.

The five who struggled the most in their new roles as soldiers were represented by Bachman, whose homesickness and daily complaining got on everyone's nerves, until Lars told him to keep quiet. Then Bachman grew inward and silent. Zimmerman the first casualty was in the hospital. Teddy continued to shirk responsibility always ready to go on sick call and never moved forward if he could find a reason to hang back. Golovin the younger followed the lead of Bachman growing more silent by the day, and Tuggel who was always sick.

Fredrick came back from mail call. "I've got a letter from the Tigers in the East."

The four Tigers in the East were younger and they entered the army two days later then Lars's group. The leader of the second group was Corporal Smuts, the son of the Mayor of the town. As a budding politician he was aggressive, loud and not the best liked of the team. He wrote twice as many letters to Fredrick as he received from the first group.

Fredrick read aloud. *"It's Smuts, he begins from the Tigers of the East, the victors of Tannenburg. Led by our great Generals Hindenburg and Ludendorff we vanquished the Russian Army at a place called Tannenburg."*

The last line brought great laughs and whoops.

The young Golovin said, "Even I've heard of Tannenburg and the great victory in the East."

Bachman. "Only Smuts would say we are trouncing the Russians. Lars, do we all work for Smuts some day?"

Lars put down his cigar. "After the war, sure we will all work for him. Holtzen will you work for him?"

The Bull quiet, enjoyed Lars's pulling him into the conversation.

"Hell no, I won't work for him. My fathers butcher shop pays too much taxes to his father now."

Teddy. "I can just see Hindenburg and Ludendorff asking Smuts advice. Smuts is not only a great politician, but a great general."

Even Bachman responded. "He takes credit for Tannenburg. I'm surprised he's aware of where it is."

Fredrick continued reading the letter. *"The Russian generals were so confused they had a fight at a railroad station. We waited for them to fall in our laps. We surrounded them near the Bossau Lake, where many drowned. The Russian's were starving and exhausted, they started to surrender in the thousands, but they became lost in the trees with no food or water. We turned giant searchlights on them then machined gunned them. They grew so desperate their General Samsonov committed suicide."*

The Squad was quiet, it was judged that a great victory would be gained in France and the war end quickly, but instead a great victory in the East against the Russians.

Fredrick concluded and then opened a second letter addressed to the Tigers. He did not recognize the handwriting. The letter was from a Corporal Ludwig, addressed to Lars and Fredrick.

"I am Corporal Ludwig. Smuts and your friends were in my Squad. We were pursuing the Russians after the victory at Tannenburg, and your four friends got separated from the main group and got lost in a swamp. When we realized they were missing I sent out scouts looking for them. The scouts heard shooting in the distance. We followed the sounds and found your four friends on a little island in the middle of the swamp. They were trapped, but they made a stand against the Russians but there must have been too many. Your friends died a heroes death defending the Fatherland, we will miss them, as gallant soldiers. Smuts always carried a picture of the team, said it was taken the day you won the championship of the city. He loved the team always talking about you all, said it was the biggest thing in his life. Sad you were separated by the war. After the war he said you were going to form a club team and keep playing. I'm sorry I have to write this letter but I wish you well and hope we all contribute to the Germanys final victory."

Teddy was weeping, Fredrick his voice hoarse couldn't continue.

Bachman said bitterly. "Not a long life, thank god they died heroes. Death if they died as cowards I would have........." his voice trailed off, his sarcasm deep and bitter.

Lars turned away, he could not face the rest of the Squad. The first Tiger deaths, but how many more before the war would be over? Lars walked away from the group, he ignored the tears of several of the Squad. This was the lowest point of the war, even worse then shooting the Belgian civilians. He was sad, but beyond that he was worried. The several months of the war and battle action convinced him of one thing. It was his job to keep the group safe and alive. The war was not a one day event, Germany didn't need dead heroes, he and the country needed experienced veterans who did their job well. By now he understood the pact he had with the promoted captain. The captain held the Squad out of harms way and they were asked to do special jobs. Twice they were held back from bloody charges and then a special night reconnaissance that was very successful. They captured a French captain who revealed important gun positions.

Lars felt himself alone, it was his leadership that kept the Squad on an even keel, aggressive, but not a fool-hardy. How long could he carry the burden by himself? Someone in the Squad had to become his partner.

Lars would give the orders, but a strong second voice was needed to confirm the Squads efforts for the good for Germany, as well as good for the Squad. Could he motivate Fredrick who was smart and much attuned to the workings of the army and Headquarters? No, the Squad didn't respect Fredrick, he was too much of a gossip, never took a stand. He was weak, not a leader and would shrink away if he was asked to take more responsibility.

The logical other was Teddy, second in rank, but he was the whiner, always complaining. Lars worked hard to make sure he did not divide the Squad.

The logical second voice of the Squad was Holtzen, the Bull. The bravest and best soldier of all the men. The night they captured the French captain, he vaulted into the French trench and tackled the man. Holtzen was not smart, rarely joining the group talk, and always silent when they ate their meals or walked on the road. But the others were afraid of him, and would never challenge any stand he took. Yes, Holtzen had to be promoted and Lars would begin to give orders to the Bull to be relayed to the others.

Lars decided when they marched he would march next to the Bull and explain what he was doing. The others would begin to see the leadership of the unit was more than one man. Lars felt better, he had made a decision. He couldn't help the dead men on the Russian front, but he had a plan to help the men under his command. Tomorrow he would make a strong statement before they marched.

Forget their friends in Russia, they had a mission, and a responsibility to each other and then he would tell Holtzen that the captain would be asked to promote him. Lars knew he would.

Lars felt better. Lars understood the unspoken pact he had with the captain. They were to perform special tasks but not be wasted in the small ebbs and flows of the war. The captain once hinted it was Lars's job to develop other leaders in the Squad. He would do that and as long as Lars and the captain lived the Squad had a chance. Lars turned back and looked at the Squad. They were half children, he must protect them. For a moment he wanted to declare the war insane, but he brushed that thought aside. Only staying alive mattered, let others debate the war, his job was to live and keep the others alive.

CHAPTER 5

The Germans approached Paris and the French led by General Gallieni, rode to the Front in taxi cabs. The peoples war, a French division supported by the taxi cabs of Paris stopped the Germans.

The Battle of the Marne proved the chance for a quick German victory was over. France proved they could take the heavy blows of the Germans and fight back. The war would continue.

Both sides noticed that a way to flank the enemy was to occupy the Channel ports. This began the race to the sea.

It started after the Marne and ended at the seacoast with the advance of winter weather, in mid November. Neither army wanted to reach the seacoast, both wanted to get around the others flank and go into open country for another attack. This was also the beginning of trench warfare. Both sides headed North with heavy casualties in Flanders.

Generals to their horror saw gains in yards and losses in the thousands. The move North continued as the temperature dropped. The Armies moved slowly, then in short jabs as troops left the Southern and Central battlefields. The Germans turning to their right, the French to the left.

Captain Percy Howatt, English Royal Hampshire heard the machine guns despite the fact the Front was miles away. The steady rattle of machine guns... many guns, and occasional artillery fire. Howatt had never heard such a continuous fire. His Sergeant Murphy, marching next to Howatt said, "I never heard such fire, we are going into that?"

His tone was surely and argumentative, Murphy's standard position in dealing with officers. Murphy an Irishman from Canada was a very good soldier, but a distraction in the Royal Hampshire Regiment. Howatt saw him under fire, he was a leader, intelligent, but a complaining and discipline problem for the captain. A steady parade of French ambulances carrying wounded heading for the rear passed Howatt's forty men.

Howatt replied. "It's a French battle, our people are South of here. We are on a special mission, I'm to meet with the Major just ahead."

Murphy's reaction was his typical defiant challenge to authority. "I hope you didn't volunteer us, we've lost enough so far in this war."

Howatt ignored Murphy's complaining. The hundreds of French wounded, sobered the captain. They were everywhere, not enough doctors and nurses to help.

The captain entered Headquarters. He left Murphy in charge of the Company and mounted stairs of what appeared to be a City Hall. The machine gun fire almost over. Four minutes of silence.

The Major sat at a desk, his ears still ringing from the battle waged less than a mile behind him. The smoke, the noise, a minor battle, but not minor if you were there.

Howatt asked. "Sir, what happened, I could hear the machine guns from miles away."

"A French division attacked this morning. It's not a Division any more, the Germans wiped most of them out."

Howatt. "Sir, why do they do it?"

The Major. "French Infantry tactics since the days of Napoleon attack with élan and courage."

"Sir, in Napoleon's time a rifle was effective from fifty yards, today without artillery support or some way to flank, modern machine guns make such attacks suicide?" His question sincere.

The Major told his French counterpart the same thing this morning, who shrugged his shoulders and said, "He had his orders."

The Major pulled out a map. "Both sides are moving to the North, if one side can reach a flanking position they can roll up the enemy. It is not a run to the sea as the papers describe it, but a run to gain an advantageous position. The French Division we lost today is the last force we have in this area. We have word the Germans are moving two Divisions in our direction."

He pointed to the map. "If the Germans could reach the area North of this river, they could sweep behind the Allies."

Howatt was silent. Did they expect his company to attack two Divisions? The Major pointed to the map.

"See this spot on the coast?" His finger pointed to a river. "This is the River Ysen, it runs into the sea at Nieupont."

Howatt could see a dam or lock where he was pointing.

"This dam holds back a lot of water because of the heavy

rains. Most of this area is swampy and wet."

"Alright I want you to get to the dam, blow it or open the locks and flood the whole section. I have a Belgian who will guide you, he feels the water will keep the Germans from passing through. It will be as deep as six feet in some sections."

Howatt looked at the map and said. "But we don't know if we have to blow it or open the locks?"

"No, all the dams in this area are different. Some have a wheel that you can turn. If that's the case, destroy the mechanism once the flooding starts, or use explosives, but you must flood this area."

"Howatt, I asked for you because when I was told we might have to blow the dam I was aware that you had engineers who had blown bridges and you carry explosives with you. I assume enough for a dam?"

"Yes, I'm sure we have."

"Did you bring that nasty Irishman with you?"

Howatt. "Yes sir, Murphy is with me, and his Squad of Canadians."

Major. "It takes such men to win wars. Good soldiers would never go to dinner with him." The Major shook his head.

Howatt looked at the map. "The dam is about four miles from the coast. Can I go straight overland? It looks like about four hours?"

"No. The area is very swampy. We feel it will slow you down. Its best to follow this Canal. it has a narrow road on either side, good walking and cleaner. I think when you get to this small bridge turn North and head for the coast and the dam."

The Belgian was at the dam several years ago and he thinks it has a wheel that will open and flood the area, so you may not have to blow it, but we can't take a chance. You must not let those two German Divisions get past you."

"Sir, the Canal runs into the River Yser, if I could find a boat could I get to the dam quicker?"

The Major liked Howatt. He was smart. This was the kind of initiative he always demonstrated.

"Yes, I'm sure a boat could get you to the dam quicker. Use your judgment. There has been fighting on the Canal, not large scale, but you could meet Germans. Avoid them if possible, your mission is to flood the plains. The Belgian lives in this town, he is

Pierre Menher, he will guide you. He is familiar with the Canal and the river."

Lieutenant Schaeffer was exhausted, his head throbbed, the machine gun fire never stopping since the attack started at dawn. Thousands of French lay on the field dead or wounded from the German Maxim Machine guns. They had replaced three barrels and at one time used urine because they had no water to keep the water cool guns firing. Schaeffer commanded six guns in his Unit but despite small casualties he was depressed. Hans Krupp, a man he grew up with ran away during the height of the battle.

Schaeffer expected he was being called to the captains dugout to officially sanction Krupp's Firing Squad. There was no excuse for desertion in the face of the enemy. Schaeffer couldn't even attempt to save him despite the fact his father and Krupp's father owned a bar together. He and Krupp went to school together, his sister was married to Krupp's cousin. They enlisted together and Krupp was a solid soldier for almost a year. They served together and when Schaeffer was made Lieutenant Hans was the first man to congratulate him, bringing a precious bottle of beer which they shared.

At noon at the height of the attack, they were changing barrels of one of the guns when Schaeffer looked to his left and saw Hans bolt from his position of ammunition carrier and feeder. They had just received ammunition so he was not going for more bullets. The Maxim was so important a weapon that it caused 90% of the enemy casualties in some battles. If one man left his position he could jeopardize the other five machine guns.

Schaeffer yelled. "Hans."

Despite the noise Hans turned and looked at Schaeffer. Fear dominated his face, a look of terror not to be forgotten. "Come back! You can't go! Come back Hans."

But Hans proved he was not hurt by running at full speed away from the action.

Schaeffer was deeply upset because the official notice of Han's cowardice would be sent to the village, and Krupp's father a veteran of the 1870 war with France would be destroyed. Schaeffer's father would ask his son. "How could he let this happen?"

When Schaeffer arrived at the captain's dugout the discussion was not about Hans Krupp or even the battle.

"Schaeffer, I have an important mission for you. You must leave at once."

The captain spread out a map. "We have two Divisions moving up in this area. See this dam near the coast? The enemy has been flooding such places and with all the rain the ground is very swampy. If they flood the plains we will never get our men through to swing around behind them. It is critical you get to this dam and hold it until advanced scouts from the Division relieve you. I can only give you fifteen men. The stupid Frenchmen may attack again this afternoon. If you leave now you can be there before nightfall. The men are being assembled. Some are Storm Troopers, but you may be lucky, we have a reconnaissance post just one mile from this small bridge over the Canal. They have horses, if they are still there use the horses to reach the dam."

Schaeffer said, "Sir, Hans Krupp."

The captain dismissed the issue.

"Court Martial. He will be shot in one hour."

Schaeffer. "Let him come with me, we have so few men I might meet the French or English on the Road."

The captain was incredulous. "Are you crazy, if he bolts again it will be my neck and yours, the man is sentenced, its over."

Schaeffer. "Sir, one man may help, it could be the difference, two Divisions escape the floods."

The captain's every instinct was no, but Schaeffer was right, they could use every man. The captain felt guilty, he gave him so few men for a critical mission. He did not answer.

Schaeffer: "Sir, he'll be in front, I'll be behind him. If he runs, I'll shoot him and if he lives, he transfers out of our Unit."

The captain looked at the map, he should have more than fifteen men, if he meets the enemy, it might be too few.

"Explain to me how you plan to use him, and I want your word you'll watch him."

"Hans is a very strong swimmer, the Canal is wide in some spots, I may need someone to cross it. If he gives me his word, I'll take him with me and I'll walk behind him."

"Schaeffer, you're a good officer, I'll give you a note to the Corporal to take Hans, but go, get on that road by the Canal, and don't fail me."

Schaeffer found Hans. The poor man was destroyed, his head in his hands he stopped shaking, but waited to be shot.

Schaeffer. "Why did you run?"

He looked down. "We were doing murder, it wasn't war, I couldn't stand to kill them anymore. The man next to me was crazy, he kept yelling, don't attack any more, don't make us kill you."

Schaeffer had a man on his guns doing the same thing yelling. "Stop attacking." Some men could only stand to kill fellow humans for so long, especially when it was clear the French generals gave their soldiers no chance.

"Hans, listen to me, I'm going to the coast. Stand up. Promise me you will follow my orders, and if you break them you will be shot, and I'll do it myself."

Hans stunned stood up. He considered himself dead. "I will." He whispered.

"One thing we'll be on a Canal, I may need someone to cross it. The water is almost freezing."

"I'll do what you tell me," Hans said.

#

Captain Howatt's group encountered the first surprise when they reached the Canal and the Cinder Road. They found a dead Belgian solder and a motor bike. Murphy pulled Captain Howatt aside.

"Look Percy the bike ran out of gas, the Germans killed the Belgian, but we've got to take that bike with us. If we can find gas we can get to the dam quicker."

Howatt annoyed said, "Don't call be Percy, I'm Captain Howatt. Now, we can't carry the bike, it will slow us down, and the mules have the explosives, we can't load anymore on them."

With an edge, Murphy responded. "Captain Howatt, I saw a horse in a field, I sent two men to get him. We can break the bike in two, and take off that machine gun. My men will carry the gun and the horse the bike. If we can find gas we will get to the dam in less than an hour."

Howatt knew he was right even if the dam had to be dynamited, it was a good gamble to find gas and bet that the wheel could open the flood gates.

"Alright Murphy, but let's be quick, we could meet Germans out here."

#

Schaeffer was two miles from the Canal when he saw Hans

running towards him. Hans was out of breath, he and two others were acting as scouts and he was returning from the Canal.

"Lieutenant, English on the other side of the Canal."

"Did they see you?"

"No, we dropped down as soon as we saw them. They were putting some equipment on a horse, I made out about thirty of them, and some pack mules."

Schaeffer on one knee pulled out his map. He motioned his second in command to come over.

"English on the other side of the Canal. They are closer to the dam then we are, they have pack mules and probably explosives. I see a small bridge on the map, if we could get to that bridge before them we might have a chance."

The Sergeant said, "Difficult, but if we send two men ahead, swim the Canal we hold them up.

"The rest of us could swing wide and reach the bridge."

Schaeffer. "That water is cold and carrying rifles difficult."

Hans said, "I could do it. We could run ahead, swim the Canal, and set up a sniper's position. With the mules, they can't move fast. We could hold them for enough time so you could get ahead of them."

Schaeffer recognized that Hans was his old self.

"Sergeant, get your best swimmer, let him join Hans. They are to run a mile ahead, swim the Canal and hold the English. Give them oil skins to protect the rifles and clothing, then send two men back to try and find some kind of motor launch, we have to try and beat them to the dam."

#

Murphy had the bike loaded on the horses. They had gone two hundred yards when he saw a sunken barge in the Canal. Quickly he had the men in the water looking for gasoline. Sending a three man patrol ahead, he was delighted when a man called from the sunken deck.

"I found a gas can with gas."

Howatt smiled approvingly.

"Good work Murphy."

Instantly the sound of shots. German Mauser answered by Lee Enfield British rifles.

Murphy turned to the captain. "Our patrol ran into Germans."

They listened clearly. More English shots then German.

Howatt. "Not many Germans, we can't flank them with the bike. The water is six or more inches deep in the field. I will take five men and crash through the German Patrol. You get on the bike and race to the bridge, they may have a large group on the other side. Use the machine gun to hold them at the bridge."

Murphy agreed, and watched the gas can emptied into the bike and the machine gun attached to the sidecar. Howatt was right. The firing was to delay the English, not stop them. The Germans must have more men on the other side. Howatt was already on a fast run with five men heading towards the shooting. Minutes later Murphy heard a fusillade of shots. Howatt hit them!

"Parks get in the sidecar, we move down the road."

Murphy gunned the bike and they churned up dirt and stones and at a controlled speed drove down the cinder surface. Murphy had to control the speed, the surface was slippery. Within two hundred yards he could see Howatt waving him on. He waved to Howatt and kept going. They passed two dead Germans, one without a shirt, that had to be cold, he thought. They had to have gone a mile, when Parks yelled.

"Germans on the other side of the Canal."

Murphy slowed down, looked to his right. Germans were running as hard as they could towards the bridge, that was not yet in sight.

He leaned over and said to Parks "Unscrew the bolts, we fire as soon as we get to the bridge." Three minutes later the staccato of the machine gun alerted Howatt that Murphy was at the bridge and firing at Germans. Should he reinforce Murphy, or cut across the wet fields and head directly for the dam? The Canal would also head North and into the river. If the Germans couldn't cross the bridge they had to go the long way to the dam. Should he divide his forces, some to Murphy, some to the dam? No, he couldn't, and have enough fire power to help Murphy and there could be Germans ahead. Clearly they had the same destination as he did.

Howatt made his decision. His group would cut across the fields. It would be wet going but they could reach the objective in one hour.

#

Schaeffer seeing the motorcycle race ahead cursed as the two British quickly assembled the gun and drove his group to cover. He signaled the Sergeant to move ahead, crawl and find a spot to snipe at the enemy, but they had to get across the bridge, it would take too long to go around it.

The captain said the Germans might have a Horse Patrol by the bridge but with all this firing none appeared. He couldn't count on help from that direction.

Murphy was worried not much ammunition left the Germans were spreading out, not many but at different angles. They could creep up on him.

A German bullet ripped into Murphy's shoulder, sending him spinning to the ground.

"Damn, lousy Kraut bullet."

"I'll load, you fire." He ordered Parks.

"Parks, listen." They heard the put-put of a small motor launch.

Parks yelled, "The Germans, they have a boat." The boat moved to the right side of the Canal, and Schaeffer and four men joined the two who had found the small launch.

At the back of the bridge with little ammunition left Murphy decided he could not stop the launch. He yelled at Parks.

"Get on the bike, warn Howatt, he's got to get to that river and stop the Germans. I'll hold them for a few minutes." Painfully, Murphy pushed with his good left arm and braced the gun between his legs with the angle of the bridge rail, but he couldn't get a good shot.

Parks started the engine as Murphy yelled. "Tell Percy, if I'll end up in a prison camp, he's to come and get me. I saved him today."

Parks roared off as Murphy let out a wild laugh. "Sure you'll come for me Percy _ _ _ _ when I'm in Hell."

Schaeffer could see that one man rode off, but the second man still was at the gun. Then he realized the man couldn't depress the angle of the gun to hit them. Firing just enough to keep the machine gunners head down they passed under the bridge and into the river. With seven men aboard the small engine could only move the craft as fast as a walking horse.

Parks struggled through the wet and drove the bike and caught up with Howatt.

"Murphy sent me, the Germans have a boat, they are on the river."

Howatt made a decision. "Take the dynamite off the mules,

and use the mules to get to the river." He pointed at five men. Stop the Germans boat."

He took off his coat and motioned another man to follow him. "Carry a rifle and a pistol, we run to the dam."

He said to the last ten men. "Carry these explosives and follow us to the dam."

He was cold and Howatt was exhausted, but despite the mud, they made good time.

Suddenly he could hear shooting from the river. He quickened the pace.

Schaeffer pulled the boat to the far shore. The English were shooting at him from the other shore of the river.

His men returned the rifle fire, but he couldn't afford a fire fight. Time was running out. He spoke to his second in command. "Get off the boat, take three men, using smoke grenades create a fog on the river."

Within three minutes the Germans developed a thick heavy smoke and Schaeffer was under way again, moving faster with only two men on the boat. The English shot into the fog, but did not hit the boat.

Schaeffer moved ahead now quickening the pace and after several hundred yards on the river he broke into daylight. The English were behind him, the dam in sight. He motioned his accomplices to fire at the English who were running along side the river. He left the pursuit and when he was a half a mile away from the dam to his horror saw a wave coming towards him. No explosion, they had opened the lock and the river was rising.

He steered the boat to the left bank and jumped out. Could he turn the wheel back and close the lock?

The river was rising. Schaeffer ran through a foot of water, and was at the dam. The stairs led to a small Wheel house. It must contain the wheel. He burst into the Pump Room, looking wildly around. The wheel was missing—the place where the wheel should be was empty.

The English captain was sitting on the floor, his pistol in his lap.

Schaeffer yelled in English.

"Where is the wheel?"

The captain didn't answer.

"You threw it into the river?"

"I threw it into the river." the captain said.

Schaeffer slid to the floor, tired beyond belief.

"Why didn't you shoot me." He asked.

The captain. "We shot too many Germans today, and you shot too many French, its time to stop shooting people, do you have a cigarette?"

Slowly Schaeffer unbuttoned his jacket and tossed a packet of cigarettes to the captain.

The captain lit a cigarette. "Whose people are closest, yours or mine?"

Schaeffer laid his pistol on the floor. "Your people are almost here, I'm your prisoner unless my Division arrives."

Percy smiled. "Are your people good swimmers?"

Schaeffer shook his head. "Not good enough, that's a lot of water out there."

Percy Howatt stood up and looked out. With the lock open the water was pouring into the river behind the Dam. He could see water for miles, the flooding would stop the Germans.

He could see his men had captured a German and were advancing to the Wheel House.

Percy Howatt said, "The water is going down the river. As soon as it gets to a certain height it will probably back up. I suggest we walk North to the coast.

Schaeffer. "How are your prison camps?"

Howatt. "I suspect better than the trenches, you may be lucky."

Schaeffer breathed a sigh, the war was over for him.

Schaeffer was a prisoner of the English for four years. He was released and lived to an old age.

Captain Percy Howatt was killed in action two weeks later.

Murphy escaped from a prison camp and made his way to the English lines. Recovering from his wounds he returned to Canada and became a hockey referee.

#

One year after the war began, the five men responsible for the English war effort met at the Admiralty where the chairman of the committee Admiral Richardson gaveled the meeting to order.

Sitting to his right General of the Army Kempton quickly scanned the agenda, for many of the questions would be directed at him. Next to Kempton, the King's brother, his representative,

Everett sat quietly. Rarely did he speak and today a particularly important meeting he prepared and made detailed notes for his brother, but after scanning the agenda did not have any question. Sitting across from Everett, the Head of British Secret Service, Mannaning, opened a book his staff prepared. A detailed paragraph or more on each issue of the agenda. To Mannaning's right the Economic Czar of England, Lord Edgar Thomas, stirred in his seat. Thomas, always upset with any joint efforts of the English and the French, was disappointed. The current effort to bring Italy into the war was low on the agenda.

The Big Five allocated resources, reviewed grand strategy and set the direction of the course of the war for the Commonwealth and the English Empire.

Admiral Richardson considered a review of the first year low on the agenda, but because of Mannaning's insistence it was the first item today.

"I have spoken to all of you and we are in agreement the war has gone in a different direction than we expected. Our government expected our small highly professional army to participate with the French in a quick victory over the Germans. That has not happened. The war is more brutal and our enemy brings many more highly trained Divisions to the country of France forces us in an apparent stand off in the trenches.

So our strategy of a quick victory and the ability of our navy to blockade the Continent and bring Germany to its knees has not worked."

Richardson looked at Mannaning, who was ready to remind the Committee he predicted the war would start earlier than the others expected. So right on the timing, wrong on the execution

"I will remind our Committee that we were all confused about the direction of the war. The Secret Service judgment that the war would start quickly was correct."

Before Mannaning could speak, the Admiral dominated the Committee, as he had done for years. "Now it serves no purpose to go over that and the first year, so I suggest we move on. We have much ground to cover."

Mannaning cleared his throat. This was classic Richardson. The man always in control, so Mannaning relaxed, his original judgment recognized.

Before the meeting continued the Admiral acknowledge the

second member of the Committee, Lord Thomas who would want to discuss his hatred of the French.

"Item six is our plan to bring Italy into the war on our side. I can see Lord Thomas will not be comfortable until we discuss the issue so Lord Thomas proceed."

Thomas passionate about France did not react to the Admirals obvious concession to Thomas's emotional weakness.

"Gentlemen we are agreed, we want Italy to come into the war on our side as do the Germans who want to induce Italy to come in on the German-Austrian side. We also have agreed we can offer Italy much more than the enemy. We can offer lands and political agreement, the Germans can not since Italy wants the lands of the German allies. What I want to point out is, this will not happen if we allow the French to meet with Italy or we jointly speak to the Italians."

"The French are liars and cheats, the Italians understand this, and will go to the German side if we do not control the offer to the Italians and the negotiation." Members of the Committee were all aware that Thomas hated the French, but never had he called the French liars and cheats in an open meeting.

General Kempton who had to fight along side the French felt obligated to speak. "Edgar, we've been friends for a long time. My men are in the trenches next to the French. I must ask you not to speak about them in that way. Your personal views must not color your thinking on the subject. If we present a treaty to the Italians they will insist that the French sign it too. The cities and geography we offer are closer to France than England. We can't exclude the French."

For ten minutes they debated the issue until Admiral Richardson closed the debate.

"Gentlemen the French must meet with us and agree to a deal with the Italians. Lord Thomas, I'll speak to you after the meeting."

Everett the only man not to speak during the debate wrote a note for his brother. Thomas hates the French, he believes they cheated him on a contract he signed with them, but the Committee wants to work with the French to bring Italy into the war on our side.

The Admiral started again. "Churchill has suggested a plan I believe has merit. A joint Army/Navy attack on the Dardanelles at Gallipoli, the soft underbelly of the Central powers.

Turkey joined the Central Powers to gain land from Russia. If we can knock her out of the war and advance in the Balkans it helps us with Italy. Each one of you agrees with the plan so I will direct the army and navy to go ahead."

General Richardson. "Admiral you said to me last week that this operation will take unprecedented cooperation and aggressiveness by the army and navy. With a war that drains all our resources your only concern is we send the military to the Dardanelles. That may not bring off a bold plan that can work."

Richardson. "The leaders will want to cooperate. They believe in the plan, but this is a new experience for both the army and the navy. I wish I was going, but General you run the war in France. I have to direct the Northern Fleet and I will explain in a moment, what is about to happen. Do you want to comment on fighting the Germans?"

Richardson. "We all thought a short war one massive effort, the Germans have proved flexible in some ways, more flexible than our side. They rely on the defense more than we do, a tough opponent at Gallipoli."

Richardson. "It works if we work together. Now let me explain what is happening in the North Sea. We think the German Fleet is about to come out. A great sea battle is about to begin. I expect our navy will defeat them. However, we think the battle will be hard and I expect to sustain losses, the Committee should not expect any easy victory."

No one spoke. Richardson's word on Naval affairs was beyond question.

Mannaning looked at his notes. The Secret Service reported very active German submarine activity in the North Sea. He decided not to mention this.

Richardson, clearing his throat. "Since we are the Committee, who oversees our base at Scapa Flow, I'll give you a verbal report. The submarine nets at the entrance to the base are in need of repair, so for the next two weeks we will repair the nets and a destroyer will be stationed at the entrance of the harbor where the nets usually are."

Everett saw a chance to participate. "You gave a verbal, does that mean I won't get a written memo on this?"

Richardson impatient said, "Everett you have a verbal, I won't send a written memo."

Richardson looked around the table. "Gentlemen, please note with a major battle looming I don't expect an attack on Scapa Flow. Now, can we get on with the rest of the agenda?"

#

The German Kaiser worried that if the original plan for victory in the West failed he was prepared to turn over management of the war to Prince Rupprecht of Bavaria. The Prince his cousin, established early his strategy was superior in the running of the war. The Kaiser used to bullying others was differential to the man he grew up with, and as a boy who he avoided, not able to ride as well or compete in shooting games.

The Kaiser before the war guaranteed the Prince – Austria-Hungary would be a formidable ally and was embarrassed by their very weak performance. He was puzzled and questioned.

"What is wrong with the Austrians, they operate our model of conscription, and our model of training, so why is the army so inept?"

The Prince answered. "Since the 1800's they have been weak. With so many different ethnic and racial groups, the generals separated the army. Troop dispositions were made for ethnic rather than military considerations. The generals over extended the army attacking Serbia and Russia at the same time. It was a losing strategy, the soldiers did their best but the plan was flawed."

The Kaiser shocked that he had believed the Austrian generals, and now was proved wrong, changed the subject.

"Our right wing did not win the war against France, now trench warfare has started. Can we win?"

The Prince did not hesitate. "We see a France that fights with a plan to attack. Attack across the whole Front totally rejecting defense. We absorbs such attack and counter after they have absorbed great casualties on several Fronts. We are about to go on the attack. The French have not read their history. The attack from a defensive position is a classic Napoleon tactic. Didn't they read Napoleon's battles?"

The Kaiser was depressed. The Prince who felt major victories were close said, "Willie the Schlieffen's plan did not succeed, our strong right wing did not knock the French out of the war but our victory at Tannenburg has greatly weakened the Russians."

The Kaiser welcomed positive news and he made a major

concession. "You asked me to ease off our pressure against the Americans and I have instructed the Foreign Office to stop any overture to Mexico and also the navy will not let our submarines attack American ships."

The Prince. "Good we need the submarines in the North Sea against the English. I have told the navy to execute the plan you and I discussed."

The Kaiser did not question that the Prince had put in motion a plan to attack the British Navy, he wanted reassurance that the plan would work.

"Willie, this is a bold plan, it could change the course of the war, I know the English are your relatives, but we wage a bloody war in France, I cannot lose the opportunity for victory."

The Kaiser. "We said Scapa Flow only if we had to."

The Prince. "Defeat the French Army and the English Navy and we win the war. I do not want the war to drag on. The longer it goes the greater chance the people will revolt. In Russia the populous already protests. The seeds of revolution grow."

A chill ran down the Kaiser's spine. "Do what you must, Germany needs me, it needs a Kaiser. I'll not worry what my relatives in England think."

#

The Russian Commander-in-Chief spoke to the Czar.

"Sire, the defeat at Tannenburg is total, over one hundred thousand men taken prisoner. Our dead and missing...

The Czar put up his hand. "I don't want to hear anymore about our losses. Is it true General Samsonov committed suicide?"

"Yes. Thousands of our men were trapped in the forest, the Germans turned search lights on our men and their machine guns slaughtered our soldiers. General Samsonov was ill and in despair, he left his staff and later they found him dead, shot in the head in the forest. It is also true General Samsonov and General Rennenkampf hated each other and refused to cooperate and that at the railroad station at Munden they started to yell at each other, then blows were exchanged and the staff had to separate them? Clearly they did not help each other at Tannenburg, so the Germans attacked each army separately? We suspect the Germans have been intercepting our radio messages. Once the Germans suspected Rennenkampf would not help Samsonov, they attacked."

The Czar sat at his desk he looked like a beaten man.

The Commander-in-Chief shared some good news. "We defeated the Austrians at Lemberg, but the casualties were high. I think that Austrian Army is destroyed."

Now he spoke. "Sire, the military in Moscow believes the Monk Rasputin has influence in your court, he should be driven out it undermines your authority."

The Czar looked down. "My wife believes he helps our ill son. I cannot send him away."

Henri Peeta, Sergeant French Army slumped against the side of the trench. He was out of breath, the attack never really got started. He saw the Corporal with the big nose was dead. The man was cut down just as they were leaving the trench. He hung down his head and neck in the mud, his legs hung out on the wall at the top of a trench. The new man Raynal had a look of horror as a fat rat scurried across the Corporal's face.

Raynal cursed and the rat ran away. He lifted up his shovel.

Henri said. "We let them alone if they only attack the dead. If they attack the living or the wounded we kill them."

Raynal cursed. "My first day. A failed attack, we didn't get past our first wire." He cursed again.

Peeta smiled. "Your first day and a good day, today is Wednesday."

Raynal looked puzzled. "You're the second man to say Wednesday when we came up this morning. The officer said it was Wednesday, we were lucky, why Wednesday?"

Peeta laid his rifle down and took an old pipe out of his pocket. "Today is the day Nevelles the accordion player comes. He always plays seven songs. We gather at least fifty, a few less tonight, it is the best day of the week. He plays in a different section each night. He is loved by the men. He plays six lively songs and one love song at the end, each different. I always keep the rhythm with my pipe."

He waved the pipe as if the music was in the background and today's attack never happened.

"Is he good?" asked Raynal.

"Nevelles was a school teacher before the war, he is clever. He tells jokes and the gossip, I love that hour. Wounded men have refused to go to the rear until he finishes. The Germans do not shoot when he's here, they listen to the music too."

Raynal who had just arrived from the real world and now

entered Dante's inferno was surprised at the change in the Sergeant. One minute a beaten exhausted hollow man, now an animated happy man, looking forward to tonight's visit.

Who was this Pied Piper Nevelles?

Peeta the anticipation almost as good as the visit continued. "When he plays the love song I think of my wife and my village and my children, sometimes tears. Several of us have cried but at the end we cheer and we all pat him on the back and he smiles and waves to us as he leaves, he is a wonderful man."

The rat was back and Raynal didn't move.

"What time does he come?"

"Always at seven. He plays to the Third Regiment first, he always comes at seven, the officers don't schedule patrols until he leaves."

Raynal was a good listener so Peeta continued. "You will never hear the birds sing in this place, you will grow to hate the smell of death.

Young man you cannot eat the food, the mud will destroy your feet, your bones will ache, you will learn to accept your fate. We are all destined to die in this place, don't think of life, it is an illusion. The only truth is Nevelles, you won't see trees, flowers, or grass, but for one hour a week Nevelles is proof God has not forsaken us."

Raynal still puzzled asked. "How long has he been coming?"

"Nine months, since we moved into this trench and he has never missed. I'm told he refused a three day pass because he didn't want to disappoint the men. I find it the only ray of sunshine in this Hell. No, Hell is better than this. This is lower than Hell. What did the poet write about Hell?"

Raynal didn't know.

At ten minutes before seven a Sergeant approached. Henri Peeta, his sad face said it was bad news.

"He's not coming."

A look of horror crossed Peeta's face. "Why has he been given leave?"

"No, he was part of the attack this morning, he's dead."

Henri grabbed the mans labels. "No! No! It can't be the truth, he can't be dead." He shook the Sergeants lapels."

"Henri, I didn't want to come, the captain is making me go down the trench. I have to tell everyone, I didn't want to do it, but they saw him. He was hung up on the wire, a machine gun cut him almost in half, he was hung on the wire."

Peeta slumped to a seat on the trench steps. "Bitch, the only thing of joy, they give us only shit, and now the officers take it away, they should never have let him attack. What did one more man mean? They kill us by the thousands, why one more man?"

"I hate this place. I hated it from the first day, I don't hate the Germans but I hate this place."

In anger he stood up and threw his rifle against the trench wall.

"That's it. I quit. They take the only joy away, I resign, they can fight the war without me. The officers killed Nevelles, let them fight without me."

Two days later under direct orders once wounded, highly decorated Henri Peeta refused to leave the trench and participate in an attack, against the Germans. Three days later he was shot.

CHAPTER 6

Gibbon Stillwell, US Navy Intelligence Officer, looked over the White House Ball Room and the twenty tables set up for the luncheon.

Most of the men were starting soup and the talk was loud as befitting a luncheon celebrating the winning of the nineteen fifteen World Series. Gibbon at six foot two inches was not out of place in a room full of Major League ball players. The former captain of the Yale football and baseball teams looked about the room to see if he could spot the President. When he did not see Mr. Wilson, he turned to the Marine Guard standing at the door. The Marine an old friend of Gibbons nodded in recognition.

"I don't see the President, he was expected?" asked Gibbon.

The Marine whispered. "Something big is happening, several of the Senior people are not here."

Gibbon notified at his office, was told to attend the luncheon, but be prepared to be called away at any moment.

"Which one is Ruth?" he asked. The Marine stared at a table across the room.

"The big guy in the brown suit. I saw him walk in, graceful for a big man. Could be a better hitter than a pitcher. Ruth pitched brilliantly in the World Series." Babe Ruth, a great pitcher, was being talked about as a great hitter.

The luncheon to celebrate the victory of the Boston Red Sox over the Philadelphia Phillies included many famous baseball players. Now Gibbon looked for his table and the great Manager Connie Mack. Mack's Athletics won the World Series years ago, but because of financial problems he sold off his players and finished last the previous season.

Mack the most respected man in the game waved at Gibbon who waved back. Gibbon, his Senior year at Yale almost signed a contract with Mr. Mack until he broke his leg in a football game that ended his career. Mr. Mack signaling Gibbon waving a rolled up luncheon program. This was so like the picture of Mr. Mack, signaling his players with a rolled up score card to move to defensive positions during a game.

At Mr. Mack's table Gibbon said, "Sorry I'm late, was held up at the Naval Bureau."

Mack introduced him to other men at the table.

"My boy, I'm delighted to see you, this is the great White Sox star, Eddie Collin and one of my former players."

Collins half stood up and shook hands. "My pleasure, Gibbons we just started, great clam chowder."

Mack said, "Ty Cobb was expected, but I don't think he's coming, business meeting. He owns stock in a new soft drink company in Atlanta, Coke."

Mack turned to Collins. "Eddie, until this young man broke his leg he was going to be our first baseman."

Eddie Collins, the best second baseman in the game and a three thirty hitter was gracious. "Gibbon, if Mr. Mack said you were going to play with us, you must have been good."

Stillwell never regretted his lost opportunity, but for a moment a twinge of melancholy.

To play with Eddie Collins against Babe Ruth, a lost moment never to be regained. Gibbons brushed his black hair back. His hand, like his face showed no emotion, he slid into a chair.

"Great team, it would have been an honor, but I don't know if I could hit Mr. Ruth's and the Red Sox pitchers."

Mack always a consummate expert. "Gibbon, you had a fine level swing, I don't think you would have hit a lot of homeruns, but you could have been a three hundred hitter and a peerless first baseman, as good as Sisler. Sisler was the best first baseman in the American League. Mack liked good fielders who supported his fine pitchers. Gibbon would have been a winning player on Mack's championship teams.

Mr. Mack passed the salt as Ray Schalk a great catcher sat down.

"How is your leg Gibbon?"

"Getting better, its almost eight years now, one of these days I'll lose the limp except on days when it rains." They laughed.

Mack continued. "Eddie and Ray, last year Gibbon went to Europe on a fact finding mission.

Can you tell us what you saw in Europe?"

The naval officer smiled. "I can't give all the details, but I was in Europe to study the English and German Navies. I came back last year before the war and wrote a report."

Collins and Schalk were impressed. He said it so easily, but here was a man that lived in a world they didn't know, and yet could have been a Major League player.

Collins asked. "Do you think America will be dragged into the war?"

Stillwell dodged the question. "I only studied the Navies, I can't give you any insights into the political conditions. Our papers favor the English. You fellows read the same articles as I do."

Collins a college man was interested. "We've heard the Germans dominate the land war, but it's mostly in the trenches, bad conditions."

Mack turned to Collins. "Eddie, Gibbon worked for his father in the oil fields of Oklahoma during college and his father almost bought a piece of the Athletics, that's how I met him. Saw him play at Yale. Now he is a career navy man and I understand you met the King. when you were in England?"

Schalk said, "You met the King?"

"Yes, we had a dinner just before I returned and the King was interested in our story. Asked a lot of questions, the English Navy was very cordial, but didn't seem interested."

"What were the Germans like?" said Schalk.

"The Germans were confident, not afraid of the English."

Gibbon was beginning to feel he was talking too much, so he changed the subject

"I was hoping to meet Ruth and Cobb today."

Mack pointed to the Babe. "The big man in the brown suit. After the luncheon I'll introduce you. He is a friendly fellow."

Schalk a feisty catcher said. "Cobb is not a friendly fellow, he spiked me last year on a slide, I don't miss him at the luncheon"

They told stories of the anti-social Cobb, a player hated by many Major Leaguers.

Schalk a very good storyteller liked to go gossip about Cobb. "In the nineteen nine World Series Cobb met his match in Honus Wagner the great Pittsburg shortstop. Cobb reached first base and called down to Wagner I'm coming down and I'm going to cut you, Dutchman."

Schalk was indicating Cobb was going to spike Wagner. He gestured with his hands.

"Cobb tried to steal second base, Wagner jumped over his slide, caught the ball and in one motion tagged him in the face."

Gibbon shook his head. "That was a great athletic play."

"Cobb was hurt. "Knocked out a couple of his teeth." Schalk smiled. He was not sorry, Cobb had spiked too many players to be concerned about mercy for him.

The Marine friend of Gibbon leaned over the table. "Mr. Stillwell the Secretary of State wants to see you in his office."

Gibbon stood up and offered his apologies and left.

Eddie Collins. "He does have a slight limp."

Mack. "His father told me two doctors said he would never walk again. We had our doctor look at him and he didn't think Gibbon would even walk without a cane. It was very bad. Gibbon went out West and since he couldn't walk he rode horses and swam everyday for almost two years. Finally the leg came back. Just before it happened he was married and his wife went with him after the accident. She nursed him, gave him rub downs and stayed with him the whole time. Wonderful girl, very intelligent. She's an architect."

Collins said, "A woman architect? Unusual for nineteen fifteen."

Mack said, "She was going to MIT in Boston. Met Gibbon when Yale played Harvard. Cancelled her engagement and married him three weeks later.

Collins asked. "How good a football player was he?"

"All American," said Mack. "Very fast, but a clever runner. I saw him play one game. Never went down with one tackle."

Connie Mack liked smart athletes. "But his real strength, very smart, level headed, kind of a man whose been captain of every team he was on. Not surprised they sent him to Europe to do a study, meets people well, I'm sure that helped him."

"He must be headed for big things in the navy, when they send you on those kinds of missions, that's a sign, the Senior level is watching you," said Mr. Mack.

Eddie Collins. "All this and he could play first base?"

Mack. "Outstanding first baseman, great foot work, excellent base runner. Yes, he could have played on our Championship teams."

Schalk responded. "Wrote a report and saw the King of England, that's impressive. Notice he was careful with his words, didn't act like a big shot. I think he'd be welcome in our clubhouse."

Collins a teammate of Schalk comments. "On the Chicago White Sox some of us would like him."

Then he looked at Mr. Mack. "But we've got an element on the team. I don't trust some of them. Too close to the gamblers that follow the team."

Mr. Mack scowled. "I worry about the gamblers and their influence on the game. We're going to have a scandal some day."

cognizant, you were the only one who thought the Germans could win. All our other people expected an English Naval victory and they were wrong. You wrote the only report that said German gunnery would out class the English and that is what happened. The English depended on a great weight of shells, but the German accuracy won. The German fire at Jutland out ranged their opponents and was more accurate. Only English seamanship saved some of the fleet."

"The battle opened with a massive explosion and the destruction of two English dreadnought, the German gunnery accurate. The two Fleets steamed parallel in a running gun battle. Both sides suffered grievous injuries. The English lost four battleships and five dreadnoughts, and many other ships suffered damage. After two days the Germans were a clear victor so your predictions were correct."

Gibbon asked. "How about the destroyers?"

"The Germans a slight edge, and everyone says the brilliant seamanship of Vice Admiral David Beatty saved the English Fleet."

The old man stood up and walked around his desk he picked up a piece of paper and walked back to his seat. He looked like he aged since the last time Gibbon saw him.

"The Battle of Jutland was a defeat for the English. What I am about to describe is a gigantic tragedy. The English Home Fleet returned to their historic home base at Scapa Flow off Scotland. It was judged they had not prevailed, but the battle would not change the course of the war."

The Secretary put his glasses back on and read from the sheet. "The Second afternoon after the sea battle the Germans attacked the Home Fleet at Scapa Flow, the survivors of Jutland. The German submarines surface ships and Zeppelins struck with no warning. The attack began with the Zeppelins bombing and when some of the big ships attempted to slip away submarines caused great damage. The German knew exactly where the barrage balloons were located and avoided the anti-aircraft fire. The English had camouflage nets, but the Zeppelins were not fooled, the submarines avoided the mines and dodged the submarine nets. When the Germans left after three hours not a large English capital ship was still afloat and undamaged. The English Northern Fleet ceased to exist as a Naval power."

Gibbon could scarcely believe with he had been told.

"Sir, I've been to Scapa Flow, it is the state of the art defenses, how could the Germans do such damage?"

"Gibbon, the Germans had the English plans for Scapa Flow, it was espionage. More disturbing, only five men had the complete plans for the defense of Scapa Flow, it was espionage at the highest level of the English Government."

It was as if a bolt of lightening hit the room, Gibbon cleared his throat.

"It had to be a top British official, they would never commit the whole plan to anyone but a top official."

The Secretary confirmed this. "The Committee that runs the British war effort is called the Big Five. The head of the Army, Navy, Intelligence, the Assistant to the Prime Minister and the King's representative, his brother, these men had the plans. The reason we know it was one of them, is the last German Zeppelin leaving the attack was hit, only the second Zeppelin hit that day. When the English reached the Zeppelin the crew was all dead. In the captain's pocket they found a crude map. It pinpointed all the key defenses. The Home Secretary told me it is their belief the captain was suppose to commit this to memory, but was afraid he would forget, and disobeyed and made himself a map. We hear discipline among the Zeppelin crews are very harsh. The map showed details only the Big Five could be aware of, so it had to be one of them."

Gibbon was stunned, the defeat at Jutland a shock, but espionage at Scapa, was beyond belief. It took all of his will power to remain quiet and listen to the events unfold.

The Secretary poured two glasses of wine and gave one to Gibbon.

"The English have no Northern Fleet to protect their island. Of course the land war continues in France, so we see no threat of an invasion. They still have the Southern Fleet, not as large but big enough."

"Captain Stillwell, this has shaken the King and the home Secretary."

His formal address, Captain Stillwell, added greater weight to the discussion.

"Gibbon, the King has asked the President for you to come to England and investigate what happened."

Sir, I'm an American."

"The King remembered you and your report. He wants someone not part of the government, they want to keep this secret. The King has faith in your ability, and the President wants to help. We don't want the Germans to win in Europe, but we don't want to enter the war. This is the kind of support America plans to give."

Gibbon. "You said five men had the plans to Scapa Flow?"

"Yes. They direct the British war effort?"

"No chance of a slip up or a mistake?"

"The Home Secretary said none."

The thirty year old naval officer could not, and would not turn down the assignment, but he must clear the air.

"Mr. Secretary, we discussed my report, a great part of it was written by my wife, she was the one who convinced me about German gunnery, I want to take her to Europe with me."

The Secretary expected this. "Agreed."

"And I need to talk to Mr. Roosevelt."

The Secretary twisted in his seat.

"You are aware the President and Mr. Roosevelt do not like each other. The President would not be happy with you talking to Roosevelt."

"Sir, if I go to England, it sounds like I'm not going to get much help from the English."

"That's true, you will have a letter from the King telling people to cooperate with you, but the mission on the surface will be a fact finding one, no talk of treason, or trying to find a spy."

"Mr. Secretary, I'll be working in the dark, Mr. Roosevelt has contacts that can help, his trip over there two years ago developed many important friendships, I need that help."

The Secretary believed he was right. "Gibbon, go speak to Mr. Roosevelt, I'll not tell the President. Ask TR to be discrete and try to limit your questions to English contacts, the whole point is to keep this secret, its one reason to use an American. The King is worried if this story gets out, it will damage the war effort."

"Gibbon, this is a difficult assignment, when the Home Secretary asked for you, the President agreed immediately, and so did I."

Stillwell liked challenges, this was a great one. His mind was racing , it was a great trust, he did not flinch.

"When do I leave?"

"The English cruiser will take you over, it leaves on the

weekend with the Home Secretary. The captain of the ship thinks your journey is to study the attack not the reason behind it. That is the cover story to be used. You will want to study the background of the five men. All our files will be sent over to your house. In addition, the Government Library is already compiling information, so you can send someone over to pick it up. We will give you all we have on the Big Five."

Gibbons stood up and shook the old gentleman's hand. "I'll begin work immediately. Do I call my superior or will you do it?"

"Better you let me call him, it will shut off questions. I'll visit you Friday night to sign off, but we have great faith in you my boy."

#

When Gibbon left, the Secretary leaned back in his chair. He thought, we picked the right man. I'll not tell the President, but his going to see TR is exactly the right thing to do. TR can help him with the background, TR is familiar with the Big Five. Gibbon is so young, but so mature, and such a big challenge. Perhaps his being so young is an advantage. Thank god he broke his leg, a career as a professional athlete would have been a waste. Someday he might run the navy, even though he did not go to Annapolis. This will be a tough test, senior English people will not welcome him, and yet this is the man the King wanted.

#

Outside the Secretary's office Westy Tyler, Gibbon's friend was waiting for him. Tyler, sixty, a real cowboy with wrinkled skin from years in the saddle was as thin as a fence post and twice as tough. The two met in a bar in Arizona when Gibbon ignored the taunts of a cowboy for a half hour, then knocked him cold. That began a close and deep friendship between the two. Tyler stood up, his cowboy boots and big Stetson out of place in the formal White House, except more Americans dressed like him then the diplomats that walked in the hall.

"Westy. You been waiting long?"

"No Amanda and I got in from New York two hours ago, saw your note and decided to come over and pick you up."

"Good, I'm glad, it's been a long day. How's Amanda?"

"She's excited, the new building is a big success and she has some drawings for another project. Took up the whole front seat of the car. I could hardly see to drive."

Westy was only happy when he was complaining.

Westy asked. "How was the lunch?"

"Good, the Red Sox have a lot of big guys. Ruth is big."

"Did you get me any autographs?"

Gibbon pulled the luncheon menu out. "Eddie Collins and Mr. Mack." Westy looked at the menu. They both signed it to Westy.

"Collins, great hitter, we saw him against Walter Johnson, Walter was real fast that day."

"Yes, and you had four beers and fell asleep in the seventh inning."

In the parking lot Westy spit out a big wad of tobacco, opened the trunk and strapped on his six gun.

"Feel undressed without it. Your wife made me keep the gun on the floor all the way from New York. That gal would have got us scalped thirty years ago. My mother traveled all the way from St. Louis to Arizona with a shot gun in her lap."

With Westy driving they got in the car and pulled out of the White House parking lot.

"I've got news, we're going to England on Friday on an English cruiser."

Westy stepped on the gas. "What the Hell.........well I'm telling the cook to have steaks every night. Goddam, we won't have one good piece of beef once we go to Europe."

For the next five minutes Westy complained about the food in Europe, the only thing he would complain louder about was if Gibbon said he was not going.

Westy drove a car like he was herding cattle. Gibbon hung on as he spun around a corner.

"Damn. What are we gonna do in Europe?"

"The English lost a big Naval battle at Jutland, they want me to do a review of the battle."

He did not mention the problem at Scapa Flow. Westy would learn in good time. Time enough when they got to Europe.

Westy remembered the report. "You told them they were in trouble that's the problem with the Europeans they don't listen to us."

Westy believed in the standings of the nations, America was one two and three. The Europeans not close.

"Well, hell, your wife will be happy. She loves England."

Gibbon felt the smooth purr of the engine.

"How did the new car drive?" They had the only nineteen fifteen Chevrolet in the neighborhood. Everyone else had a Ford.

Westy loved the Chevy. "Just the electric starter makes the car better then the 'Tin Lizzie' hand starter. Also we drove some at night. Our electric lights are so much better then Fords lights. When the Ford slows down the lights dim. I go past them and give them a toot on the horn, a little more money, but worth it."

They pulled in the driveway and Amanda came out of the house. She was as pretty as the girl he fell in love with in Boston ten years ago. Only gone three days, he missed her and he knew she had made Westy leave before dawn to get home. They did not have a perfect marriage, it was better than that. They both had careers and each supported the other. Only two people believed he would walk again, and he was married to one of them.

They held each other for a long time, but before he could tell her the news she said.

"Where are we going?"

"How do you know we are going on a trip?"

"Westy parked the car and pulled out the trunk with his mothers shot gun. Whenever we go on a trip he gets that shot gun first."

Gibbon liked it, they both assumed they would be going.

"Amanda, it's serious business."

"Of course it's serious, or they wouldn't have sent you."

Amanda believed he would be head of the navy some day. It wasn't just that he was smart, he was a leader. Gibbon had a natural presence, maybe because he was such a great athlete, Gibbon radiated leadership. Her parents were shocked when she broke her engagement to future writer and reporter Matty Stevenson, but understood when they met Gibbon. The two years in Arizona she never heard him complain or feel sorry for himself. Rarely did he mention the pain. Life was always a mountain to climb for Gibbon and her work was as natural to him as it was for her. Of course, she was a great architect, not a great female architect. A great architect, what was the point if you didn't do it well.

"The English Navy was defeated at Jutland"

"Where's that?"

"Just off Denmark."

"So your report was right?"

"Our report." He corrected. "And beyond that the Germans

staged a surprise attack at the English Home Base. The King believes one of the top people in the country gave the Germans the plans. Our job is to find out who did it."

"Gibbon." She pulled back. "Police work, intelligence work, I can't help you."

He disagreed. "Don't be sure, we didn't know anything about German gunnery before the last trip. We'll learn."

"This is serious." Her face was drawn. It would take some time before she accepted the challenge.

"How do we start?" she questioned.

"You get us organized. We leave Friday. Get to the library, they are gathering background reading including all the English papers. I'll give you five names to research. It's best we start here. Westy will drive me to New York tomorrow to meet TR. He knows some of their people and he can open doors for me in London."

TR thought of Gibbon like a son. Both retrieved their health in the West. It was TR who suggested Gibbon go to Arizona and their personalities were the same. Gibbon a little quieter, a little more of a reader, but just as positive as Mr. Roosevelt.

After dinner Amanda and Gibbon sat in the library. She rereading the report they wrote about the German Navy, and he sitting at his desk making notes. It was classic Gibbon to be writing out a game plan for the investigation. When they went to Germany, Gibbon, an expert on codes and communication read every book he could on Naval guns. The Krupp Steel people opened many doors for them to speak to senior German naval officers, but Gibbon's tact and aggressiveness allowed them to see the guns. Krupp wanted to sell steel to the Americans and Gibbon used this leverage to get them to places no foreigner had ever seen before. When Amanda said the German steel was better, Gibbon arranged to see a test firing of German Naval guns.

She remembered she had met two of Gibbon's teammates on the football team after they were married. The players explained that Gibbon was not only the captain of the team, but also an assistant coach.

When the coach put in new play Gibbon was always the first player to understand the assignments and help the coaches direct the walk through of responsibilities. They marveled at his great patience as he shared his knowledge with his slower teammates. This leadership transcended to the games. Gibbon was always at his best in the fourth quarter, and the team always played, best at the end of games. Just as he was a born teacher, he had a very stable, calm personality, and in the ten years of marriage the only time she had seen him lose his temper was with the drunken cowboy in Arizona.

His self confidence also showed in his competitive nature. Not as handsome as her former fiancée, his black hair and rugged continence attracted her to him immediately. They met at a fraternity party the night after the Yale-Harvard game. They danced for over an hour and she knew that night she would marry him, but still was surprised to learn he was the star of the game that afternoon.

Mostly they talked of what courses they were taking, he asked many questions about her work and was more relaxed than most men when he found out she was the only woman in her engineering school. Her fiancée occasionally questioned her career but Gibbon accepted it as the most natural thing in the world. When they went to Arizona, he would discuss the books she read. As she continued her studies and when they returned East, he insisted she join her fathers firm even though it kept them apart when he joined the navy.

Just as competitive as he was , there new venture was daunting, she wondered how they would start.

"Gibbon." Her voice was a statement and a question. "This is going to be difficult?"

He looked up from his notes, and smiled. She wanted a pep talk.

"I know."

She was the smartest person he had ever been close to. They were a team just like college.

"Let's start talking about the plan."

"We've got some advantages, the problem isn't impossible, the fact we are strangers and Americans work in our favor."

She listened.

"One, we don't have any preconceived ideas or feelings whose guilty. That helps. It's a fresh start. I think if something appears odd or out of place we might see it before someone who is part of that society. I'm going to see TR, I know him, he'll tell me to keep a fresh, open approach."

"Two, the people we question won't know why we are there. Maybe the guilty party will suspect and tip his hand."

He did not convince her.

She said, "We are strangers. They may refuse to be candid with us. They are important men, we will be younger, Americans, and not familiar with their convention rules and standards. They will be defensive even if the King directs them to talk to us."

"Yes, I expect that, but we are not going to England to make friends. If it gets tense so much the better exert some pressure. Remember the German officers that didn't want to show us the guns? Once the Krupp people made them, they told us more then they intended too. I want it to become adversarial and your right about being strangers. I have an idea I want to run past TR. Remember when we were in Arizona, we were a bit out of place until we became friends with Westy. He helped to understand the place, I intend to find the English Westy."

She asked. "Your not concerned that the President will be annoyed you went to see TR?"

"If we solve the case it won't matter and if we can't find the traitor it won't matter anyway."

He was saying the case would make or break his career in the navy.

She nodded. "How can I best help?"

"Do your research on each of the Big Five, we have a lot of material coming from the Library of Congress, then study the Naval battles at Scapa and Jutland. The captain of the ship we are crossing in to England commanded a cruiser during the engagement. He can help."

"Do you want architectural drawings of the battles?"

"Yes, at some point I intend to show them to the Big Five."

"Gibbon, your developing a plan but we are not trained detectives, isn't that a disadvantage?"

He stood up and walked around the desk. "It is if we let it be. I plan to develop a team in London to help us. That is part of the reason to see TR, he has police contacts in London. I have some other ideas I am going to ask Mr. Roosevelt about. The whole idea is to be aggressive, the King told the Secretary that's why he wanted us.

I'm told the King was impressed though disappointed. We were right about the German Navy."

She stood up, walked to the desk and put her arm around his waist and laid her head on his shoulder. "The King loved Westy, he represents Wild West Americans," he said.

I have one last question. Do we study the Germans in any of this?"

He kissed her hair. "I thought about that. If one of the team in London can help with the Germans we use him, but I think we concentrate on the English side. Time is a factor, if we spread out to thin, we may miss things. Remember the English spy is a guilty man, the Germans were doing what their government intended them to do. I think it will be easier to find a guilty man."

CHAPTER 8

Westy drove Gibbon to Long Island to visit Gibbon's friend the former President Theodore Roosevelt. When the car arrived at Sagamore Hill in Oyster Bay the enthusiastic rotund outdoorsman was waiting in the driveway.

He pumped Gibbons hand. "My boy, my boy, I'm delighted to see you, welcome."

Roosevelt was the only friend of Gibbon who never asked him about his leg. That was the past, not to be remembered. Like a strikeout early in the game, the next at bat was the one that counted.

Then the President turned to another man he liked. "Westy, you old cowboy." He pumped his hand vigorously.

"The only man to be with me at San Juan Hill and with Custer at Little Big Horn." He patted Westy on the back. Roosevelt always said the same thing when he saw Westy. Something very few of Custer's men could have done, served at San Juan Hill since most were dead.

"Of course I did better than Custer." He laughed heartily.

Westy truly admired the two men, one was Gibbon, the other Roosevelt.

"Colonel." Westy came to attention and saluted his former Chief of the Rough Riders.

In many ways Custer and Roosevelt were much alike, brave in battle, but Westy considered Roosevelt a winner and Custer a loser. Roosevelt was aggressive, Custer was reckless. Westy was with Major Reno at the Little Big Horn, not Custer. The reason he was alive today was he was just behind TR at the charge up San Juan Hill.

Westy worked on the car and Gibbon and TR went to the library.

Gibbon. "TR I've been assigned to England and I wanted to talk to you before I left."

"Of course my boy, any way I can help."

The press was beginning to report about the battle of Jutland, so Gibbon explained to TR the press reports were not accurate and that the English Fleets losses were much greater than stated.

Roosevelt rose from his chair. "My God. My God, this can't be true. You were right about the Germans."

Stillwell always felt compelled to set the record straight.

"My wife is recognized for her architectural work, but her real expertise is metals. For the Woolworth Building she designed and directed all the steel work. When we were in Germany she and I toured German Steel companies. The German engineers were astonished at her knowledge. That was a great deal of the report."

TR laughter. "I can see the gentle and beautiful Amanda asking questions about tensile strength."

"She did," said Gibbon.

Gibbon then added one other dimension that he omitted from the report. "When Amanda and I considered the report we reasoned the British as a great world sea power had to be everywhere. The Germans could choose only one place and concentrate, so the British advantage in numbers was not as great as it appeared."

TR looked at him. It was so simple and clear, an idea this young man deducted, but that veteran Admirals ignored. Some day Gibbon would run the US Navy.

Gibbon tried to keep the tone of his voice level, trying not to betray his emotions.

"Beyond that I am asked to discover the spy on the Big Five Committee. We have proof it was one of them who gave the Germans the plans for Scapa."

TR's nervous energy would not let him stand still, he paced the floor. "Gods, that can't be.

Could it be one of their associates is the spy?"

"No, the Big Five were given verbal secrets only they knew. One was on a notation on the map we found."

TR put his hands on his hips and shook his head violently. "You say your direction comes from the Home Secretary, and the King believes it was the Big Five?"

TR sat down. Seldom such shocking news, he was breathing hard.

Gibbon could see he was upset. TR liked the English and considered the Germans future enemies. He had given speeches damning the Huns, blaming them for the war. The Naval Captain plunged ahead. TR would get over his shock.

"Sir, you're the only American that has met the Big Five Committee, could you give me your impression of these men?"

"Yes, of course, but I must tell you I cannot, I cannot believe any of these men would betray his country. The only one I haven't met is Everett, the King's brother. He was on the Committee only as a concession of the King." Roosevelt stood up angrily.

"The one I knew best was General of the Army Kempton, a career officer. His father and grandfather served on the Army General Staff. He loves the army, the man could not be disloyal, the army is his family and his life."

Gibbon was taking notes.

"How old a man is he?"

"Almost sixty and my favorite, a man who was very kind to me. He likes Americans and we went hunting together. He likes to hunt, so of course we got on well. I stayed at his house.

The second member of the Committee was head of the Fleet, Sir John Richardson. If Kempton was the man I liked, the most, Richardson was the man I liked the least. Arrogant, pompous, a terrible reputation of sleeping around, rumored to have made love to some of his subordinates wives. Hated by many members of the Government and clearly the most brilliant of all the members of the Committee. Richardson in twenty years never lost a Naval war game. The man is so smart, he was declared out of the games and the navy has a lot of smart men, like Beatty."

Gibbon at the mention of Beatty said, "Beatty's seamanship saved the Fleet at Jutland, they were beaten. Could some kind of rivalry between Richardson and the other Admirals get him to give the plans to the Germans?"

Roosevelt looked into space. "Hard to believe, but he doesn't love the navy, the man is too egotistical, he loves himself too much."

Roosevelt looked at Gibbon. "Do the Committee members know they are suspected of treason?"

"No, I'm investigating the battle as an observer, but they don't know the real reason I'm involved."

TR. "Gibbon, most of them won't welcome your questions, and one may really consider you an enemy."

"I know, difficult days are ahead but I couldn't refuse the King."

TR said, "Of course not, and I'm convinced we will fight the Germans some day, that's if Mr. Wilson gets up the courage."

Mr. Roosevelt's antipathy to President Wilson was well

known.

As a member of the navy, Gibbon did not comment on his Commander and Chief.

The former President returned to the subject.

'The Assistant to the Prime Minister is Lord Thomas, a politician on the Committee so that the Prime Minister has representation."

"Thomas is an old sixty-five, and very rich, a genius at production, not as smart as the Admiral, but married to one of the most attractive women in England, his second wife Hattie. Hattie, is thirty years younger then he is and one of the most buxom women in high English Society. I sat next to her at a dinner party one time and all the men on the other side of the table kept sneaking looks at her low cut gown. He is fabulously wealthy, much landed estates, and his father bought the Star of India Diamond many years ago, now estimated as worth five million pounds."

Gibbon looked at a note on the pad. "Do any of these men have any German contacts, or history of supporting the Germans?"

"The next man Theodore Mannaning, is married to a second cousin of the Kaiser. You know there are several blood relations of the Kaiser's in England including the King. Mannaning is head of British Intelligence."

Gibbon was writing furiously.

"Mannaning is considered clever, not as smart as Richardson, but not to be trusted, and he doesn't like Americans. Leading up to the war, he was the one man who always believed war was inevitable, so he was right about that."

The one man on the Committee who Gibbon met on the previous trip was Mannaning.

"When I wrote my report that the German Navy could compete with the English he called me. He asked me questions. He wasn't friendly, but when I told him we believed German gunnery would be very good, he didn't argue. He asked me a lot of technical questions. Most everyone else ignored my report because it was negative."

The older man issued a warning. "Mannaning is a bit paranoid, if anyone will resent you and think it's a conspiracy against him, its Mannaning."

"Sir, you were a police official, this is really an investigation, how would you proceed?"

TR once head of a major Police Department responded quickly.

"The best detective in England is Walter Dew of Scotland Yard. You can't use any of the people in British Intelligence because of Mannaning. Dew is called the Dapper Detective. Great dresser, worked his way up, solved more crimes then anyone else. He is a real life Sherlock Holmes. I met him and liked him. I'll give you a letter of introduction. Dew is a very patriotic man, you have the letter from the King that will really energize him. He's a man who doesn't have to consult his superiors on what he is working on. He is perfect for you."

Gibbon felt the rush, trip to Sagamore Hill was as productive as he hoped.

Teddy Roosevelt. "If this case is like the ones we worked on don't go in with preconceived ideas, you will have many surprises. But a game plan will help. Do you have a plan?"

The naval officer looked up. "Just one, at one point I've got to eliminate someone as a suspect and then get the man to help me. The members of the Committee have been meeting for two years, there must be a store of experience I could never reach, especially since they live in a special world. The reason is so unbelievable that someone betrayed the country, they are the country. Not one could leave England and find a life anywhere in the world that he could be happy with. No amount of money or power or hate or jealousy can justify what has happened. I hope none of them are involved." He paused.

"But if I can enlist one of them to help me, I'm sure it will help the investigation."

Roosevelt jumped to his feet. "Gibbon that is an excellent idea, this is a closed social and political society. Your going to need help. Good idea. Bully, very good idea."

Roosevelt respected this young man, his comments proved at once a higher level of responsibility and dedication, and penetrating the inner circle and finding an ally of a member of the Committee was an excellent approach.

TR said, "We've been looking at this from the English standpoint. Imagine what the Germans must think, one of the great espionage wins of our time. They must have a great deal of confidence and little respect for the English to let this happen. I believe if the Germans win the war in Europe, they may want to extend their power over the whole world and we may have to fight them here. Gibbon you are working for your own country as well as the English."

#

Gibbon and Westy drove for thirty minutes, when Gibbon motioned Westy to pull over. They parked on a hill. A lone sailboat moved in a stiff breeze down Long Island Sound. Gibbon told Westy the full story about the trip to England including TR's comments and the detective Walter Dew.

#

Westy produced a silver flask, took a nip and offered it to Gibbon who refused a drink.

Westy first reaction, this was a very difficult assignment for this young man, but he knew Gibbon was well past that assessment.

"Gibbon, people tend to fit in a pattern. When the hostiles scalped Custer and cut up his men that was what they do. Its part of their way of life. The English traitor will fight to protect himself. You're a stranger, the man may realize you are a threat and feel it will reduce his danger if he kills you. Its what he does."

Gibbon never thought of the potential danger of the assignment.

"Now this fellow Dew may help." Westy spit out a chew of tobacco.

"But we have another advantage, they view us as crazy Americans, especially me and my boots and hat and my gun. If I stay close the traitor may not want to try us. He may believe I'd be crazy enough to shoot first, which of course I would. Its what I do, so I believe you and I should never be apart."

His logic was hard to refuse.

"Westy its not the Wild West."

"No but remember when we met. The King and I told him all the stories about fighting Indians. He considered me a crazy cowboy. He loved the stories. If I shot someone the King would pardon me."

Westy dealt in a world half civilized like baseball and the frontier which in some parts of America was still pretty wild.

"Westy what you say makes sense. If the man is a German agent he could be very dangerous, and I appreciate your help."

"Gibbon remember the day you knocked out the cowboy?"

"Yes."

"You took your time because you're a gentlemen, and the circles you have to move in requires a gentlemen. These are important people, the Germans, and they are not gentlemen. You do your job and I'll do mine, if we meet trouble I'll step up, besides if you get killed your wife would never forgive me."

They both laughed. "Not one word to Amanda. She and I hadn't thought of what your talking about. Westy, I told TR about Amanda walking through German steel plants. He was impressed."

"Its what she does, Gibbon people do what they're good at."

CHAPTER 9

The dinner party at Lady Mitilda Owens palatial home outside London proceeded on schedule with course after course served by waiters dressed in white livery of the French Court of Louis the Fourteenth.

Lord Thomas, the industrial leader of England and Assistant to the Prime Minister ignored the white wigs and tight pants of the waiters. Since the dinner began his anger was directed at the absence of his wife and Admiral Richardson from the table. He ignored the wonderful onion soup, the excellent wine and the talk of Lady Carenington on his right.

When Mitilda Owens spoke to him when he first sat down he was curt with her, suspecting she was probing to determine if Richardson and his wife were having an affair. That his wife would cheat on him was disgraceful or that Richardson would gamble with his relationship with a fellow member of the Big Five, was traitorous.

The Big Five was the cutting edge of the war effort. Anything that disturbed the cohesion of the group was an aid to the Germans. Richardson was not only insulting Thomas, he was acting to hurt England.

Richardson, notorious for his pursuit of women in British high society seemed to smile at Hattie at the beginning of the meal. Thomas sitting at the far end of the table was watching his wife, her usual low cut dress with the Indian Star Diamond draped over her ample bosom. The Indian Star Diamond held by a necklace was brought to England by Lord Thomas's father, and was now considered the most valuable jewel in the British Isles, worth over five million pounds. Of course, Hattie was wearing an exact copy since the original necklace never left the safe at Lord Thomas's home in London. Thomas was not thinking of the Diamond. For the last two weeks Hattie treated him with cold disdain, refusing to sleep with him, and thus arouse his suspicions about Richardson.

Lord Thomas a brilliant industrialist but previously weak in the ways of the sexual intrigues of London society was correct in his suspicions.

Upstairs on the second floor Hattie waited for Richardson. Familiar with the house, yesterday she sent word to Richardson to meet her in one of the visitors apartments that Lady Mitilda Owens reserved for her guests. They slipped into the apartment and kissed passionately. It was hot, no windows were open to the outside. Richardson said.

"There is a crisis at the Naval Bureau, I have to phone, I'll be back in ten minutes, wait for me my darling."

The apartments two rooms, a sitting room, and bedroom was very warm, the windows were closed. She took off her clothes and went into the bedroom and unlocked the floor to ceiling windows and immediately a breeze stirred the drapes. The heavy air of the sitting room was oppressive so Hattie sat on the bed in the bedroom waiting for him. She opened a second window encouraging cross ventilation. Hattie took a bottle of Merlot off the night table and poured herself a drink. Admiring herself in the bedroom mirror she agreed she was the most voluptuous woman in London. She smiled, she did not take herself seriously because Hattie was smart, and confident and witty, not like the paramour she waited for. The Admiral was a pompous and insufferable man with no sense of humor. The house was magnificent, including a grand salon and crystal dining room where the enormous dinner tables were set up. She could see her husband stirring. At one point he would miss her. Part of the plan.

The dinner party continued, the bottles emptying faster, the laughter louder, but the mood of Thomas did not improve.

Now mad at the blatant absence of Hattie, Lord Thomas left the table and walked up the winding stairs to the bedrooms on the second floor. He tried three doors before he found one open, the hall way into the room held a single candle. The bedroom beyond dark, but a breeze from the open windows of the summer night made the candle flicker. The husband recognized Hattie's shoes by the entrance to the bedroom.

He paused as his wife's voice came from the dark bedroom.

"My darling close the door, my husband may be wandering around looking for me. Come to bed my dearest, I've been waiting for you, and lock the door behind you."

Thomas his temper rising blew the candle out and waited in silence, until his eyes became accustomed to the dark. The summer breeze and moonlight came through the open window. As he entered the bedroom she spoke.

"My darling, take off your jacket, last time your medals scratched me." He thought, *Hattie you are waiting for Richardson, that bastard.*

"Your so quiet, does your passion silence your voice." She laughed.

Thomas clinched his fist, she barely spoke to him, these days, but saved her prattle for the Admiral.

Then the door to the hallway opened and Richardson's voice was heard. "Hattie are you there?"

Lady Thomas was confused, if the Admiral was at the door who was in the bedroom. She lit a candle and seeing her husband uttered his name *"EDGAR?"*

Admiral Richardson heard the cry of shock. He turned and quickly exited the room.

Thomas, furious at his wife lashed out. "Hattie, you harpy, you were waiting for him. I'm disgusted, don't deny it."

She sat up in the bed and covered herself with a sheet.

She could only answer weakly. "NO. NO."

Thomas's rage boiled over. He slapped his wife. "You whore, I hate you, you've disgraced us both."

His yelling attracted the attention of Mitilda Owens who was walking by. She quietly opened the door to hear him shout.

"Hattie you were waiting for Richardson, I heard you, call his name. Lying in bed with no clothes on, what were you the desert for this dinner party."

Owens listened to the soft tearful denials of the voice she recognized as Hattie Thomas. Then she scurried away to tell two of her friends what she heard. The story gained strength throughout the next hour and some guests believed that Thomas caught Richardson and Hattie in bed together.

The next morning Admiral Richardson was concerned about his career. All of the city was a buzz of conversation with the story. He had been warned by a representative of the King's that during the war all members of the ruling elite of the country must serve as models for the citizens of England. Now it would be only days before the story would appear in the press coupled with the defeat at Scapa. Would the King dismiss him, especially since the scandal involved the wife of another member of the Big Five? The strange twist was, he didn't pursue Hattie, she threw herself at him. It was difficult to ignore the beautiful and voluptuous Hattie and against his better judgment he entered the affair.

Richardson left the party immediately after Thomas found

Hattie. In the car on the way home he searched for an idea to save his career. Captain Fitzwith was at the party, he was a cousin of Mitilda Owens and by the time Richardson reached his house the beginning of a plan was forming in his mind.

Richardson called the weak and untalented Captain Fitzwith to his office.

"Captain, you were at the dinner party last night, you've heard the rumors about my affair with Lady Thomas?"

The captain stammered and tried to pretend he was ignorant of the whole episode since he was afraid of Admiral Richardson.

"Sir, I do not know of any rumors of last night."

Richardson explained what London was talking about and said, "Captain, we are in a great war, I cannot be accused and gossiped about, this way you can do your country and the navy a great service. You will leak to the press you were the man Lady Thomas was waiting for. My name came up through the confusion of which Naval officer it was. You are a bachelor, your life will not be effected."

The captain sat down in a chair speechless. Finally he said. "Sir, that would be a lie." The captain turned white.

The Admiral was cognizant of the man he was dealing with.

"Yes, and I and England would be in your debt."

The Admiral a great manipulator of men continued to describe this as patriotic duty.

"You would be serving your country, you know my services are critical to the war effort and I would be grateful." He continued. "We are about to win a great victory at Gallipoli. I would send you with dispatches to that war zone, you would be out of the country. In a year or so when the Fleet returns you would be in command of one of our battleships, your career made."

This was a great incentive, since the captain could never hope to command a battleship.

"What about Mrs. Thomas?" he asked.

"She will admit it was you, she understands how important this is to the country."

The Admiral had not spoken to Hattie, but gambled the Lady would refuse all comments about the affair. As would her husband, and so a bargain was struck and the captain did as he was asked for the good of the navy. Richardson as he often did, manipulated the event in his favor, but it was strange. The women threw herself at him, and yet it was almost as if she wanted her husband to catch them. Why the party at Owens house, they could have met somewhere else? Today she reacted to his message with cold disdain like she didn't care He vowed not to see her again.

When she reacted to his message in such a cold manner the Admiral thought. Could this be a plan by Lord Thomas and his wife to discredit me? A plan to force the King to dismiss me from the Big Five? Were they working for a third party, the Germans?

When Amanda and Gibbon reached the hotel in London the story of the scandal was front page in all the papers except the *Times*. The two leading tabloids had divided stories. One said Hattie was caught in bed with the captain, the other she was waiting for the Admiral. The two Americans devoured the news. Finally Gibbon spoke.

"Could this whole treason be about a marriage gone bad? Thomas hates the Admiral because of his wife."

Tired from the trip Gibbon was not in a good mood. The thought of the disaster in the Orkney Islands because of a domestic quarrel was bitter and depressing.

The first biography compiled was Thomas. Amanda pulled out the folder and started reading. "Lord Thomas was a very rich man, second marriage, he was thirty-five years older than Hattie, and acknowledged as an industrial genius in production. The most important man in the military industrial complex of England. A very nasty divorce from his first wife, caused a split with his oldest son. Now the son Derek was back running the family business, autos.

Amanda made a judgment. "The man is conservative, this event with the public must be killing him."

Gibbon asked. "Does the record show any conflict between Thomas and the Admiral in the past?" "No, but they didn't work together often. Thomas did most of the developments with the army. I can't find projects with Richardson."

Gibbon closed no door. "The Germans would like to see Thomas out of the war effort."

Amanda. "We're both so tired our minds are wandering. That the Germans could orchestrate a scandal that would hurt Lord Thomas, is pretty far fetched."

"Your right." Gibbon recognized he had to put the

investigation on track.

"First I've got to see Walter Dew then meet with each of the Big Five. The scandal is not part of the investigation, this begins and ends with Scapa. The last change of plans the placing of the submarine nets just weeks before the attack, I want to pursue that."

The scandal story was important for three days in the press until gradually the story was clouded by the confession of the captain. Now high society was laughing at Mitilda for getting the story wrong. The confusion only upset Lord Thomas more, who went into a deep depression, not going to his office and drinking heavily. His wife at first embarrassed began to enjoy the attention where ever she appeared in London. She began to see herself as a film or stage star.

                                   #

Two men in Germany reacted to the scandal, Baron von Below Chief Advisor, to the Kaiser and his Head of Intelligence, General Lugger.

"General, this is amazing, two members of the Big Five feuding. The Admiral sleeps with Lord Thomas's wife and it effects the war effort."

"Yes, Baron our man in London reports that Thomas their most effective industrialist has stopped working. He rarely appears at his office."

The Baron twirled his white mustache. "You don't think the cursed Prince Rupprecht could be behind this?"

They hated Rupprecht, his star rising their patron the Kaiser falling. Germany winning the war was not as important as careers.

The general hesitated. "I can't believe Rupprecht could influence the behavior of English society. His success at Scapa Flow is the talk of the nation, and now his armies are on the move in France. No one is talking about the Kaiser. What does the Kaiser think?"

"He is morose, not afraid the Prince will usurp him but jealous."

The Baron asked the question he asked many times before. "How was the victory so complete. Did the Prince's spies invest Scapa and does the Kaiser know the Princes secret?"

The general was analytical. "The Kaiser may know, but he will not discuss it. He won't discuss the Prince, especially if the plan was the Princes idea. Now the Zeppelins and the Gotha bomber, they were directed by the Prince. The man Zastrov, he pretends to be royalty, but he is an ex-auto parts salesman. He met the man who designed the Zeppelin and took, it for his own."

"He sold parts to the Zeppelin company, stole the idea and developed the fleet of air ships. The man is very ruthless, threw one of his captains out of a Zeppelin when the man displeased him. Rupprecht heard about it and told Zastrov that could never happen again. Zastrov obeys the Prince, but would be loyal to us if he had the chance."

The Baron. "I've met Zastrov, Rupprecht is his sponsor, but he would come over to us if the opportunity presented itself, but lets talk about London."

The Baron had a plan. "The Swiss delegate to London is in our pay, he is a friend of Derek Thomas, the son of Lord Thomas. The young man has big gambling losses. We offer Thomas money to find out if one of the Big Five helped the Prince at Scapa. Once we find out we release the information and embarrass the Prince. He can't protect his sources."

The General recognized the Baron was desperate.

General. "Yes he could not protect his spies and also the Prince stooped so low as to orchestrate the scandal. This would be a black mark on his reputation."

The ruling classes of Europe could let millions die in the trenches, but a trick to embarrass the royalty of another nation was considered criminal.

#

The Swiss delegate spoke to Derek Thomas.

"Derek, I represent people who believe there was treachery at Scapa. We would pay if you could investigate your father and any other member of the Big Five. Also this might be related to your step-mothers incident with the Admiral. You move in the social circles of the Big Five, perhaps you can help us?"

Young Thomas accepted the German money, then Derek Thomas met the French Ambassador Vivile.

"Vivile, you are going to find this hard to believe. The Swiss Ambassador approached me this morning. He wants me to investigate if someone from the Big Five gave the Germans the plans for Scapa Flow, and also he wants to know if the scandal was staged. I agreed to work for them, the money was excellent, but I cautioned them I might not be able to help. Clearly about Scapa, I don't know, and yet I'm confused. If the Swiss delegate is working for the Germans, they must be aware of the espionage."

Vivile. "There are rival German Secret Services, the one for the Prince had the Scapa plans. You must have been approached by the Kaiser's people, their rivals. They want to discredit the Prince. When we paid you to stage the scandal we wanted to embarrass your father Lord Thomas. Your father has favored a separate peace with the Germans that would leave France at the Kaiser's mercy. We wanted Thomas off the Big Five."

"Hattie did stage the incident and she still thinks it's a plan to destroy my father's health so we can inherit the money on the Star Diamond. She is in love with me and has no idea about his politics," said Derek.

Vivile understood the English aristocracy, like the French, only cared about themselves. Vivile cared about his country. He thought, *We must destroy Thomas, he might be the traitor and hurt the English war effort.*

"I worry about the war, the General Staff has no idea how low the morale of the French Army is. If any word leaked out the English wanted a separate peace with the Germans our army would surrender. I think some units are close to revolt now. The killing on the Western Front is terrible, our generals think they are Napoleon. The great General Napoleon must be turning over in his grave. He would never fight the Germans the way they are they are criminally stupid."

Derek Thomas did not care about the war or the French or the English. "Vivile what should I do, I can't tell them the incident was staged, and I'll never find out anything about Scapa."

"Well, I suspect we'll never find out anything about Scapa, the scandal tells them what they want to hear. Tell them you suspect the Prince, but can't prove it, they bribed your step-mother."

After Derek left, Vivile speculated. The war is crazy. We pay Derek to stage an incident to discredit Thomas the Germans come to him to find out if the Prince is the designer of the scandal. Young Derek would never tell the Germans, but we will have to continue to pay for his silence. If the scandal continues to incapacitate, Lord Thomas our plan worked.

It is amazing the Germans are winning the war despite the deep divide between the Prince and the Kaiser's people. The world has gone mad.

CHAPTER 10

Chief Inspector Walter Dew met Gibbon Stillwell at the Laters London hotel to receive a letter from Theodore Roosevelt. Dew was impeccably dressed, his herring bone suit and matching vest made him look more like a banker then a policeman. Broad shoulders of medium height he put on reading glasses to read Roosevelt's letter.

When Dew finished he handed back the letter to Gibbon who then gave him the King's letter. Dew read the second letter and finally took off his glasses. Both letters urged the reader to give full support to Gibbon Stillwell.

"You have impressive credentials Mr. Stillwell. What can I do for you?"

"Gibbon, please call me Gibbon, I have accepted a job I'm not qualified to do. I'm to find a man that committed treason against your country. I need help and I'm told you are the best qualified man to help me."

Dew did not respond.

Gibbon explained the events at Scapa. He declared that one of the Big Five committed treason. Each man on hearing the events at Scapa reacted differently. Dew uttered the words, "it cannot be."

Then he picked up the King's letter and read it again. Gibbon waited. This was the first Englishman he explained the events at Scapa to. The reaction was deep and emotional. Dew needed a moment.

"Gibbon, assume its one of the Big Five, what's the motive?" His voice trailed off.

"Motive and opportunity, this group paralyzes the senses. They are England, I've pursued high government officials but never a crime like this."

Dews mind was racing.

"If the man wanted to destroy the Fleet, how could he be sure the Germans would be victorious enough to drive the whole Fleet to Scapa and then destroy it?"

Gibbon responded. "That's been troubling me too. We suspected but none of us were sure the Germans would win a battle that would send the whole Fleet to Scapa. So the motive might not have been to destroy the Fleet, but blackmail or money, but with these five men its hard to accept any of that."

Dew never on a case like this wondered if the American had a plan where to begin.

"Have you plotted how to begin? Do you have a plan?"

Before calling Dew, Gibbon wrote down his opening to commence the work deliberately he said.

"At the direction of the King I will question each of the Big Five. It will be a study of what happened, a review of a losing battle by a Naval person from another country. At some point I'll ask questions about the defense, strategy and where the plans were kept and this will be under the guise the King asked me to write a report on Scapa. Scapa was clearly not the only project these men worked on. I'm not overseeing the Big Five only one aspect of their work. There will be a follow up of questions and at some point you and I will determine one man who could not have done it and enlist his aid. Clearly that man will understand the other four better then you and I could. I believe a member of the Big Five will be our best insight into these men."

Dew realized why the King and TR had so much respect for this young man. He had courage and a simple and clear approach for an amazingly difficult and complicated problem.

Dew said, "Yes, these men operate at a different level then the rest of us. We need someone who will see things in a perspective we never could. I like your idea of getting help from a member of the committee. I like it very much, you have my full support."

Gibbon was pleased they passed an important hurdle. He asked his new partner. "Inspector, do you have an idea you'd like to develop?"

"I'll begin round the clock surveillance on these men. With the two military leaders difficult, but I can begin security checks on their associates investigate on the edges. I'll develop a file and also I'd like to see the notes your wife worked on."

"It would appear the guilty party does not know we are pursuing. Reaction to your questions could give us a lead."

"Gibbon is it possible someone gave the plans to the Germans inadvertently?" Said Dew

"Almost impossible. The last changes in the submarine nets were made just before the attack and given to the Big Five verbally."

Now Gibbon had a question for the Inspector.

"Assume the man is not a career criminal and has never committed a major crime before what is his state of mind?"

"A normal human being deep guilt and you would assume only a normal human being could attain such a high office."

"Except for the King's brother."

"Except for the King's brother, but I met him doing charity work. He is a likeable man, very popular with the people in the Police Department who came in contact with him."

"It's not going to be easy Inspector."

"No, and may I ask why did the King pick you?"

"I'm an outsider, my wife and I wrote a report. The German Navy would acquit themselves well. I am a naval officer and we met on my last trip and the meeting went well with the King."

Dew said, "Sir, may I add I think it was a good choice, I am honored to serve with you. Difficult it may be, we shall give it a good go."

The two men shook hands.

#

The first member of the Big Five that Gibbon met was General Kempton. They met at Army Headquarters in London. Gibbon was nervous despite the letter of introduction he carried from the King. This was new to him, not pure research for Naval Intelligence, but a criminal investigation.

The friendly General Kempton immediately put him at ease. A large white mustache, big smile, slightly heavy, but immaculate uniform with polished boots.

Gibbon explained he had been asked to meet with members of the Big Five to discuss the events of the Naval defeat at Scapa Flow. He expected some resistance, but the general was very open and even began with an explanation of how the Big Five was formed, and the history of the committee.

"Gibbon, England has a classic foreign policy in relations to her many wars on the Continent. We traditionally formed Alliances with the weaker nations to form a coalition against the strongest military powers. Certainly you've read our coalition against

Napoleons France. With Germany building a large army and navy, we formed an alliance but beyond that with the development of modern weapons we took it one step further. For the first time a Committee was formed, the Big Five was to promote greater cooperation among the military and political arms of the government. The Committee was to recommend allocation of resources and develop an oversight of our war effort."

Gibbon felt the need to ask a question. "Did anyone in the government dispute or criticize the organization of the Big Five?"

"No, for such a powerful group it was amazingly tranquil. I never met anyone who disputed the need for the Big Five. In fact most people felt this was one of the smoothest war time leadership groups we ever structured in England."

The general smiled, proud that he could report the concept was so well received.

Gibbon still feeling his way asked. "Was the inner working of the committee smooth?"

"Yes, and no, four of us worked together well. Admiral Richardson was the only one to lose his temper or complain about our decisions. I'm a close friend of Assistant Prime Minister Lord Thomas, we went to school together, rowed for the schools and have always been close so we usually agreed on most decisions that came before the Committee. Everett, the King's brother, was very quiet, he rarely did anything but agreed with the majority."

The American was fascinated with the inner working of the powerful organization and the personalities involved.

"General, I met the head of British Intelligence Mannaning. He strikes me as a very brilliant man."

"Yes Mannaning was clearly the second strongest personality and his judgment that there would be a war when many said it wouldn't happen gave him great creditability, but he could not match the intellect of Admiral Richardson and Richardson's knowledge of the war effort."

"Can you give me one example? Gibbon asked.

"Yes. The Gallipoli invasion was approved but only Richardson recognized the problems that the navy was facing and his insistence the navy must attack the bottleneck of the Dardanelles and the army must land and keep Turkish gunners from firing at the ships."

"So, Richardson was right?"

"Brilliantly right, if the army had not landed the Turkish gunners would have thwarted the ships and the invasion would have failed."

Gibbon felt the need to pursue the question.

"Even after the initial landing, there will be difficult fighting."

"Yes, but we have a chance, it could change the war," said Kempton.

"Sir, along with the Admiral you on the Committee reviewed the defenses at Scapa Flow. Did the Admiral dominate the strategy of those defenses?"

"Yes this was totally his decision, none of us felt we could dispute his judgment."

At this point the general began to review his military history and for the next hour Gibbon listened patiently to the General's family history that included his grandfather and fathers service record. Clearly the General loved the army. The General explained he spent half his time in London and half at the front in France with the army.

The General explained that Lord Thomas was head of tank production and he said the tank was the only way to break the stalemate in the trenches in France.

Gibbon asked. "General do you think the stalemate in the trenches could produce a truce or an armistice?"

"No, the French General Staff will never agree and yet I question if they have the support of their troops. The French Infantry has taken great casualties. Our men have not suffered nearly as much?"

This was interesting, but Gibbon wanted to return to Scapa Flow. "Sir, the King wanted me to discuss the defenses of Scapa Flow. Do you think they were adequate?"

"Obviously not."

The phone rang, the General picked it up, listened then hung up.

"The Germans are massing on the Western Front, I've got to return to France. Can we continue this later?" he stood up and Gibbon shook his hand and left.

Gibbon felt disappointed, he had not handled the interview well, they got off the subject and he was not aggressive enough with his questions.

The Big Five were all going to be distracted and busy and

sometimes defensive. He would not do what the King wanted if he remained timid. Yes, he was a stranger and these men national leaders but they hadn't saved the Northern Fleet. He vowed to be more positive on the next interview. Of course this man was so dedicated to the army, he could not be the traitor. But Gibbon perhaps with good questions could have gotten more insight into the four others. Gibbon judged the interview a disappointment.

CHAPTER 11

The King's brother Everett was the only one of the Big Five to invite Gibbon to his home to grant the request of the King for an interview. Gibbon immediately liked the man. He was shy, but open and friendly. He spoke in a low voice, but the interview quickly turned as he wanted to know all about Gibbons background and what the Americans thought of the war. Gibbon welcomed the open communications for he was learning about the man by the tenor of his questions. Getting an insight into what he thought was important. When Everett found out that Gibbon was a history major at Yale, with a major in Military History and had written his senior thesis on the Napoleonic Wars, Everett was delighted.

"I have a treat for you, please follow me." Everett opened a door to a room in the basement and turned on the light. On a large table perhaps twenty-five feet across was a model of a military battle with thousands of toy soldiers.

Gibbon recognized it immediately. "Its Waterloo."

"Yes."

Gibbon moved to the table, scanned the French side and pointed to a figure on a white charger. "Napoleon?"

The host delighted nodded and pointed to another figure. "Ney."

Gibbon was transfixed. "It's magnificent, the only model I've seen this size was Gettysburg, at West Point."

The older man delighted at the reaction stepped back to let the guest scan the table.

They discussed different stages of the battle. Gibbon as familiar as Everett with the events of the historic day when the French and English met Napoleons last battle and greatest defeat.

Gibbon could see the model figure of Wellington, the head of the English Army was slightly larger than any other. For ten minutes they examined the farmhouse, 'Hougoumont,' then Everett said, "Boney was not good that day."

The American responded with the classic reason Napoleon did not show his best as a general. "They say he was sick."

Now Everett pointed to the toy soldier representing the Duke of Wellington. "The Duke was at the top of his form, but he was always good, very consistent on the battlefield."

The pride in the statement was obvious and it was true. Everett moved the figure slightly and said. "Do you know the effect of the English Infantry on the French Infantry?"

"What do you mean Everett?"

The man motioned to the Red coated toy soldiers standing on the hill facing the French Blue advancing.

"The French always advanced with flags flying, drums beating, a sight that intimidated most of Europe. The English stood very still, not a man moved. Finally as the French drew near the English solid line unnerved them. The Red Coats would wait to the last minute and fire when the French were very close. It was a hallmark of Wellington's troops."

Gibbon remembered this story and recognized that Everett took pride in telling him about the steadfast Infantry. After an hour Gibbon started to ask him about Scapa Flow.

"Did you have much input into the defenses of the base?"

"No, not being a military man I didn't offer advise. Actually I was only there once, cold place."

"On looking at the plans did you see any weakness?"

"No, again I felt General Kempton and Admiral Richardson were far more professional than I was, so I was very quiet. But on most matters of the Committee I didn't speak up."

He sat down, a wave of sadness touched him. "All our brave men who died at Scapa, I still can't sleep when I think of that terrible day."

He was not talking about model soldiers, but flesh and blood. Gibbon thought, if this man helped the enemy he is a very good actor. He loves his nations military.

They continued to talk, Everett was candid in his answers to every question.

"I know Mannaning and Thomas well. I don't know General Kempton or Admiral Richardson except for our meeting. Have you talked to them yet?"

"Only Kempton, I'm having lunch with the Admiral in two days and playing golf with Mannaning on Friday."

Everett sighed. "I played golf with Mannaning once, he beat me soundly, not a friendly person. I think he only was cordial to me because of my brother. Not unusual. I don't mind. My role is best when I show my diorama. Even the Kaiser was impressed when he saw it."

The three dimensional table did command respect. "Your related to the Kaiser?" asked Gibbon.

It was an innocuous question, but Everett trying to help the young American volunteered an answer in depth."

"He is an honorable person, you can trust him, but he has an inferiority complex. I think because of his withered arm, and he's not too smart. He and the Russians blundered into the war. We all let Austria send us down a path of destruction. Now I think he doesn't even control the war effort, the Prince does. It would be better for us if he did. Maybe we could negotiate a peace treaty. Of course, after Scapa, if I know Willie, the terms would be unacceptable. He is a man that cannot see the other fellows point of view."

Gibbon felt this interview was so much better then the one with the General, and decided to ask a leading question.

"Where did you keep your set of plans for Scapa."

Everett smiled. "I'll tell you, but I've told no one else. A fake set of the plans were in my safe down stairs, but the real plans are in one of the draws over there." He pointed to a series of cabinets with many draws.

"The day after the attack I rushed down here and went to the draw. They were untouched. I'm sure no one even saw them. I always laid a pencil on top of the plans, it was unmoved."

"And of course you never discussed the verbal changes you were told about?"

"No never, in fact some of the details of the Committee I didn't understand."

Everett stared at Gibbon for a long moment.

"You think Germans spies got the plans?"

Gibbon shrugged his shoulders. He would not tell Everett his real mission.

"Well to evaluate the attack, I've got to examine all the aspects of the defense."

"Gibbon, by brother has a great respect for you. He has told all the members of the Big Five to help you and I'm sure we will. One thing, you might consider. Everyone knows the Admiral is brilliant and Mannaning very capable, but the real key to our war efforts is Lord Thomas. My son-in-law worked with him, the man can't be replaced. His genius is to take complicated industrial projects and mass produce them. Since the incident I hear he is very troubled, not working, drinking. When you see him, hopefully he will come out of this problem he has with his wife."

"Will the incident make it impossible for Thomas to work with the Admiral?"

"Yes, but I don't think it matters, all of Thomas's work are with the Army and the Air Force which my son-in-law is in command."

He turned philosophical. "Gibbon, it must be difficult for the people of America to see the common people making such sacrifices where the argument appears to be between the ruling classes."

Gibbon waited for he could see Everett had a point.

'"We believe on this island we care for the people and some of the warring fractions don't. We didn't want this war and some like Thomas would want to end it today, but can we? If you know the Kaiser his ego won't let him end the war without a victory, so we keep on fighting, no matter what. Our Southern Fleet will protect the island. The Germans may bomb us but no German soldier will ever set foot on British soil."

#

Admiral Sir John Richardson was annoyed the King asked him to meet the American Gibbon Stillwell. He arranged to meet Stillwell at his Club despite the fact no American had ever eaten there. Sir John was furious when Gibbon brought his wife. The only other women to enter the Club were members of the English royal family. The lunch in the bar was strained, the Americans tried to be polite, but Sir John only gave curt, short answers to the questions. The Admiral who guaranteed the King the Germans could never defeat the English Fleet, was incensed that Gibbon predicted the Germans would be competitive, and would have been more outraged if he was aware Amanda influenced Gibbons thinking. That she saw the Krupp Steel and recognized it was better than the English never occurred to him.

By the end of the lunch Gibbon was tired of trying to question the Admiral. Patient but not timid Gibbon used the direct approach.

"Sir, the King asked me to talk to you, we can continue to try and have polite conversations and you can continue to be rude, but I want to ask you some direct questions and we get this over with."

The Admiral was outraged.

"Sir, you are no gentlemen to bring your wife to this Club, it is a flagrant disregard of manners."

Amanda understood his husband. She had seen him in frontier bars, crash the line for Yale football, stand up to German officers on the Rhine who did not want him to see their artillery. He would not back off. Gibbon did not have a temper but there was a line you could not cross with him. That line was his promise to the King, and the President, he would find out what happened at Scapa Flow.

"Admiral my wife knows more about steel and Naval guns then I do. I thought she could help. Now I'm going to ask questions. If you choose not to answer I will tell the King. All the others cooperated with me, and I'll omit your name from that list."

The Admiral almost got up from the table, but he recognized the King did not like him, because of the defeat of the Northern Fleet, the incident, he was not on firm ground. He would stay and grit his teeth. This interview would not end his career.

"Go ahead ask your questions," he said with a snarl.

"Sir, you and the Committee had the plans for the defense when the Germans attacked? Did not the Germans execute the attack as you would have in a war game?"

Richardson rocked back. Once, a week after the defeat the idea crossed his mind but because he was so troubled he ignored the implications.

"Yes, if I was the attacker I would have used the Zeppelins and the bombers and ended with the submarines, it was a perfect plan."

"So, the strategy was perfect, the execution just as good?"

"Yes, just as good." The Admirals voice was less aggressive.

He began to realize what Stillwell was saying.

For the next twenty minutes Amanda and Gibbon asked questions about the details of the ships that were damaged and destroyed. Amanda had an architectural drawing of the anchorage and what ships were hit by bombs or torpedoes. It was so painful for the Admiral, he realized that this was the first time he replayed the battle in such detail. The young Americans had done their homework.

Gibbon asked. "Sir, in the fog of war, it is unusual to see such execution. Could the Germans have done this without the plans of the defense?"

This was the question they were leading up to. The question he avoided in his own mind for months. The question he would have considered an insult one hour ago, but the question he knew they would ask. The answer he decided on when he saw the terrible drawing and the destruction that was so painful that his answer was a whisper.

"No. No. They must have had the plans." The table was silent, all three participants quiet. The room empty except for the waiters who stood a good forty yards away at the bar. Catching snatches of the early talk the waiters and the bartender organized a pool when the Admiral would ask the young Americans to leave the Club. Not hearing any details but watching his body language and expression and knowing the Admirals temper, all four joined in the pool. Now kept away because the Americans were showing him clearly highly classified material the bartenders saw the expression on the Admirals face.

The bartender who knew him best said, "Forget the pool, the Americans are not leaving."

The Admiral said, "Please put your papers away, I need a drink. Do you want a drink?"

They did not.

After the waiter retreated to a respectful distance Amanda brought out her rendering of the Battle of Jutland. The battle was displayed with exact movement of ships and times. The detail even better then Scapa.

Gibbon was polite and respectful. "This may sound harsh but to seek the truth we feel the Germans had the better guns and gunnery. The English superior seamanship and some advantages in breaking the Naval code. The Battle of Jutland, a small German advantage."

Everyone said the Admiral was brilliant and after the very painful hours he proved it.

"What you really have proved is the Germans could only win big if they had a traitor helping them.?"

"Yes, that's what we think."

The Admiral said, "The Germans had the plans at Scapa but no help at Jutland. So if someone helped them it wasn't the navy because the traitor could have given ship dispositions and tactics and they didn't at Jutland."

"Yes we think there is a traitor but not the navy, the positions of the guns, the submarine nets, the balloons, they came from the plans at Scapa."

The Admiral did not feel relief he only felt empty. Proving the navy didn't do it, did not bring his ships back. He was still the man who lost half the English Navy. He felt nothing about the Americans, they were like the teacher who tells you your not number one in the class anymore. He would not thank them for the excellent work, and his career was it over? Probably.

"What do you want to do?" he said.

"We have a list of questions, mostly about where the plans were kept and who worked on them. Could we send them over?"

Again he responded quickly. "The position of the outer submarine nets, that was verbally given to the Big Five."

"We understand, and critical to the end of the battle."

"Do you want my help with the Big Five?"

Gibbon. "Sir, I have no authority other than to investigate. After I make my report to the King we may call on you again. Clearly you can't talk about this luncheon."

Outside Amanda said to Gibbon. "I'm exhausted, that was far more difficult than any meeting on bidding for a building project or even when we visited Krupp. Why didn't you accept his help, now that he knows there is a traitor?"

Gibbons looked at her. "Everything says the navy probably didn't do it and could help defeat his own men? I don't think so, but I'm not sure about him."

Amanda. "You wanted some help from one of the Big Five."

"Amanda did you see the look on his face when we praised the seamanship of Beatty and his behavior in the scandal. Little things but I'm not sure about the Admiral, his ego is so big I still don't trust him."

CHAPTER 12

Sir Theodore Mannaning was the head of British Intelligence and President of the most exclusive Golf Club in England outside of London. The drive from the highway to the clubhouse was two miles. Named The Club it featured long green fairways, great elms and quiet ponds. A stream ran across the first fairway and giant sand traps protected the greens on the back nine.

With only one hundred members in his Club, Mannaning, the fourth member of the Big Five, debated if he would invite Gibbon to play golf at The Club.

He decided to extend the invitation because he viewed the meeting as potentially confrontational and necessary because the King sent him a letter requesting it. Mannaning remembered their first meeting when Stillwell warned him about the might of the German Navy. Dubious his respect for the young man grew when he was proved to be right. Still he did not like Gibbon because he was an American, and he viewed America as an uncivilized nation.

The British Intelligence Chief had mixed feelings about the opportunity to exchange information with Stillwell. The man right once, belonged to an Intelligence group that Mannaning had little respect for. One declaration Mannaning did bring to the match, the resolve to defeat and embarrass the young American at the game of golf.

The opening tee shot gave him confidence that it could be achieved, using a long swing from his six foot four inch frame. His ball was almost forty yards past Gibbon.

Gibbon Stillwell was the finest all around athlete in the history of Yale. His greatest strength was his eye-hand coordination. On his second shot, hitting a long iron he drove the ball to within four feet of the pin. On the second hole the same thing happened. Mannaning hit his tee shot well past the American, who using an iron hit his ball almost to the cup to go one up for the match.

The Club Secretary standing in a small group that was following the match turned to Mannaning and said, "He hits an iron like a professional, he has great hands and touch."

Mannaning deflated responded. "If he hits irons like that all day I can't beat him.

The Club Secretary sought to reassure his boss. "Sir, I've heard he has a bad leg, I noticed a little limp after the second hole, stay close, he might really weaken on the back nine."

The subject did not believe he was on the course for a game of golf. His second meeting confirmed his opponent was smart, arrogant and a bit of a front runner. His change of stride after Gibbon hit his second iron told Stillwell that he could be knocked off balance. So he probed.

"Mr. Mannaning, the King asked me to investigate the defeat at Scapa Flow, can you comment on it?"

As they walked to the short third, the Englishman was shocked by Gibbon's directness and impertinence. Annoyed, he recognized that the question would come up sooner or later.

"Mr. Stillwell, the navy was caught unprepared, I'm surprised the Prime Minister and the King did not replace Admiral Richardson."

Gibbon pressed on. "The Germans seem to know where the submarine nets were. Has your agency investigated?"

This really caught Mannaning unprepared. He blurted out. "We believe German spies must have penetrated the base. We investigated in depth. Have over fifty agents at Scapa checking everyone."

Gibbon pulled a five iron out of his bag for the one hundred eighty yard third. He was very deliberate turning back to get a different club. This was to give him the time to think. The head of British Intelligence a suspect in a treason case and not aware he was a suspect, annoyed that a stranger was questioning his responsibilities. The caddies and four others stood a respectful distance, not hearing Gibbon whisper.

"The submarines cognizant where the nets were, the Zeppelins bombed exactly where the big ships were berthed. Have you tried to penetrate German Intelligence to find out how they were so knowledgeable?"

Mannaning leaned over the brush, some cut grass off the tee, and said in a low voice.

"There are two German Intelligence's. The one that works for the Kaiser, and barely knows what day it is and the professionals that report to Prince Rupprecht. I monitor the professionals and what they study and research, but that is none of your business.

Your suppose to be checking on what happened at Scapa."

Seeing the conversation was heated the spectators shrunk back and gave the participants even greater room.

"I am asking for the King, I direct you to answer my question," said Gibbon.

This stunned Mannaning and he said, "Rupprecht's Intelligence people did no work on Scapa. The emphasis was on France and Russia and the land war."

Gibbon judged he could ask one more question before the man walked off or hit him with his clubs.

"You deduct from this?"

"That Rupprecht had spies at Scapa that reported to him. None of his top people were involved, it was all his show. He supports the Zeppelins and they proved him right. He is stronger then even the Kaiser's people. They are not involved in running the war. Now damn you, hit the ball."

As they walked off the third tee, Gibbon thought. "I didn't want to have this conversation on a golf course, but it works for me, he's distracted, but I better let him win a couple of holes."

Mannaning won the third hole when Gibbon missed a short putt. He began to feel better and walked to the fourth still puzzled at the questions. What was the American getting at?" As he mounted the steps to the elevated tee an idea struck him.

The American believed one of the Big Five gave the Germans the plans. Of course they used someone outside of Government circles. The King feared a spy and wanted an American to probe. This so unnerved him, he dubbed his next shot.

The play was erratic. Neither man playing as well as when he started. The Club Secretary was satisfied when he saw Gibbon limping badly at the ninth hole. Westy Tyler, Gibbon's caddy opened a small folding stool he carried in his bag and Gibbon sat down in the shade. Refreshed he hit a fine drive. Westy trailed the group as he folded the stool.

The Club Secretary walked over to Westy and said, "You cannot use that stool, its against Club rules. We don't allow anything like that."

Westy said gruffly. "My man has a bad leg."

"Well then, he shouldn't be playing."

Westy decided to use his finest western diplomacy. "Since we are not members, the rules don't apply to us."

"I decide the rules, I am the Club Secretary and if I call the Security people they will take the stool away from you."

Westy pointed to his hat and then pulled his jacket open to show a six gun.

"I spoke to your King, he laughed at my hat and gun. He called me a crazy American cowboy. If I pull this gun and shoot you in the knee, it will hurt a lot and the King will ask me why I did that, and I will say I was just showing it to you and the gun went off. He may not believe me but your knee will still hurt. Now go away before I get mad."

He picked up Gibbons golf bag and left a speechless Club Secretary staring at him. On the next hole Westy opened the stool again.

The match ended with Gibbon winning by one hole. They went to the Clubhouse and Gibbon savored the finest gin and tonic he ever tasted.

He decided to change the strategy.

I'm sorry if you think me forward, I am a great admirer of the King and I want to pursue his charge to me as best I can."

Then he returned to the subject. "Is it possible the Germans got a copy of the defense by careless handling of the material, or a robbery?"

"No, I checked, we all agreed if any security breach occurred I was to check and to follow up.

No one called me about a problem."

He was referring to the copies that members of the Big Five held.

Now Mannaning took the offensive. "You keep coming back to the breach of security and how it relates to the defense plans of Scapa."

"Sir, the Germans were very lucky or very smart to do such damage. Your navy broke their code, we must be suspicious of the actions at the anchorage, and you have to be concerned with treason."

"Young man, I have been involved with intelligence a lot longer then you. So much information is obtained that is useless. The enemy sends out false signals, right now I have bigger concerns then our defeat at Scapa."

Gibbon did not react, but Mannaning decided to tell him.

"On several occasions in the past few weeks the French

Infantry refused to attack when ordered by their officers."

Gibbon was surprised. "Is it widespread?"

"No, not yet, but two days ago in the Central Sector not only did troops refuse to leave their trenches, they shot a Major. This is of deep concern to me, I have to study our Allies not our enemies."

Gibbon refused to be distracted by the unsettling news from France.

"Did you work with the navy on the breaking of the German Naval code?"

"I regard breaking of codes like reading a private letter, I don't approve of such things." Mannaning said.

Gibbon attacked. "The Germans would do it to you."

"The Germans are not gentlemen."

Gibbon sipped his drink. His tongue pushed the lime over the ice. He decided to upset Mannaning again.

"If the plans of Scapa were given to the Germans isn't that your responsibility?"

Mannaning recognized the American was deliberately trying to upset him.

He spoke slowly as if explaining to a child. "The Big Five are the only ones who had the complete plans. No one reported them missing or stolen."

Then Mannaning thought. "Was this the King sending the American to give him a nudge to quit? No, the King knew he would never quit."

"If there is any negligence I would say it was Admiral Richardson, and since you persist in asking me questions about Intelligence, I will answer you this. We work at a high level of analysis, not guess work, and spying and I will tell you, I don't like you or your country. When I visited New York five years ago I was amazed how many of your gentlemen did not dress for dinner. You are not a civilized country and now I understand why you are asking me these questions."

"Mr. Mannaning, you and I disagree about a lot of things, except your Club makes great gin and tonics and you have an outstanding golf course. I will write my report but I may have to ask you more questions. My charge comes from a man I respect greatly, your King, so if I appear overly forward please know it is not personal, it is my way."

Mannaning tried to end the meeting with a friendly exchange.

"Did you play golf in college and were you the best player on your team?"

"Yes, I did play, but a man named Kinner was better than me, he is playing professionally now."

#

In the car on the way home Westy said, "Not a friendly match."

"Yes, some harsh words. Chasing spies is hard work. What about that conversation you had with the Club Secretary?"

Westy dismissed it. "Just a difference of opinion, nothing serious. Didn't like my hat."

"What did you think of Mannaning, is he the one? Asked Westy.

"I don't know, complicated man at times, I think he cared more about his golf game then his country. He suspects what I'm doing."

Westy said, "Well the head of Intelligence, how can he not be aware that the Big Five are under suspicion?"

"Westy I'm going to say something that you have hinted at. Some, not all of the European aristocracy felt a greater bond to their enemy leaders than their own people."

"Well some are related."

"Yes but it's a class thing, they think gentlemen don't spy on other gentlemen. The war threatens their very existence, the great casualties and suffering will change the map of Europe."

Westy, a good newspaper reader.

"What if the Germans win?"

"No matter who wins, Europe will change and many of the countries that started this war certainly Austro-Hungary won't be the same or exist," said Gibbon.

CHAPTER 13

The French general staff took most of the heavy guns away from the Fortress at Verdun believing the Germans had little interest in the historical bulwark opposite the German city of Metz. The lack of military significance did not diminish the historic importance of the place as a symbol of France and a citadel that withstood the attack in 1870 during the Franco-Prussian War. No one understood better then Prince Rupprecht the importance of Verdun, and that the French character would force them to defend the Fortress, so he planned a battle of attrition. The French Army would be drawn to the battle and their blood sacrificed for honor.

Prince Rupprecht explained this strategy to Count Zastrov. "Our strategy at Verdun is to lure the French to battle a war of daily attrition, casualties the mark of our success. The enemy shouldn't even occupy the Fortress, its an awkward position, but because we attack they defend. A single road with truck convoys is their only source of supply. I have flown over that road it's a continuous line of vehicles and we encourage them to supply an area our guns pulverized. For us it is a short Front. Our gun command, and once they are on the verge of collapse your Zeppelins will end the battle."

Zastrov asked. "Sir, are you sure the French will not retreat? As you look at the map, it does not seem worth defending."

"Zastrov, the French do not make war like we do. Frequently they show me that they view war as a test of manhood. Long after we stopped straight ahead attacks they continued to send their Infantry against our machine guns. No. They will defend Verdun and we will break their backs. This will be a critical battle if the place has no military value. What better place to show they will fight just to prove us wrong. Mostly our assaults will be made by guns not men. The massed artillery fire will be in great depth. I shall probe with the Infantry, but our guns will crush them."

#

The Tigers were not party to high level strategy, but were part of a probing attack, a terrible day. They attacked in a snow storm, at first a ground fog, then the German Infantry advanced over bleak landscape, shell holes, a lunar picture, light snow then heavy snow, it was difficult to walk. Bachman fell in a shell hole and had to be pulled out and Zimmerman was wounded a second time. Finally the

Germans moving forward blindly, were caught up with a French Infantry attack. The groups broke down to individual combat with bayonets. Night brought an end to the terrible battle along with rain.

The Tigers were cut off from the German lines, wet, cold and hungry, they could not go forwards or backwards. To return, Lars believed they would be shot by either side. Dawn brought an end to the snow and rain and the firing. The battlefield was one large mud hole. Lars woke the rest of the Tigers.

"We're going back, now stay low and try and keep those rifles from getting muddy, we may have to fight our way back." They walked less than a quarter of a mile when they saw a man who was buried in mud up to his chest.

The Frenchmen was trapped in a large shell hole, the more he struggled the tighter he was stuck. His heavy coat weighed him down and only his arms and head were visible.

Fredrick reacted. "He's French, do we shoot him?"

The powerful Holtzen. "No, he can't get out, don't waste a bullet. Besides you might be caught like that someday. He's a soldier, leave him alone."

The man yelled in French for help. He was exhausted and tiring fast.

Lars paused, he couldn't endanger his Squad by taking him prisoner, there might be other French around. The five Tigers turned towards the German lines. The Frenchman screamed the cry of a wounded animal. Lars had seen many men die, but never a cry like that. The Tigers walked a few steps and Lars ordered.

"You go on, I'll get him out and catch up."

The four watched as Lars moved to the giant shell hole. Lars put one leg down the side of the hole and slipped. He rolled down the hole and when he tried to stand up his left leg sunk into three feel of mud. He tried to pull loose but he couldn't and the side was slippery. He was trapped. The powerful Holtzen at the top of the shell hole leaned down and extended his rifle. Lars grabbed it and Holtzen pulled him out.

Frederick was critical. "Leave him, you can't get to the Frenchmen its too dangerous."

Lars answered. "Yes, I could never have gotten him out by myself, we will have to leave him."

Then Lars felt rain drops, that quickly became a steady rain.

Lars looked at the Frenchmen, and the man looked at the sky. Pure terror on his face. He would drown in the god- forsaken hole.

It was Holtzen who felt all soldiers were comrades, who said, "It's going to be heavy, he will drown." He looked at Lars for direction.

Suddenly the war came down to one man. None of the killing made sense, but one human being trapped and frightened, it all came down to this moment.

Lars yelled at the Tigers. "Get wood! Get some wood and hurry."

The Tigers found wood and began to lay a path closest to the side of the Frenchmen. Lars started down the planks to help the man out, but Holtzen stopped him.

"Let me do it." Lars backed away. He knew Holtzen was stronger. Holtzen edged down the planks and at the bottom of the hole grabbed the mans free arm. With two Tigers holding his legs Holtzen pulled the man free and gradually they both made it to the top of the hole. Exhausted they sat down as it began to rain harder.

Fredrick asked. "Do we take him back?"

Lars. "No, we are too tired, we have to get back ourselves."

He made a sign to the Frenchmen which direction the French lines were.

The Frenchmen pulled a picture out of his pocket. It was a woman with two small children.

Fredrick. "His wife and kids."

Suddenly Lars hated the war more than he ever had before.

He pulled Holtzen to his feet. "Bachman carried Holtzen's rifle. We go now." He could not bear to look at the man again.

Lars supported the exhausted Holtzen and they started to walk.

Holtzen said, "Wait." He turned and waved to the Frenchmen who waved back.

Holtzen always quiet said. "We did the right thing."

Lars. "Yes and I would do it again tomorrow."

He looked at the hole. It was rapidly filling up with water. The Germans plan of attrition was short one man that day and the Tigers were glad.

When the exhausted Tigers regained their lines they were quiet and a meal of black bread and potato soup was a feast. The youngest Golovin sought out Lars.

"Lars, I hate this, but today was the best day we've had,

saving the French soldier. I hate the killing, I'm tired of the war, I want to go home."

He was very young, his face scared by pimples and his glasses always seem to have mud on them. He was the quietest of the group, seldom complaining, never bragging or joking as the others would do.

Lars realized he needed a big brother.

"Golovin you're a good soldier, you never give me trouble, your rifle is always clean, as clean as it can be in this mud. You cannot go home, we all have to stay until the war is over."

Golovin blurted out. "I don't want to die, I'm only eighteen, you all talk about the women you've been with. I've never been with a woman, I never kissed a woman, I don't want to die before I kissed a woman, its not fair." He began to weep silently.

Lars took his hand. "Golovin, we didn't know it was going to be like this, but we all volunteered."

Lars could see an appeal to patriotism would not help and he frankly didn't want to anyhow. The young man put his head in his hands, he seemed inconsolable and Lars for a moment felt like yelling, he hated it too, and he wanted to go home. But just like the Soccer Team, Lars was captain of the team now. He was the Sergeant, he wasn't allowed to yell or complain or quit.

"Look I understand how you feel. When we get relief I'll find you a woman."

With that Golovin's head popped up. "Will you?"

"Yes."

"I only want to kiss her."

"That will be alright."

With Golovin quieted down Lars faced his second problem of the day. Zimmerman, wounded a second time was returned to duty. He protested.

"The captain said it was only a scratch and I can't go back to the hospital, but my hand hurts and if your wounded twice you should be relieved."

Lars marked him fit for duty.

Later that afternoon the new captain who was very strict spoke to each Squad. The Tigers not use to such communications listened silently."

"Men, we are winning the Battle of Verdun, the French are about to give up. They have only one road to re-supply their soldiers and that road cannot defeat us.

General Falkenhayn is amassing great artillery on a short front. The artillery will open the way for us and we shall advance tomorrow morning. Then after we have achieved our objective the artillery will open the way for us again. I expect every man in the Company to advance like a heroic German soldier, no one should hold back."

The new captain motioned Lars to follow him. Out of earshot of the squad, the captain said, "Sergeant, you are a very good soldier and I understand the former captain used you and your Squad in a special way. That is over, this is a life and death battle, and I need every man, so your Squad will follow me when we attack."

Lars stood at attention. "Yes sir."

"Sergeant, I have one question. You have a very good soldier in your Squad, the man you call The Bull. I need a new Squad leader, can you spare the man?"

Lars had never questioned a Senior officer, but he said what he believed.

"Sir, Holtzen is an excellent soldier, but he is not ready to be a Squad leader."

"Sergeant, your not thinking of what is best for you. This is what is best for the army and the man."

Lars did not flinch. "Sir, I am thinking of what is best for the man, and the army. He should stay with me."

The captain dismissed Lars and after he left, the captain thought, this man is ready to be an officer, he can make decisions and he is not afraid of his superiors.

Lars spoke to The Bull. "The captain asked me if you are ready to be a squad leader. I said you should stay with me, but its not too late. If you take it, its more money and another stripe."

The Bull looked down. "I'll stay, I don't care about the rest of them, but I respect you Lars, you give the orders I'll follow."

True to the captains word, a massive German artillery barrage began the next day.

The French guns limited to a supply of ammunition from the one road couldn't answer and the German Army and the Tigers advanced.

The gray clad Infantry equipped with flame throwers moved rapidly at first. Lars behind the captain who waved his pistol and yelled for the men to follow him. Then the French, firing machine guns from the many shell holes caused by the artillery began to inflict great casualties. The captain rose from a hole and was almost cut in half and fell back on top of Lars. Lars struggled to get free and saw the captain was dead. Lars crawled forward and moved past Zimmerman who was dead and would not complain anymore.

A hail of fire and suddenly a hole in the French line and the Germans poured through. Lars saw Golovin go down, he reached the young man who lay spread eagle in the mud, his mouth open staring lifelessly at the sky.

Lars muttered. "Never been kissed, too young too die."

He cursed. "We're all too young to die damn you all, we're all to young to die."

Lars got up and moved forward.

#

The Kaiser delighted with the victory at Scapa, and the progress of the war. He was worried about one thing. He believed he could defeat his relatives in Britain, but he could not and would not accept their contempt if he was caught spying on them. Gentlemen did not do such things, especially Kings or Kaisers. The Prince continued to assure him that only the Kaiser and the Prince knew the British spy, but the Kaiser worried that Count Zastrov recognized the man and would somehow disclose the secret. Despite the Prince's guaranty that Zastrov had been warned that he was not to speculate about the English spy, the Kaiser wanted to speak to Zastrov himself.

The Count called to visit the Kaiser, and was overjoyed and believed he was receiving the recognition he deserved for the Zeppelins victories. Aware that the Kaiser was a strict man Zastrov knew his background as one without noble blood, was against him. He decided he would continue to present a humble and modest presence despite the fact he believed himself the most valuable man in the German war effort. Expecting to be complemented he rehearsed his response which was to thank the Kaiser for his opportunity to serve the Fatherland.

At attention before the Kaiser, he was surprised when the leader talked for twenty minutes about great German victories, all of which were under his direction and never mentioned the Prince or Zastrov once. Finally the Kaiser at the end of his diatribe said.

"Zastrow, I had my eye on you, I expect great things in the

future."

Zastrov felt let down, the future, what about the great things he had already done."

"Thank you sire."

"Now Zastrov, one thing I want to question you about. Your trip to Scotland? Do you remember the details?"

Puzzled Zastrov responded. "Yes Sire."

"The man you met, what kind of a mood was he in?"

Now Zastrov was confused, and answered as best he could. "Quiet, we did not talk for long, he read the letter, and gave me the plans."

"Did he mention the royal family?"

"No, he said nothing about the English royal family."

"Did he mention my name?"

Zastrov struggled to decide how he should answer the questions said, "No, he read the letter, recognized the signature, shook his head and handed me the plans."

"Any comment about the plans? Did he seem worried he was handing you one of England's greatest secrets?"

Of course Zastrov had thought about this but it was well over one year ago and much had happened since the meeting.

"No. Again, he was quiet we parted quickly, I cannot honestly say what he was thinking."

The Kaiser to show how important the next question was arose from the desk and walked in front of Zastrov. He poked his finger into Zastrov's chest.

"Do you know who he was?"

Zastrov shocked at being touched by the Kaiser sputtered. "No I don't."

Now the Kaiser turned his back, then turned back again, leaning against his desk.

"The Prince has told you, and I will repeat, these are great state secrets, you are never to discuss the meeting with anyone else, only the Prince and I. Do you understand?"

Zastrov recognized his orders, clicked his heels and said.

"Sire, I will obey your orders on the subject."

The Kaiser assured that his secret was safe said, "I have my eye on you. Continue to fight hard against my enemies. When we win I will be generous to you and your men."

A shaken and disappointed Zastrov left the office. What was

that all about? Reward, my men, I am the Zeppelins, didn't he know that?"

A general stopped Zastrov and told him the Kaiser's advisor Baron von Below wanted to speak to him. Zastrov was ushered into von Below's heavily carpeted office, the drapes pulled closed. von Below was the Princes rival and rumored to be very political. He had gone out of his way to shake Zastrov's hand at a dinner recently. Zastrov judged the man to be a dangerous enemy and besides he wanted to open conversations with someone besides the man who supported the Prince.

"You deserve a great deal of recognition for what the Zeppelins have done."

"Thank you Count"

von Below recognized the man looked disappointed.   He quickly guessed the Kaiser did not compliment him at the meeting. Classically, the Kaiser would tell a man like this how the Kaiser was winning the war and disappoint the visitor.

von Below.   "I sometimes think our leader believes the victories of the Zeppelins are due to the Prince and forgets the man who commanded such forces."

Zastrov did not answer and von Below knew he was on the right track.

"Zastrov, you are a great soldier, but you need friends in Berlin, men who will promote you.   Men like me could be your friend."

Zastrov. "Thank you Count, I would welcome your support."

von Below decided to strike quickly. "Did you and the Kaiser speak about the English spy?"

von Below could see the fear in the mans eyes and knew he had gone to far.

"Look Zastrov you cannot disclose what you spoke to the Sire about, but if I am to promote your career I must begin to take some of the luster away from the Prince. I must understand some of the secrets he shares with the Kaiser. If I knew the English spy and his connection with the Prince I can help you."

Zastrov decided to gamble this could be the break through for his career. "I met the English spy but I don't know who he is, I've sworn not to disclose any more, I trust you Count, but I can only go so far."

von Below. "I understand, and you are right, you cannot cross over the promises you have given the Kaiser, you understand if I find out who the man is, it weakens the Prince, and that helps you."

Not sure, Zastrov responded. "I think I understand."

"It would prove the Prince could not be trusted. I will not ask you anything further except one thing. Do you think the man is an important leader in England?"

"Yes I do."

That ended the meeting and Zastrov left.

CHAPTER 14

At the end of 1914 the Germans and the Allies faced each other in opposing trenches on the Western Front.

The English directed by sea by Lord Winston Churchill resolved a plan to flank the Western Front with an amphibious landing on the Gallipoli Peninsula, Turkey. The plan was to knock Turkey out of the war and open communications with Russia. The first phase was a Naval operation to bombard and destroy the Turkish forts on the peninsula.

Admiral Richardson warned the leadership of the operation, that land and sea operations had to be coordinated, but this was ignored and contributed to early failures. A series of Allied mishaps hampered the opening days of the campaign. The Transport ships were incorrectly loaded and had to be reloaded causing a long delay and surprise was lost.

The next problem, preparations for the landing were amateurish and inadequate and without proper reconnaissance. The English leadership frequently out of touch with the troops, were disliked by the Australian and the New Zealand troops who were called *Anzacs*.

The troops landed on the Peninsula at Cape Helles and stalled with heavy casualties.

Admiral Tom Gordon the new sea-land Admiral called the *Anzac* leaders to his flagship and listened to their complaints.

Gordon agreed with Richardson that coordination was important and also respected the *Anzacs*. One night he went ashore and personally scouted the hills where the early fighting occurred, so when the *Anzac* leaders complained he welcomed their thoughts which were strong and bitter.

"We had too many orders given from officers who are not familiar with the terrain," said one.

Captain Mike Bottomly was irate. "We don't have maps, that are any good. The defiles and hills of Gallipoli are tricky, too many men have been killed unnecessarily."

A third said, "One assault wave landed in the wrong place. The navigation in the boats poor, we got lost and they didn't understand the currents.   The command doesn't coordinate the different companies with group separated by a short distance not helping each other."

Gordon also believed that not only was the leadership unprepared but it lacked fire and enthusiasm.

"Gentlemen you are right, all your criticisms are correct and I intend to change the leadership. I will send you someone tomorrow who should do a better job."

Mike Bottomly was standing with other *Anzac* officers on the beach the following morning when his friend Bob Collins spoke to him. "The Admiral is sending his brother to lead us. More English politics."

"He's from India. No one knows anything about him except he taught math at Cambridge and writes poetry."

"Poetry?" Mike Bottomly cursed and pointed to an ugly path up the side of a nearby hill. It was a killing ground the day before.

"He's going to order us to go up that defile same as yesterday. The Turkish machine guns are spotted all along the path. It can't be taken."

Collins looked at the twisted ugly brown hillside. "I count five machine guns on that hillside, we had two hundred casualties yesterday, I don't think we can take it."

Bottomly said with clinched teeth.   "If an English officer orders us up that hill he goes with us or nobody moves."

With that two Englishmen came down the beach, a Colonel and a Sergeant. They wore Australian bush hats, khaki jackets, and scotch kilts with boots. The two looked lost.

The Colonel wore a beard, granny glasses and acted if he was intruding. His demeanor was so modest and shy that Bottomly whose rising anger was about to explode barely remained in check.

Roger Gordon said, "Sorry we're late, we took a wrong turn on the beach."

He extended his hand and shook Bottomly's hand.   "I'm Gordon, this is Sergeant McAllister, I've got some maps."

He opened his case and a sudden wind whipped three maps out of his hand. The four *Anzac* officers and the two Englishmen chased the maps down the beach. Bottomly pulled up. He spoke to himself. "My God, who is this. This man has no military bearing at all, I'm not going to follow him."

Now Gordon gathered up his maps.   He stood next to

Bottomly and pointed to the path two hundred yards away. "That path leads to the top."

Bottomly thought. "He's going to order us forward."

Gordon looked at the path and said, "Why don't the Sergeant and I take a look."

None of the *Anzac* officers moved as he un-slung a Lee-Enfield rifle. Gordon dropped his pack and took out a fine looking sniper scope.

Bottomly stared at the scope. Gordon was apologetic. "It's German, better optics then ours."

Gordon and the Sergeant set off for the cliffs. Forty yards before the path the two crouched down and started to creep forward. Then McAllister hid behind a rock and Gordon ran ahead. He ran twenty yards and flopped down just before a Turkish machine gun opened up. McAllister fired several times and the Turkish machine gun was silent. Gordon moved up the hill positioned himself and waved McAllister to follow him. Again a second machine gun started to fire. Gordon fired his rifle and the second gun was quiet.

Bottomly looked at Collins. "Are they mad, they are going up alone?"

Collins. "My God, this is insane."

For the next hour every twenty minutes this tableau repeated. Machine gun fire then Lee-Enfield shots, then quiet. Finally Sergeant McAllister returned to the beach.

"Sir, the Colonel is at the top. He requests you bring your men up the path and join him."

Bottomly weakly said, "We'll be right with you. Are you all the way to the top?"

"Yes sir."

Bottomly looked at Collins who had a blank expression.

"We did something wrong yesterday, we had two hundred casualties. Lets go and get up there."

As the *Anzacs* climbed up the path they passed two machine gun posts with Turkish soldiers as casualties. Bottomly stopped at the second machine gun post, four Turkish gunners all had head wounds, two were dead. He pointed to the enemy soldiers. "Sergeant that's some shooting."

McAllister answered. "That's the Colonel, he never misses."

Bottomly was incredulous. "Just the two of you?"

"Yes, one draws fire, the other does the shooting. First time we did it in India I was nervous, but the tribesmen were very poor shots."

"I wouldn't want to try this against the Turks too often."

The Sergeant took the lead as Bottomly followed thinking. "If I didn't see it I wouldn't have believed it."

At the top Gordon was crouched down, he pointed to a line of trenches.

"We can Enfilade the trenches where the Turkish Infantry is holding, by using that draw and using our grenades. We can roll up the line." Before Bottomly could answer Gordon said.

"Of course I'm new here, if you have a plan please speak up." Again his speaking was so modest he disarmed Bottomly.

"Colonel that's a good plan, I can bring my men along on the right and we can work our way down the draw."

Bottomly moved next to Collins. Who was breathing hard from the climb.

"The Colonel doesn't give orders, but he suggests we move down the draw and attack the trenches."

Collins was beginning to be amused by the most amazing operation he was ever to take part in.

"No, you want me to run forward and draw fire first?"

Bottomly checked his pistol and turned to Collins. "No, Captain, lets do it the old fashioned way. Lets sneak up on them."

The Turkish Infantry thinking they were protected by the machine guns were surprised by the *Anzacs* Infantry moving down the trenches. After two hours Roger Gordon had still not issued an order but over one thousand Turkish Infantry were cleaned off the hills of Cape Helles. The *Anzac* reinforced, cut off a large enemy Infantry Division. With the Australians on one side, and Tom Gordon's battleships shelling from the sea, the Turks finally surrendered.

Bottomly said to Collins. "With less then one hundred casualties we won this battle, and if Gordon tells me were marching to Berlin tomorrow, I would follow him."

#

The next day American reporter Matty Stevenson interviewed several *Anzac* officers at Gallipoli.

"You gentlemen have stunned the world. Your success at Gallipoli is the envy of Europe, where the armies are stuck in the trenches. How did you do it? How did you vanquish the Turks?"

Collins said, "The New Zealanders are the best soldiers in the world. Every male is trained from school age to be a soldier. Our Australians are very good. Once we found great leadership we beat the Turks."

Stevenson questioned. "The leadership?"

Bottomly. "The Gordon brothers, Tom Gordon the Admiral have pushed the Fleet up the Peninsula, they turned back German submarines and defeated the shore batteries. A great man."

"Well we walked the hills of Gallipoli yesterday with you, you said you were surprised how narrow the Peninsula was."

Stevenson. "I was very surprised, the hills were steep and its really a narrow battlefield, lots of high ground."

Bottomly. "This made Rogers leadership more effective."

He saw immediately you had to get to the high ground, we take a position and be ready to sit and have tea and he'd be moving out to the next ridge and pushing the Turks."

"I understand and he never gives orders?" Said Stevenson.

"No. He goes down a gully and he'll say." "I think this turns to the water, do you think if we set up a machine gun and push them forwards and we can trap them? So we do it and next day two hundred Turks would surrender in the gully. Collins said Gordon came from India, these hills and gullies are what he was used to in the mountains of India. The man is a dead shot, he almost apologized for the fact that he uses a German sniper scope."

"I can't get Gordon to give me an interview," said Stevenson.

"No, he's probably reading poetry. He's not much for talking about himself. I think he's a teacher in private life but he doesn't talk much."

Stevenson asked. "In my article, I'm gonna to say he's one of the best soldiers I've heard of in the war, fair statement?"

Bottomly replied. "He's the best man I've ever soldiered with."

Admiral Tom Gordon discussed strategy with his brother. "Roger good work, but we've got another tough nut. The Turks have an artillery observation post at a bottleneck on the Peninsula. They spot our ships, set the range and shell them. Knock out the observation post and we can get past the Chanuk Bair Ridge."

"I can't get ships in close, the water is too shallow, and the machine gun fire will not let you land on the beaches on a straight ahead attack, so we need something special."

Roger puffed on his pipe. "Do you have a plan?"

"I do, but it depends on a landing at dawn, can you get someone to swim ashore in the dark and set fires to guide your men ashore?"

"I can." Roger thought of Tom Winn, the best athlete and swimmer of the *Anzacs*.

"All right, this is what I suggest."

#

On a cold morning one hour before dawn, Tom Winn slipped into the icy sea at Gallipoli. He carried a waterproof bag and reached the beach after a fifteen minute swim. He lit a flare at the waters edge and quickly moved one hundred yards further down the beach and lit a second flare. The 'Collier Atlantic' swung towards the beach in the dark of dawn. The old vessel used to carry coal, offered a low silhouette to the Turkish sentries who did not react until she ran aground fifty yards off the beach. Turkish machine guns fired at the front of the ship to be met by rifle fire from Roger Gordon and two others. Two of the four machine guns stopped firing as *Anzac* Infantry spilled out of a sally port in the side of the ship onto a lighter tied to the side that acted as a bridge to the beach. In effect the New Zealanders flanked the machine gun positions as Rogers and his team used the hesitation to kill three other gunners, and silencing the third machine gun.

A Turkish officer tried to rally his men but was cut down. The *Anzac* Infantry charged up the beach and overwhelmed the sleepy Turks in a trench.

As the sun broke through the horizon Mike Bottomly waved his fist at Roger who waved back. Many prisoners were captured and the Observation Post taken.

Bottomly yelled. "Well done Roger, I'd follow you to Hell."

He waved his fist and his men stormed up the hill. The Turks tried a counter-attack, but the *Anzacs* drove them off.

After the battle Roger Gordon returned to his cabin on the flagship. He locked the door and knelt by his bunk.

"The Lord is my Shepherd, I shall not be in want. He makes me lie down in green pastures, he leadeth me besides quiet waters, he restores my soul."

He opened his eyes and his prayers became personal. "Oh Lord, I was afraid today when the battle started. I was afraid I would let these brave men down. Then I felt you at my side and my fear passed. You steadied my arm, and I even smiled, you were with me today. I could feel it, as our brave fellows stormed up the beach. We do the Lords business and it is important. I show no fear."

He returned to the prayer the 23rd Psalm. His voice rose as he repeated his favorite line.

"Even though I walk through the valley of the shadow of Death I will fear no evil for you are with me, your rod and your staff they comfort me."

Again he shared a private thought.

"I do not ask for my life, only that it appear I am as brave as the men want me to be, for they are the finest men I have ever know, and for your steady hand I thank thee O Lord."

He ended.

"Surely goodness and love will follow me all the days of my life and I will dwell in the house of the Lord forever."

CHAPTER 15

Matty Stevenson, the American reporter, peered into the dark wine cellar. The bar in the village was two miles behind the Front Line and a French rest area. His eyes, coming out of the rainy Verdun sky adjusted quickly. His friend Captain Renee Sarrall was sitting hunched over a table by the far wall. A flickering candle high-lighted a bottle of wine and the two glasses.

Stevenson shook Sarrall's hand.

"Renee, I came as soon as I got your message."

"Good Matty." Sarrall one of the most highly decorated officers in the French Army poured Stevenson a glass of wine.

"I wish this was a happy occasion Matty, but I want to tell of monstrous events."

His tone was serious, Sarrall was not a man to inflate or dramatize. Stevenson rapt attention confirmed this.

"This morning I and two others went to see General Gerald, commander at Verdun. We brought a petition signed by five thousand men from our division. The men want the French Army to discuss a truce with the Germans."

"A truce?" Stevenson's voice cracked.

His surprise complete, the veteran reporter drank his wine to regain his poise. Newsmen were not suppose to hear thunderbolts from Front line troops. Why hadn't he heard of these events from Headquarters?"

Sarrall. "Other Divisions have petitioned senior officers for a truce. The idea is spreading through the French Army like wildfire. Not a surrender, we just want to see if the Germans will talk."

Renee wounded four times and promoted from corporal to captain was the logical man to approach senior officers.

"Renee how long has this been going on?"

"We have been at Verdun for six months, it's a meat grinder, over four hundred thousand casualties, a war that has gone on for two years and no change in French strategy. The generals and the government ask for sacrifice of French blood but give no indication they know how to win the war."

If Renee felt this way what did the other men think? "Renee, what does the average enlisted man think?"

"I and my two associates had to argue with many of my fellow soldiers, not to start walking home, we fear some men will start leaving and shot officers who try and stop them. Two weeks ago we heard rumors that signs were appearing in the trenches saying, only maintain a defense, but do not attack. Then the petitions started to appear, when there was no response, talk of going home."

"Renee, I have been in Paris at Headquarters, no talk of this, no inkling of trouble, don't they know?"

"They know, they want the front line generals to deal with it. The French Army is on the verge of mutiny and the politicians and the generals have no ideas. But what can you expect from leaders who send Infantry into German machine gun fire?"

Matty. "You've been wounded four times, do you believe in mutiny?"

"Matty, from my village one hundred and twenty of us volunteered, now after two years only four of us are left, the rest wounded or dead. Most of us died for nothing, even the Germans know straight ahead attacks won't work. But our officers speak of Élan, all out attack, the Napoleon way, but Napoleon would not have chosen this against modern weapons. The generals are stupid, this Élan thinking is criminal. The Germans have new weapons, stronger artillery and Zeppelins. The French answer is only more sacrifices. We are saying give us a chance or at least discuss a truce."

"Are you saying if the Government tries for a truce the French Army might go to all defense? No attack and the war would still continue?" Stevenson was still trying to understand what he was saying.

"If the Government can convince us they care we will still fight, we know that the people of Paris still eat well, while we eat swill fit only for pigs. Let me explain about an incident that shows their stupidity and lack of concern for the troops. Three weeks ago a Division of French Moroccan Troops was on my left. I warned the generals that the Moroccan officers were inexperienced, not likely too stand up too strong German advances, and the troops might run. I said I would help the Moroccans, but I was told to stay at my spot on the line. A strong German attack routed the Moroccans and they started to run. I could see their line failing and I raced to close the opening with my troops, and I heard French machine guns fire and watched as hundreds of Moroccans were killed by our machine gun fire, directed by French officers. I could have closed the gap and I and my officers could have rallied the North Africans Division, but Élan again synonymous with stupid. Victory is not the goal of the generals. Fool hardy courage is what they want. The generals never appear at the Front and speak to the troops. If they don't adjust we will lose the war."

Stevenson a good reporter was shaken that he had no inkling how bad conditions were.

"Renee, will the generals respond?"

"I don't know, all we ask is, an attempt to talk to the Germans. No more wasteful attack, lets us stay on the defensive, and let us develop better weapons like the Germans did. We hear the new English fighter the Sopwith Camel will help, and better food. The Government has to convince the French soldier they care, and if the war continues it will be pursued with more intelligence and concern for the troops. But if the generals think terror and punishment will stop our movement, they will lose the army," Renee coughed.

"I heard rumors this morning an officer who presented a petition was shot. This will be the worst thing they could do."

Later that day Stevenson heard that Captain Renee Sarrall was arrested and shot. The next morning thousands of French soldiers were seen leaving Verdun.

The office of Lord Thomas was gloomy and quiet. A reflection of the mental state of Thomas. Gibbon Stillwell entered the office, the last member of the committee to be interviewed. Before they could begin a Secretary handed Thomas a note.

Lord Thomas turned to Stillwell. "They want us to come to the Prime Ministers Office immediately."

They walked to the Prime Ministers Office who was standing by his desk.

"The French Army has mutinied." He pointed to a map on the wall.

"It started at Verdun and spread across the whole Front. In some cases the soldiers have left the trenches without orders. In others they are still at the Front but have refused to obey orders from their officers. The army on the English flank has melted away and we are in danger."

Gibbons was quiet. Lord Thomas and the Prime Minister looked at maps of the Front Lines.

An army officer came into the room. "I just spoke to General Kempton. He has ordered the army to retreat to Dunkirk. The navy is sending ships to bring the army home."

The Prime Minister looked at the map. Dunkirk to Dover somewhat over thirty miles, the war in France was over.

The Prime Minister said, "We are doing so well in the Dardanelles, the navy and the army have pushed ashore at Gallipoli, it's a complete victory."

Lord Thomas said, "We have to bring the Southern Navy home, the country will demand it. Clearly the Germans may pose a threat of an invasion."

"Gibbons asked. "What do you hear of the Germans?"

The Prime Minister said. "The French have asked the Germans for a truce, I suspect as the French Army melts away it will be an Armistice dictated by the Germans. With the Germans at the channel ports, we must protect our country. No German soldier will ever land on our shores."

#

General Kempton conducted a text book retreat, the troops gathered at Dunkirk and were taken by ships back to England. The German Army continued to hold its position and did not pursue the English.

CHAPTER 16

The Kaiser entered his office. Baron von Below was waiting. "Sir, I have the latest news from France. Along the front the French Army has deserted, in some cases they remain in their trenches but clearly not obeying their officers. Prince Rupprecht ordered our army to pause, we are not attacking. He told the generals to let the French continue their action without our interference. I suggest you speak to him."

The Kaiser who discussed the major issues with Rupprecht one hour ago did not respond to von Below.

von Below seeing the hesitation on the Kaiser's part said, "Sir, we need a policy, the war has taken a new turn and we have to react. The Russians have signaled they want a truce. I suggest we negotiate and they must turn over vast areas in the East in return for any truce."

The Kaiser was prepared to answer this and he repeated what he and Rupprecht agreed to.

"Yes, negotiate with the Russians, give them a truce and a treaty, but make the price high for any armistice."

von Below was surprised the Kaiser made the decision so quickly.

"What about France and England Sire?"

The Kaiser responded again quickly. "We shall divide France and occupy half of the country, especially the industrial areas. A government friendly to us will be allowed to rule the South."

von Below not use to such decisive judgment and not knowing this was agreed to by Rupprecht was puzzled.

"And England, we can crush the army without the French support?"

The Kaiser slammed his fist on the desk. "No, let the English retreat, we shall negotiate with them after the French question is settled. Do not destroy their army and harden their resolve."

"Sire?" he questioned.

The Kaiser sat down. He enjoyed setting the agenda with his confident and arrogant supporter.

"von Below, I plan to offer the English a treaty. They shall give us many of their overseas possessions and even half of India or else we shall invade my relations in England. They are not use to being dictated to, but we shall dictate terms."

He pulled on his mustache, well pleased with himself. This was all agreed to by Rupprecht, and clearly they set policy well beyond what von Below was thinking.

Von Below could see the leader was at his most triumphant talking even more of German control of Europe then the diplomat envisioned.

"Sire, one question, the Prince is loved by the soldiers and the public. Your supporters will be concerned they will be replaced by the Princes people. Do we continue to concede his peoples powers?"

The Kaiser was not a great military leader, but recognized power politics was mindful, he had to respond. The Prince had no aspiration for greater power, and told the Kaiser he wanted to retire to his country home. The Prince was weary, the long hours and the pressure of running the war. Still von Below wanted confirmation. It was wise to be loyal to the Kaiser and the Kaiser realized he had to confirm such loyalty was warranted.

"What do you suggest, von Below?"

"Sire, I know you appreciate the Princes contributions but at the Foreign Office, one of his people is talking of forming a new committee to change the settlement of all future geographical boundaries and border disputes. I would like to chair the Committee. It will decide the future map of Europe.

The Kaiser sat down." "I agree to that, what else?"

von Below inwardly heaved a sigh of relief. The Prince might have his ear, but he was still the Kaiser.

"Sire, if the war is winding down, you must have a higher profile. Can you attend all future planning meetings with me at your side?"

The Kaiser spun his chair and looked at the courtyard. He thought. For all intent and purpose the war is won even if they invade England. Did he really need the Prince anymore?

von Below was right, he could not concede any more power. The dictates to England must come from him. The invasion was dangerous, but they could pull it off.

"Von Below, you are right. Speak to the Prince, tell him I will attend all future meetings. Be respectful, but I agree I must attend."

There was another reason the Kaiser was willing to subvert the Princes power. The Prince tired of the war agreed they would pressure England and even invade if necessary, but he did not want to continue the war in the East. If Russia would concede the land he wanted, a harmonious non-threatening ending to the war, not one that Russia would feel they must avenge and war would again break out in two or three years. This was in conflict with many of the Kaiser's more ardent supporters, the rich land owners in Prussia .

#

A Committee awaited the Kaiser that morning. They wanted German farmers to colonize Lithuania and Poland ruled by a German Prince, with much of the land controlled by Prussian landlords. Laws would be harsh by the occupiers, political activity forbidden, newspapers censored and all courts and schools under German control. The Kaiser agreed to this idea even though he had not told von Below about it.

Prince Rupprecht would never agree to this since in the long run it would threaten the Russians and certainly bring about another war. So the Kaiser believed he had to appease his followers and ease Rupprecht out of power.

#

In Russia the Czar was gloomy. The General Brusilov claimed a great victory, but over one million casualties. The people were hungry, and the revolt of the French Army would spread to the Russian people. The war was over for Russia. Food riots dominated the landscape. The Czar's Chief Minister brought him more bad news. Several army divisions had arrested their officers. It was France all over again.

"Sir, we have captured a train heading for Moscow with a well known revolutionary sent from Germany. The Germans sent him from Switzerland with the purpose of starting riots in Moscow."

"What is the mans name?"

"Lenin. He is a Communist and well know to the police."

The Czar asked questions without enthusiasm. "And the news from France?"

"All reports state the French Army refuses to fight. The Germans are on the verge of a great victory."

The Czar hung his head. "I'm tired, Austro-Hungary gone, my government finished, the war is destroying the leadership of Europe. The Royal House, finished. Even Germany will not survive the war."

"Sir, the Kaiser will be the victor."

"Yes, but his people and all the people of Europe will see the death and suffering, they will not forgive the leaders."

The Minister did not believe the Czar.

"What if Germany invades England?"

"If they succeed, that may save the Kaiser, but only a complete victory. Meanwhile, I abdicate, tell the Duma to form a government"

#

The overall commander of the successful Gallipoli campaign Tom Gordon received his orders from London. He was to bring the Fleet home to provide the first line of defense against a possible German invasion. With the loss of the Northern Fleet, his Southern Fleet was the defender of the British Isles. Gordon discussed with the Admiral Tittus, who was in charge of all battleships, a future strategy. "If we get into a running fight with the German Navy escorting the Invasion fleet, I intend to engage them with all but two battleships and six destroyer. You will take those eight ships and ignore everything else, but destroy the troop carriers. They must plan to bring soldiers over on Transports and probably barges pulled by tugs."

Tittus questioned. "Sir, that is very risky on the Germans part, do you think they will still try an invasion?"

"I'm not sure, perhaps they think the Zeppelins and Gothas can provide air cover, but you and I know they are ineffective against a moving ship. Any attacks by Zeppelins or bombers here at the Dardanelles caused little or no damage."

When Morgan called a meeting of his Naval and ground commanders to embark and leave Gallipoli, he was disappointed when Tittus was too sick to attend.

He began. "Gentlemen, I have issued orders, we are to leave immediately for home. The Germans control France and have signed a Peace Treaty with the Russians. The Kaiser has issued an ultimatum to us which we have rejected. London believes the Germans next possible move will be an invasion of England, they control the skies, but Admiral Tittus and I don't think that will stop us from destroying a great many of the invasion ships and the army we bring home will defend the beaches....."

Gordon was about to continue when General Adair stood up.

"I don't feel well." Perspiration beaded on his forehead. He held onto the table and started to shake.

The General fell to the floor. Admiral Gordon called the doctor who came to the cabin. The doctor examined him. "Sir, he's burning up, heavy fever. The doctor signaled two assistants to take the General to the infirmary.

The doctor took the Admiral aside. "Sir, I've got fifty cases like this and word from the mainland is that fever is spreading there."

The Admiral turned white. "What do you think it is?"

"Plague."

"Plague? How bad?"

"Very bad."

By the end of the week half the men of the British expedition were sick and with in two weeks the military force was barely able to limp to Egypt where three quarters of the men were marked unfit for duty. The Southern Fleet could not return to England. England had no navy to defend it.

CHAPTER 17

When the war started the Kaiser and his Ministers planned for a quick victory. Denied, the Staff found the Kaiser was not willing to continued to lead and turned the direction of the war over to Prince Rupprecht. This raised the ire of his Chief Advisor Baron von Below, who was shunted aside. The Prince built an excellent staff and the strategy of the meat grinder at Verdun worked. The Prince also promoted the development of the Zeppelin and the Gotha bomber. When these weapons began to swing the war in Germany's favor, the Baron jealous, sulked in his office. It was Prince Rupprecht who masterminded the strategy of the attack on Scapa and was recognized as the father of the victory. The mutiny of the French Army caught most senior officers by surprise. Rupprecht quickly gave orders the Germans were to let this unwinding of the French side go on and not to provoke the enemy. A truce, then an armistice was signed.

The war between France and Germany was over. The Kaiser and the Baron quickly assumed control of Headquarters in Berlin.

Their Staffs took over the bureaucracy in the city. The fighting men in France and Russia did not see the change, but clerical personnel sensitive to power shifts at headquarters did.

Prince Rupprecht a loyal man, resented the intrusion of the running of the war, but trained to follow orders acquiesced to the new direction of the Kaiser.

Count Zastrov an ambitions man, recognized that his patron the Prince, had lost power and quickly switched allegiances to Baron von Below. Everyone knew the critical decisions would cover the invasion of England. Zastrov wanted to attack a concentrated spot, it would make his bombing more effective. The navy wanted to invade at the closest spot, Dover. Their ships would carry the first wave to the coast then tugs would pull barges from Calais to the English coast. While they knew no opposition was expected from the English Navy, they did not have enough Naval vessels to protect the barges. Crossing at the closest point, it was expected it would work so they agreed on the one concentration area theory. In addition, Admiral Scheer did not like Prince

Rupprecht, so he quickly joined Baron von Below in his plan. The Prince who had been developing a strategy of invading in two areas was not aware of the concentration plan of invasion. He was told a planning meeting in Paris would decide the next course of the war, he instructed his offices to develop a plan for two landings on the coast of England. The Prince was convinced two landings would favor the experienced and fast moving German Army and results in far fewer casualties. This was important to the Prince with victory so close, his concern was his loyal soldiers.

The Kaiser not used to chairing the Military Planning meeting since the war started, sat awkwardly at the head of the table. Rupprecht sat on the left and Baron von Below, who urged the Kaiser to chair the conference sat on his right.

The Baron recognized the Kaiser's feeling of inferiority to the respected Prince Rupprecht. He told the leader, with the victory of the German military machine he must be more visible. That too many Germans viewed Rupprecht as the War Leader. Reluctantly and nervously he took his place at the seat of power. He told the Baron he did not intend to go into great detail for his lack of knowledge would be exposed.

The Baron. "Sir, you should settle one major issue, then leave the meeting. Let the other officers settle details, you are the Director, the Kaiser."

The Baron wanted a conflict between the Kaiser and the Prince, for a sharp break would enhance his power. He suspected the naturally belligerent Kaiser would chafe at any criticism of his plan. The Baron told the Kaiser that the navy and Count Zastrov totally supported him.

The navy began the meeting with a review of how many ships would be used and the difficulties they expected to encounter. All agreed no English Naval ships would appear. Then the Admiral asked, has a decision been made on the width of the landing area and is it agreed a landing in one spot? The navy strongly favored one spot, they were worried especially about the barges being protected if two beaches were invaded.

The Kaiser took this opportunity to advance his plan. "Gentlemen I have decided on a narrow front. We will land in England in an area four miles wide, we shall pound the English on the beach and advance to London."

Prince Rupprecht cleared his throat. "Sir, the original plans were to land in two places, ten miles apart. That way the English defense could not concentrate against us. Which ever landing met the last resistance would be supported by our reserves, and then the victorious wing would circle and destroy the enemy."

Prince Ruppercht's brilliant strategy, had won many victories for the Kaiser. Clearly he deserved recognition, but the Kaiser was not a gracious man and decided it was time to take over the war.

"Prince Rupprecht, we the German Army do not need deception. Our military army and navy will crush them, I have been told by Count Zastrov that his Zeppelins would be more effective against a concentrated foe. We will land in a narrow area that is decided."

Rupprecht stung by the unwillingness of the Monarch to debate the issue tried again.

"Sir, with all due respect, it is our army that will land on the beaches, they will have to win the battle. I am convinced we will have less casualties with two landings."

The Kaiser forgetting all he owed this man let his temper answer.

"The decision is made, I expect you to support it. If you cannot you can stay home."

This stinging rebuke to the Prince silenced the room. No one moved, everyone turned to look at the proud soldier, father of so many victories and now treated with a complete lack of respect.

The Prince pushed his chair away from the table. "Sir, if you wish to proceed without me I will follow your wishes, if my advice is not needed I will not intrude on this meeting."

Rupprecht and his Aide von Hotzendorff both stood up and left the room.

As the Prince closed the door, the Kaiser was heard to say "Let him go, we don't need him."

When the son of Prince Rupprecht heard his father would not be part of the invasion, he was dumbstruck. The younger man Kile was an important member of the communication team of the invasion force. He left his office and went to his father's house, where he found the Prince still shaking with anger.

"Father, what happened?"

"Kile, he didn't want me, after all I've done for him, he insulted me in front of the whole Planning Committee, and it's a dangerous plan besides. A narrow landing, do then think the

English will not fight? A landing is always dangerous, once the army gets inland the only support is the Zeppelins. The Zeppelins are best against fixed fortifications, but what if the English attack from all sides not from a fixed position? The army could be badly hurt."

Kile did not answer. He was aware his father was a brilliant planner.

The Prince. "Our army is at its best when moving, two wings will allow this."

The Prince continued. "The English are very dangerous. They are fighting on their own soil, men whose blood traces back to Waterloo, beat the great Napoleon and the fools think it will be easy. Our general will be surprised.

Kile. "Will the English have new weapons?"

The Prince responded. "I'm sure they will, over confidence is a disease and we have the disease."

Next day the Kaiser dismissed the Prince from the army. The only man as devastated as the Prince was his Aide General von Hotzendorff who was demoted and assigned to the Communication Unit, a dead end to his career.

Von Hotzendorff a friend of the American newsman Taylor met him in Paris

"I was sorry I couldn't help your friend Stevenson, that was the beginning of von Below gaining control. I saw the Prince, the other day. He is bitter of course, who wouldn't be?"

Taylor smoked his cigar. "I'm suppose to be a neutral, but I don't want the English to be destroyed. I can't believe you want the Kaiser to win."

Von Hotzendorff agreed. "It will be bad for Germany. The Baron and his Prussian friends will grind everyone under their boots. Some of them hate the Prince. I believe if victorious the Prince's life could be in danger."

Taylor didn't think they would go that far. "They're not that vindictive?"

"They are, it will be an opportunity to destroy all the Moderates, this group will press to attack America, and rule the world."

Taylor asked. "Do you want to help the English?"

"Yes, and I can, I'm assigned to the Communication Center at Abberville. So is Kile the Princes son. We've talked, we can help.

Can you let the English know they have friends?"

"Yes."

"One other thing, I believe the English have a traitor, the Prince had the plans for Scapa, he got them from someone very high up. He never told us who it was. It could even be a member of the royal family."

Taylor said, "Matty Stevenson's been arrested, do you know where he's being held?"

Von Hotzendorff. "He is being held at a castle about forty miles outside Paris. It was Baron von Below's men. He was caught interviewing General Bettsloff, the generals been arrested too. I can't help."

"Is he in danger? He once interviewed the Kaiser."

"I think he is safe for now, but I hear they may take him to Germany. There he will be in danger."

Taylor puffed on his cigar. "I think I know someone to help him, but tell me more about the English traitor."

"Not much to tell, the Prince never told me who it was, but it had to be someone important and someone who could be trusted."

"Trusted?"

"The man kept his word, they made some kind of bargain," said the German.

"Do you think the Germans will use the traitor again?"

von Hotzendorff said, "They're pretty confident, the only question at Headquarters I heard was the height of the barrage balloons. The Zeppelins and the Gothas, want to bomb from low height and they are afraid of the cables of the balloons."

CHAPTER 18

At the American Embassy, Gibbon Stillwell's small office held two file cabinets, a desk and a picture of the nineteen twelve Philadelphia Athletics. When Gibbon felt blue he would look at the picture. He was not homesick since he liked the English and his wife Amanda was with him. But the mission was not going well, and he was impatient for a breakthrough event that would put him on a track to the solution. Working long hours he agreed to see Alvin Taylor head of the American News Bureau in Paris.

"Gibbon, I've come looking for help. The Germans have arrested Matty Stevenson." Stevenson was Amanda's ex-fiancée and not a friend of Gibbon.

"Why? What did he do?"

Gibbon always felt a friendship for Stevenson not shared. He watched as Taylor puffed on a cigar, classic hand drinking, cigar smoking newsman.

"Matty was working on the German invasion of England. They are all bragging, thinking its going to be easy. He met with a big German general who repeated a quote from the Prince. The Prince said it's a crazy war, the historians will never believe the Scapa agreement."

Gibbons head snapped up. Taylor recognized his interest. "Gibbon I don't believe your on some fact finding reviews of the battle of Scapa and neither did Matty. Your one of the inside people in Washington, and they wouldn't send you over here unless it was important. After Matty met with the General he told me the General's comments might relate to what Stillwell was in England investigating. The general was a man who supported the Prince and was afraid the Kaiser was going to destroy the Prince."

Stillwell asked. "Before he was arrested, did Matty meet again with the General?"

"Yes, and the General promised to show him some unique papers. He wasn't exposed to great secrets, but Matty thought the man wanted someone to understand the Prince's contribution to the war. Now I'm not going to ask you what your doing because you won't tell me. But I want you to save Stevenson as the Germans are acting like he's in danger. I want you to go over to France and get him."

Gibbon asked. "Can you tell me anymore about Stevenson's story?"

"We are neutral, the Germans recognize the Americans are sympathetic to the British. In Paris, German officers say they want to invade England before America joins the war and helps England. Matty is a great reporter, I bet he found out something. You know there are two German Intelligence Services. Matty might be caught in the middle."

He puffed on his cigar. "But I guarantee Stevenson has something the Germans want to keep secret. My contacts tell me they are holding Stevenson outside Paris and they are going to transfer him to Germany."

Gibbon wasn't going to mislead Taylor. "I can't tell you what I'm doing, but I'll go to France and get him if he has something that helps. I will tell you and Matty what I can when I can."

"Gibbon, the story doesn't come before his safety," said Taylor.

Gibbon smiled. "I always knew the press had a heart."

"Don't believe it, some day I want to know what this is about."

Taylor stood by the door. "Two things Gibbon, the Germans want to know the height of the barrage balloon, and your traitor didn't get paid, he made a deal."

Gibbon didn't react but did ask. "How do you know?"

"A German general told me. He doesn't know the name, but it was a bargain not a payoff."

"Your sure?"

"Very sure, and Stevenson may possess more information then I do."

#

Gibbon sat by his desk thinking. Taylor has guessed I'm after a traitor, he wanted to see my reaction to his mention of the man. I didn't react, but this confirms the Germans reached someone at the top level of the English government. I've got to go to France to rescue Stevenson. He might help me. Everett's son-in-law Arthur Denny told me a great English military leader is here in London. I'll ask for his help. The man is an expert in this kind of mission.

The fifth day after the meeting with Taylor, Gibbon, Westy

and the English commando leader were peering through field glasses at a Chateau just outside of Paris.

Gibbon spoke to the highly regarded English leader. "Our contact said the Germans are going to move him this morning. See the two big cars? They will take him to Paris."

He answered, "My men are at the bridge, let them pull out. We'll stop them well away from the Chateau. We follow on the motorcycles."

At 9:30 the Germans pulled away from the Chateau in two Daimler limousines. In the first car, two army men sat in the front with two Military Police in the back. In the second car Stevenson was bound and gagged, sitting in the back seat with a Military Policeman.

Westy whispered. "On these country roads, they won't make speed. Fancy cars to be driving around in."

The German cars pulled away. The commandos followed in two motorcycles with side cars. The English leader was first a man with a rifle in the side car. Gibbon drove Westy who held his six gun at the ready. On the road the loose tongued and active Westy was silent and intense. At ten miles from the Chateau the German cars broke from a forest to a rolling meadow. The Germans slowed, a French farmer with a hay wagon was stuck on a small bridge that crossed a wide shallow stream. The first driver stopped his car and waved a pistol and cursed in German at the farmer who shrugged his shoulders and pointed to his horse indicating it was lame.

One hundred yards behind at the edge of the forest the English leader drove into the bright sunlight and fired a flare pistol.

"Come on men he yelled." Five men burst from the hay, and four men hiding under the bridge emerged. A series of shots and all the Germans in the first car were out of action.

The English leader swung to the right, but the Germans second car with Stevenson spun wheels, moving left in cloud of dust that obscured the vision of the first motorcycle. Gibbon moved to block and Westy shot the man on the passenger side who was half raised and firing at Gibbon. The driver spun the wheel but Westy shot him before he could accelerate away and the car stalled and halted. The German sitting next to Matty put up his hands in a sign of surrender. It was over in less then a minute. The English leader renown for his ambushing proved his genius. Out of the motorcycle he grabbed Westy's hand. "Excellent shooting, excellent shooting, I could use a man like you. Where did you learn to shoot like that?"

"Dakota Territory, against the hostiles." The famous Lawrence of Arabia exclaimed. "Oh, you mean the Indians?"

Westy. "Yeah, the hostiles."

Lawrence looked at Gibbon. "Is that your man?"

Gibbon saw the English help a battered Matty Stevenson out of the car. His eye was blackened and he had a cut lip. The Germans were not great hosts.

"Alright." Lawrence of Arabia waved, a large truck to drive out of a close set of trees. In the desert or in France the famous man and his crew moved fast. The German cars were driven into the trees and covered. The hay wagon pulled off the bridge.

"Everyone in the trucks! We go to the fishing boat and be off before they find the cars."

He turned to Westy. "I go back to the desert with Allenby next week, I could use a man like you."

Westy shook his head and pointed to Gibbon. "I go with him."

Stevenson looked at Gibbon.

"Never though I'd be glad to see you."

Gibbon helped him into the truck. "Never thought I'd meet you this way."

They drove for two hours with Stevenson sipping tea. When they reached the boat Gibbon felt he had to question him.

"Taylor told me you were meeting with a big German general, is that why you were arrested?"

"He gave me files, I was caught by the Military Police with the files and maps. They worked me over, but I wouldn't tell them where I got them. The group in France were so overconfident, they were not that concerned and because I once interviewed the Kaiser I didn't get the worst treatment."

Gibbon. "I have to ask, what did you see?"

"They have fifty new Zeppelins to be completed with trained crews. They will lead the attack against the English. The Germans told me the air Amada can't be stopped and the English should surrender now. If they don't the Germans won't be as easy with the English as they have been with the French. The collapse of the English Navy opened them up to the first invasion since ten sixty-six. The Norman invasion."

"Did you see any invasion plans?" Gibbon would not wait for

them to get back to England.

"Yes, the first ships will bring over half a million men including men in barges. Then in the next two days they will go back and bring over the rest. The army will land one million men, supported by the Zeppelins, which they think can't be beaten."

"What do you think, can the English stop them?" Stevenson asked.

Gibbon looked away. "Only if they stop them at the water edge, once they begin to move into the countryside, they will control it. The English left a lot of their heavy equipment at Dunkirk, they don't have much left."

Stevenson responded. "The Germans let the English escape to Dunkirk?"

"Well, they had a truce." Said Gibbon.

"No, the Germans were negotiating a truce with the French. They just stood aside and let the English leave? I saw the maps, they were marked so the German Army halted and the English could leave. Wouldn't it have been better to destroy the English Army in France?"

Gibbon speculated. "Maybe at that time the Germans didn't want to invade England."

Puzzled Gibbon said, "Are you sure the maps showed the German Army halted. The English escaped at Dunkirk, lots of canals and waterways, tricky landscape."

Stevenson. "I was in Paris when it happened, but we heard the Germans didn't bomb the English. Wouldn't bombing made it more difficult to embark the army?"

Gibbon asked. "What did the German general say about this?"

"It was a decision made at the highest levels, the Prince or the Kaiser. He guessed the Kaiser, still had respect for his relatives in England and didn't want to destroy their army. With most of the equipment lost, perhaps it didn't matter."

Gibbon. "You met the Kaiser, does that sound like him?"

"No, not the man I met. Does this have something to do with what you are working on?"

Gibbon stared at Stevenson. "I will tell you in time, the Kings in this war seem to care more about their peers than their subject."

#

The medical officers in Egypt worked day and night, but many men died and others were so weak they couldn't resume duties for weeks.

Tom Gordon spoke to his brother. "We can't gather more then ten percent of the Fleet, I decided you should return to England, Arthur Denny needs experienced officers. I hear the army is very short of equipment, most lost at Dunkirk. I'm going to wait here, I'll leave with all able bodied men the minute I hear the Invasion starts. We can catch them the second day in the Channel. I'm sending two destroyer to wait in the Channel. They signal us when they think the time is close."

CHAPTER 19

The small Conference Room at Police Headquarters had recently been refurbished. A deep brown carpet supported the walnut table where Walter Dew piled his folders. The growing piles of folders represented long hours of work by Dew's staff. Dew's prestige was so great not even his superior knew the details of the case he was working on, only that it entailed national security. The only outsider allowed was Gibbon Stillwell who visited three times a week. Stillwell was welcomed by both Dew and his staff, who recognized the young man whose work ethic paralleled theirs. Dew liked the American and believed Stillwell's future career would take him to the highest office of his nation. Initially surprised that such a young man was given such a difficult and important assignment he commented to his number two man, that Americans had sent the right man.

Today when Gibbon arrived he was a weary man. His eyes and body movements told the Inspector the trip to France and the long hours and strain of the mission were wearing on him.

Dew asked. "Sir, I hope you are getting your rest? A tired mind can make mistakes."

"Inspector, your right, I'm working too hard, but in my defense, I've just returned from a mission in France. Due to the fall of the French government things are moving very fast. Hopefully you can help me."

"Sir, I have two leads. The first one might explain a lot. In the eighteen nineties a scandal centering on a homosexual brothel in London, indirectly leads to one of the Big Five. A man convicted in the Cleveland Street Scandal died of a heart attack in eighteen ninety-eight. I checked on his past, he was in the navy and served as an enlisted man on a battleship commanded by Admiral Richardson. He testified that a Naval office was once at the house dressed in civilian clothes. It could have been the Admiral, right age, and he was stationed in London at the time. I know it is thin, the man didn't say it was the Admiral."

Gibbon grimaced. "We had almost eliminated the Admiral, but a homosexual blackmail would explain a great deal what happened."

"Why were you about to eliminate him." Asked Dew.

"The Germans received the help at Scapa, but not at Jutland. We felt if it was the navy, they would have gotten to both."

"Could it be the blackmailer only extended to Scapa and there was no way to help them at Jutland?"

Gibbon nodded.   "Yes, and the Admiral did dominate the placing of the defenses at Scapa,. He is the logical traitor."

"We know the Admiral leads an active life with many women. Can he be active on the other side too?" asked Gibbon.

Dew. "It happens." Dew, rather then pursue the case for the Admiral gave his second lead.

"The second incident is even more unusual. We arrested a Swedish diplomat for carrying drugs for sale in England."

"The man told me he had diplomatic immunity," to which I responded, "no such thing in a drug case. Trapped he explained that he worked for British Intelligence, and directly for Mannaning."

Gibbon's attention was completely on Dew who continued.

"The Swedish agent told me he last saw Mannaning and informing him German submarines were joining together in the North Sea. Sir, he placed the date just before the Scapa attack.

Mannaning knew about the possibility of an attack and didn't warn the navy."

Gibbon was tired but his voice rose. "Inspector, its treason or at least negligence. What possible reason could Mannaning have for not warning the navy?"

"Yes, he certainly should have and he didn't, and I believe the Swedish Envoy, Mannaning was informed."

Gibbon didn't want to pass up this clue. "The Swedish Envoy, and you believe him? Is it possible Mannaning didn't trust the man?"

Dew answered. "The man is very corrupt, drugs and other crimes, its possible Mannaning thought he was a double agent. I'm not even sure he might not have worked for the Germans at one time, but I'm sure he told Mannaning about the submarines. He showed me a note he kept. It was dated just before the attack and stamped with the seal of Mannaning's Office."

"Did Mannaning sign it?"

"No."

"Inspector, this question of conflicting loyalties, runs

throughout the case. I went to France to rescue an American newsman. He was working on a story about the German invasion. He described a German general staff that is divided and the strategy is erratic. It appears that they let the English Army escape. You wonder about a tie with the Royal family to the Kaiser? But I find it difficult to believe Everett is not loyal to his country. From no suspect to two leads."

"I don't like Mannaning, Inspector," said Gibbon.

Dew adjusted his jacket. "Sir, he's a complicated man, of all the men on the Big Five, he was my last suspect. No one is more elitist, hates foreigners more, lives for his golf club, helps the Germans? I think he looks down on the Germans, considers them barbarians."

Gibbon walked around the table. "I've only met him twice, but that describes the man I met.

Hard to believe he would even consider working with anyone not English. Of course, he's very ambitious, would do anything that would help his career, or discredit other leaders to help himself." Dew closed the second folder.

Gibbon said, "We face the first actual invasion on your island since William the Conqueror in ten sixty-six . Did the Norman's have spies?" he omitted Napoleon and the Spanish Armada. He asked the question because he was tired, it had no logical relationship to what they were discussing.

Dew answered. "The English and King Alfred lost because an Englishmen of royal blood led the Danes to invade, and after Alfred beat them he was too exhausted to beat the Normans."

"So the French won?"

Gibbon rubbed his chin. "So it was indirect. The French were the second opponent?"

He stood up and looked out at the London traffic. "Inspector, we always approached this that the traitor wanted to destroy the English Fleet. What if that was not the main reason for the treason?"

"Blackmail or some other reason, but the plans given to the Germans was to protect something else?"

Dew looked up. "So it was indirect?"

Yes, why else would someone of these Five do it? I asked myself one thousand times and the only answer is the traitor did not do it to destroy the Fleet. Not one of these Five could have done that, even for blackmail."

"Not one of them?"

"Inspector, can you concentrate on Mannaning while I continue to follow the other men?" asked Gibbon.

"Yes, I can and I will." Dew wrote himself a note.

"I don't believe we are close to designating one for assisting us."

Gibbon shrugged his shoulders. "No, I can't say any one of the Big Five is above suspicion and no one is clearly guilty. We'll keep working. However, lets think in terms that the plans for Scapa were not given to the Germans, to destroy the Fleet."

CHAPTER 20

The sudden Armistice and basic surrender of the French Army caught the soldiers of both sides unprepared. The French soldiers in the South were mustered out and could be seen walking along the road heading home. The French soldiers in the North and the East faced a mixed reception, some were sent home, but many were pressed into work groups and sent to Germany. There was little rhyme or reason other then the German officers were given quotas to fill for French work battalions.

Outside of Paris the Tigers were on duty to form a work battalion of French prisoners. Lars watched as three French soldiers, all Privates waited to walk to the railroad that would take them East. The three were in stark contrast to the marching. singing, victorious German soldiers heading for Paris. The oldest still had his steel helmet, but his worn, ragged and torn coat told of past actions. The youngest had a mixed outfit, the red pants of the early French Army with a dirty gray jacket of the defeated. His uniform was muddy and forlorn. The short one was wounded, his right arm in a sling. The bloody bandages had not been changed in days.

Fredrick the gossip and talker of the Tigers was making fun of the defeated. "Look at the one with a bad arm, no chance we will get any work out of him. Send him home to his fat wife."

The other two a sad sight. "Amazing it took them so long to give up."

Holtzen the Bull liked to make fun of Fredrick. "If they saw you coming it would have ended sooner."

Fredrick ignored the jibes. He would not cross swords with the Bull.

Bachman, the cynic. "If they hadn't quit I was going to suggest we give up. I'm tired of the damn war. Where is the column walking to the rail head? Let's put this group with them and get on to Paris."

He craned his neck to look down the road awaiting the column of French prisoners marching to the rail head. When they arrived, the Tigers would add the three to the prisoners then join their comrades heading for Paris.

Lars could see the prisoners knew the Germans were talking about them, and one looked down at the dirt, but the short man looked with glazed eyes. He looked hungry, no food available to the French until the rail head.

Lars thought I would hate to be a defeated soldier.

Bachman asked. "Lars do you think the English will surrender…..?"

Before he could answer Teddy volunteered the latest scuttle butt. "I hear we are going to invade. The English will be easy, the war over in a few weeks. They ran away at Dunkirk, the talk is, they surrendered as soon as we land."

Bachman lit up a cigarette and blew a ring of smoke. The wounded French soldier looked on with the attention of a smoker who had missed his cigarettes for many days.

Lars turned to the Squad. "Cigarettes, I want three cigarettes from everyone." The Bull took three cigarettes from his vest pocket. Lars was the one Tiger he respected without question.

Bachman handed over three cigarettes.

Teddy as always questioned. "You can't trade with the French they don't have anything we want."

Lars motioned with his finger, he never debated, with the Squad. Teddy groaned, and reached in his pocket.

Lars. crossed the road and extended his gift to the French soldiers.

The two men eagerly took the cigarettes. The wounded man said, "Merci. Merci."

Lars not speaking any French reached into his bag. He had a half loaf of black bread he was saving. He handed the bread to the injured man.

The man's eyes bridged the communication gap. He took a bit of the bread, then handed it to the man on his right.

He said Merci, and extended his good hand. Lars shook his hand and extended his other hand to pat the man on the shoulder. Lars turned and rejoined the Squad. Now a column of French soldiers appeared and they all moved in the direction of the rail head.

Teddy ever the whiner. "I don't know if we're suppose to give them food."

The Bull gave Teddy a shot in the arm. It hurt. "Don't

question the Sergeant."

The Bull smiled at Lars. He supported the Sergeant and also he liked to quiet Teddy when the chance presented itself.

#

It was 9:00 p.m. and Gibbon Stillwell was exhausted, working twelve hour days without a break. He couldn't read another report from Walter Dew's surveillance team. His eyes were so tired that the words seemed to run together. He arose from his desk and descended the stairs to the London street.

He paused, his new friend Jerry the newsboy was yelling out headlines from his corner stand. Neither Jerry or Gibbon could fully understand each other, but they bridged the gap in communication with common interests in sports. Gibbon not having time to go to see any English soccer games was kept abreast of all the London teams by Jerry.

Jerry shouted. "Read Mr. Churchill's speak. Mr. Churchill speaks at the Commons."

Jerry yelled again and waved a paper.

Gibbon handed Jerry a coin and picked up a paper off the newsstand. "What did Mr. Churchill say?"

The newsboy stuck out his jaw a classic imitation of Churchill. "We shall fight them on the beaches. We shall fight them in the streets. We shall never surrender."

Gibbon was moved. "A strong speech."

"Yes, everyone is signed up in my neighborhood for the Home Guard. If they get off the beaches my neighbors will be waiting.

Gibbon could hear the pride in his voice.

"Jerry what do you think?"

Jerry answered in English soccer parlance.

"We in the finals ain't we, we're playing at home?"

He was saying it was the English vs. the Germans, head to head, and the battle would be fought on English soil.

Gibbon turned back to his office. "Aren't you going home Mr. Stillwell."

"No, Jerry, I've got a few more hours work." He mounted the stairs, the English were going to fight, and the Germans better be ready, it was not going to be pretty. He had to find the traitor, he had to work harder.

CHAPTER 21

The King's brother, Everett, asked Gibbon to bring Westy to his house. He believed Westy represented the American Wild West, a cowboy wearing a big hat, six guns, spitting tobacco and drinking whiskey from a silver flask. Hearing that Westy served with George Custer at the Little Big Horn, Everett told Gibbon he had a surprise for his friend.

Everett ushered Westy and Gibbon into a room filled with toy soldiers. It was the Little Big Horn.

Westy was pleased. "You got it right, that's the way it was."

He pointed to the table. "I was over there in that clump of trees with Reno, that's why I still have my scalp."

He brushed his hair. "I was with Major Reno, we were suppose to draw the Indians off, but Crazy Horse wanted Custer. We were exhausted, marched miles the day before, we should have rested but Custer was afraid they would get away."

He moved to the table and pointed to a set of figures. "That's Benteen. He joined us and we formed a defensive position."

Everett asked. "Were you afraid that day Westy?"

"No, I was too young, didn't know what I was doing. I wasn't afraid, I was too excited. I remember my rifle getting hot from firing so much, I didn't hit too many of them but I got a few, but they got most of us. We couldn't help Custer. They cut us off. It was over in less then a half hour."

He was talking faster now. "What I remember most was my rifle getting hot. I had a Springfield, had to clean and reload after every shot. Some of the Indians had Winchester 44 repeating rifles. Five years after the battle I met a gun salesman in a bar who sold rifles to the Indians. After some drinks I took him outside and beat him up, would do it again today."

Everett and Gibbon stood transfixed. Westy took a deep breath. "Hell, Everett, it was a good fight, I don't hate the Hostiles. The Sioux were good people, proud, brave, no they whipped us that day .....Don't like the Apache, mean, nasty, no patience with the Apache. Don't resent what the Sioux did to Custer's men, they don't know any better."

He moved several figures on the table. "It was really Custer's fault. Tired out his men and mounts, had the wrong numbers, too many. For a while, people liked Custer, but now everybody knows he was wrong. Crazy Horse was killed, he was the best Chief. You have Custer's brothers separate, they didn't die all together. I've never been back, forgot about it but sometimes I think of it. Glad I didn't die that day. Lots of a good life since and still some more time I hope."

He was rambling.

Gibbon and Everett didn't know what to say.

Westy was silent. "The Black Hills, Yellowstone River, the memories flooded back.

"I can smell the bacon, the day before I was glad I was so young, if I was older I might not have made it."

"Can I have a drink? Give me a double scotch."

Everett went to get a drink. Everett poured Gibbon a drink. "Your friend is an amazing man."

Gibbon responded. "He is a true man, the kind of man you see is the kind of men he is, he is a loyal friend."

Everett looked at him. "I think you attract such people."

This was a wonderful compliment and Gibbon responded. "That is nice, thank you Everett."

Everett. "Gibbon, I want you and your wife to meet my son-in-law, he is a Senior officer in the Royal Air Force."

"I've heard of your son-in-law. He is very well respected."

Everett. "You might be able to help him."

"Please come to dinner and bring your wife."

Of all the people Gibbon and Amanda met in England their favorite was Everett, the King's brother. Everett was very gentle and humble and extended dinner invitations several times to the couple. He was in intrigued they were so young, yet so poised and successful especially Amanda. A professional woman was very unusual in England, as they were in America.

Everett invited them to dinner along with his son-in-law, Arthur Denny. The senior officer of the Royal Air Force, Denny was thirty-five, a meteoric rise in the fledging service. He liked his father-in-law, was low key, calm yet confident. For a chance Gibbon answered more questions than he asked. Everett was tired and went to bed but Denny wanted to talk. He turned to Gibbon

"A German invasion is certain, but we may have some

surprises for the Germans. If we can develop and use our new weapons, we can win."

Gibbon poured port wine. "Can you talk about it?"

"Yes, and I want to tell you because your involved."

Gibbon didn't blink, but he was cognizant that Denny was close to the King.

"We have the finest fighter plane in the world, the Sopwith Camel, it will defeat any German plane including their bomber, the Gotha. Our biggest problem is we don't have a bullet that will penetrate the skin of the Zeppelin. If they can roam at will we may lose the battle. Our second problem, we only have two hundred and fifty planes. I don't know if that is enough planes to defeat both the Gotha and Zeppelins even if we develop a bullet. If we could determine the invasion route of the Germans that would help. In addition Lord Thomas before he collapsed developed a Flying Boat that can attack German barges if we catch them at sea. The key is find out the path of the Invasion. The two engine Flying Boat won't damage large ships, but it would be perfect against their barges."

Both Amanda and Gibbon waited to hear what he wanted Gibbon to do.

Denny continued.

"My father-in-law, told me about your questions regarding Scapa Flow and I know the King has great confidence in you. Well, I hope you succeed in your mission, it's important to all of us."

"My mission?" Gibbon questioned.

Denny folded his hands on the table. He spoke in a low tone, intense and earnest. "The German attack on Scapa Flow was too successful to be chance. They must have had the plans for the anchorage, those plans could only come from the Big Five. The King asked me to head the defense against the Invasion, he told me what you are doing."

Gibbon asked. "Do you have someone you think is the traitor?"

Denny smiled. "No, I wish I could help, it can't be Everett and I doubt its Lord Thomas, his collapse does trouble me. Thomas is a true genius in manufacturing and production, I've got to get him back, in the war."

Gibbon asked. "You want my help?"

"Yes, we kept the Sopwith and the Flying Boat secret, but the traitor may find out and tell the Germans. I believe if you could catch him that would help us."

Gibbon felt the weight double on his need to catch the man.

"I'm not close, but we've done a lot of work, and I believe something will turn up. Walter Dew is helping us, he 's a great policeman."

"Yes, I know Dew, you've got Dew helping, that's excellent, I'm confident you will catch the man."

Amanda questioned. "What is your problem with the bullet?"

For one hour he explained the problem which came down to, the bullet would not penetrate the skin of the Zeppelin.

Finally he said. "Amanda, I can tell from your questions you've done a lot of work in metals, would you like to speak to our top engineer?"

Arthur was low key, but he was discussing momentous issues.

"So, I've got a great weapon, if I can bring them to the battle at the proper time, we can win.

"I hope you can catch the traitor and also if you could find out the invasion route, we could make our weapons in one spot. Gibbon, get the traitor to help us find the route, it would be as important as catching the man."

Arthur was clearly in charge of the defense of England. The King asked Arthur and the Morgan Brothers to prepare and manage the defense. The older Big Five, the past; these young men, the future.

Denny explained the strategy but it always came back to the problem of the Zeppelins.

"The field guns of the British could not reach the height of the Zeppelins, it had to be the Sopwith charge to defeat them."

Next day the Amanda met with the head of the Science Department of the Royal Air Force. After two hours the man named Clarke said.

"Amanda, I think you're a wonderful architect, but I'm more impressed with your knowledge of metals."

Amanda was used to such comments. "One of my teachers said you can draw all the lines you want, but if you don't understand the materials your working with its sterile knowledge. We frequently went on field trips to steel mills, poured our own concrete, and worked with building materials. Can you let me see all the bullets you've made so far?"

All afternoon he showed her bullets, primer, the propellant, powder and the walls of the bullets they had use. Clarke tried many variations but none of the bullets would penetrate the skin of the Zeppelins.

Two days later Amanda was back at Professor Clarke's lab.

She said, "This is a bullet I made with a brass jacket or soft metal jacket. Let's see if this adds destructive power."

He fired the bullet at the same material the Zeppelins used as an outer skin. The bullet exploded and tore a large hole in the material.

He yelled. "You've done it! How did you do that?"

She was as delighted as he was. "The brass jacket expands on contact, increasing the destructive power. It has an incendiary effect."

They fired four more bullets, all had the same effect.

The Engineer Clark was overjoyed. "Amanda, Amanda, your wonderful. Arthur will be overjoyed. He works so hard, this will be a great victory for us. I think there is something else we can do. If we put a chemical compound in the base of the bullet, it will have a tracer effect and our pilots will know the path of the bullet and prove we are scoring hits."

She agreed. "Yes, that will help your pilots aim."

Clark was writing furiously. "I'm writing down the formula for the compound, we worked for months on the bullet, now everything is falling into place. We couldn't reach the Zeppelins, now." He waved his arm. "First they were too high, then our bullets did no damage, the Royal Air Force was subservient to the army and the navy who didn't want us to help, but Arthur kept working."

He stopped talking, he was so excited after months the problem was solved.

"Your background is amazing, tell me about the building you designed in New York?"

She shared in his joy. "The Woolworth Tower is a landmark for its day at seven hundred and ninety-two feet. I worked on designing the steel frame, we had wide piers and a tall tower that rose to carry the piers to the summit."

Caught up in the moment she recognized he did not fully understand the detail she was talking about.

"But this is your moment, the Royal Air Force moment, you said it was hard for you in the beginning?"

"Yes, we were part of the army and limited to reconnaissance.

Then Arthur and Lord Thomas convinced the Big Five to build the Sopwith and the Flying Boat. After we worked on the Flying Boat, we were afraid Admiral Richardson and the others would take it over for the navy, but none of the Big Five has looked or inspected those planes. They don't know how good they are."

Amanda asked. "We met Richardson, he's a smart man."

"Yes, but since the disaster at Scapa he changed." He continued. "I think, not as sure of himself."

"Were many of his friends killed at Jutland and Scapa?" she asked.

The engineer felt comfortable with Amanda. "He doesn't have friends." He was embarrassed for the moment.

"Well, I mean he's not close to many people," said Clark.

Amanda welcomed his candor. "It's a difficult war, so much pressure and pain I understand people have changed."

She wanted to learn more about the Admiral. "His decision not to use the Flying Boats was strange after the damage the Zeppelins did at Scapa, you would have thought he would be interested in air power."

"His last big decision was Gallipoli, and Scapa, since then he's been very quiet except for the scandal."

Amanda said, "I'm told someone else tried to take the blame and went to Gallipoli." She was probing. Maybe she could help Gibbon.

Clarke replied. "No one really believed that story, in fact his behavior was the beginning of the Admiral's slipping in power and of course the decline of the Big Five. I don't think they've had a meeting in months."

The Engineer was not only candid, but incredibly knowledgeable. Then Arthur arrived.

He was exhilarated. "You've done it! We can shoot down the Zeppelins, Amanda. You're brilliant."

Amanda not use to seeing the English so excited was quiet then she said, "The war in the trenches is so terrible, these new weapons can change the war."

Arthur. "We fight for our life, our island and our people, ideas more powerful than weapons."

CHAPTER 22

The Head of the Royal Air Force Arthur Denny and his Wing Mate the famous Sholto Douglas crossed the Channel flying at fifteen thousand feet. This would be the first combat test of the Royal Air Force's *Sopwith Camel.* The plane that Denny considered the best plane in Europe. At two thousand feet below them they saw four German Albatross Yellow Colored Fighters. Denny pointed down and they nosed over. The *Sopwith Camels* new design was compact with guns and pilots seat all at the center of gravity. Immediately the design was proved as Denny and Douglas both scored hits on the first pass. One twisted away and Denny followed the German pilot who tried the famous Immelmann turn. The maneuver began with a dive to gain speed, then a loop, at the top then the plane turned sidewise. This always lost the pursuit, but Denny caught him and shot him down. The *Sopwith* was the class of the sky.

Douglas shot down the last German plane and they turned for home. They had gone ten minutes when Sholto signaled a Zeppelin well above them. Arthur responded and the two fighters climbed and attacked, but their gunfire was ineffective, the bullets missing or not penetrating the bag.

Sholto tried a new tactic gunning his engine for maximum power trying to climb above the airship.

Denny yelled above the engine. "He's going to try and drop a bomb on the Zeppelin. In the thin air, Sholto's plane stalled and he went into a violent spin. Sholto did not regain control until below four thousand feet. Once he gained control the two pilots turned for England. Back at the base Denny and Sholto conferred.

"It's a great plane Arthur, it beat the Germans easily and not many would have come out of a spin like that. Lord Thomas's design changes worked."

"You were trying to bomb the Zeppelin?"

"Yes, I lost control at that height, its not going to work."

Denny was happy with the *Sopwith*. "It will dominate the skies, but we've got be able to shoot down the Zeppelins, and we don't have enough planes to spread out, to attack the bombers and the Zeppelins.

"I'm going to see the American Stillwell, I want to see if he learned anything more about the traitor."

Then Arthur turned back. "Sholto, I was waiting for the moment when our production produced a vast supply of bullets, but I'll tell you now, we have a bullet that will penetrate the Zeppelin."

Sholto said, "Are you sure?"

"Yes, Stillwell's wife made an incendiary bullet. It explodes and tears a hole in the skin. Now, we're got to make a plan to attack the bombers and the Zeppelins."

"The question, do we have enough planes?"

Sholto. "The Americans are with us, they want to defeat the Germans as much as we do. Have you heard the story of what happened at Mannaning's Golf Club?"

"No. What happened."

Sholto started to laugh. "You've met the stuffy club Secretary?"

"Yes."

"Well, Stillwell's caddy was his friend Westy, and the club Secretary insisted Stillwell couldn't use a stool despite the fact he has a bad leg. So Westy pulled a gun on the man and made him back off."

Denny started to chuckle. "Wild West Golf, it may start a trend. Shoot your way into the lead. We could use Westy. I need someone to protect Roger Gordon. Roger takes a lot of chances and his men think he's invincible. I'm told they don't think he could be shoot. We can't afford to lose Roger."

Sholto. "Will Roger want a bodyguard?"

Denny. "You know the Wild West of Westy and the hills of Indian are very much the same, small arms, ambush, the two think the same way."

Douglas said, "You've got to stop flying on missions like this, we can't lose you."

Denny nodded his head in agreement. "Your right, I don't want to admit it but that's correct. This war is about being smart not brave. Douglas who can believe how the war had changed. Before the war started I sat with French generals who told me French dash would beat the German Army. It didn't. Millions died because people didn't realize that artillery, wire and machine guns ended the aggressive frontal attacks of past wars. Our

General Staff said the war would be short war one mighty effort. Instead nations were willing to sacrifice all mass armies. The trench, the symbol of the standoff, the treaties as deadly as French money, built Russian railroads so they went to war against the Germans. We British said we have no eternal friends only eternal interests and now we stand in a live or die ending to the war. The Kaiser's so erratic we couldn't refuse to help the French. I never thought we be on the same side at the Russians."

Douglas. "We can shoot down the Zeppelins, a small bullet could decide the opening air war, but will the traitor find out and tell the Germans?"

Arthur. "We don't arm the planes with the incendiary until the last minute. We also have a bullet, a tracer that will help us aim at the Zeppelins. I talked to Stillwell. He won't say, but I think he's getting closer. In fact, I asked him, did he think he could use the traitor against the Germans? He smiled and said the traitor could be a great weapon against the enemy."

"How?"

"Not too fool the Germans, just to disrupt their plans. We have a great coast to defend, but an invasion is not easy, no one has ever coordinated land/air and sea like they are doing. I'm guessing they see the problem as a difficult river or bay crossing and who better then the traitor to help us to take advantage of that."

Arthur. "Early reports tell me this will not be the well timed imaginative strategy of the Prince. They are using a committee system. Everyone has a vote and a say. Good for us. We catch the rhythm of this attack and we can do great damage with the *Sopwith* so we hold back the planes to surprise the invaders."

Walter Dew arrested the Swiss diplomat Klaus Harrker. Harrker was caught trying to sell the Star of India Diamond to a police informant who posed as a diamond smuggler. The Star of India, the famous diamond owned by Lord Thomas was worth several million pounds. The famous Inspector began a patient examination of the diplomat who refused to answer questions. Harrker, irate kept insisting he had Diplomatic Immunity.

Dew reserved and cool prepared for a long cross examination.

"Klaus we found other gems and a German code book at your house, your Ambassador is embarrassed by you, so forget immunity. The Germans stand poised to invade this country, your life is hanging by a thread. Tell me what you know and I may save you."

"I don't know where the Code Book came from, the Diamond was given to me by Derek Thomas to sell, I believed it was his to sell."

Dew pulled out a typed statement.

"The diamond smuggler tells us you were very talkative. Lord Thomas did not know the Diamond was missing and Derek submitted a copy and you bragged about having important foreign connections."

Klaus tried to remember what he told the smuggler.

"The smuggler will testify against you to save himself. He will tell us about your connections to the Germans, enough to send you to the gallows."

"A lie, I never told him that."

Dew straightened his tie. "Justice will be swift in these times. A Foreign Diplomat whose own Government doesn't want to protect him. You don't have any friends, the Germans won't help you, I'll make sure their too late."

Klaus slumped in his chair.

"Young Thomas was desperate for money, he gave me the Diamond to sell. He needed to pay off gambling debts. The old man is so distraught he would never suspect the copy was in the safe."

The Inspector had opened the door now to pursue the real reason or the interrogation.

"Tell me about Derek Thomas and the Germans?" asked Dew.

For five minutes Klaus dodged the question about the Germans.

Dew. "If I arrest young Thomas, he'll tell me everything I want to know and I may not need you."

That broke the dam with Klaus. "The Germans asked me to recruit him to inquire about the Scapa attack. They believe someone on the Big Five gave the plans to the German Military. With his father on the Big Five, they hoped he could find out, and he also knows the Admiral."

Dew would ask a series of questions that would determine why the Germans did not know the details of this.

"There are two German Intelligence Services, Baron von Below wanted to find out if the Prince had a spy at the highest levels of the English government."

Dew from this answer ascertained Klaus was knowledgeable about the conflict on the German side.

"Was Thomas any help?"

"No, his relations with his father are bad and he never did see the Admiral. Young Thomas is wonderful with women but in the world of Government and information he lacks any skills at all."

Dew would hammer at this point. "Did you think it was puzzling, the Germans would even think of him?"

"No, von Below believed Thomas as the traitor and that he hated the navy and Richardson."

The Inspector recognized the Diplomat did have deep sights into German Intelligence.

"Klaus, I can try and tell my superiors you were helpful, in which case you'll go to jail, but not be hanged or I can tell them you volunteered to work for us and we will pay you and no jail time."

Klaus volunteered to work for the English.

Dew probed. "Did the Germans ever ask you or Derek to spy on the English defenses?"

"No."

Do you think they have other agents checking on the defenses?"

"No."

"Why?"

"The Germans are very confident, they bragged to me the invasion would be easy, as easy as the fall of the French."

"They don't respect the English weapons. They think the Zeppelin will overpower anything. One agent told me he could give them a map of where we are coming and they couldn't stop us."

Dew asked. "Land in one place or several places?"

"I would guess one place."

Dew. "Did they tell you anything else?"

"Zeppelins. Zeppelins. All they talked about was Zeppelin. They will land where the Zeppelins will lead."

The Inspector wrote down the strategy of a very confident victorious army but there had to be something more. "Did the Germans question anything?"

"I was once asked if I could determine whether the the English barrage balloons would be as heavy on the coast as London."

#

Dew wrote a report to Gibbon Stillwell.

Best evidence the Germans intend to attack in one area. Zeppelins will lead and they are concerned about the height of the barrage balloons because of the bombing. They are very confident but the leadership was divided, but now the Kaiser and von Below lead. I have no proof but because of the rivalry we could penetrate a senior German officer and get him to help us."

Gibbon gave the report to Arthur Denny.

Amanda's stride down the hall of the hotel was quick and determined. She was in a hurry to speak to Gibbon. The lunch today was enlightening and she wanted to share it with him.

Amanda opened the door to the hotel suite and walked into the living room. She kissed her husband, sitting on the couch reading the paper.

"Did you get to see Lord Thomas?"

"No, he wouldn't see me, claimed he was sick." Said Gibbon.

Gibbon put down the paper. "I think the rumors are true, he is so depressed he can't function."

Amanda seated herself in a big overstuffed chair.

"I met his wife today at the luncheon."

"What was she like?"

"Imposing, physically very beautiful and delightful and charming."

Gibbon responded. "Sounds like you were impressed."

"I was, very impressed, we sat together and she told me about three new dresses she bought. I believe she's in love."

Gibbon listened intently. Amanda was going to make a point.

"She's in love, but not with Admiral Richardson."

"How do you know that?"

"The woman sweeps men off their feet. There is no way she impressed with the man we had lunch with. He's too old, his personality isn't close to hers, he would bore her." Gibbon was interested."

"Maybe its his brain or his power."

"No, its neither the women is a romantic, she told me the books she reads. The plays she seen, she is in love with a younger man and I bet very much in love."

He looked at her. "Are you sure?"

"Gibbon I'd bet on it. The whole scandal is a fraud. She used the Admiral just like she used her husband. This scandal is a joke to her. I asked her if she read the papers. She laughed and said only the theater column. I'm afraid I'll be on the front page. She isn't the least impressed with the scandal."

Gibbon. "Amanda one of the Big Five is destroyed because of a mythical scandal. A whole country is in danger and you think the whole thing is nonsense?"

"I'm sure of it."

He folded his paper. "Can she be a German spy?"

"Not unless the Germans are making spring hats, her world is fashion, the theater and her social life."

Gibbon called Walter Dew and told him what Amanda said.

Dew called back and Gibbon repeated what he said to Amanda.

"You're right. She is in love with the oldest son of Lord Thomas Walter thinks the whole thing could be a plan to get the old mans money."

The next day the King's brother Everett and Gibbon called on Lord Thomas.

Thomas did not refuse to see Everett and he sat with the two visitors.

Gibbon said, "Sir, I do not have time to waste. You are a critical man in your countries defense, your leadership is important and I must ask you about the plans for Scapa Flow."

There was no life in Lord Thomas's eyes. He answered questions like a man drunk.

After twenty minutes Gibbon did not believe he was the traitor. He asked Everett to leave them and looked at Lord Thomas.

"Sir, you are being deceived by a hoax."

"What?" Thomas's head came up. "Your wife did not cheat on you with Admiral Richardson, that's a smoke screen. She's in love with your oldest son."

Thomas was dumbstruck. "Sir, I don't know all the ethical and moral codes of your country but you're a smart man. You know them both. This can't surprise you?"

For the first time Gibbon saw the fire in his movements.

"What are you saying?"

"I'm saying, your country needs you. Some bogus affair shouldn't detract you from your duty."

"Bogus?"

Gibbon had hit him hard, the ball was on the goal line. "Did you give the Germans the plans for Scapa Flow?"

"No, of course not. Young man you say some disquieting things."

Gibbon got up. "If it was my country I wouldn't be sitting here feeling sorry for myself, I'd do my duty first and settle my domestic problems later."

He got up and walked out.

CHAPTER 23

London traffic was light, an early Saturday morning.

The head of British Intelligence Mannaning shifted his brief case from his left hand to his right. Two Naval guards saluted as he mounted the steps to the Admiralty. Mannaning did not notice them, his mind was fixed on the information he was about to share with Admiral Richardson. Richardson would take it badly, but Mannaning wanted Richardson as an ally and this should cement the relationship.

The Big Five was in decline, no meetings for several months and now the American, Stillwell. Mannaning worried the King would blame him for the lack of warning about Scapa and the collapse of the French Army. He needed Richardson's support.

He entered the well decorated office of the Admiralty. Models of great English vessels from the classic ships that defeated the Spanish Armada to Nelsons flag ship at Trafalgar. He always recognized that none of the ships at Scapa or Jutland were in the office, but his mind did not dwell on this fact.

Mannaning immediately got to the point. "We haven't had a meeting of the Big Five in a long time. I have something to tell you."

The Admiral listened.

The *Morgon* brothers are being talked about by the Prime Minister. He wants to bring them back."

Richardson was alert. "Well, I intend to bring the Southern Fleet back, so *Morgon* would lead it. That was before the plague news." Mannaning eyes went up.

"*Morgon* would not report to you. He and his brother and Arthur Denny would form a Defense Committee."

The Admiral's belligerent response. "He follows my plan, I designed that strategy for Gallipoli."

Mannaning did not argue with him. "I agree, but they want his brother too. They think both are a winning team. Have you heard what he did?"

"No." Richardson said in a low voice.

"The younger *Gordon* was attacking the Turkish Rail Lines

North of Gallipoli. The Turks brought an army to destroy him. He set up a phantom Calvary Unit, horses made up of wood and canvas, and they appeared to the Turks to be trapped in a valley. Then *Gordon's* real Calvary swung in with an ambush behind the enemy and now the battle. He is the idol of his men and the press is spreading stories of his victories despite censorship."

The Admiral sat down. "I feel so tired, the war goes on forever. Ever since Scapa it weighs on me."

When Mannaning didn't answer he said, "Have you spoken to the American, Stillwell?"

"Yes I had him to my Club. He believes one of the Big Five gave the Scapa Defense Plans to the Germans."

The Admiral did not answer, then he said, "He's clever, and I met his wife. I wish she was on my staff. I could use her."

"Does it trouble you the King turned to an American to do this study on Scapa?" asked Mannaning.

"No. I don't care."

Mannaning tried to rouse his spirit. "Admiral you are considered the most talented man on the Big Five, we haven't always agreed, but I've tried to support you. With Thomas not involved anymore, if you decline to lead, the King may disband our group and the Arthur Denny cabal may supplant us."

Richardson sighed. "The Big Five, we presided over the greatest Naval disaster in English history. The country that dragged us into this war has just quit. The Germans plan to invade, what would you do if you were the King? Just to keep up the morale of the government he has to make changes."

Mannaning left.

He though of Richardson. "He truly doesn't care anymore. The war has beat him, that and the scandal."

The Admiral sat for a long time thinking of Mannaning. "Mannaning could be the spy, I don't trust him. His wife is related to royalty in Germany. He could be working for the Germans, he professes to be a gentleman but what kind of man would do the job he has and still be a gentleman. Mannaning has never really fit in. That Golf Club he runs is a pack of rich businessmen, none of my friends belong. Why did he tell me about *Morgon* to disrupt our Committee?

The Committee is falling apart, Thomas, me. Can the Southern Fleet recover and defend our island?"

Richardson continued to suspect Mannaning. He is telling me about the spy, could be a way to deflect attention from him. If he brings it up he can't be the traitor.

Mannaning returned to his office and called his Assistant Guy Bingham. "Bingham I've spoken to the Admiral, told him the *Morgon* Brothers are returning. He doesn't care, the man has absolutely given up. Doesn't care who wins the war, we can't depend on him anymore. I would not have believed it."

Mannaning was annoyed. If the leader of the Big Five abdicated his responsibility how long before the King dissolved the Committee and Mannaning's role in government was diminished?

Bingham picked up Mannaning's concern about his own role, several times before. He mentioned lack of Big Five meetings and Government Bureaus setting policy without any input from the Big Five. However, Bingham had other security concerns. "Minister. We are listening to the phone messages of the Swiss Legate who we know is a paid German agent. We have intercepted several Diplomatic pouches sent here but intended for German agents. He is careless and last week he met with Lord Thomas's son Derek. That Derek could be compromised did not surprise us, he's a gambler, drinker, womanizer and even uses drugs, but my men were surprised when they recognized a familiar police agent. One of Walter Dew's men. Dew's man was seen following Derek and the Legate. We immediately pulled back so as not to alert either party."

Mannaning was alert. "Are you sure it was one of Dew's men?"

"Yes, my man served with him many years ago."

"Walter Dews' man?" Mannaning said the name with respect. "What could this be about, the Swiss Legate wasn't involved with any domestic crime?"

"No. The only idea we could deduct is somehow, Dew identified with the American Stillwell. He is investigating members of the Big Five in support of Stillwell.

Mannaning scowled. "No, Dew is England's greatest detective, he would never associate with the American."

Now Mannaning changed the subject. "Guy you told me Stillwell was an excellent athlete, but you didn't tell me he was almost a Professional Golfer?"

"Sir, we didn't have any information on him as a golfer, we didn't know how good he was. He played sports in college."

Mannaning curled up his lip. "I rely on the Department, I want to know these things. Make sure it doesn't happen again."

"Sir, what do you want me to do about Derek Thomas."

"Look into it and write me a report. I want a study in depth about Thomas."

Bingham left the office more then a little annoyed. He was to write a report about what? Typical, Mannaning gives an order without research or direction. The Department was busy but productive, no. The Minister was intelligent, but lacked imagination and foresight. In three years the only true intelligent victory, his judgment there would be a war.

Bingham put on his bowler and walked six blocks to meet his friend and idol Walter Dew.

"Walter, the Minister has asked me to write a report on Derek Thomas. We are aware your people are following him. Can you help me?"

Dew responded. "You mean Mannaning is interested in something besides his golf game?"

Bingham did not answer. Then he said, "Walter we are British Intelligence. We are sworn to protect the Crown and the people"

Dew pulled out a folder. "We arrested a Swedish agent on a drug charge. He told us that he worked for your Ministry and that he wrote Mannaning a report that German submarines were massing in the North Sea just before the Scapa attack. What did your Minister think they were doing getting ready to attack downtown London, or go after the Loch Ness Monster? Why didn't the Minister call the Navy, an attack against Scapa had to be a possibility?

Guy. "I don't know." He hesitated. "I wasn't told about the submarines."

Dew decided to continue to be aggressive.

"He is either stupid or a criminal, tell me which?"

Guy was defensive. "He has a tendency to make snap judgments. He'll guess, and frequently he is wrong. I know the man your talking about and Mannaning wouldn't believe him."

"Believe him or not, it was his duty to sound an alert."

Dew pursued the question. "Is it espionage. What possessed him to keep this quiet? If Richardson heard of this he would demand an investigation or, did they both know?"

Guy. "I've worked for him, he is a strange man, he cannot

stand to be wrong. He hates to be embarrassed, that's why he would not gamble on being wrong. If there was no attack he would be embarrassed."

Dew wanted to lash out. He thought defenders of the Crown, Mannaning treated his responsibilities as if it was his option, or was he a German agent?"

"Are you working for Stillwell?" asked Guy.

"Does the Minister think so?"

"No, he believes you wouldn't work for an American."

Dew laughed a bitter sardonic laugh. "With his great intelligence skills what does that mean?"

"You are working for Stillwell?"

Dew brought out a copy of the letter from the King to Gibbon. "That's who I'm working for."

Bingham read the letter.

"My God, what is this about. Stillwell is the Special Agent of the King? Mannaning said he was to check Scapa but its more isn't it?"

Dew said, "This letter gives me authority over you. I am deputizing you to help us.

"Help you do what?"

"Find out if Mannaning is a German agent. We believe one of the Big Five works for the Germans."

Bingham rocked in his chair. "Walter, he is my Minister."

Dew leaned forward. "And you are working directly for the Crown, through me, your in it now, no going back. I want you to check his papers, research his contacts and help me."

Bingham asked. "Are you following him?"

"Yes, but its difficult have you ever seen any suspicious actions?"

Bingham was slow to answer.

"No, I don't think he's pro-German, in fact he doesn't like the Kaiser."

"What about the Prince?"

"He admires the Prince, but would never help him. He's not English and not English nobility."

Dew thought. Yes, Mannaning would only associate with English nobility or his golf pals.

Bingham questioned. "Walter did you suspect, I was going to come here?"

"Yes, my men told me you spotted them. Sooner or later I expected you. Ever since I spoke to the Swedish agent I've been thinking of how to recruit you, your loyalty is not to Mannaning, it is to the Crown."

The new recruit shifted uncomfortably in his seat. "Walter, you've put me in a difficult position."

Dew was not sympathetic. "The King didn't use your Agency when he needed to investigate Scapa. He turned to an outsider. This is for King and country. Once more, have you in any way seen evidence that Mannaning is disloyal?"

Bingham was still shocked at what he had heard and tried to think. "Our Agency has not penetrated the Germans in any way. Could our failures be Mannaning's leadership? Yes, but that doesn't prove disloyalty only incompetence. Walter I don't like him, he's petty and selfish, but I've never seen an incident that would make me suspect him."

Dew fingered the button on his vest. "If he were a German agent or arranged a deal with them, is he clever enough to hide it?"

"Yes. He is intelligent when his mind is not blocked into a position, he is clever."

"Is the Agency trying to penetrate German Intelligence?"

"Only the Prince. He thinks the Kaiser's people are stupid."

"How come you didn't warn us of the French collapse?"

"We saw it coming, but we weren't sure. We suspected but didn't want to go out and declare it."

Dew. "The picture your drawing is of a man who protects his reputation above his country, a very selfish man. Could the Germans be blackmailing him, and what about his wife? She's related to the Kaiser?"

Bingham. "I can't say he would betray England."

Dew waited. Bingham would not say if he would or wouldn't betray the country and an amazing response to a question about the head of British Intelligence.

Bingham said, "You know Mannaning fought in the Boer War in South Africa? Is it possible that he was involved with something that he could be blackmailed for? The Germans found out from the Boers that it was a dirty Guerilla war and he was at the siege of Mafeking."

"Was he a soldier?"

"No, an intelligence officer."

Dews mind raced, how to check on the mans participation in the Boer War. Was it blackmail?

CHAPTER 24

Walter Dew spoke to his two Lieutenants, the physically imposing Hefty Buster Posner and the intellectual Michael Barnard.

"I've talked to Bingham, he doesn't think Mannaning could be the spy. He hates the Germans too much, but his behavior is very suspicious. Not to react to the German submarines is treasonable on the surface."

Barnard. "He is so unpopular maybe he feels alienated from the rest of us."

Dew listened intently. "True."

You've followed him, any signals?"

"One amusing incident. When Stillwell was playing golf at the Club the officials tried to harass his cowboy caddy and the man threatened to shoot them."

All three men smiled. Dew recognized the wall that existed between the stuffy elitist Club and the rest of London society.

"What about General Kempton, Buster?"

Buster sat up. His ample barrel chest bulged out of his jacket.

"Can't believe he is the traitor. Before the retreat from France, an incident at the Front proved his patriotism and love of the army."

"He was inspecting the Front trenches where senior officers never go. Suddenly a German attack, infantry without artillery. The General's aides tried to get him to go to the rear but he pulled out his pistol and yelled. 'Hold men! Hold!' "

Our soldiers seeing the commander cheering them on unleashed a wall of fire on the Germans stopping the attack."

"His Aides relieved, were stunned when Kempton mounted the steps of the trench and started waving his arms. 'Come on men, lets show them what the English are made of.' He rallied the men who advanced to the German trenches and won the day. The officer who told me the story said there is not another senior officer in any army, French, German or English that would have done that."

Dew shook his head in amazement. "And most would have had informed the press. He didn't. Anything else Buster?"

"Well since he returned from France, he hasn't held any

meetings with his top officers. He stays in his house. Rumors are he's picked up some kind of flu in France."

What about Thomas, Michael? "Well the Germans think he is the traitor. They tried to get his son to prove it and he's been outspoken that he thinks our support of the French was wrong. Now he doesn't come to work at all, and is drinking heavily."

Dew fixed his tie. "He always opposed our Treaty with the French."

He designed a plane before the war. It was suppose to be a joint effort with the French, but they built the plane and broke the partnership. Thomas wouldn't forgive them."

Dew. "I have agreed to continue to watch Mannaning. Stillwell will continue to research the others."

Barnard a deep thinker. "Walter, is Stillwell the right man to talk to the Big Five? He's not a trained investigator, could he miss clues?"

Dew responded. "Stillwell is an unusual man, he is open and strong. People react to him, he brings people together. He is a lot like Arthur Denny. He was a great athlete in college before he got hurt, but the injury did not effect him. His wife is a career woman in a time not many men would be comfortable with such a marriage. In all my dealings with him I find no ego, no agenda, only a dedication to meet the commitment. America has sent the perfect man for the job. Look he was smart enough to pick our team!"

Dew and his men formed the greatest Police Task Force in Europe. They had no false modesty. Dew felt compelled to share with his team another idea building between him and Stillwell.

"Several of us have worked with the King's brother Everett on projects for the poor and men hurt doing police work."

"We've talked about this before. You and I don't believe Everett is the traitor despite the fact the Kaiser once visited his home. I can tell that Stillwell doesn't think Everett is the traitor if for no other reason, than Everett's love for his daughter and Arthur Denny. Stillwell is new to England, but he likes the right people, like Everett and instinctively confronts a man like Mannaning. I understand the golf game was like a war with Gibbon challenging him every step."

Barnard nodded. "We had a man at the Club. Mannaning almost lost his poise several times. Our man thinks Stillwell could have beat him badly, but let up."

Dew. "Stillwell would do that. He wants to get the job done, not win silly golf games. He keeps an open mind. Richardson maybe innocent but Stillwell is still not sure. Our tie to the homosexual scandal is very thin, we can't place the Admiral at the scene."

Buster Posner, a bull dog of a man asked. "If he's not part of the Cleveland Avenue Scandal, that doesn't mean he didn't do it and to think the traitor didn't help the Germans at Jutland so he's innocent. That's not good enough for me. He and Mannaning are alike selfish, not patriots, I don't trust either one of them."

Dew. "We've heard that Richardson took the defeat at Scapa personally, but never have we heard any concern for the men killed in the battle. This troubles me."

"Arthur Denny plans to plant a story that is untrue about our defense on the beaches and release it to the Big Five. We want to see if the story surfaces in the German High Command. We're going to give a slight twist to each man including Everett. We have someone in Germany who will monitor the reaction."

#

Gibbon Stillwell received a letter saying the writer had information concerning the treachery at Scapa. The writer would meet Gibbon at an undetermined place and that Gibbon post a notice in the *London Times* accepting the meeting. This he did after conferring with Walter Dew, and then received a second letter telling him to be at a street corner in London.

#

Standing at noon on a quiet street in the suburb of London, a black touring car pulled up.

The driver, a swarthy man said, "Mr. Stillwell, please get in."

Gibbon got into the back and the car roared off down a side street. Gibbon turned to see a large truck block off the street they just came through. The touring car pulled to the side and both Gibbon and the driver switched to another car.

These people don't want to be followed, he thought. He was uneasy but he felt the gun in his jacket and the fact that Dew was aware of the encounter and he felt better.

They rode for an hour into the country side and finally pulled into the drive of a small farm house besides a quiet lane. The driver pointed to the house and leaned on the fender of the car.

Gibbon alert, entered the house. A thin man in a trench coat, vest and black tie stood by a small table in the kitchen.

"Mr. Stillwell, please come in, I've been waiting for you!"
"You wrote the letter?"

He said yes and sat down. The man was precise, his suit
pressed, his cuff links matched his tie clip. He was a banker or a
diplomat.

"Mr. Stillwell you have shown great patience and faith to
come here. Let me explain myself and my background and you will
better understand my letter. I am the French Ambassador to
England. I arranged the incident with Admiral Richardson through
Lord Thomas's son."

"Why?" Challenged Gibbon.

"Lord Thomas is the enemy of France. He doesn't believe it
is England's advantage to fight Germany. He wants to make peace,
we cannot accept that, we tried to destroy him."

Gibbon settled in a small chair.

"Mr. Stillwell, I respect you, I am going to tell you things not
another man in this country knows. Things that are more
international then the war in Europe. Things that in the long run
will effect all of the world including your country."

In addition to representing France, I am in the employ of a
Consortium of Banks. Banks that represent the greatest financial
power in the world. We are concerned. We lent money to all the
leading dynasties of Europe, the Romanov of Russia, the
Holenzollern of Germany and the Hapsburg of Austro-Hungary.
Now we are worried, the war drags on the, Communist of Russia
threatened a new economic structure that will never pay back the
legitimate investments we made. I share this with you because we
have common interest to save England and catch the English
traitor."

Gibbons was trying to understand what the man said, "I
assume you represent Swiss interest, why did you make the loans if
you thought they were risky?"

The man ignored the reference to his employers. "Sir, we are
in the business of taking risks, but we never thought the war would
last this long and that the lunatics that govern these countries would
not find a way to make peace. Monarchy and Kings, not one real
statesman amongst them. Mr. Stillwell, did you know how many
great men these three royal families in hundreds of years have
produced? I will tell you four and one Peter the Great of Russia was

mad."

Your Thomas Jefferson said it best. "Kings live in idleness, great food, sex, their lives spent in the company of courtiers and they become all body, no mind. We have idiots with the last word in a world of magnificent technology. The car, radio, the plane, where your country proves the bureaucracy is to work for the people. In places like Russia it exists only to make the Czar happy. They and the military kill millions over a feud that could be settled in days, and they run the danger that all of us will live with anarchy the rest of our lives!"

The man was so passionate, spittle appeared on his lips. Gibbon felt compelled to speak.

"If your banks are so strong, why don't you reason with them?"

"We did, in the late eighteen hundreds we helped them settle their differences but the Balkans kept pulling Europe apart. Some of the leaders are good. Franz Joseph of Austria works ten hours a day. He has tried to develop some social problems but he is old and surrounded by fools. They start a war over Serbia. Serbia for god sakes, what great statesman wouldn't have settled that conflict peacefully. The money spent in the first two days of the war was greater then that little heap of dung was worth."

He was speaking like a banker.

"The Czar lets his country be torn apart by a drunken Monk Rasputin. I met the man once, he smells to high heaven. By the way Rasputin was in the pay of the Germans. The Czar is a classic King letting a country be destroyed because of he has a Treaty to protect Serbia."

"Well, he will pay with his head and the greatest fool of them all, the Kaiser. Do you know he has made overtures to Mexico to attack America? Did you ever hear of anything so stupid? These people are hopeless, it would be a joke, but so many are dying and the money lost is criminal. Some think if Germany defeats England it will bring peace to Europe. We believe that it is wrong. Germany will have a Civil War. Millions believe in the Prince and the suffering is great. The Communist will spread their poison and the Germanys will split in two."

Speaking very fast the man continued.

"The Kaiser's sending Lenin to Russia in the long run endangered his own government to unleash the forces of anarchy.

He let the genie out of the bottle. The Bolshevik idea is spreading in Germany by soldiers and prisoners of war returning from Russia, revolutionary propaganda. These people will flock to any one who opposes the government and will be joined by people loyal to the Prince."

" The Kaiser has never been near the Front, in his own interest he should make peace with England. If the invasion succeeds he will still lose. If it fails he won't last two years. Of course, to let Austro Hungary begin the was he deserves to lose his Crown. But I fear for Germany and France. What will follow maybe far worse then what we've seen."

Gibbon wanted to get to the issue of Scapa, but he recognized he had to let the theme of the destruction of the Monarchy continue.

"What about the Hapsburgs" he asked.

"Well the people who make up the power base of the country want to take the clock back to the 1700's, in self interest of course. Of course, many of the people they rule in the Balkans want to turn the clock back to the 1500's.

"So a pox on both?" Said Gibbon.

"It's a shame we can't put them on the moon, the earth is too good for the Balkans."

The man was a philosopher. He laughed.

"Every war has a winner or a loser, the Austrians are the designated opponents. France always marched against them. First the tragedy, the Austrian nobility doesn't realize the rest of Europe is laughing at them. They take themselves seriously and have millions dead to prove it."

"Do you fear the Communists?" Said Gibbon

"Yes we do, they represent the worse evil. The future is England and America, countries where the common man is more then fodder for the trenches. Have you ever been to the trenches?"

"No, I haven't."

"It is worse then Hell, the smell, the noise. I was there when a bombardment occurred. I huddled with a private, he was shaking. I was afraid he was petrified. Tons of metal raining down on us, men screaming. Men told me they almost looked forward to charging at the enemy. At the Somme 400,000 casualties with no ground gained. In the beginning of the war French officers with white gloves led the charges, now they are all dead. If the Kings and Generals were in the trenches the war would be over in one day."

He was so intense he was gripping the table with both hands. Gibbon recognized the man was a fanatic for his cause, Peace.

"Ambassador what news of the event at Scapa." Asked Gibbon.

The Ambassador calm now said, "We think the traitor is Thomas. If you can confirm this we will save you the trouble of arresting him and a trial. We will take care of him."

Gibbon slumped. The man could not help him. Gibbon responded. "I don't know who the traitor is. I can't prove anyone did it."

Now the Ambassador became the banker. "Give me someone and I will pay you one million dollars. I want to save England the same as you."

The American disappointed recognized the Frenchmen was desperate.

"I can't help you, I came here because I thought you could help me."

The Frenchmen stood up walked to the door in deep thought. Then he turned, he had a pistol in his hand.

"If we can't work together, I can't let you leave. My employers need to remain anonymous. Help me I beg you."

Gibbon could not draw the gun in his coat. "Killing me won't stop the war."

"No but it will convince the people who pay me I am trying. With enough money I can escape this mad house but I don't want to kill you."

A voice behind the Frenchman said.

"Well if you don't want to kill him put the gun down."

Gibbon was never so glad to see the dapper Walter Dew.

Dew pulled the pistol from the Frenchman's hand and shoved him into the chair.

The stunned Frenchman said, "You can't have followed him, we changed cars, we blocked the street, you can't have followed him."

Dew chuckled. "We didn't follow him, we followed you, you led us here."

After the Police took the Frenchmen away Gibbon asked. "How did you know it was him?"

"We didn't. After you got the letter I started trailing ten suspects. He was one of them. We spotted him with young

Thomas. When the car was left in North London I came here on a hunch."

"And a damn good one Inspector."

"Well Mr. Gibbon, you picked us because we're the best team, couldn't let you be disappointed. Did he offer any help?"

"No. The man hates the dynasties and the generals. Reinforced the idea this is a feud with rulers among the aristocracy of Europe."

"A feud with rules?"

"Yes, the war goes on, but they observe courtesies with each other."

"Someone related to the Kaiser, that's Mannaning or Everett." The Inspector frowned.

"Or someone who makes a bargain with them," said Gibbon.

Gibbon. "Walter, I think I understand what happened and who is the traitor. I am going to speak to Arthur and then prove it. I was hoping the Frenchmen could help but he didn't."

Arthur Denny spoke to Gibbon. "When we agreed to plant a false story to see if the traitor would pass it on to the Germans, the story was we would use gas on the beaches, the day of the invasion. We told each of the Big Five including Everett. Our man in Germany reports no word has reached the high command, so either he didn't communicate it or no traitor within the Big Five. Gibbon was silent for a moment. "Arthur he didn't tell them and I think I know why and I know who it is."

Denny waited.

"Arthur I want to confront the man. Give me two days and I'll explain. We may be able to use him."

Arthur's respect for Gibbon was great. He would wait. He shared the plans for Defense against the invasion.

"When Tom Gordon and I looked at the maps our biggest problem was a two hundred mile coast line, that is a lot of area to defend. In studying the Princes former battles we suspected a series of faints then landing in two areas, but now with the Kaiser in charge we think it will be different. I spoke to my father-in-law. Everett is familiar with the Kaiser. He said expect him to believe he can roll over us. Expect one big landing on one spot. Everett talks about his toy soldiers, but he has a great eye for military history. Tom Gordon also believers it will be one landing and the shortest distance between France and England. The Channel is a very rough piece of water, very difficult tides and currents. The barges with inexperienced crews will have a hard time steering. If you could learn the landing spot I could give them a very rough timer with our Flying Boats."

Gibbon said, "I have an lead, I'll work on it. Walter Dew questioned a German agent. and he also said one spot."

Denny. "One of our landing parties in Belgium captured a barge, not the most sea worthy vessel. We are playing games with the Germans. They build barges in Belgium and Holland and tow them along the coast-line to France. We use small crafts to intercept them, and they have horse drawn artillery to protect the barges. We attack, they set up the artillery and drive us off, I could use the Flying Boats, but I don't want the Germans to be aware of them."

Denny continued. "Everett told me when Napoleon planned to invade us in 1805 he ordered a rehearsal. A storm was blowing up and the navy asked him to call it off. He refused of course, dictators don't let the weather change their plans. When Napoleon got to the beach boats were overturned, hundreds of men in the water. He and some others got in a row boat and were swamped. Too bad the Kaiser isn't riding over in a barge might change his mind. Mid-channel in a small boat is rough."

What is the weather forecast?" asked Gibbon.

"Unfortunately good for several weeks. But we do have a surprise for the Germans. We had to leave a great deal of our artillery in France, but I have ordered guns from Scapa to be brought South including guns off our sunken ships. I don't think they will expect that. We must find the landing spot."

CHAPTER 25

Gibbon pulled up the collar of his coat. The rain steady, he wore a rain hat, but he looked forward to the hot tea Everett would have waiting. Today was important, the culmination of his theory of finding an ally, not a gamble anymore he was sure of the traitor, but Everett would clinch it.

Gibbon met with Everett. It was time to ask for support. "Everett, I think we've become friends. I need your help."

"Yes, anything Gibbon."

"I was asked by your brother to question and research the defeat at Scapa Flow and beyond that to find the spy that gave the Germans the plans for the Defenses."

"A spy?"

"Yes. We have absolute proof someone on the committee gave the Germans the plans for Scapa Flow."

"Tears welled up in Everett eyes. "A spy on the Committee? I knew it, your investigation, I knew it was more than you told us. But I didn't want to believe it. Why would someone do it?" Tears ran down his checks. The man so loved England, the news was devastating to him.

"My brother picked you to investigate?"

"Yes, he did but now the investigation must take a new turn. The warm-ups are over, we start the game."

His football analogy activated Everett, his head snapped up, he was alert."

"Anything, yes anything. How can I help?"

"Coming from America I had an advantage. I didn't know the Big Five thus I had not preconceived ideas. Now I need the help of someone who is familiar and has worked with the Committee. You can distinguish insights I need to be informed of, so I want to ask you a series of questions."

"I think I can help, I understand the men better than they understand me. They do important things. I just make lead soldiers, so I listen to them."

Gibbon smiled. "This is important. If you want to analyze the question fine, but sometimes the first answer is the best."

Everett was listening intently. "Does Admiral Richardson love the navy better than he loves England?"

Everett did not hesitate. "No, England is what give him his power and prestige. The Navy is the vehicle, but he doesn't love the navy better than England."

"Could Mannaning live without the Secret Service?"

"Yes, he's only been at the Secret Service three years. If a bigger post like the Prime Minister came along he would take it."

Everett surprised himself. How quickly and positively he was answering, but he was the listener on the Committee.

Gibbon thought of the third man. "The scandal almost destroyed Lord Thomas. Has he ever confronted anything like this before?"

"No, his life was perfect from his standpoint. This is his first real conflict since he was a boy."

"So, Thomas showed no signs over the last year that anything was bothering him, until the scandal? Could he hide a problem?"

"No, never, he can't be the spy. He could never hide it."

"Does General Kempton love the army more than he loves England?"

"Yes." Everett answered so quickly Gibbon paused then said.

"Would General Kempton sacrifice part of England to save the army?"

"Yes." Everett rocked back on his chair. Stunned at what he had just said.

"Does Kempton hate the navy or Richardson so much he would sacrifice them for the greater good?"

"Not the navy, Richardson."

Everett stood up walking to the table and brushed his arm against the lead soldiers, knocking some over. He did not see what he had done."

"Kempton," he muttered.

Gibbon stood still looking at the toy soldiers, then Everett questioned.

"You believe its Kempton, but why? What possible reason?"

"I understand the reason, the Prince once said its bizarre, and it is. I have to speak to the General to confirm it."

Gibbon sat in the study of General Kempton. The man looked terrible, unshaved, clearly he was not sleeping.

"When did you perceive the French Army would revolt?"

Kempton looked at Stillwell with sad eyes. "Two months before the war started I was on field maneuvers with the French. They were terrible, members of the Senior Staff were openly discussing blanket courts martial. If the men wouldn't fight, the head of the army told me they were going to send the men forward into German guns. Better to die than not attack."

"So you knew the French would fall apart and your army would be trapped in France and be destroyed?"

"Yes, I tried to tell the Prime Minister, but he didn't believe me and besides we had Treaties, we had to support the French."

"Is that when you decided you must rescue the army?" Gibbon was calm.

The questions were not argumentative.

"I thought of it, but I didn't know what to do. I met a German general in Paris. He urged me to speak to the Prince before the war started. We met secretly in Belgium. The Prince told me he and the Kaiser did not hate the English, and that I could not trust the French. That the French cabinet would flee if the war went badly. Then he said the Germans discovered plans for the French to send their Navy to Scapa Flow. He told me if I would give him the secrets of the anchorage the Kaiser would sign a letter that if the French quit, the Germans would not destroy the English in France. The war would end in a stalemate. The Germans could never cross the Channel. I believed the Kaiser would never go back on his word to his relatives in England."

"But the Battle of Jutland changed everything. Our Navy was driven back into Scapa and the Germans attacked, I was dazed but the Prince sent me word our original deal stood and they did keep their word."

"At first I planned to kill myself, but when the scandal hit and Thomas fell apart I believed both of us should not leave the Big Five."

Gibbon interjected. "You were also worried if you left Richardson would gain control and appoint his friends to run the army?"

"Yes, I hated Richardson. You understand why I wanted the army to escape, but let me tell you why I hated Richardson. My mentor and friend was the Prince of Wales. In 1890 there was an illegal card game at a famous house party. One of the guests was accused of cheating. We agreed, including the Prince of Wales, to cover it up. The Admiral leaked the indiscretion to the papers and the accused sued some of the guests for slander. The Prince of Wales was hurt by public opinion and attacked by the press for his association with the gambling and the cover-up. I have never forgiven the Admiral for his cruel treatment of my friend!"

The General hung his head. "If you propose to court martial I will confess.

"What I propose is you do what everyone else is doing. Fight the Germans. I talked to Denny who is heading the Defense. This is what he wants you to do, first get Thomas back at his post, then contact the Germans."

General Marshall Kempton called his old friend Lord Edger Thomas to meet at Henley-on-Thames a spot in their boyhood they both enjoyed. In school they rowed against each other. The Henley Regatta a one mile course. Standing under beautiful trees they peered down the wooden slope to the river.

Kempton said, "It still is beautiful, I love it. Remember my senior year, you beat us?" The morose Lord Thomas didn't answer. Kempton said slowly. "I know this part of your life is very difficult, I didn't call you here to criticize, I want to implore you to come back to us.

"I can't." He mumbled.

"The Germans will invade in a few weeks, you can get the tanks I need, I beg you to think of your country."

Kempton put his hand on Thomas's shoulder. "Forget your wife, she is a silly woman, the whole thing doesn't matter. The workers will respond to you, I want you to go to the Tank Factory and work twenty-four hours a day, I need the tanks."

Kempton. "It's not my wife, I can't face the workers."

"Edger the men don't care about your private life, they like you and believer in you. Think of the country, think of the King who is preparing with Mister Churchill to fight a Guerilla battle in Wales. What would your father say if you didn't help?"

Thomas looked up. "The King is going to fight as a Guerilla?"

"Yes, wake up man, were desperate and I will tell you I've made far greater mistakes than you, but when the Germans land I will lead my men to the waters edge and drive them back."

"Marshall, you're a general."

"Edger once the first German steps on English soil we're all soldiers. We won't need generals, we need fighters and with tanks we can stop them. The leaders will be young men like Denny and Gordon, not men like Richardson and me. Young Denny has taken your planes and is preparing a nasty surprise for our visitors."

Thomas reacted. "I like Denny by god, he will stop them, and I will go to the factories and get you your tanks. I think I know one of the problems, but can we hold them? Is it too late."

"Denny and Stillwell have a plan. They sent word to the Germans. Many of our people don't want to fight, the Germans are sure we're done. They may land in one place and we can gather all our artillery there and beat them even without the navy. I pray the Germans won't land in two places."

"Thomas felt alive for the first time in a long time. "What about the Americans, they sent Stillwell and I understand Pershing is in London."

The General looked up at him. "I met Pershing last night. He told me the Germans sent secret word to the Mexican Government they should begin a war with American and the Germans will support them. If we can hold out for three months Pershing will bring American troops to help us. When the American people find out about the Kaiser's Mexican adventure they will help us."

Thomas shook Kempton's hand.

"Take care of yourself, General."

"You too, Edger."

CHAPTER 26

The head of the German Bombers the Gotha was the enigmatic cold haughty Prussian Baron von Shaeffer. The Gotha, a heavy engine bomber, carried bombs under the fuselage. Not as large as the giant Zeppelin its bombing was not as accurate or as damaging. The heavy publicity accrued to the Zeppelins infuriated Shaeffer against Count Zastrov and his Zeppelins. This surfaced when it was time to assign bombing targets to the air wings for the invasion of England. Both Shaeffer and Zastrov wanted the prestige of bombing London. This conflict increased when each found out the other wanted the assignment. When the Prince was in charge this would have been quickly resolved, with his decision final.

The Kaiser declined to get involved and left it to Baron von Below to decide. von Below called a meeting, concerned it would be difficult in dealing with these two head-strong men.

von Below tried to head off the argument and harsh feelings with an opening compromise. He suggested the two air leaders split their forces, each bombing part of London and share the stopping of English reinforcements leaving London then heading for the beachhead and the invasion force.

Zastrov reacted quickly. "Insane, the bombing cannot be organized if the Fleets are mixed. The Zeppelins fly higher and carry greater bomb loads. I will not permit the forces to be mixed." This was a protest. Zastrov never would have made to the Prince, not daring to dispute the former leader.

With Zastrov's belligerent answer Shaeffer felt he must respond.

"Out of the question, I will not let my bombers share an attack with the Zeppelins. Out of the question."

von Below sat back, stunned by the vehemence of the two men. For ten minutes they argued, both air leaders demanding the predominant position in the planning. Finally Zastrov stood up and pointed at Shaeffer.

"Damn junker, damn Prussian aristocrat." This insult, the classic epithet describing a Prussian aristocrat landowner infuriated Shaeffer.

Shaeffer jumped to his feet and threw his swagger stick at Zastrov striking him in the head.

von Below grabbed Zastrov to hold him off from attacking Shaeffer.

Zastrov yelled again. "Damn junker."

Now Shaeffer yelled. "Damn auto parts salesman! Damn auto salesman!"

Zastrov broke free and swung at Shaeffer striking him on the shoulder. von Below and his aid separated the two men and the meeting broke up.

The failure of the meeting lingered as von Below met with Shaeffer. "That low class auto parts salesman, once threw one of his captains out of a Zeppelin. I will not fly in the same sky with him. It's out of the question."

von Below appealed to the Kaiser, who wrote a letter to Zastrov ordering him to attack the beach head and assigned London to his friend Baron von Shaeffer.

Zastrov had no choice but to follow orders but his anger overflowed. He court-martialed a junior officer for no reason. The morale of the victorious Zeppelins was very low.

Shortly after the assignments were set, Zastrov was ordered back to England to visit General Kempton.

Both the Germans and the English were aware of the wide-spread sickness in the English Southern Fleet. But a new energy prevailed in the English government the spark, Mr. Churchill and Arthur Denny.

The Germans confident, were sure of victory and with no fleet to challenge the invasion forces it would be easy. Zastrov ordered back to Scotland was unhappy when his ship touched down on the coast.

Count Zastrov pushed open the door of the hut, the dampness of the wet Scottish morning did not penetrate the smell of the oil lamp that lit the room. Last time the Englishman met him at the door this time General Kempton sat by the table looking at the oil lamp. He did not look up when Zastrov entered the room. Zastrov scanned the room. They were alone, he pulled his briefcase to the side and walked to the table.

"General." There was no need for secrecy this time. The General, a great coat draped over his shoulders to keep out the cold, never looked up.

"Count?"

"I have come at the direction of the Kaiser." The Count went directly to the task at hand. The coast was empty and the morning fog hid his three Zeppelins, but still with victory in sight he did not relish being captured by an English Patrol.

The General looked up a defeated man. "Your agent said you want the disposition of the barrage balloons on the coast?"

Zastrov. "Yes, in return I will give you a letter from the Kaiser confirming you will be the official in charge of the England we do not occupy."

"A letter from the Kaiser?"

Zastrov was impatient. "Yes, that's what you received the last time and we kept our word, your army escaped from France."

The General looked down at the table, every inch a beaten man. When he didn't answer

Zastrov spoke again.

"When we conquered France we took half the country and let the French govern the Southern half. You shall have the same opportunity, we will not occupy all of England."

Zastrov wondered if the man understood the proposal or was he so beaten he could not respond.

The General turned. "Which part of the coast do you want to know?"

The Count lied. "We have not decided where the invasion shall take place. Give me the heights at Harwich, Gravesend and Manston."

"At Harwich our Balloons are at five thousand feet, at Gravesend, eight thousand feet and at Manston more than ten thousand feet."

The Count wrote the three figures in his book.

General Kempton looked up. "If you invade we shall see great casualties on both sides, we should have peace."

Count Zastrov gave him the answer the Kaiser told him to give to the General. "If it was up to the Kaiser he would agree, but the generals want to finish the war. We will not sign an Armistice unless the King signs on our terms."

The General shook his head. "That will not happen, the Government plans to fight."

Then Kempton repeated what Gibbon told him to say. "However, many of our people are tired, you may find it easy. Will you command the Gotha Bombers as well as the Zeppelins?"

The Count reacted. "No, I command the Zeppelins, because

of jealousy the Gotha are commanded by someone else."

For a moment the Count did not move, then he sat down at the table.

"I will tell you something that will impress your fellow leaders. You can tell them the Gotha are scheduled to bomb London. The Gotha are also scheduled to bomb your reinforcements coming from London to the coast."

The General saw the look of hate on his face. "One other thing, the new Gothas have a weakness, the rear machine gun does not have a clear field of fire. Your planes can attack from the rear."

The General remembered Gibbons question. He was to ask. "How many Gotha will you send?"

"Approximately two hundred with fighter protection. My Zeppelins do not need fighter protection."

The Count seemed to sit taller as he bragged about the invincible Zeppelins. The General had learned a lot, one last question the flight plan, but before he could ask the Count volunteered.

"Here is the flight plan of the Gotha, see they fly from Holland." He laid a map on the table.

Stillwell said the psychopath wanted to see the Gothas fail. The young American was right.

#

Four hours later the General handed the map to Stillwell. "This is the route they will fly from Holland. Two hundred planes with escorts. Zastrov wants them destroyed."

The young American. "All our information points to the fact the Germans think it will be easy. They don't realize they've trapped us and that Mr. Churchill is setting a tone that we won't give up."

His reference to *we* made the General feel good.

"You think we're going to win Stillwell?"

Stillwell. "I know your going to win. I've been here a short time, but the English are a great people you're the hope of people throughout the Western world. You will not let the Kaiser bring a new Dark Age to Europe, you must not let him beat you."

The General looked down. "I should disqualify myself."

Gibbon held the General's hand tightly. "No! No! Our George Washington lost more battles then he won, but he won the last one. You should be on the beach with your men, win the last battle. The last one counts."

The General could barely speak. "I promise I will win the last battle, England will win."

One week later General von Hotzendorff spoke to Taylor, the American newsman in Paris.

"I don't have the place but the Zeppelins plan to bomb from eight thousand feet. I've been assigned to the Communications Center at Abberville. We will coordinate the Zeppelins, Gotha and Barges that go to England. I know they intend to overwhelm the beach defense, which beach I can't tell. The second day they will land the balance of the troops."

Taylor said, "I've had generals tell me America is next, you have a confident army."

Von Hotzendorff shook his head. "In one of our wars with France, our young officers sharpened their swords on the steps of the French Embassy in Berlin. One month later they were marched as prisoners through the streets of Berlin."

"The Prince would never allow the kind of talk, you are hearing."

"The English on their home soil will be dangerous."

Von Hotzendorff continued. "The finest military mind in the Germany Army is sitting in his estate getting ready for spring planting and fools like Zastrov and von Below are suddenly military geniuses."

Taylor. "The one thing I've heard you generals saying, crossing the Channel is like crossing a wide river."

The General laughed. "Only a great land power could think that way. England has not been invaded for one thousand years. The Spanish Armada, a great force didn't even come close. The most dangerous moment will be the first few hours. We will be exposed but not dominant, and if the English have an answer for the Zeppelins the whole thing will be a tragedy."

Taylor. "I have friends who would like you to help."

"Land at Abberville and take the Communication Center and I will help. I do this to defeat von Below, he is such a fool. I despise him. Let the Kaiser return to the Prince that is the path of Germany."

CHAPTER 27

The day was warm by London standards, a morning rain wet the streets. The sun tried to peek through but the noon clouds gave an overcast dank look to the afternoon. Gibbon and Westy rode in a London taxi cab in silence. It was unusual for Westy to be so quiet, but meeting General of the Army Pershing was not an everyday event.

The General of the Army, Black Jack Pershing arrived in England and called Gibbon and Westy to a meeting at the War Department. Westy respected Pershing who he soldiered with against the Apaches. Unlike the magnetic Theodore Roosevelt who he considered a friend Pershing was vigorous, firm, efficient and a great soldier, but not a friend. Pershing stiff, direct, and demanding was respected by the hard bitten Westy.

"Gibbon, I was with your friend in the Arizona Territory, great shot, best scout we had, liked the Apaches about as much as I did, and I suspect feels about the Germans like I do," Pershing said.

"Yes sir." Westy nodded.

"Heard you shot up a couple in France." Pershing spoke but did not smile.

"Yes sir, I did."

"Good, well you probably have to shoot a few more."

"Now we've got a lot to talk about. Gibbon where are you on the investigation?

"I know who gave the Germans the plans for Scapa."

"Who was it?"

"General Kempton."

"You can't be serious?" Said Pershing.

Gibbon answered, "The best detective in England is Walter Dew. He and I have proof and the reason is bizarre, but it all fits."

"Kempton determined the French Army would mutiny and leave his army at the mercy of the Germans. He loves the army and made a deal with the Germans to let it escape."

Pershing said. That's the craziest thing I've ever heard, but I'm going to tell you an even crazier idea. The Germans sent a message to the Mexican government. A man named Zimmerman.

They want the Mexicans to prepare to take back California and Texas. They promised the Mexicans help and also unrestricted submarine warfare against the United States. The Kaiser must have lost his mind. He thinks he can conquer the whole world. The President doesn't want a war but the Germans are forcing it on us. I'm to determine if the English can hold out and stop the Invasion, we will bring troops to England."

Gibbon said, "I thought the bargain over Scapa was lunacy, but a message to Mexico by the Germans, that the Kaiser is forcing the United States into a war."

Pershing. "Years from now historians will shake their heads over the Zimmerman overture."

Pershing continued. "America has a great decision to make. Do we go to war with Germany or will it be too late? Is the war lost in Europe? What do you think Gibbon?"

"The war is not lost. If the invasion fails the English will fight on."

"Well, that's a decision about to be resolved quickly. What's your best judgment when the Germans will invade?"

"In a few weeks, no later then September."

Pershing always in charge asked. "Why do you think the English can win, they have no Navy, their army is much smaller then the Germans?"

"Their fighting spirit is intact throughout the country. They are ready and their new fighter the *Sopwith Camel* will dominate the sky, critical in battle."

Pershing recognized he knew little about air power but was intelligent enough to inquire.

"Why is the English new plane so important?"

"The Germans will try and bring barges of troops over. If the *Sopwith* dominates the sky the English may sink those barges and control the beaches. If the *Sopwith* drives off the Zeppelins the German troops could be at the mercy of the Defenses, at the waters edge."

This was a new kind of warfare to Pershing. "An invasion by the sea? Do the Germans recognize how dangerous it is?"

Gibbon responded. "We hear the High Command is very confident England will be easy and America is next."

The General frowned. "I spoke to Churchill yesterday, the former sea lord. He said what kind of people do they think we are?

They think we won't fight? I was impressed."

Gibbon. "If that is the spirit of the people, the Germans are in for a rude shock."

#

After the meeting Gibbon said to Westy. "You don't warm up to Pershing do you?"

"Americans like a general who smiles. Pershing is too stiff," said Westy.

Gibbon didn't comment.

Westy. "He's a great general, but my friend Buddy got killed scouting for him. It all started at the town of Columosus, Texas, fifty miles west of El Paso. God forsaken place. Sun, sand, and rattlesnakes, even the Apaches hate the place. Pancho Villa, the Mexican bandit, attacked with a thousand Mexicans and Yagus Indians, they came in two columns. Killed sentries and then the troopers started fighting back. The whole business section, gunfire and Mexican horsemen rode up and down the streets shooting everything up. Firing into houses and setting the stores on fire. The towns people and troopers drove them off, killed two hundred of the attackers. Buddy and some scouts followed the Mexican rear guard chased them South of the border. Pershing pushed it hard, they had two Calvary columns, a very good officer named George Patton led one column and Pershing rode around in a car with Apache scouts heading the chase. They caught Villa at Guerreno, a victory for our side, but Buddy was killed and Villa got away. I can't blame Pershing, but he did push his scouts hard and Buddy wrote me a letter saying, this could be bad."

"Pershing got mad at the press. It was hard to supply the columns in Mexico. Some good fighting. Pershing organized his forces in districts. Sounds like what Roger Gordon did in India."

"Gibbon, the Americans wanted to love their general, if Pershing could smile once in a while it would help."

Westy explaining. "There's one other type of leader that's, Captain George Patton, *Georgie*."

"We were on the border, a shoot out at a Mexican Ranch, the Mexicans had us pinned against a low stucco wall. Patton came riding up, cursing at us. When nobody moved he yelled at me.

"Get up you bastard Westy lets see some guts."

"I didn't move. With that he spurred his horse over the fence and firing with his damn pearl handled pistol engaged them. I followed him over, so did some others and we won. You have to win when you do that. Lose and your Custer."

Later that day I said, "You called me out today?"

He said, "That's because I knew you'd follow me over."

"I decided to forgive him going to be a great general someday, George Patton."

Gibbon knew Westy admired men like Patton and Roger Gordon.

"The English are going to attack the Communication Center in France."

"You going?" asked Westy.

"No. Arthur Denny wants me to stay here and coordinate. Roger Gordon will lead, but he wants you to go."

"Why?"

Gordon's men think he can never get hurt despite the fact he always in front. Arthur wants you to watch his back."

"A bodyguard?"

"Something like that."

"So, after all these years they do respect the colonials."

Westy. "Gibbon you like Gordon and Arthur don't you?"

"I do, very much, they have fire, good leaders of men, I'm glad we're with them."

"They believe you and Dew solved the Scapa thing, they must be impressed. What will they do with Kempton?"

Gibbon turned to Westy. "We talked, we can't turn Kempton out at this stage, the army believes in him. England needs to be united, he is going to help us beat the Germans."

Westy. "If you court martial him it would split the army."

Gibbon. "He can help us."

CHAPTER 28

Westy was drinking heavily two nights in a row and he stayed up well after Gibbon and Amanda went to bed. Gibbon found an empty bottle lying on the table and his friend snoring loudly on the couch. The rail thin cowboy awoke, stretched and shambled over to the dining room table where Gibbon deposited a mug of hot coffee.

He looked at Gibbon. "You look worried Gibbon."

Gibbon sat down at the table. "You've been hitting it pretty hard Westy!"

A slight smile and he yawned. "Oh, you mean the drinking? I'm meeting Roger tomorrow, we go to France in two days. Last night was the last drink and I made it a good one."

Gibbon was satisfied. He had seen the same thing before they went to France to rescue Stevenson. He suspected when Westy was young these adventures were spontaneous and natural, now they were organized and formulated. Westy was gearing himself up for the attack on the Abberville Communications Center just like an athlete before a big game.

"You nervous Westy?"

"Naw, not even keyed up, just catching my rhythm. I'll start cleaning my guns this afternoon."

The previous mission in France the two coolest members of the group Westy and Lawrence of Arabia.

Now Westy looked at his friend." This is a big fight coming up Gibbon."

"I know Westy."

"Gibbon, there is no such thing as a fair fight, the Germans will do what they have to and so should we."

His face was serious. "I never told you about Twin Forks, but am going to tell you now."

"Twin Forks Wyoming, ten years after The Little Bighorn, my brother was Deputy Sheriff. Times were hard, lots of banks going under, people losing ranches bad times on the Frontier. A gang called the Wayne Gang led by Billy Wayne dominated the town. Billy was young, nineteen, mean, wild, he and his brothers and three others. The Wayne Boys and the others were out of work, trail hands, so they held up a couple of banks, maybe even a stage. A total of seven in the gang. My brother was taking a prisoner to the County Seat so I went along. When we came back we found out the Wayne Gang beat up the Sheriff in a saloon one night. Beat him so bad he died. We knew my brother was next. They were going to run all authority out of the town. Kill the town, they didn't care so we came up with a plan. We couldn't run, no jobs anywhere else, now I was his Deputy and our only help, an old Indian fighter named Tex. Tex was a hard man. He saw we had to pick the ground, three against their seven. No one in the town would help.

Every Saturday night the gang would get drunk in the saloon, and then walk down the street to the local whore house. We turned up the lights up in the Jail and positioned ourselves between the Jail and the house they would visit.

We heard yelling and screaming at the saloon. They were beating up some poor local, but we didn't intervene. They probably thought my brother was afraid. It was about midnight when they left the saloon yelling and carrying on. One of them threw a bottle at the Jail and cursed at us. Loud laughter and hoots and Billy yelled for us to come out, that we were old women. There was more cursing and laughter.

We were fifty yards down from the Jail. Tex and I in the livery stable and my brother across the street in the hardware store. Tex had two sawed off shot guns, nasty but good, in close, my brother had a rifle and I had this. "He patted his colt." And I carried a back up.

When they passed us they were thinking of the women, real drunk, one of them howled like a wolf in heat. After they got ten yards past us, we opened up. My brother first, he told me he aimed for Billy but they were bunched up, Tex jumped out leveled the shot guns. I can still remember the smell of the smoke. He empties both guns. I kept firing until they were all on the ground and no one was moving.

Gibbon was incredulous.

"Did you warn them?"

"Hell, no that was the point, shot them in the back like they would have done to us and not wait. So that three or four of them catch one of us like they did to the Sheriff and beat us to death."

Westy emptied the coffee. "The only one still moving was the youngest Peter. My brother told me to bring a horse over. We put him on the horse and my brother told him if he ever came back he was a dead man. We would give his brothers a Christian burial, but he was never to come back. He rode off just glad to be alive, and he never did come back. They never got off a shot and no one in the town said a word but every day for a week people were bringing us food. Had some of the best meals I ever ate that week. We couldn't pay for a drink at the saloon."

The former Yale captain and naval officer was silent.

"Gibbon, that happened a lot on the Frontier in those days. Criminals and the lawless element shot in back alleys, good people had to protect their women and kids."

Gibbon poured him another cup. "That's what we should do to the Germans."

"Exactly, they're coming to invade this country. The English will resist and the Germans if they gain the upper hand will take revenge for their casualties. It's just like the Frontier. Besides, I like the English, they talk funny but their good people, Almost as good as the Americans, especially people like Everett and Arthur. I'm glad we're here."

His only concession to the danger was, he reached over to a letter and handed it to Gibbon.

"This is a letter to my brother. If I don't come back send it to him, he's pretty old but we keep in touch."

In a short twenty minute meeting Arthur Denny explained to Westy why he wanted him to support Roger *Morgon.*

"He takes too many chances Westy, we can't afford to lose him. It's a miracle he hasn't been hurt. His men think the bullet hasn't been made that has his name on it. I can't afford to gamble. The man can't be replaced. Like Lawrence of Arabia he's very good at deception. On the Peninsula his famous trick was luring the Turks into a trap in a valley with a phantom English Calvary Unit. But he always leads from up front, I can't stop that, but I want a good shot at his side to watch his back. That's you."

Westy was pleased, Arthur was like Gibbon, open, direct and unlike so many of the officers he served, explained the mission.

"Arthur, will he resent my coming along?"

"No. He likes you, Roger experienced all his early training fighting the hill tribes in the mountains of India. It was all small arms and ambushes. He told me listening to your experiences in the

Southwest his experiences were the same. He will welcome you."

CHAPTER 29

Westy and Gibbon hurried to a meeting at Everett's house. Westy pointed to a group of old men drilling in a park across the street.

Westy growled. "The Germans don't think these people will fight, that's smart, real smart."

It was early, 6:00 a.m., and the morning fog was burning off. Seeing the men execute a smart about face Gibbon commented. "They look good, some must be old soldiers." It was early and his voice was horse, another late night."

Westy. "Summers almost gone, they must be coming soon."

He fixed his gaze on a senior officer watching from a house. The man looked to be in his seventies, but he never moved. His fist clinched, a stick under his arm, he was lean and impressive. A man to be respected.

"The officer is older then me, he sits well on a horse." Westy's expert opinion of the rider registered with Gibbon.

"They are drilling all over the country. I saw a group of women yesterday. Amanda continues to work long hours on science projects. She said everyone is dedicated. No one thinks the Germans will defeat them."

A London bus pulled up to the corner of Everett's house. With so many men in the army a woman bus conductress helped a little old lady up the rear steps. The young woman did not realize she dropped her change purse.

Westy saw the miscue.

"Miss wait you dropped your purse" He leaned over and picked up her purse. She looked at his big Western hat. His cowboy boots and said.

"Your American?"

Westy, a sly grin. "Not American, I'm from Texas"

The three laughed. The alert young woman saw the two athletic men.

"You here to help us?"

Gibbon nodded. "Yes, we are."

A serious look came over her face. "That's good because we're going to kick their German…"

Because she was a well brought up young woman her face turned scarlet. She caught herself and put her hand over her mouth.

Gibbon. ever the diplomat said, "Posterior, is the word your looking for."

"Yes, posterior," she said.

They all smiled.

Westy couldn't resist. "And your going to kick their ass too."

Her head came up. "Yes we are."

The bus pulled off and she waved to them.

Westy said, "That's toughness. I think there people will fight house to house if the Germans land and if it happens I plan to be with them."

Gibbon. "Westy, if we upset the German plans it won't come to that. Take a good look at the Communication Center. Denny believes the Germans have made a major mistake. The Prince always coordinated operations from a headquarters close to the battlefield. The Germans are so confident the priority is to keep the various generals apart."

Everett built a model of the German Headquarters at Abberville, France. The headquarters was the Communications Center of the German invasion of England. They had converted a resort hotel on the French coast that would coordinate signals to air, sea and land for the Germans wanted overwhelming weight on the spot on the English Coast. The hotel would not direct but relay the signals for the agreed invasion from the hotel in the dock area. The giant transmitter was on an island that ran parallel to the dockside. Two small bridges crossed from the mainland to the island. Denny's plan was to attack the transmitter and throw off the timing of the Invasion. The meeting to plan the attack included Everett, Gibbon, Westy, Roger Gordon, Arthur Denny and Matty Stevenson.

Gibbon pointed at the model and handed photos of the German Commander Krattzer to the group.

"We believe the Germans have one thousand men guarding the hotel and the island. So it will be bloody if we attack head on. If we can capture the island a German General Von Hotzendorff will send false signals to begin the invasion. If we can throw off the timing we expect Arthur's *Sopwiths* will attack both the Zeppelins and the Gotha. If we send the Barges before the Germans have a beachhead we may have a big surprise for the invaders. The key is upset the timing."

Westy looked at the picture Count Zastrov's brother Krattzer. "He has long hair that's unusual for a German."

Matt Stevenson knew Krattzer. "Yes, very. He's considered a smart officer, but weird, very erratic and not liked by the other officers. That's why he's not part of the Invasion. This is a blow to his career."

Stevenson could see Gibbon was staring at the photo. Matty said, "On field maneuvers Krattzer was suppose to hold a road block but he saw a chance to attack and sent a Division forward. This got him in trouble when he left part of the line uncovered. The Senior generals were mad."

Westy turned to Gibbon. "He looks like Custer, long hair, a wildman."

Gibbon asked. "What would Custer do if told to protect a position but had a chance for glory?"

Westy. "Not even a question."

Arthur Denny. "So we tempt the commander, get him to leave the area, give him a real chance for some fighting."

Gibbon. "Arthur, make the price so big not only he leaves, but he takes most of his men with him. Do you have something the commander would like to attack?"

The Royal Air Force leader. "We can come up with a diversion of course. You Colonists want something that looks like the great Western Plains. Don't know if the Germans recognize they're suppose to be the Indians. Westy you want to send some smoke to Commander Krattzer?"

Westy enjoyed the English humor. He responded. "Can we dump some tea in the harbor that way the English and the Germans can both be fooled."

Both Roger and Denny laughed heartily. Gibbon shook hands with Denny. This was a winning team. The English and Americans were not only Allies they were friends.

#

Next day as the destroyer pushed off, Roger Gordon stood next to Westy.

"You know Westy, one of my relations was shot by one of your relatives at Lexington almost one hundred and fifty years ago during the Revolutionary War."

Westy disagreed. "Can't be. My folks only landed in New York in 1850. Good Danish stock. When our wagon pushed West my father still couldn't speak English, but it could have been Stillwell's people, he's from New England."

"Arthur Denny told me Gibbon was a great athlete."

"Yes. Best football and baseball player ever to come out of Yale. If he didn't hurt his leg would have played in the Major Leagues."

"Did you ever see him play?"

"No but I saw him at batting practices against a Major League pitcher. Struck every ball with authority. Just like he hits a golf ball, god given talent, great hands."

"Yes, I've heard he can hit a golf ball."

Westy. "He can hit it to the cup on almost every hole. He's a better iron player than any pro."

Roger wanted to talk. "I heard you were at the Little Big Horn?"

"Yes, took a licking that day. Still trying to make up for it. Like to be on the winning side."

Westy didn't mention San Juan Hill and numerous battles in the Southwest.

"What about your Roger?"

"Went to India to teach school. Got caught up in the Frontier wars. My brother called me to meet him at Gallipoli. Don't like fighting much, but what we do today is important, we can't let the Germans invade. They hate us, it will be terrible. They killed innocent people wherever they landed." Roger never spoke about his feelings but he was open with Westy, perhaps because he was a stranger.

"I hear you take a lot of chances Roger?"

"Yes the *Anzacs* are great soldiers. I'm trying to prove I'm one of them. Did you ever try to prove yourself?"

"No. No, I like fighting. Just trying to stay alive. Don't even hate the Germans, but I guess if they were about to invade America I would. Only group I hate is the Apache, miserable people."

Gordon didn't know about the Apache.

"Was your ancestor wearing a Red Coat at Lexington?" asked Westy.

"I'm sure he was not great camouflage among the New England Green Trees. Your people weren't sporting, hiding behind trees."

"Are we going to be good sports with the Germans Roger?" Westy joked.

"No, we're going to shoot them anyway we can, but please, no scalping, I promised Arthur Denny we wouldn't scalp them."

Westy broke up laughing. This was his kind of humor, sardonic exaggerated.

"Now Roger, was this only for me or did you tell the *Anzacs* no scalping?"

Roger decided to stretch out the joke. "The *Anzacs* are so uncivilized I never gave orders, they would laugh at an English officer telling them what to do."

He turned serious. "Westy the *Anzacs* are great soldiers. They perfect men for this attack. It's requires quickness, bold men, we can't hesitate. Our advantage is surprise."

Westy. "Not like the Western Front."

Denny. "No. This is going to be in close, these men are excellent small arms experts. The Communication building and the hotel is a perfect skirmish area. Westy, you've engaged in this type of thing in the Southwest, first reaction?"

Westy. "We looked at the model, but until we get there I'm not sure, but my instincts tells me stay on the island, don't cross over to the hotel, make them come to us."

Roger. "Exactly. The Germans will suddenly be confronted with the problem they are out of position. They are suppose to be guarding the transmitter. If our plan works we catch them in the open."

#

Captain Fitzwith stood at attention in front of Admiral Tom Gordon.

Gordon was not as familiar with Captain Fitzwith as he was with his other captains. Fitzwith was sent to the Fleet by Admiral Richardson with orders to take command of the Battleship *Invincible,* was treated with great disdain by the rest of the Fleet. The story spread he was given his command because he accepted the guilt for Richardson's part in the scandal. This dislike spread to the crew of the *Invincible* and resulted in many brawls in the bars of Egypt and the rest of the Fleet's nicknamed the ship the *Pariah..*

"Sir, my Second in Command is on the Intelligence Committee for the Fleet, tells me the Germans have massed twenty big Transports at Le Havre for the Invasion. We have a plan to attack those ships."

Gordon responded. "Captain, besides the Transports, the Germans have five heavy cruisers defending that anchorage. Because you were on a scouting mission your crew is the only one with enough men to man a ship. One battleship against five cruisers, what can you do?"

"Sir, when the Spanish Armada stood off England, Drake and Hawkins attacked with fire ships and the Armada scattered and was destroyed. I plan to pull motor Barges into Le Havre loaded with combustibles and sink as many ships as we can. We have volunteers who will go with us on the mission. Then I will take the *Invincible* into the middle of their Transports and sink any ship not on fire. The cruisers will have a hard time shooting at us since we will be in the midst of their ships."

Gordon was silent. If it worked a great victory for the English. These were elite German troops, some of the Germans best. Gordon wanted very much to see this plan work. Could Fitzwith pull it off? A battleship in the middle of transports, the casualties very high, very high.

"Captain, what you describe is a suicide mission."

Fitzwith looked over the Admirals head at the large Union Jack on the wall.

"Sir, I have brought disgrace to my ship. My men resent the embarrassment and the ridicule by the rest of the Fleet. I beg you for the opportunity to prove on this mission we are worthy of the ship we sail. If we succeed we will damage the German Invasion. I think damage it greatly, and I respectfully request the code name of our mission be called Operation Pariah."

That night the Battleship *Invincible* slipped its mooring, and pulled four barges slowly left the harbor. No whistles were sounded, but the word traveled fast in the fleet and every officer and enlisted man stood at attention and saluted as the ship left.

A captain on a destroyer summed up the feelings of the Fleet.

"Go get them Mates."

The English Battleship *Invincible* entered Le Havre harbor at 11:00 p.m. A wet cold haze hugged the water during the moonless night. A German picket ship grew alert but realized when he saw barges that barges had been arriving for days, no schedule, or control, tomorrow they would leave for the Invasion.

The Battleship *Invincible* eased into the Channel and headed directly to the lights of the vast collection of Transports. The captain issued his final orders. "Pass the word England expects that every man will do his duty. The immortal words of Lord Nelson at Trafalgar. The first to respond were the forward gun crews with loud and continuous cheers. The men in the engine room, and the bridge and the barges. A roar then a chant PARIAH...PARIAH.

The captain made no attempt to quiet the noise as his right arm rose to begin the signal to fire.

CHAPTER 30

The German General Staff was so confident of the success of the Invasion of England that the Communication Headquarters at Abberville, France was the dead end for two careers.

The two men shunted aside from the glory of the actual Invasion were German officers in disfavor with the General Staff. Conrad von Hotzendorff was in charge of the Transmitters that would send the order for the barges to leave France and follow up the initial landing on the English shore. This was not considered important. The origination of the orders would come from the battleships standing off the English mainland. In addition the battleships would send a signal to Abberville asking for the support of the Zeppelins. The bombing of the Gotha would proceed independently. Conrad, standing on the small dock just outside of the Transmitter Building ignored the slight breeze from the clear September morning. The beautiful day was in stark contrast to what he considered an incredibly amateurish plan for the attack on England. During the war von Hotzendorff frequently directed communication for the Prince, always timed and coordinated to the split second. A thing of beauty.

Today he considered the plan so amateurish it was almost treasonable. The bombers and the Zeppelins should be moving in tandem to overwhelm the English Air Force. By sending the bombers first, if they could be defeated, the English *Sopwith Camels* could then turn and support the defenses on the beaches. Worse, the German Air Force made no provisions to protect the Barges. Not only was the timing wrong, but so was to let decisions be made independently. The Gotha general should not be flying on his timetable, but under the Prince. He would adhere to a master plan even if he was a friend of the Kaiser.

Von Hotzendorff's disdain with the plan supported his judgment to help the English today. When he rose that morning any guilt he had was quickly dispelled when the officer in charge of Security refused his offer to inspect the Transmitters.

Major Krattzer the other officer on the Senior Staff was disliked and acted with total lack of interest for his responsibility as

Head of Security.

von Hotzendorff heard the story that Krattzer planned to spend the morning hunting.

Conrad looked at the small harbor at the head of the river leading to the ocean. No German ships in sight. No protection. Did any army even appear so overconfident on the eve of battle?

Major Krattzer loaded two shells into his shotgun and focused on the high grass behind the hotel. The grass covered dunes that led away to a beach was not an idyllic spot for hunting quail. But he ordered his servants to stock the dune grass with the foreign birds this morning. Angry , he was not included as part of the Invasion he was determined to spend the day in other pursuits then the Invasion. In fact, he planned not to cross the island and check the Transmitter until the day was over. His brother told him tomorrow he would land a Zeppelin by the hotel and fly him over London.

His duty was at his office, but he was so furious at being left out he didn't care if senior officers called for him. He shook his head and his long blonde hair fell on his shoulders. He concentrated on one of the dogs pointing to the high grass.

"Major! Major!"

He turned, it was his Aide Captain Bunz, out of breath from running and waving his arms."

"What did the fool want?" he thought.

"An English Flying Boat on fire has landed on the river."

Krattzer handed his shotgun to the Sergeant, all interest in the hunt gone.

"Where?"

The captain pointed up the river. "About one mile up the river, it came past our windows. I sent a Motorcycle Patrol to pursue it."

With that they heard gunfire. Rifle fire from the Germans, machine gun fire from the English plane. Krattzer started to run towards the river followed by the captain. Arriving at the hotel he jumped on the hood of his car to get a better view of the River.

Then the sound of twin engine planes, two English Flying Boats zoomed over the island heading up river.

Krattzer yelled. "They go to help the plane on fire."

The double wing Flying Boats were low, the side gunner not one hundred feet over the water. The two pilots sitting just behind the nose were focused on the downed plane. The new arrivals firing at the Germans on the shore of the river. The shooting stopped with an English victory. Now the Flying Boats swung in a circle and made ready to land.

The Major waved his arms in excitement. "They go to rescue the plane on fire, send trucks with men to stop them."

The captain ran forward to the dock and Germans began piling in the trucks.

"Sir." The captain yelled again and pointed two miles down stream to the harbor entrance. "Sir, one of our destroyer is entering the harbor with launches following. They must be after the Flying Boats."

Krattzer looked at the destroyer heading into the harbor. He hated the German Navy, they acted in concert with the army to preclude his participation in the Invasion.

Krattzer cursed. The Navy was after his targets.

"I want everyone after those planes, only men manning the Transmitter and on Guard Duty stay, everyone else up the river." He ordered his aide Bunz.

Captain Bunz yelled for more men into the trucks. Suddenly he hesitated. They were directed to protect the Communications Center, this was wrong. But Krattzer waiting only to see his orders were followed, impatiently pointed at Bunz. He was in command. They would pursue the planes.

Krattzer yelled to his driver. "Go up the road, they are not to get away."

Krattzer standing in the front of his open touring car watched as the wounded plane taxied away from the pursuing Germans on the road by the river. One seaplane came directly at the Germans firing its machine guns, the other swung around in preparing to land on the river. The Major was besides himself with excitement. The destroyer would be too late, he would get one plane, maybe two.

Most of the Germans on the island were working on the Transmitter. A few guards standing on the pier waved to the destroyer who pulled even with the island and began to make smoke. The Guards were puzzled and distracted, not observing the launches.

Bunz's truck pulled even with Krattzer. He must protest.

"Sir, we've left less than two hundred men to protect the Transmitter."

"I don't care, I want those planes."

The captain issued the orders and Krattzer pointed to the driver.

#

Roger Gordon leaned on the railing of the first launch.

"He's biting Westy, I see more trucks heading up the river. The destroyer is level with the island. Roger turned to the men crouching in the launches. "Get ready, we land in five minutes."

Several German Navy personnel behind the men at the hotel not working, were at the windows watching the drama unfold.

The destroyer continued to make smoke, within a minute the dock on the river was covered with a fog like smoke.

Roger turned to Westy. "Two minutes and we land on the island. First group right to the Transmitter. Westy you and I dash right across to the two bridges, cut off the mainland. I see less then fifty men in front of the hotel. The Germans on the pier are watching the destroyer."

The smoke from the stopped destroyer engulfed the pier and in the confusion Rogers launches landed within minutes. Rogers first group burst into the Transmitter Building and took control. Roger and Westy followed by one hundred men raced to the two bridges using rifle fire swept the street in front of the hotel of all Germans. The men on the pier surrendered.

Roger issued orders. "Prepare for a defense, Krattzer and his men will be coming back, set the dynamite on the bridges. Get back to the island."

Three Germans appeared by the side of the hotel. Rogers rifle and Westy's six guns leveled the Uhlans. Roger looked at Westy and smiled.

"Good shooting Yank."

"Good shooting yourself. The plan is working, they chased the planes."

An English officer came out of the Transmitter Building.

"We are sending signals to the Germans, von Hotzendorff is in control. We had no trouble with the radio crew, I'm setting dynamite in the building."

Gordon nodded approval.

"Good, we'll hold here. You continue with the signals."

#

The Major was frustrated. The two English seaplanes continued to taxi up the river staying two hundred yards ahead of the pursuing Germans.

Krattzer was yelling, but he looked back to see the destroyer by the island making smoke. What was that about?

Then the captain was by his side. "Sir, shooting by the hotel. Some kind of raiding party has attacked the hotel."

Krattzer stiffened. He was in charge of Security of the Transmitter, the Invasion of England and he had left his post.

Now Krattzer was calm. "Captain, follow me, I want all the men to go to the hotel and the island. I'll drive the first truck, you follow me with everyone else."

Krattzer deliberately walked to the truck and told the driver to get out. He signaled twenty men in the truck, got ready and started the engine. Driving down the road in the direction of the hotel he picked up speed and saw a gun flash from the destroyer that exploded behind him hitting a second truck. He heard the screams of men behind him.

Roger saw the German trucks racing down the road toward them. One truck exploded, then a second was on fire.

Roger signaled to blow the bridges. One blew, the second did not.

Roger turned to the English riflemen. "Prepare for an attack. They'll probably abandon the truck on the other side of the bridge and rush us."

Westy could see the driver of the first truck had long blonde hair.

"Roger, he's going to drive that truck right over the bridge. Don't expect him to stop."

Roger glanced at Westy and yelled. "The truck will come over the bridge, hold your fire until he is within fifty yards."

The *Anzacs* positioned themselves. Westy could see they were professional. No wasted motion, weapons at the ready.

Kneeling next to Roger he heard him whisper.

"Even though I walk through the valley of the shadow of death I will fear no evil."

Westy loaded his pistol and said.

"Get ready, Roger."

Some British tried to fire at the speeding truck, but the bridge blocked the fire and Krattzer racing at twenty miles an hour barreled over the bridge. The truck stalled just over the bridge with many rifle shots causing smoke from the engine. Krattzer and the

Germans spilled onto the bridge and found cover from the steel side. A heavy fire front ensued as a second and third truck brought more soldiers into the battle. Both sides were pinned down, to move forward impossible.

Westy spoke to Roger. "Pretend to move back. He'll rush us."

Roger signaled his troops to retreat twenty yards to a pile of sand bags. The English executed a side slipping retreat motion with almost one hundred men moving back twenty yards.

Krattzer was on his feet and leading his men across the bridge to be met by a hail of British fire as they gained the island.

Krattzer hit in the chest fell to his knees. Half his men were down, but he struggled up and yelled and led a second rush. Westy's colt bullet hit him in the shoulder, spun him around and he went down. The British withering fire finished the rest of Krattzer's men, well over two hundred German casualties. The German Infantry pulled back, most moving behind the hotel for cover as the destroyer began to fire at them. Krattzer lying against the end of the bridge was covered with blood. He looked up to see a man pointing a six gun, wearing a cowboy hat and boots.

"Who are you." Asked Krattzer

"An American," said the stranger.

"What are you doing in France?"

"Helping friends."

Krattzer. "You look like a cowboy."

"I am a cowboy," said Westy.

Krattzer dying said, "I left my post, I am disgraced."

Westy knelt on one knee. "You're a brave man Major, you go for the fight."

The Major sighed.

"You know me?"

Westy wiped his forehead. He was covered with blood. Westy gave him a handkerchief for his lips.

"I know someone like you.

"He was a brave man too."

The Major died.

"Your just like Custer Major, I wonder if you ever heard of him?"

He started to reload his pistol and he had a flash back to Sioux Country. How many years, how many shoot outs?" It was time to

...er and good riddance. He can join Rupprecht in sitting on
...h after the war is over."

...ow they talked of another officer they didn't like.
...he auto parts salesman Zastrov, will be bringing his
...ns over in a few hours. I have decided we may need him
...t clearly we don't need to share the glory of the landing."
...heer answered. "I agree, we don't need him now. He is a
...le man. Yes, land before he gets here. The man calls
...a Count, he is no such thing."
...ready German troops were loading the landing craft. The
...re in positive mood. It was like a exercise. The Admiral
...e signal to begin to fire on the English shore.
...hen Admiral Scheer read a message. "This is from Le
...he English attacked."
...udendorff. "Attacked? With what?"
...heer. "Battleships and fire ships, we sunk one battleship,
...he dark the others got away. Much damage almost all the
...rts destroyed, much loss of life. That was eighty thousand
...est men. They were to land in England tonight."
...heer was speechless. Finally he said, "Fire ships? Have
...he mad, at Le Havre? The English used fire ships against the
...Armada in the days of wooden ships. Do they see the ghost
...e? Hawkins the message must be wrong."
...dmiral Scheer read the rest of the message.
...Very little damage to our cruisers, the English concentrated
...ransports. They sacrificed themselves. A suicide mission."
...e thought, "If the English fought that hard at Le Havre, what
...hey do on the beaches."
...e looked. The first landing craft were approaching the shore.
...eneral Ludendorff read aloud. "We sank one battleship, they
...o bravely, no sign of the others."
...e asked. "Could our men be wrong? It was only one big ship
...all that damage?"
...heer for the first time felt concern.
...dmiral Scheer, Captain Teeder is on the radio."
...eeder was the well respected officer in charge of the cruisers
...avre.
...eeder, what happened?" asked Scheer.
...t was foggy, they were in amongst the ships before we saw

stop.

It wasn't he was too old, it wasn't exciting anymore. His brother told him he would reach the end of his love of gun-smoke, and in 1917 in France it happened. This was the last one.

He looked up, they had taken the Communication Center at Abberville. It was a good mission. His mood brightened. Maybe I'm not done. Roger was walking towards him.

He made a fist and said, "Roger good mission, this was like a border fight in Mexico."

Roger was at Westy's side. "We've got control, the destroyer can keep them from attacking the Transmitter.

von Hotzendorff stays until the barges and the Zeppelins are sent. He looked at the dead Krattzer. "He drove that truck directly into our fire, tough man."

Westy. "I said to him he was a brave man. This is a cold war, no place for knights and romantics, he should have been in Sioux Country. Lots of wild charges out there."

CHAPTER 31

The Great German Fleet contained ove
ships. In addition many Transports with nur
approached the English coast.

The Wine Steward offered a silver tra
champagne to Admiral Scheer and Gener
Ludendorff. Ludendorff did not drink alcoho
took a small sip. He lifted the glass.

"To our success. The Invasion of Engla
Scheer raised his glass. "We make h
English ship in sight and the beach is empty
surprise."

"Is your plan to avoid London?" asked t
Ludendorff adjusted his monocle. "
whoever is in front of us, march toward Lon
take the army into the city. We shall starve th
Admiral Scheer said, "I don't miss Ru
in the Invasion, do you?"

Ludendorf shook his head. "No, he w
will be better off without him. The English v
The army will be off the beaches by tonight."

Scheer. "There is another reason for no
is a descendant of the English King Charles
convinced the Kaiser that if Rupprecht won
some might want him to rule England and
Kaiser."

Ludendorff, a career soldier cared littl
high office. But he recognized many in th
General was pushed aside.

"I had to reassign some of Rupprecht
support our plans."

The Admiral was interested in one offic
"Where did you put his aide von Hotze
"I put him in a place where he wou
Communications Center at Abberville. H
officer then Krattzer, but Krattzer is in cha

"Fire ships. What nonsense," said Scheer. "They had Navy motorized barges, and they built a high structure to roll oil drums onto the decks of our Transports. Once the oil spilled onto decks, they used flaming pitch to ignite it. A barge would pull up, pump oil on a deck, set it on fire and be off before we could defend. They set ten ships on fire before we knew we were under attack."

"How many battleships?"

Teeder. "I think only one."

"He was in the middle of the Transports, we couldn't reach him he never fired at the cruisers only sinking Transports."

Sheer was aghast. "It was a suicide mission?"

"Yes, and I captured one of the officers when I asked him the name of his ship, he said the *Pariah*"

Scheer. "There is no English battleship called the *Pariah*"

"I know, but the man insisted the ship was the *Pariah*. There were no other English ships, we sank all the barges."

Scheer. Looked at the horizon. No English ships on the sea, they couldn't attack with suicide ships against his Fleet. Perhaps he should spend more time firing at the beachheads. Scheer gave an order. He directed the firing to target further inland.

General Ludendorff was shaken. "Those were some of our best troops. I planned to use them to break out if the English held us. Do you think the English knew they were attacking elite troops?"

Scheer. "I do, it was so effective, motor barges setting ships on fire, who could suspect that?"

The German fleet shifted into the line. Battleships, cruisers and destroyer began to fire rapidly at the English shore. Continuous flames and explosive destructive clouds of dirt and noise rent the coast line.

The air was filled with brown smoke.

Admiral Scheer. "The English are overwhelmed, continue the Invasion."

With that, hidden English shore batteries answered and a German cruiser disappeared. Fire and flames marked the death of one of the Invaders ships.

The din was indescribable, the Germans were surprised by the opposition, the duel of big guns, echoes of the battle of Jutland. A German battleship hit and was on fire. Admiral Scheer's battleship blasting the distant cliff with broadsides from her main battery. But the English from inland batteries continued to answer. This was not the easy landing the Germans expected.

The English waited until the first German soldiers landed on the shore before they fired so almost all the Infantry was in boats or unprotected on the beach. They fell in large numbers. Hidden machine guns in the dunes raked the men. Artillery hit the small boats with loud screams of terror and pain.

Scheer was stunned where was all this English fire coming from? They must be very well camouflaged. He saw a flash, it came from a hay-stack, the English had hidden big guns on the shore. Flashes came from caves, but how could they have so many guns in one place? The whole idea of a narrow front was to outgun the British. Now the clear sound of machine gun fire, the English from hidden dugouts were shooting the Infantry as they landed.

Scheer. "First Le Havre, now the beaches. We were overconfident."

A terrible idea struck him. He said to the General. "The Prince would never have made these mistakes. The narrow front we had, the advantages in men, we gave it back to the British, a wide front was better."

The English artillery concentrated because they knew the destination of the German Fleet. They began to win the gun duel with the German Fleet.

Many German surface ships were on fire so the English shifted their targets to the Transports. This took a heavy toll on German troops who were climbing down rope ladders to waiting assault boats.

Of the first wave of German troops on the beach of England, fifty percent casualties. The English artillery shifted again and started to shell the beach.

General Kempton raised his arm. "Now."

Hay-stacks fell away as Mark IV English tanks emerged. In one area the German soldiers were stunned to see the giant tanks moving toward them firing six pound guns and machine guns. The Germans had no way to stop the tanks and died or were driven back into the ocean.

Kempton waited for the troops in another sector to land, then he attacked.

Scheer gave orders. "Send the signal to Abberville. Tell them to hold the barges and bring the Zeppelins here immediately."

The signal officer returned. "Admiral we can't reach Abberville. No one will answer our signal."

Scheer was frustrated and cursed. "What the hell is going on? Keep trying."

He turned to Ludendorff.

"Can you call the troops back?"

"No, once they were ordered to invade, they were not to turn back. We have to proceed. Ludendorff trained his glasses on the beach, his men were being slaughtered. This was worse then France. He was helpless. He realized a major mistake was made not to have recall orders and not to wait for the Zeppelins.

#

At Abberville the operator sent the wrong orders at the direction of von Hotzendorff. The barges headed for England and the Zeppelins waited.

General Kempton continued to send tanks forward. It was a massacre.

He turned to his aide. "German soldiers have landed, if you call this a landing. They are not even shooting back. Most of them have not gotten beyond the tide line."

The aide pointed out to sea. "Sir, our guns have hit another battleship. Look, its explosions rent the sky. Our guns are leaving the beaches to the tanks. We've overwhelmed them."

Some German barges who had left early were now beginning to attempt to land.

The General signaled. "Fire on the barges."

The barges tormented by sea planes met unexpected fire from the beaches. The sea was a mass of burning ships, sinking Transports and bodies.

Kempton could see the opening of a great victory but he realized more Germans would be coming. He said to his Second in Command. "A sea Invasion, I suspect they can't stop it, they'll keep coming. Get the tanks ready. I'm going to the waters edge?"

#

The Tigers were cold and wet sitting in a small barge that was to be pulled across the English Channel. Some were seasick, some scared, all uncomfortable. They embarked as the first streaks of dawn crept through the sky. Now four hours later they still waited for the signal to proceed to England. Around them hundreds of boats and barges waited. The sea placid at dawn was now rolling and water was splashing into the barge, using their helmets they tried to bail but the water at the bottom of the barge did not recede.

Lars was miserable, never on the ocean before he expected a lake, not a rolling, dashing body of water that knocked him against the side of the barge and hurt his shoulder. He did not know how much more he could take. Frederick was throwing up again, he had not spoken for an hour, the longest anyone could remember his being silent. Holtzen the bull chewed his tobacco, holding his sub-machine gun. Lars knew he was looking forward to the landing and hoped the English would oppose them on the beaches.

Holtzen was the only one who really liked the war and Lars considered him his best soldier.

Teddy, his hair wet from the spray leaned on Lars. "God is he going to get sick again. I have his vomit all over my boots. Damn Fredrick."

Lars did not answer. He brushed his hand against his mouth. The salt stung his lips, but it was a way to distract himself from the misery of the moment.

The heavy Bachman, looked in Lars's direction with eyes that said, "How did you get us into this."

The Tigers after weeks of good food and rest in France were hoping England would surrender after they landed. No one but Holtzen wanted a drawn out battle. Teddy told Lars if it lasted more then a few days he was going to shoot himself in the foot to go to the hospital. He couldn't take the fighting anymore.

Bachman stood up and looked in the direction of the shores of France. At dawn he eagerly climbed aboard the barge. Now he wanted to go back. He peered up. Zeppelins very high waiting for the signal to attack England.

"Lars." Bachman pointed to the sky.

"Zeps waiting for the signal, it can't be long now."

Lars nodded. "Yes, we'll be leaving soon."

Teddy rested his head on Lars shoulder, he was exhausted and the day had not even begun.

#

Count Zastrov looked down. The sea was covered with hundreds of boats, the German Armada. The guns of the big shops would be battering the English shore, just after all clear the first wave would land. The troop ships and the barges being towed across would be the second wave. He would follow the second wave. His radio operator came to his desk in the Pilot house.

"Sir, I picked up a message from the Gotha headed to London. The English *Sopwith Camels* have driven off the escorts and are now shooting down the Gotha. It sounds like some have asked permission to turn back."

Zastrov tried not to smile. The failure of the Gotha was sweet and the English fighters could not damage his Zeppelins.

"Any word on the shelling of the beaches?"

"Yes sir, Headquarters reports no English returned fire and our first wave has just landed. We should wait and delay until the army meets resistance."

This was a false report from Abberville.

The Headquarters report was from an English operator on the island with von Hotzendorff showing him the correct code book to use. The actual report from the Channel said the ships faced heavy English fire. The early landings were struggling at waters edge with heavy casualties.

General Ludendorff. "We can't get off the beaches. None of our troops have gone Inland. Can the English have so many guns or did they guess we were landing here? We must have the Zeppelins, Hold the barges."

The German Albatross fighters escorting the Gotha were no match for Arthur Denny's *Sopwith Camels*. They scattered and fled.

Then the English fighters began attacking the Gotha from the rear and shooting them down. Within twenty minutes half of Baron von Shaeffer's bombers were down and the rest turned for Holland.

Arthur Denny gave an order. "Tell Abberville to send the Zeppelins, we'll meet them on the coast.

Count Zastrov listened to the messages of the retreating Gotha and was delighted. His enemy the Baron, disgraced while coming upon the English coast. He could see the Invasion in trouble. This was his moment of triumph. A thought crossed his mind. He would win the battle, then he would approach the Kaiser and request joint leadership of the war effort with von Below. After all, the Zeppelins were the most powerful force of the Germany army. He ordered the Zeps to proceed to England.

The Zeppelin captain. "Count many English fighters approaching. The groups that attacked the Gotha. "

The Count sneered. "Signal the Zeppelins to climb. If we're

high enough their bullets have no effect and they can't fly above us to drop bombs." He shouted above the engine noise.

"We are not the Gotha, we are the Zeppelins."

Shanto Douglas gunned his *Sopwith* into a steep climb. The Zeppelin Armada was gaining altitude. In the lead Zeppelin was Count Zastrov, distinguished by a large black eagle on the bag.

Douglas cocked his twin machine guns. "Count your about to get the shock of your life. His first burst was under the climbing Zeppelin, but the tracers showed him he was shooting low, and the veteran pilot raised the nose and his second burst incendiary and tracer bullets tore into the Zeppelin.

Another English fighter on Douglas's right sent machine gun bullets arching into the Count's Zeppelin.

The crew of the Zeppelin and Count Zastrov were dazed. Bullets hurting the Zeppelins? Flames spurted out of the bag and smoked filled the command cabin. The incendiary bullet worked in combat as well as the lab, the first encounter by the Zeppelins with an enemy that could hurt them. The Count's Zeppelin began to lose height as waves of English fighters passed them and headed for his other ship.

Zastrov shocked was in a stupor while the captain yelled orders for the crew to put out the fire. He could think of only one thing. The Zeppelins because of there invulnerability did not carry parachutes but he had one in his cabin. He stumbled down the corridor to his cabin. When he opened the door an officer on one knee was trying to pull the chute from under his bed. Zastrov pulled out his pistol and shot the man in the head.

He strapped on the chute, but did not hear the noise behind him. Suddenly everything went black.

When Zastrov awoke he was sitting in the bomb-bay of the Zeppelin, his hands tied, his legs dangling in space as the Zeppelin continued to lose height. The bag still burning.

A voice behind said. "Your hands are tied, but it doesn't matter, I cut a big hole in the chute, it won't work. Interesting you have the only chute on the Zeppelin."

Zastrov groggy shouted. "Who are you? I am your leader."

"Count I am the best friend of the man you threw out of the Zeppelin."

"Don't do this, I offer to make you to be made captain of the Zeppelin." The smell of smoke was strong, even in the bomb-bay.

"Count you would be better off telling the English to stop shooting us down, more than half of our ships are on fire. You, the fearless leader telling us the English could not stop us, but you had your own parachute."

The man continued to mock him. "I will tell you something else, that is not our man at Abberville. Somehow the English are sending us false signals, I am the radio and telegraph operator. You have been fooled, they were waiting for you."

The Count, afraid, but also mad, answered. "It can't be, my brother is defending Abberville."

The Radio Operator laughed. "Your brother is considered a fool like you, the disgrace of the family. You're a bully and a coward and unless you can fly your going to die like you killed my friend."

With that he pushed the Count out of the Zeppelin.

The operator could see Zeppelins burning and falling. The English would never be defeated by the great air ships.

CHAPTER 32

After the Barges were pulled a few hundred yards in the direction of England, the Tigers heard the sound of a motor. Lars peered over the side.

English two engine seaplanes were roaring down at them, he could hear machine gun fire.

He yelled. "Everyone down." They huddled at the bottom of the Barge. The English Flying Boats were firing three machine guns, one in the nose and one on each side. They swept in low dealing death to the defenseless Germans. The German troops tried to defend themselves with rifle fire, but it was totally ineffective against the fast moving sea planes. By mid Channel half the German soldiers were wounded or dead.

As they got closer to the English coast German Warships drove off the sea planes, but the damage was done.

Besides Lars, Holtzen who had fired his machine gun was the only one in the barge not dead or seriously wounded.

He yelled. "Why didn't they tell us about the planes or give us protection? Where are our planes?"

Lars shrugged his shoulders. "They didn't expect those planes. Most of the barges we started with are sunk. I see some on fire. Not many of us left."

With that the tug cast off and the Barge one hundred yards short of the beach was alone. The tug raced away. The sea was very choppy with high waves pounded on the shore. Without the tug to give it forward motion the Barge began to take on water from the many holes in the boat.

Holtzen yelled in terror. "Its sinking, I can't swim."

Lars made a decision. He couldn't save the others, only Holtzen. "Get rid of your belts and ammunition, drop those heavy boots, we go over the side you'll hang on to me."

Lars cursed, where was the easy landing they were promised. Lars began paddling to the shore. Holtzen hanging on to him. Avoiding bodies, he pulled the powerful Holtzen who kicked his legs. Both swallowed sea water, but a giant wave pushed them to the beach. Lars fell to his knees coughing, salt water in his nose, and his mouth but he was alive. Two dead German soldiers were a few yards ahead of them. There were abandoned weapons, an artillery piece and bodies all over the beach. They never saw such death or destruction even at Verdun. He looked to the ocean. Many German ships were sinking or burning. Others still dueling with the English guns. The noise was deafening. Where were the Zeppelins, who were suppose to clear the way

Finally, to his right twenty men spilled out of a Barge one of the few that made it to shore intact.

Lars poked Holtzern. "We can join up with them."

Holtzen nodded, his eyes searched for a weapon.

As suddenly as the barge appeared, an English tank came around a dune and machine gun fire sprayed the just landed Germans.

Lars helplessly watched and then a shell exploded over his head. knocking him flat. He was stunned and a great pain in his shoulder. He saw Holtzman half his head blown off. Lars looked away to see the English tank a Mark IV moving at four miles an hour, moving down the beach driving German soldiers back into the ocean. Lars passed out.

German soldiers started to surrender, to fight the tanks impossible. Not one spot on the beach was held by the invaders. A few landing crafts tried to return to the Transports but so many were on fire, this proved hopeless.

#

Admiral Scheer a very intelligent man quickly recognized that the English artillery was far greater then could be expected at any one section of the coast. He turned to General Ludendorff.

"They were expecting us."

"What?"

"They knew we were landing here, the guns are too well hidden, we can't see any of them, and they must have placed all the guns they had at this spot.

The English judged the height of the Zeppelin verses the balloons, and understood it was Gravesend, the invasion beach.

Ludendorff. "How? "How would they recognize this was the spot."

The Admiral saw another cruiser bracketed with shell fire. The English fire was very accurate.

"Those are Naval guns, they must have taken them off their

ships at Scapa. We are facing the same guns we faced at Jutland."

The General yelled above the din. "I see some smoke from the cliff and the hill but no flashes."

With that an English shell hit the Admirals Flagship. Flames rose in the air igniting the ships magazine. The ship exploded and broke in half. In less then ten seconds the bow and the stern section stuck vertically out of the water.

English gunners cheered when they saw the Flagship break in half. One man yelled.

"That's for bloody Scapa you bloody bastards."

Now the German fire from the sea was non-existent and the English gunners were hard pressed to find targets. The smoke covered the ocean. Never in the history of the world such a great Invasion force, and never such a great defeat.

The captain of one English gun crew directed his men. "All the warships are out of action, I still see some Barges. Fire on the Barges."

#

The English General Kempton surveyed the burning equipment and hundreds of bodies on the beach, almost all Germans. Many bodies were in the surf rolling in and out with the waves. Clearly this was a great German defeat. He could see five downed Zeppelins and many German warships beached and burning. Several others were sinking off shore. He could hear English tanks moving off. They were firing at the enemy who were not firing back.

He started to turn when he heard a faint voice.

"Water!"

It was in English but with an accent. A German Sergeant had pulled himself up on a sand dune. He rested his head on the dune. A huge hole in his shoulder, signaled he was close to dying.

In English the young man called again. "Water!"

Kempton hoisted his pistol and took out his water bottle. He held the water bottle to the young mans lips.

The German struggled for breath, then said, "thank you."

The General could see he was a brave veteran with several medals, but young probably not twenty.

"Where are you from soldier?"

"Stutgart."

The General could not leave him. His breath came in great

gasps, he was almost gone. Kempton held his hand.

"I've visited that area, pretty countryside. What did you do in Stutgart?

"I was a *Tiger*."

The General was puzzled. "What did he mean?" The man was slipping in and out of consciousness. He was not coherent.

The German explained. "I was a soccer player."

"Soccer player?"

"Yes."

"What position?"

"I was a goalie."

"A goalie?"

He heaved trying to catch his breath.

"Did you have a good team?"

"A very good team, we won the Championship."

The General realized this was insane, but he could not leave the young man. The soldier was not in pain, but kept slipping in and out of consciousness.

"I'm the last of the *Tigers*."

We lost Golovin our youngest, never been kissed. He cried he never was kissed."

The General was listening intently.

"Fredrick was our gossip. Never lived up to his responsibilities, but I promised his mother I would take care of him."

The General gave him another sip of water.

"We saved the French soldier in the mud, that was the best day of the war…. the best day of the war."

The General held the young man. He could have been the General's son.

The soldier looked at him. "You're a general?"

"Yes. But I'm not a very good one."

A wave of sadness passed through the General. This fine young man was dying and he could not help him. Suddenly the General hated war. His whole life a waste. The soldiers head dropped to his chest, he heaved and then, quiet.

He spoke to the quiet soldier. "Soldier, I am sorry that people like me couldn't stop this war. When I met the Prince we should have talked peace not a deal. Events carried us along. We had to defend our country on the beach today, but it never should have come to this. This war will go down as one of the great blunders of mankind. The time of Kings and Czars are over, the Kaiser will never survive today's defeat, but so many died to prove we were wrong."

What if the Kaiser continues the war, did England need General Kempton? The General felt very tired.

The General stood up. He felt sad. All these young men dead because old men couldn't resolve their differences.

The General took out his pistol and said, "Thank God we won, but my crime.... my crimes go on. Watch over our country. He put his gun to his head and pulled the trigger."

CHAPTER 33

For the Germans the worst disaster of the Invasion Day occurred late in the afternoon. The German High Command finally realized the English had massed all their guns on the invasion beach at Gravesend. Transports filled with two hundred thousand men were directed to land twenty miles south of the initial invasion point.

Because of the communication blackout with Abberville and the sudden change of plans, no German capital ships would escort the Transports. The English *Sopwith* fighter planes controlled the skies. They spotted the convoy and began attacking. The Transports with no ability to fight back took heavy casualties from the Fighters, Suddenly real danger loomed when Admiral Tom Gordon appeared with three battleships and several destroyers. The battleships with the ability to fire from further than ten miles closed to within a mile of the slow unarmed Transports. It was the worst slaughter of the day. Gordon's skeleton crews worked furiously to sink the Transports before any German battle ships would appear to protect them. Very few Transports escaped back to France, and as it grew dark thousands of German soldiers were in the ocean as the English turned from attackers to rescuers. Soon other boats from England began to rescue prisoners of the defeated Invasion force, from the water.

The Channel was choked with bodies, German soldiers were strewn on the beaches of England, many thousands were dashed ashore in France. Hundreds of Barges littered the ocean drifting helplessly some with wounded but no one to help. German ships drifted some burning, many beached or sunk and oil slicks covered the surface of the ocean for miles. Because no one envisioned the magnitude of the defeat, support for the wounded was overwhelming. Burial provisions were hastily revised, but even the dead on the French beaches could not be cared for.

No senior officer, naval or army, was alive to respond to the calls from Headquarters asking for an Intelligence report. The knowledgeable at the Headquarters to the Kaiser's question as to how bad was the casualty report, wrote a terse "bad."

The church bells in England started to ring at 9:00 p.m. and continued for hours.

As dark descended, German Quarter Masters stood forlornly on the docks of France.

The docks piled high with supplies, ammunition, medical and food sat waited for ships that would never come to take them to England.

A deadly silence dominated the German Headquarters in Paris.

#

After two days the Kaiser boarded his railroad car for a train trip to Berlin. As a steady rain reinforced the deep gloom.

The Kaiser's biggest decision, should he let von Below ride with him back to Berlin. He realized he would need the Prussian landowners support and von Below was their man. He did not react when his disgraced Councilor boarded the train just as the engineer signaled he was ready to go. One hour before they arrived in Berlin the Kaiser called von Below to his State Room.

"von Below these are sad times. Answer me truthfully, all our fates may hang on the decision we make."

"Is my throne in jeopardy?"

von Below opted for the truth. "Yes, your Majesty, the defeat is so great your position may be in danger."

The Kaiser looked out the window. The rain had stopped, but a cold shiver ran down his spine. He did not think of the dead and wounded in the Channel or the families that would never see fathers, sons, or brothers again. He did not think of the proud ships on the beach of England, burned out hulks. He thought only of himself.

The Kaiser turned to von Below.

"What are our losses?"

"Over one million dead, wounded or missing. All the Zeppelins, most of the Gotha are gone, and most of our equipment lost."

The Kaiser put up his hand. "How could it be so bad?"

He did not ask if the one landing strategy was partly to blame.

"Sir, our first wave was surprised and destroyed. We lost almost 100,000 at Le Havre. The English Flying Boats destroyed our Barges. But an unforeseen disaster, the four English battleships from the Mediterranean, they must have used skeleton crews, attacked our second wave of Transports. We suffered almost one hundred percent casualties. We didn't coordinate cover and support. These ships, the Transports were at the mercy of the English. We still don't understand what happened at Abberville.

The Kaiser, his face white, leaned his cheek against the window of the train. He never felt so low.

"We can't have lost the war in one day, can we?"

"No sir, but it has been a long and hard war. The troops thought the Invasion would end it. They want to go home. Word of the failure of the Invasion has swept through the army. Just before we boarded the train some of the troops in Belgium and Holland had started to desert. A whole Company was seen walking to neutral Norway. We must react immediately."

"A look of fear crossed the Kaiser's face.

"What do I do?"

"Your Majesty, we can't let this grow like the French mutiny. I urge you to form special Military Police Units to stop the desertion before they grow and to put Otto Ellenbacher in charge.

"Ellenbacher I dismissed him on the Eastern Front because of his cruel treatment of civilians. The man is a sadist."

"Yes, but we need a hard man, we cannot let the desertion grow."

The Kaiser let his hands fall in his lap. "Do it. If you must, bring Ellenbacher back. Is that all?"

No, again I received word from the Prussian landlords. Word is the Communist in Russian are arming. Our friend thinks they mean to take back the land from the treaties we negotiated."

This news turned the sad Kaiser to the mad Kaiser. "We signed Treaties, they gave their word. You cannot trust the Communist, they are liars. He stood up walked to the door prepared to leave then he turned back."

"What must I do?"

"Sir, to revive the morale of the army send word to the English we want peace. If our people think we want to end the war this may help to support us."

"Well the English will give us peace, only at a price. If we leave France, Belgium, and Holland and, they may ask you to resign."

"Impossible, not only must I hold my office I will not give them France back," the Kaiser said.

"What will they do?" he asked.

"If they can convince the Americans to help they may invade France and take it back by force."

The Kaiser his jaw slack didn't even ask a question so von Below continued.

"America will follow English banking interest and if they do they only man to rally the army will be the Prince. We must ask him to come back."

Of all the cruel news, a call to the Prince was the most bitter.

The Kaiser said, "We continue to attack American ships, with our submarines. Will that cower the Americans?"

von Below a strong advocate of attacking American ships confirmed the policy.

"I know the Americans, they will retreat if we make the pain great enough."

"Will that frighten them?" asked the Kaiser.

"Yes, we may intimidate them and also convince the Mexicans to come into the war on our side."

"Yes we should treat the Americans like the cowards they are."

This talk of aggression made both men feel better.

"Your Majesty one small item. A squad from Stuttgart was lost in the Invasion. They were called the *Tigers*. The Prince called them his Lucky Squad. In the war for three years they never were in a losing battle, they fought at Verdun, and yet only lost two men during those years. Almost unheard of. The story has gone around the army that the lucky charm was lost and it hurts morale. I plan to announce that two of the *Tigers* have been found and are alive."

The Kaiser. "A squad, a squad is important. What has the army come too?"

von Below. "Yes your Majesty is right, what do the lives of eight men matter. But they influence our superstitious troops. I am trying to maintain morale."

Eight men did not matter to von Below or the Kaiser. Eight young men dead before the prime of life who neither started the war or understood it. Who saw life as a good meal or pretty girl or a glass of beer, who shoot men or were shot at by men who did not hate them. The *Tigers* did not understand it was a feud with rules and the rulers did not apply to them. The rules were made up for the Kaiser and the Czar and the feud was over Serbia and similar backwaters. Future generations would wonder why anyone would fight over Serbia and if you asked the current leaders they couldn't answer either.

von Below left the Kaiser's state room. He paused to look out the window at the suburbs of Berlin. He saw a long line of people waiting to buy food as the train slowed, passing through a small station. Food lines not a crisis if the war a victory, but if the war would go on the food problem could be trouble. The Kaiser would continue, that was good. von Below was afraid he would resign. If the Prince came back he would control the war but the nation would be controlled by the Kaiser and von Below. von Below needed to appease the Junker families in Prussia who would not give any land back to the Russians. This had to be a condition for the Prince to come back. Not to give anything back to the Russians. Would he accept the conditions?

Could they keep America out of the war? A strong threat against America would work best, make them afraid of the might of Germany.

von Below paused, but Teddy Roosevelt appeared to be a fierce man. If he were President a strong policy might be wrong. Von Below also worried. Would the French Government in the South continue to cooperate. Could they recruit French soldiers to fight for Germany? No that was doubtful.

von Below felt troubled, perhaps he should join with the Prince who would almost surely want to make concessions and end the war. This would not be welcomed by the Kaiser and especially the Junkers. Von Below's life could be in danger if his friends suspected him of wanting peace.

CHAPTER 34

Taylor and his reporter Matty Stevenson arranged to meet the Prince in Switzerland. The Prince living in exile since the defeat of the German Invasion of England agreed to speak to the press on the condition he would review the text of the interview and have final approval.

The Prince while not part of the German government, wanted to explain to the American people that Germany was not their enemy. He recognized if a powerful potential enemy stayed neutral it would help Germany. The Kaiser also wanted America to stay neutral, but his approach was far different.

Taylor and Stevenson agreed to a strategy they would begin with a very innocuous questions then as the interview proceeded, review more controversial material.

They met on the restaurant roof of a fine hotel in Zurich. The hotel at the head of the Lake, commanded a excellent view of the sparkling waters. The morning before the restaurant opened for lunch, they were served coffee by a white jacketed waiter who quickly left to give them privacy. The breeze from the lake and the surrounding mountains gave the interview an unreal atmosphere, considering the subject matter. The scene so peaceful, and tranquil, but no one would ever describe the war as tranquil. The Prince dressed in a blue blazer with gold buttons, seemed very relaxed and in good spirits. The two reporters were not surprised the Prince, a modern man familiar with the technology of the media and known for using the cutting edge of modern weapons, was far different from the Staff of the Kaiser. The Kaiser's people were used to directing a war and a country in a vacuum. The soldiers and the non-combatants were robots mindlessly following royal directions. The Prince a great disciplinarian but he believed the war was hands on as the years passed he found communicating with his officers important. The army performed better if the mission was clear. No general on either side worked harder at this.

For the first question, a broad overview about the beginning of the war and how it was fought.

Rupprecht very good at grand strategy decided to add details.

"It opened the way we expected, but the speed of build up probably surprised the French and English as much as it did us."

Munitions, multiplied and so did field pieces. Must greater artillery support of the Infantry. A brigade of artillery for each division.

Then the guns were fired from deep earth pits to foil counter fire.

The stronger the artillery the less important the Infantry. It was difficult for Infantry to advance at all. If an attack was ordered, you had to pound the enemies barbed wire and hopefully his guns. "Sir, were you surprised that the French generals continued to attack your machine guns?"

Rupprecht had an ulterior motive for the interview. He hoped to begin a dialogue with the American public and keep America neutral. Thus he decided he would be candid with the American press.

"We were very surprised, they continued to attack our machine guns. Their generals were as surprised by trench warfare as we were. However, they continued with methods that didn't work."

"What was wrong with the generals?"

"They were not at the Front, too many of the colonels were in command at the front lines, but all the French generals were in the rear and this led to immobile fronts, and generals that did not understand the war."

Taylor was writing as fast as he could, candid talk.

"People concentrated on mundane things like where to pick up rations, locate water points, check storage areas, small things, moving supplies up, routines established, and trench systems became more sophisticated. Trenches were the forts with fire bays, and earth bulkheads so that once one shell burst it would be confined to a small area. Support trenches and communication trenches backed up the front line, and machine guns fired diagonally, high ground for observation. We all had listening post. The high command refused to yield ground genius was considered a good concentration of barbed wire. The artillery tried to level the barbed wire."

Stevenson again. "Sir, you broke the deadlock at Verdun."

"Yes, we made it a killing ground, used the Zeppelins and expected the French to bleed to death."

"So you expected the French to fall apart?"

"Yes, I expected it sooner."

"You've heard General Kempton died on the Invasion beach?"

"Yes, before the war started he saw the same thing we did. That was why we made the deal when the French Navy didn't go to Scapa and after Jutland, We felt compelled to attack."

The Prince's body motion said he wanted to change the subject.

Now Taylor asked. "America is neutral, but American ships are being sunk bringing supplies to England. What are your thoughts on this?"

"That is a mistake, we should avoid any confrontation with America. I would not let the submarine attack American ships."

Taylor marveled at the man, he spoke with an authority and honestly, believed that only a strong man could.

What about Austro-Hungary?"

The Prince shook his head. "The sick man of Europe, they ruled a diverse, disparate group of races ridden with corruption and bureaucracy and then to prove their competence they started the war."

Clearly he had little respect for the country that broke off diplomatic relations and mobilized and caused Russia to mobilize.

"With the Emperor dead, is there any chance the Empire can be held together?"

"No." Then he proved he would not sit on the fence.

"Let it break up, to hold it together will start a war that will last forever. The Bosnians, Croats and Serbs don't want to live together"

Taylor asked. "Prince the Communists have taken over in Russia, what do you make of that?"

"I expect trouble from that area. The revolutionary feelings are strong and may spread to the rest of Europe. Communism will be with us for awhile, not good for Germany, England or France. I suggest this threat should force us to bring about peace with the warring powers. The opposite of government of royalty without responsibilities or consent, anarchy in the street will be the legacy of the Communists."

Taylor said, "How would you deal with the Russians?"

"Give them back some of their lands. That Government will avoid war if they can, but the generals in the East may exert the same kind of pressure that started this war."

"Talk about Verdun?"

"Yes, we led with Storm Troopers and flame throwers, picked men."

"Can you give us a one word comment on the French generals at Verdun?"

"Uninspired." The Prince looked out at the mountains. He did not want to comment further about men he might have to fight again.

"They had supply problems, only one road," said the Prince.

Now a happy thought crossed his mind. "My *Tigers* of Stuttgart, only two casualties in a group of that size, you could almost count on two hundred percent dead or wounded. Sixteen, they were my lucky charm.

Now Taylor wanted to get back to hard facts. "When did you actually believe the French would mutiny?"

"Even before the wear, our spies were saying the army would revolt, the senior officers had no feel or concern for the men."

Taylor. "You made a deal with General Kempton?"

"Yes, the General was smart, he realized the French would fail him."

The Prince looked down at his coffee. The next questions would be hard.

"Did you break the contract when you attacked Scapa hurting the English not the French?"

He dodged the question. "We kept our bargain we let the English escape."

"What about the Kaiser?"

The Prince continued to be candid, but wanted to be diplomatic with his former leader.

"He and I agreed to the whole thing, we told no one else."

Taylor had studied the agreement. "My view, the Kaiser would not let his relatives in England believe he broke his word and also he didn't want the King to think he went behind his back."

The Prince nodded. "That is exactly right."

Stevenson said, "A feud with rules?"

The Prince asked. "What do you mean?"

Stevenson. "That the royalty on both sides had a set of rules for the war?"

The Prince said, "Of course you Americans are not entirely neutral. I understand a young Naval officer was quite active in the English defense."

Stevenson said, "He rescued me in France."

The Prince waved his hand. "That was von Below's people."

"I'm sorry I didn't want that."

Taylor. "Were the Germans overconfident?"

The Prince was prepared for the question.

"When you put a Major in charge of your communication and don't have a recall for your landing you are very confident.

I won't comment on the strategy."

Taylor decided to probe. "The German strategy appeared to be a very narrow front, they had no plans to land any other place then the Invasion site. In reviewing your past battles when possible you always attacked in two directions, supporting the attack that made the most progress early. Were you at odds with the Invasion plan?"

The Prince blinked., the newsmen were more aggressive than he expected.

"I'm not going to comment on that, I was retired at the time of the Invasion."

"What other aspects of the war were new?"

The Prince looked out at the lake, a small boat was moving towards them. "Ah, look at that boat, that's where we should be gentlemen, not talking about the war."

He was stalling, but then showed he had analyzed the question.

"In previous wars battles lasted for hours or days. Not like Verdun, months. At Verdun our battle plans were fire power, not man power, made easier since the French withdrew their artillery. Felt the French Army was close to its breaking point and that what happened."

"Did you do anything different with your Infantry?"

The Prince was impressed with the questions, they had done their homework. "We used Storm Troopers and refused to challenge strong points go around."

The Prince probed, it was his turn to ask questions. "I don't understand American ways, do you want to come to Europe?"

Taylor puffed on his cigar. The well traveled Stevenson responded.

"America does not speak with one voice. The only thing we agree on, we're on the move, you could never put Americans in trenches and expect them to stay. So many of us don't care about

Europe including me, after speaking to many of the rulers. Of course, some of us have families and relatives in Europe, and we do care."

The Prince interrupted. "What about the rich and powerful?"

"Mixed, the same as the population in general. I can mention three papers that want to join the English and three that are totally against any involvement in the war. But I can tell you one thing, we seem to agree on we don't like the Germans. You bullied your neighbors, killed non-combatants and now this strategy with Mexico. How afar do you think you can push us?"

The Prince looked sad. "Zimmerman was a big mistake." Then he said, "You Americans have a toughness, when does it come from?"

Taylor chomped on his cigar.

"We are all from underdog status. In every family you can find someone who came from somewhere else. You had to be tough to be a stranger and leave the old country behind. The Pilgrims and the latest arrivals the same, a gut toughness. Now united, we live in a society that loves winners and achievers. You can be small and poor and not speak the language, but don't be lazy, and not try, and if you are born to advantage you better produce. The government works for us, we don't want Kings or Kaisers."

The Prince still trying to understand said . "I spoke to von Hotzendorff who said at Abberville an American cowboy led the English, are you all cowboys?"

"No, in fact a friend of his a woman, discovered the bullet that shot down the Zeppelin.

The Prince. "A woman?"

"Yes she is an architect and a good one. The trend is for talented people like her to contribute."

The Prince. "Do you have women in your military? The Russians have women in the army."

Stevenson looked at Taylor. "No not in the army or in the press, it's a long way off, but I suspect someday. America is not a country that is just going to coast along and let half its citizens not contribute. Women, if they can do it will participate."

The Prince listening to the positive and strong Stevenson suspected a negative outlook for the old world.

"You should like you think America will rule the world?"

"No, not rule the world, lead it, we could be comfortable with our two oceans, separating us and just sitting back, but that is not our nature, we're far from perfect, we will make aggressive mistakes, but......."

Stevenson stopped. It was beginning to sound like a sermon.

The Prince an intelligent man did not criticize the Stevenson enthusiasm

"You sound a lot like your Mr. Teddy Roosevelt."

"Yes, TR is a good symbol for us, loud, brave, patriotic, he loves the country, set aside land for National Parks for future generations. We know we have a good thing and we want to keep it."

The Prince asked the question that was on his mind.

"Will you join the English?"

Taylor. "For sure if the Kaiser tries to bully us."

The Prince. "He will."

Stevenson. "I agree."

The Prince rubbed his nose. He was learning, but it was not what he wanted to hear.

"You don't like the royalty of Europe do you, Mr. Stevenson?" asked the Prince.

"No, I don't. With the exception of a few like yourself most of them couldn't run a small store or hold a job. They break our test of an American leader, not responsible to anyone, not talented and not hard working. They bungled into the worst war in history, fought it to maximize the casualties and....."

Stevenson stopped talking, he realized the Prince had probed his deepest feeling. The man was a good listener, one of the reasons he was such a great leader. Stevenson had one last word. "We have our leaders too, but they earn our respect. Americans will do great things for a true leader, but he must be talented and deserve our support."

CHAPTER 35

After Taylor and Matty Stevenson spoke to the Prince they returned to England to interview his former aide Conrad von Hotzendorff. von Hotzendorff helped the English to confuse the signals to the Germans the day of the Invasion. In England he intended to write a book about the war.

Taylor asked. "You were at the Princes right hand, who do you think started the war?"

"We all deserve blame. Russia, France, Germany, England, the real villain the comic opera empire Austro Hungary."

His contempt was overt about the government in Vienna.

"We had meeting with their generals, in fancy uniforms, but stupid men. The villain Berchtold the foreign minister, who fooled us, we never thought he would attack Serbia. The Kaiser believed we could pull back, so did the Prince. The only sane man in Austria, the Emperor Franz Joseph who recognized his country was weak and not united, was urging caution. Berchtold was determined there would be a war. Gray of England tried to stop it. Gray recognized no stopping the war once it began. Berchtold, told us he only planned to frighten Serbia, we took that as he would never move without us. A Habsburg ultimatum struck Europe with as much force as the murder of the Grand Duke. Berlin was stunned and Russia was compelled to react. They mobilized to deter Austria Hungary from attacking the Serbs.

Vienna's provocation, and Russia's reaction we were on the path to Hell.

Gray acted as peacemaker in 1912. The fool Berchtold would not let it happen again. On the brink of war, General Conrad of Austria hesitated, but Berchtold would not let it happen.

The Prince and Hollweg tried to speak to the Kaiser, but he was cruising on his yacht.

Worried German diplomats spoke to Gray of England. If the English would stall, neutral Germany might invade Belgium and France. But if the war ended quickly the Germans would give back those countries and peace would return to Europe. Of course, Gray would not agree to that idea. Such a concept showed how desperate and out of touch we were. The leaders of Europe were not as evil as we were stupid and arrogant."

"Can there be peace?" asked Stevenson.

"No and I'll explain, but let me continue, I want it on the record how I feel about the beginning of the war. If only Berchtold distinguished between members of the Serbia Nationalism Party and the actual country of Serbia itself. Of course, the man was adamant for a war. You saw how his forces performed. What a brilliant strategist his judgment worthless. The Austrians moved against Serbia, Russia armed to protect Serbia. We were drawn into the conflict to side with Austria. Then France and England came in. Austria attacked the Russian forces, but a second army to invaded Serbia, and the little country that Austria believed they could defeat easily beat them. Fancy uniforms weren't enough. Now the main battle - Austria on the northern frontier with Russia. Here the unreality of parts of the army became clear. The Austrian Army spoke nine different languages. Conrad the Austrian general attempted to outflank the Russians with a weakened force. That didn't work. It was not the soldiers fault, they fought bravely. That was a theme of the war the leadership got better than they deserved."

"You were in Italy for the Caporetto Campaign?"

"Yes amazing, again, fighting in the mountains. I will never forget artillery being lowered down a sheer rock face and ammunition and guns taking all day to climb one position. We had an outstanding officer, Erwin Rommel, always in front, ignoring the high peaks, but moving through roads and valleys to sever the Italian communications. The Prince always said when you have a great leader give him his head, so I let Rommel proceed, with small numbers he defeated and captured units many times his own size, the man will be famous some day.

Stevenson. "What about the future?"

"An uneasy quiet but the Communist control Russia. They are going to want to take back the lands Germany controls today."

Conrad. "We will have a war in the East. The French want their country back and England will not forgive the invasion attempt. An American must see the German attempt to arm Mexico and the sinking of their ships as a provocation. The great war, World War I is not over.

Of course the whole thing is absurd. Nations at the height of success and wealth choose to fight this war to risk all? Worse than starting the war the inability to stop it, when it was obvious that the Treaties and the pain and the death were outdated. A false and naïve belief in the leaders supported by the clergy, the press and business, a whole generation gone insane."

Taylor looked at Stevenson. A recurring theme, the insanity of, what happened, but the unwillingness to stop it.

Taylor asked. "We spoke to the Prince, he will come back if the Kaiser asks."

von Hotzendorff shook his head. 'The man is a patriot, he will always put his country first, I won't, the war will go on, the energy and the drive, the Junker in the East supporting the Kaiser........"

He shrugged his shoulder. "How long the people will support the government?" England is not strong enough to invade without America. Germany is divided. Russian a new Communist government."

Stevenson asked one last question.

"With the Monarchies in place it was called a feud with rules, now it's a new war. The idea a ruler could sign a letter and an army could escape is over, isn't it?"

von Hotzendorff. "Yes, the Ruler starting the wars like it was a private grudge on his part and he was not held to any responsibility by his subjects. But the new dynamic, the interest of millions of people fighting over land, oil, food, there will not be rules, the new war could be worse than the one we just finished."

Taylor gasped. "Worse?"

#

Mannaning discovered a new driver that added length to his already powerful golf tee shots. He invited Gibbon and Arthur Denny to his Golf Club for a friendly game. Convinced the extra length would negate Gibbon's great iron play, he was horrified when a replay of the first two holes produced the same results as the first game.

Gibbon hit solid irons to within three feet of the pin, sank putts and beat him on the holes. By the sixth hole the flustered Mannaning was losing to the steady unspectacular Denny as well as Gibbon. Clearly Mannaning was rattled. His play erratic, and on the eleventh hole a par three, he put his iron shot into the pond. Frustrated he picked up his clubs, threw them into the pond, and stalked off to the Clubhouse.

Gibbon leaned on his iron. "I guess its over."

Denny responded "We're close to the parking lot, lets get to my car, and drive to my house for a spot of lunch."

The two players and Westy walked to the parking field. Arthur got in the drivers side and started to giggle. Then Gibbon couldn't hold back, laughing uncontrollably. Westy let out a wide guffaw.

Gibbon held up his hand. "Does this mean we won't be asked back?"

Denny pounded his fist on the steering wheel, now laughing so hard his side hurt.

Westy, leaned forward. "At least I didn't threaten to shoot anyone.

With that, the great war leaders lost all control. The invasion of England 1917 was over, all the evil people defeated.

Invasion France 1918
Projected 2004

Author Biography

Arthur Rhodes, a former bond syndication manager and thirty year senior executive in Wall Street, continues his life-long interest in military history with a series of books about World War II and the Cold War. Not content to mirror history, he tries to keep alive the warriors of the greatest generation. We have fictional heroes with real battlefields, Guadalcanal, Midway, Lexington and modern jets with World War II weapons. It is a blend of nostalgia and what-if history.

Currently, Arthur Rhodes is working on a book about the attack of the Spanish Armada on England.

Books by Arthur Rhodes

On the INTERNET at
http://3mpub.com/rhodes/

𝕿𝖍𝖊 𝕷𝖆𝖘𝖙 𝕽𝖊𝖎𝖈𝖍

America 1960: After nearly ten years under the control of the Nazi regime, the United States is suffering through a period of severe economic depression and spiritual despair. However, as the oppressed citizens plod through their grim lives, there is a whisper of hope. The underground movement — a dauntless network of American patriots working tirelessly against the German forces that occupy the country — is preparing to make another major strike against the hated Blackshirts. The weapons are different at the second Battle of Lexington, but the courage is the same as two hundred years ago.

The Last Reich is a riveting thriller that imagines a stark dystopia created by Hitler's success inn his campaign to dominate the world. In this ingeniously conceived post-World War II fantasy, the balance of power is about to shift again. While insurgence escalates to open warfare in the United States, Germany is also contending with internal conflicts and civil war. As a ravening Reich Chancellor desperately grasps to maintain Germany's authority, the American Army, the legacy of the land of the free, strikes with unprecedented speed and power in the climactic battle.

The Return of the Rising Sun

Endless War

The year is 1964. The Second Battle of Guadalcanal rages in the South Pacific as the United States makes a bold attempt to free ten thousand Allied prisoners who have been languishing in Japanese prisoner-of-war camps since the disastrous defeat of 1950. Surely a modern navy, equipped with giant aircraft carriers and flying the latest jets, will prove more than a match for the undefeated Japanese Imperial Fleet.

It is a time of change. Germany has finally been defeated after decades of war. The Russians are expanding into Eastern Europe while the Japanese Secret Police wage a relentless unconventional war against America from the Pacific to Central America. Drug dealers are among their most lethal weapons ...

Return of the Rising Sun is the second book in Arthur Rhodes' Alternative History of the Second World War. Come read how things might have gone differently.

Invasion England 1917

A timeless mystery. The home fleet destroyed at Scapa Flow, Scotland.

The Germans poised to invade England, and evidence points to one of the five most important men in England as a traitor.

The King asks an American naval officer, Gibbon Stillwell, to find the traitor. There is conflict on the German side. Prince Rupprecht who defeats the French is the architect of the Scapa victory. The Kaiser's jealous aides plot to eliminate Rupprecht. The Battles rage from the Atlantic to the trenches of France. Will the Kaiser win World War I?

The Swiss Pikemen

The Swiss Pikemen is the alternate history of the actual invasion of Switzerland by the Austrians in the year 1386. Will the Swiss prove they are the greatest soldiers in Europe and defeat the much larger army of Austrian Knights? The men of Switzerland defending their homes have a military moral weapon......Freedom.

The Red Menace

Against the backdrop of the Korean War, the FBI pursues the Nazi underground in America. There is a mighty fight in the Politburo for control of Russia. The FBI closes in on Nazi and Russian fugitives.

The third book in Arthur Rhodes's alternate history of World War II continues where its action-packed predecessors left off.

The Derby Day Murder Mystery

The murder of the most famous child in America triggers an official response. The President sends the FBI's most famous team to investigate. Unique in style, they are as ruthless as the criminals they pursue.

THE
SWISS PIKEMEN

By

ARTHUR RHODES

AUSTRIA-HUNGARY 1386

Third Millennium Publishing
A Cooperative of Writers and Resources
On the INTERNET at 3mpub.com
http://3mpub.com

ISBN 1-929381-97-2
100 pages

Production Manager – Lennie Adelman

Third Millennium Publishing
1931 East Libra Drive
Tempe, AZ 85283
mccollum@3mpub.com

THE BATTLE OF SEMPACH
1386

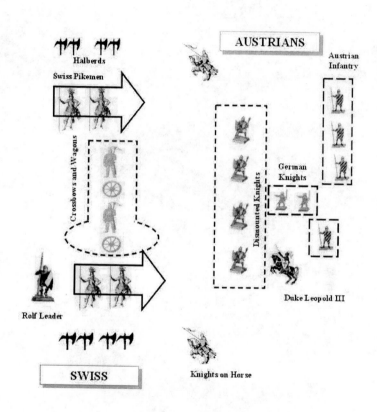

Halberds

Swiss Pikemen

Crossbows and Wagons

AUSTRIANS

Austrian Infantry

German Knights

Dismounted Knights

Duke Leopold III

Rolf Leader

SWISS

Knights on Horse

iii

Table of Contents

CHAPTER 1

In the summer of 1386 Duke Leopold III of Austria organized the largest military expedition of his career. The Invasion of Switzerland. The Duke, not an educated man was the prototype Prince of his time. Ruthless, narrow minded, greedy and driven to rule over people he considered inferior. The Invasion of Switzerland was not only to reclaim the lands his Grandfather ruled but to avenge the Dukes startling defeat ten years before by the Swiss.

Before he could march on the Swiss, he had to acquire the tools to make his conquest effective, and the most important tool was money. He assumed the money will be given by the Italian City-States. The details of the loan bored him, but suddenly a question about the loan caught his attention. The Italian Bankers were raising problems and the Duke was concerned. The Duke disliked the Italian Bankers and the arguing over the terms of the loan.

The interest rates were not in dispute, it was the collateral. How much of his estates the Italian City-States would require to secure the loan?

Ten years ago, when he borrowed money from Venice and Milan his counselors negotiated and he only appeared at the final signing. Today the son of the Doge of Venice, Gillani insisted on a head-to-head meeting with the Duke before the closing. The Duke a warrior, did not like Bankers or respect them. The control of his lands was by his sword and their power financed by commerce, and trading, occupations he considered inferior.

Florence, Venice, Naples and San Marino the Syndicate, with several smaller cities joining to lend him twice the size of the previous loan. Money! The life blood of this war.

This time he intended to lead an army twice the size of his previous invasion of the Swiss.

For days knights were arriving at the castle and in due course they expected to be paid. Never expecting a "No", he had no other source of money. Thus when Gillani requested a meeting the Duke at first hesitated, then agreed to meet Gillani. Gillani was given the purpose of the loan even the line of march to the Swiss Cantons. He was expected to support the Duke.

The historic tribute collected for almost two hundred years by the Habsburgs, was cut off as the Swiss Army proved it could defend and defeat the Austrian Armies. The Duke denied the money, resented his loss of funds but also was offended by the Swiss who denied his Royal right to rule them. The Cantons lived by commerce and actually elected officials and Mayors who served at the forbearance of the people. A very dangerous and radical concept in the fourteenth century. If the Canton lived by commerce, the Swiss farmers were great soldiers.

Gillani half rose from his chair and nodded more than bowed as the Duke entered the room. Leopold III, Duke of Austria was over six feet in height. Impressive in stature unless measured against the Swiss giants, he intended to fight. Gillani, representing the wealth of Italy, was not impressed by the tall and handsome Duke, and especially not impressed with his castle, not more than a tower with an outer wall. Gillani's fellow Banker and aristocrats would scoff at the Duke's home, but not at the steady parade of knights Gillani met on the road to the Dukes castle. The numbers were impressive and the diversity of Nobles with retainers even more impressive, clearly, skilled warriors distinguished by banners, pennants and elaborate canvas surcoats. The crests – eagles, lions, bulls, hawks, and many others covered coats of mail or stiff leather. Gillani recognized professional killers, men whose whole life was dedicated to destroying opponents. Best they were, for the Swiss were not the usual peasant opponents, afraid, weak and dominated by Nobles. For the last fifty years the Swiss had gained ascendancy over mounted knights.

Western Europe dominated by the aristocrats on a horse for centuries, now were seeing a powerful Infantry. The Swiss and the English long-bow-men who did not concede the field of honor, and especially the Swiss with long pikes and eight-foot halberds. Gillani heard rumors the Duke planned new strategy to face the Swiss. He would not besiege the Swiss cities and that some knights would fight on foot. However, the Duke's retainers told him the initial campaign would begin with a scorched earth burning of some small towns on route to intimidate the larger towns who supported the Swiss Army. The Swiss always fought against larger numerical opponents, but no one had seen an Army as large as the Dukes, five thousand knights, and ten thousand Infantry.

The Duke felt uncomfortable. "Gillani, I don't understand why you wanted this meeting. The terms of the collateral were agreed to this morning. The interest rates were set four days ago. Why are we not signing the document?"

Gilliani cleared his throat. "Duke, we are satisfied that the financial terms are correct. What I want is more background to the venture."

The Duke, his temperature rising reacted. "You question my right to conquer the Swiss? Those are my lands, my family taxed the peasant when most of them walked without shoes, they are scum. The emblem of the Lion of Habsburg will fly over their towns again."

Thinking this settled the issue the Duke sat back in his chair, still puzzled at the question. Did this Banker think they would just avoid the Swiss, and keep the money? A more dark thought occurred to him. Did Gillani think they were afraid of the Swiss?"

"No, of course we recognize the right of Royalty to do what they will with their historic subjects, but this is a very large loan. Twice what we gave you ten years ago, and we just want to ask questions."

Duke. "Questions? What questions? I take an Army of great knights to war."

He did not mention the Infantry.

"Such a venture is not cheap. We paid you back for the last war."

Gillani would not be cowered by the Duke. His father trusted him to make the final decision and protect their money.

"Duke the loan was for five years, it took seven years before you paid it back."

The Duke rose from his chair, his hand moved to his sword side, but he relaxed and held his temper. "You, are on difficult ground. Do you question the honor of the House of Habsburg?"

Gillani did not flinch. "Sir of course not, or we would not be here. Four large cities put up the majority of this loan, I will have to explain to each of them why this is a good investment. I believe this is the time I must be sure I am making a wise decision."

Gillani understood the Duke did not care about the logistics or endeavors that raised the money. The prosperity of the cities Gillani represented depended on trade, art and lending money, a cornerstone of the despots who ruled them. Florence with Cosimo De Medici and Milan ruled by the Viscounts Family while Venice an Oligarchy of leading families including Gillani. They traded with the Moslems, all the time preparing to go to war with them. The Turks were very aggressive and Gillani's father told him, protect our money, but someday we may hire the Duke to protect us against the Turks. It was a world of shifting alliances and the Swiss form of Government dangerous. Men electing their Leaders against Gods law, Gillani believed in the divine right of the Nobility.

Uprisings and Civil war by the lower class was always a threat even in the City-States. In Florence a very dangerous riot a few years ago. Since then both Venice and Florence employed secret police to control their cities. The Duke was an absolute dictator, a tyrant, his was the only voice. The Italian City-State Oligarchy, governed by a few. Only in Switzerland did the common man decide the direction of his government.

The Duke was so upset he had forgotten Gillani's name for the moment.

"Sir Banker, the Swiss, with their rustic approach to war, are formidable fighters. They successfully use the terrain. Their sub-human culture and lack of Military ethics are dangerous. I will take away that unity that makes them strong. I will defeat the sub-humans." His voice rose with the word sub-human. The Duke hated the Swiss.

Gallani felt a need to assure the Duke he was not an enemy. Knowing the Duke was not a scholar he decided to give the Duke a history lesson and confirm his loyalty to the feudal system.

"Duke we have researched your enemy. Originally three small Cantons formed a defense system and revolted against your Grandfather, then joined by Lucerne, Zurich and Berne now making up a confederation."

"They combine against outsiders, but they quarrel among themselves. Perhaps you could divide them?" He asked.

The Duke. "We have a spy among the Swiss, your money is not moving into a blind trap." The Duke was proud of his subversion of the Swiss

"Duke. That comforts me. I bear a great burden. This is my

decision and mine alone."

When Gillani made it clear this was his decision and his alone the Duke sat down. There was no one else. Already a significant number of the Army was gathering, he must get this loan. Better to answer the question and get it over with.

"Ask your question, but my patience has limits."

Gillani decided to get right to the point.

"For the past fifty years the Swiss have demonstrated they are the greatest Infantry in Europe. Frequently out numbered, their pikes and halberds destroy the enemy. I mean no disrespect, but your Army ten years ago, was defeated by elected Leaders and men with the halberd which has a greater reach than knights with a sword on horseback. My own cousin was pulled from his horse by the hook from a halberd and pinned to the ground by the sharp point. He survived and returned by the grace of god. Clearly we are sympathetic with you. We don't want common people like the Swiss to challenge the right of royalty to rule them, but I must ask if we give you this money, can you defeat them?"

The Duke was stunned he would be asked this question. His response was the same one he was telling the knights he was recruiting.

"The divine right of Kings and Royalty must not be challenged by the common man. I ride to defend our civilization. This is a Holy War."

Gillani. "Duke, I believe you ride with God, God does not want the anarchy of the common people, but the Swiss appear invincible. Do you have anything new that will stop them?"

The Duke leaned forward. "I have new tactics. If you ride with me you will see that. Beyond that, you have financed the House of Habsburg many times, you know I, Duke Leopold am one of the great knights of Christendom. You see the knights that are joining me, we have never flinched in our duty. This is a stronger Army than last time and I pledge my word we will erase the peasants that will oppose me. The forest of the Cantons will be filled with my enemies hanging from trees. Men, women, children, they will bend to my will or die."

Gillani recognized the statement, ride with me was a challenge. "Give me the money and have the courage to join my crusade."

Gillani, would not jump at the challenge — his cousin who survived the last time would join the Duke again.

"Duke my cousin Count Magglie will join you again. I am going to request he ride at your right hand. Magglie is a valiant knight and believes in your cause. His own serfs bend to his harsh will. No estate in Italy demands more work from the peasants and Magglie wants the Swiss crushed."

The Duke thought. Italian Bankers, money is all they care about, but knowing they faced the Moslems from Africa and they needed profits to build a defense against the Infidel, he relaxed.

"I remember Count Magglie, he was unhorsed on our first charge. When the battle moved miles away he survived and walked to our camp the next night. He returned with us with grave wounds but a true knight."

Again unwittingly the Duke praised knights but not Bankers. Gillani ignored the remarks.

"Duke, I am going to approve the loan but I'd sleep better if you pledge to me your supreme effort and let Magglie and his ten knights ride at your side."

The Duke stood up. "I, Duke Leopold, Leader of the House of Habsburg pledge I will not return until the Swiss kneel before me. Your representative Magglie will ride with me and will share in our great effort. He will protect your money and defeat the sub-humans we face."

After the meeting the Duke and Gillani rode to the growing encampment. The Banker was impressed. It was the largest gathering of men-at-arms in this part of Europe since the Romans. Gillani noticed the Duke was more familiar with the agents who negotiated the hiring than the knights themselves.

That night to prove how serious he was, the Duke also served notice. Under pain of death no one would loot or carry off booty, tents, animals or money until after the Swiss were defeated.

The Duke hung two men from his ramparts the next night saying they were spies, but observers suspected it was to serve notice his threats were not idle. The men tried to steal from fellow men at arms.

The day after the meeting with the Banker the Duke walked to his study. It had the best view of the countryside. The sunlight coming through the window was warm on the back of his chair. He remembered the first time he was in the room, he was twelve, his Grandfather sent his body-guard Mengler to bring the boy to speak to him.

The Grandfather terrified the Duke as he did everyone else in the castle. The old man wasting away with a disease the doctors couldn't cure had a ugly purple pimple on his nose and a hacking cough.

"I heard you jumped the canyon with your horse, was the bridge too far away?"

He coughed and the boy could barely speak mumbling a weak "Yes."

"Speak up! Speak up! You can't give orders in that tone."

"Yes, I jumped the canyon." It was a little louder, for he expected to be punished.

The old man laughed, drool on his chin. "I jumped that canyon when I was your age and I heard your brothers were afraid too. Yes or no?"

"Yes."

The old man continued. "Remember when you fought your older brother in the dining room at our supper and you hit him with the foot stool and your father wanted to beat you and I wouldn't let him?"

Now the young boy was sure he was going to be punished.

Again a weak, "Yes."

Suddenly the old man pointed at him. "Where is Switzerland?"

He spoke up louder trying to please the old man. "Switzerland is north of here."

The old man sat down in the same chair as the Duke was sitting in today. He pulled the chair close to the boy.

"And who do they – the Swiss belong to?"

"To you Grandfather."

"Yes. I took those lands when I was a young man. Made the peasants pay me taxes and now your father is losing them because he doesn't have… " The old man put his hand on his groin, "…the balls."

The young boy puzzled, shivered as the old man held his arm.

"Your father and your brothers are going to kill you when I die. They think your too much like me and they fear you."

The boy was silent.

"I from the grave can save you, but before I do I want a promise. I want you to take back Switzerland. I want my lands back, promise me that and with the help of this man." He pointed at Mengler.

"I will make you Leopold the Third, owner of all the lands of our family."

The boy looked at the brutal and dangerous Mengler and took the oath.

For the next year the boy was brought to his Grandfather's study where he was tutored. Just before his Grandfather died his older brother had an accident and was killed. Two months later Mengler killed the Dukes father. Now the Duke's oldest son proclaimed himself Leopold the Third of Austria. When one of his Nobles revolted the Duke at fourteen marched and regained the property in the same fashion his Grandfather would have.

As the Duke looked out of the castle window he did not think of his Grandfather. No, his thoughts were focused on the hated Swiss. He did not think of his killing of Mengler before he marched ten years ago, that was history. Only the war to return his lands occupied him now.

He was sure his Infantry could not stand up to the Swiss. He had more knights this time. The key was to put his Army in a position to go to war with the Cantons where the enemy would not dominate the battlefield with a solid wall of pikes. To beat the sub-humans you had to destroy their wall of pikes and turn the battle into a series of hand-to-hand combats. The knights were brave enough but could he put them in an advantageous situation? The Italian Banker was impressed with his Army. If we beat the Swiss he might hire me to beat their enemy the Moslems when that war starts. The Duke smiled. He would like to be asked to help the City-States.

CHAPTER 2

The Duke hired a group of German knights with an outstanding reputation. They agreed to join him only on the condition he speak to a professor from Berlin whose reputation was that, he was a preeminent authority on the military of Europe.

The knights hearing of the defeat ten years ago wanted someone familiar with the Swiss to brief the Duke. The Duke amused, but wanting the two hundred and fifty knights, agreed.

The Professor arrived at the Dukes castle with a thick dossier and proceeded to compare the Swiss with the Romans to which the Duke reacted.

"What are you talking about, the Romans used short swords, these people have long pikes."

The Professor. "Yes, your right. The weapons are different but it is the speed of the attack and the work ethic that are both the same. Busy bees, working bees, the opponent must be prepared for an enemy who never stops."

Seeing the Duke perplexed he said. "The weapons….. it is like the Macedonians of Alexander the Great, but that was with ten foot pikes, not eighteen like the Swiss."

The Duke still unsure said. "Were the Romans ever beaten?"

"Yes, Hannibal lured a Roman Army into a soft center and attacked from the wings. Difficult to do with the Swiss because they move so fast not only on the battlefield, but they march thirty miles a day."

The Duke. "What can you tell me about the Leader Rolf?"

"As a young man he studied to be a Priest, very well educated, can read and write."

The Duke who could do neither was not impressed.

"He was elected General and developed the Swiss tactics with a coordinated defense. Pikes, cross-bows and halberds. The rear guard will fight off the flank attack."

The Duke remembered the shock of seeing knights pulled out of the saddle. The Swiss were not afraid of men on horseback.

"I hate them. Do they hate us?"

"No, the Swiss are not emotional, they are patriotic, but they treat all enemies the same. They are very business like. Why I think they are like the Romans. They wear a helmet and a breastplate, they follow a red banner with a white cross. They have a saying. "You may cross our border, but you will never go home."

The Duke grew bored with the meeting. He outlined the size of his Army and that he had new tactics. Then he left the room.

The Professor realized he never asked for advise or a suggestion on how to beat the Swiss.

Later the Professor spoke to the leader of the German knights.

"He is a great knight," said the Professor.

"I didn't ask you that, can he beat them?"

The German knight knew the Professor would not lie.

"I don't know. He has impressive knights, but his Infantry won't stand up to the Swiss. I don't know."

The German knight said, "I want to talk, but not here, lets ride."

They rode two hundred yards outside the Dukes castle. Horse drawn carts moved to let them pass. The huts of the peasants with doors open displayed animals walking in and out and children playing besides heaps of manure. A peaceful scene compared to the field where knights and soldiers were gathering for the coming war.

Arriving at a quiet stream, they dismounted. The knight said, "I have returned from the Holy Land. We held out in a castle against the Moslems for six months. Their catapults killed half my men. I led several night-time raids outside the castle and I suffered three wounds in an attempt to destroy the catapults, but they were protected by strong shelters. Once I was burned badly by the oil we used to attack the damn weapons."

He opened up his sleeve to show serious burn marks on his arm. The Professor noted he never mentioned the name of the castle or what part of the Holy Land. To mercenaries all places were the same.

"My Prince was furious I had lost half the men, my valor expected, my failure noted. If the Duke wins the war but we suffer great casualties, I cannot return home. I asked the Duke to talk to you, I need to have some feel for this campaign, he keeps saying he has new ideas. The Swiss beat him badly last time and he barely escaped with his life. My rewards are not that good, if he wins, I won't collect the money to cover the risk if he loses."

The Professor realized this was what he was paid for.

"The Duke uses his weakest soldiers to soften up the enemy, he holds his best for the last. He will hold you for the end. At that time make a judgment, if your winning fight hard, if losing......." His voice trailing off.

The German knight looked away. If this was anybody but the Swiss he would ignore the advice, but this was the Swiss.

To the German knights war was a business. They were well paid because they were good. His Prince did not want to lose his assets. The German knight decided to be cautious.

CHAPTER 3

Normally tournaments were organized as great spectacular with elevated seating, but this tournament was organized to spot talent.

At every tournament one knight seemed to dominate. The last tournament, before the war with the Swiss, was held twenty miles from the Dukes castle, at a grassy meadow that was Mache Rouchmelle. Marche a twenty-one year old Norman was the second son of the Count of Rouchmelle. He was poor, his surcoat frayed and his armor in bad condition.

He was poor because when his older brother inherited the estate, he was excluded and forced to leave under pain of death. At seventeen he could have killed his brother but not the two knights who always accompanied him. Now his performance at the tournament vouch safe he could win against all three at the same time.

At five feet six inches he was of average height. A veteran knight watching the two early combats said he had the fastest hands he had ever seen. Fast hands and quick feet were displayed before noon.

The first combat was with a lance. A mounted combat against the respected English knight, Holland, ended when Mache dipped his lance and drove it under Holland's chin killing him instantly.

One hour later he fought on foot, with a kite shield favored by the Normans, covering between the shoulder and the knee. Both knights used the flail, combined of a wooden shaft with a multiple chain ending in spiked balls. His fast hands struck his opponent twice with a single ball before his quick footwork positioned him to the side where twice he struck the man without ever receiving a blow to his person. The audience was dumbstruck when his first killing blow toppled the man, and his second caught the man on the back of the neck just before he hit the ground. No one could remember two such fast strikes and ordinarily that would have ended any challenges to him.

However, a member of the Dukes court was drinking and took great pride in his long-sword, — long bladed and double edged.

Seeing he was bigger De Cornaut believed he had the edge because the weapon was so heavy and this was Rouchmelle's third combat of the day. It was standard procedure for a more experienced knight to challenge someone who had already fought, and gain an advantage by being fresh. Because he was drinking De Cornaut didn't realize Rouchmelle had dispatched his two opponents quickly.

Their battle lasted three minutes, distinguished by Rouchmelle's quick foot work and a killing blow after parrying De Cornaut's thrust.

When he took off his helmet, Rouchmelle screamed a challenge to all the Dukes retainers sitting in front of a large black tent. The younger brother of De Cornaut started to rise but was stopped by his friend.

"Look he's frothing at the mouth. Don't challenge him, it is sure death."

Not only great skills were on display, but among the assembly of killers, a man who would froth at the mouth after killing another was considered a psychopath and to be avoided. Since most of the knights displayed some maniac characteristics it was three kills in one day that carried greater weight.

One of the Dukes agents examined Mache's horse and his equipment. He beckoned a servant to him. "Give him wine, but don't speak to him, he may kill anyone in his presence. After he has eaten and had wine and if he speaks to you offer to pay him two times the wages."

The servant recognized this was a very dangerous man. "What if he says no?"

"Tell him, much fighting and no quarter and tell him he rides with Schaeffer, a man who has killed eighty opponents. That will appeal to him." The servant realized he should be afraid said, "How can I tell when it is really safe?"

"He will be weak and tired. The equipment is normal. He is not bewitched, but….." The agent made a circling sign next to his head indicating Mache was crazy.

The servant appeared at Mache's side and handed him a glass of wine. Rouchmelle drank the wine and followed the stranger when no one else would fight him that day.

The servants tent was large and well outfitted. Rouchmelle

cursing because he wanted to continue instead, accepted a plate with meat and bread. The servant helped him with the armor, but did not speak recognizing this was a man who could strike him and kill again today. Such a man in this mental state was so dangerous that the servant kept pouring wine and retreating to a safe distance.

Mache had not eaten in two days and between the wine and meat began to calm down.

"Whose tent is this?" he asked.

The servant on one knee responded. "My Master is Peter Schaeffer, Leader of Duke Leopold's guard. He welcomes you as champion of the day."

Mache. "I am going to Leopold's castle. I understand he marches in three days and I intend to join him."

Mache now under total control suddenly felt very tired.

He asked, "Who does the Duke war against?"

"The Swiss," said the servant.

"Who are the Swiss." Mache asked.

The servant recognized a man poorly educated and probably oblivious to anything but killing and fighting.

"The Swiss are a mountain people who refuse to pay taxes to the Duke."

Rouchmelle asked the logical question of a man who lived for fighting.

"What kind of weapon does your Master use?"

"My Master uses the ball and chain." The ball and chain was a very heavy metal ball attached to a wooden handle by a three foot chain.

"Is your Master adept at using the ball under a mans shield?"

Mache always used the ball and chain under the shield.

"No, my master is very tall, he tends to come over the top of a mans shield, occasionally by the side. The servant recognized he was talking to a serial killer and quickly offered Mache a position in Schaeffer's elite, at double the pay of a regular knight. More fighting against a brave opponent. Mache instantly accepted.

Peter Schaeffer hearing of Mache's skills matched him with a skilled opponent in a mock match with wooden swords. Mache displayed his extraordinary talent and matching mental makeup. Schaeffer quickly adopted him as a companion. Schaeffer at thirty-four unlike Mache was going on the campaign for money and decided that Rouchmelle riding at his right side would enhance his being alive at the end of the campaign. Schaeffer had no illusion about the difficulty of the war against the Swiss.

He carried a large scar from his chin to his hairline. Ten years ago a Swiss Pikeman knocked his helmet off. The second pikeman slashed his face. Half unconscious and his face covered with blood, his horse despite two wounds, carried him to safety.

That was ten years ago, and hearing that the Duke had new tactics and would pay him a special bonus, he joined the venture.

Rouchmelle was impressed when he learned Schaeffer killed eighty men and was an expert on the Dukes weapon of mass destruction. Mache traveling from tournament to tournament had only one small campaign experience and he marveled at the Duke's killing machines.

Riding behind a large siege engine, he asked Schaeffer, "What was it?"

"That's a trebuchet. It is a counter weight machine and has the large framework. The beam has a container that holds rocks, and stones, and a sling at the end of the beam, the projectile is held by a catch. The weighted end falls and fires the projectile, as heavy as forty pounds, two hundred to three hundred yards away. It is very effective."

Mache. "I thought we would avoid towns and kill the Swiss Army."

"We will but the Duke intends to make an example of some towns that refused to pay taxes during the last ten years."

The first city the Dukes Army encountered was Carssene. The town pleaded to a surrender but the Dukes answer was to hang the envoy.

The Duke had a two pronged motive for attacking Carssene. One revenge, two Gillani from Venice asked him to embarrass the Florentine contingent sponsored by the Medici family.

The city of Florence sent five hundred men led by a Captain Messine. For a week the Duke tried to convince Messine to marry his older sister. Today he addressed Captain Messine.

"We attack Carssene, they only have five hundred soldiers so the Florentine has the honor of leading the attack."

Messine. "Do you plan to use siege engines or mine that

gate?"

The Duke. "No. We don't have time, I will give you scaling ladders, and I expect you to lead in the war. I will lead when we meet the Swiss, you follow the example. I want you first on that rampart."

Messine realized it was sure death to be first on the ramparts. He quickly acquiesced to the Dukes plan to marry his sister. The Duke nodded his approval and the Florentines were sent forward without Captain Messine. The attack failed with fifty percent casualties belonging to the attackers.

The Duke rode up to Peter Schaeffer. "I intend to use the trebuchets to knock down that gate. I'll send three hundred men in and you follow with your elite. The orders are to kill everyone in the city. I want to be on the march in six hours, so be quick, this piss-ass city won't pay anyone taxes after today."

Schaeffer recognized the Duke was unique as a war leader. Most military leaders send in their best troops first, this Duke frequently sent in his weakest, let them tire the defenders and follow up with his strongest.

The Black flag of Habsburg flew over the city three hours later.

Relaxing in their tent Schaeffer recognized Mache was bored. "Today was easy, killing several people who tried to surrender."

"Today was not typical of a siege, I was with the famous John Hawkwood in Spain," said Schaeffer.

"We built a great siege tower and Hawkwood was very smart, he disguised it so that we were going to undermine the wall. The extra supports on the bottom were really to build strong ladders to the top four stories. We would place archers at the top then assault by placing ladders onto the ramparts.

Pushing the tower to the ramparts was dangerous, the Spaniards used missiles and arrows to kill our men. Our cross-bow men drove the archers off the wall but they used flaming pitch and despite the wet animal skins the tower caught fire and burned.

We cut down all the local orchards for wood, so we had to get wood from a further distance. We built a ramp for the front gate and pushed that on wheels but they dropped down ropes with hooks, caught our ramp and pulled it over.

Finally we used Greek fires in one spot, and drove all the defenders from the wall, then we used scaling ladders that got us to the top and we took the city."

"What about the Swiss?" Asked Mache.

Schaeffer paused. "The Swiss are big, most six foot or over."

Mache. "I've defeated men taller than me."

Schaeffer. "They are agile and move quickly and have small armor and great discipline. They are on you before your ready. Once committed to the attack they press forward and its almost impossible to stop them or break their defense."

Rouchmelle whose whole life was individual combat. "Are they afraid to meet you one-on-one?"

Schaeffer could see he didn't understand. "They don't think in those terms. The Swiss do not take prisoners, they are as ruthless as we are, but they don't fight for pay. They refuse to let the Duke rule them, but if they continue someone will someday pay them to fight as mercenaries."

"Are you afraid of them Peter?"

Schaeffer pointed to his scar. "This my gift from the Swiss. I'm not afraid to fight them, but I want to win, so I believe the Duke when he said he had new tactics."

Another man was also greatly concern over the question of the Dukes strategy. A French aristocrat visited Gillani and was told the Duke left on his venture. The aristocrat was disappointed.

I would have liked to provide some soldiers for the Duke. I understand he attacks the Swiss, I've not met them, mostly I provide soldiers in Spain and France." Gillani explained the tactics of the Swiss.

The Frenchman responded. "Infantry is gaining over the mounted knights. I was at Poitiers in France, the whole English Army fought as Infantry. The English long-bow-men defeated us despite the fact that we outnumbered them at more then two to one. It was balanced Infantry and dismounted Cavalry tactics. Our knights were helpless. Your Duke should have a plan to attack the Swiss."

Gillani felt concerned. The Duke said he had one, but did he? Was the loan in danger?"

The Frenchmen could see Gillani was upset. "The Duke is a respected soldier and the House of Habsburg beyond reproach. Your money is safe."

Gillani thought. "The damn Swiss, we don't have the initiative, they do. We have to prove we can beat them."

The Frenchmen wondered if the Duke planned an ambush such as the one he experienced in the Holy Land at Nicopolis. The Sultan positioned a light Cavalry on a hillside.

The French knights out of control charged up the hill and finally attacked both Cavalry and Infantry. It was a trap with the Sultans main body attacking from the far crest of the hill.

"But could you do that with the Swiss? Men who moved so quickly and maneuvered to either side, to trap the Swiss, would take a very clever plan."

Gillani did not mention the Duke had a spy in the Swiss camp. He relaxed the more he thought of it. This time the Duke had a better plan.

Ten years ago he was over confident, but at this time a bigger army, and superior knights. The Germans were the best knights in Europe.

Gillani was glad the Duke hired the Germans. They were professionals and he should have listened to their advice, but would he? The Duke was arrogant, it was not his way to listen. The Duke was also fearless, he would die before he would retreat this time. If he would fail again, he could lose his kingdom and his followers would revolt. The money he paid the Duke to bloody the soldiers of Florence was a good investment. The Duke appeared more intelligent this time and was willing to work with Gillani to help Venice and also to have a spy in a senior position in the Swiss Camp. That, was something he would have disdained ten years earlier. Gillani was surprised, usually the Swiss were united and loyal. Medici of Florence was considered to have the best secret service. Could he have helped the Duke? No, the Duke would never agree to put the soldiers of Florence in danger if Medici helped him.

CHAPTER 4

The Count Dati of Florence was ushered into the tent of Rolf, the Leader of the Swiss Army. After he was given a glass of wine he explained. "I am the Ambassador of Florence, where twenty-one families represent the government — the Medici family as Governor General of our city has instructed me to visit you."

Rolf never visited by a dignitary before was aware of the Italian City-States and also that they were bankrolling the Duke.

Dati continued, "You are aware the Duke is planning on paying you a visit?"

Rolf, a small smile on his lips was amused. An invasion called a visit. Diplomacy was interesting.

Dati seeing he was amused thought. The Swiss are confident, and decided to go directly to the subject.

"I must tell you we have paid for a loan to be given to the Duke, and a contingent of soldiers from Florence will be joining him."

Rolf sipped his wine and did not react.

Dati seeing he was not upset leaned forward and placed two hands on the table.

"This is business you understand, we have no animosity to the Swiss people and no great desire to see the Duke best you, in fact we would hope you would prevail."

Rolf felt compelled to speak. "Strange you bankroll my enemies and send soldiers to fight us, but you want us to win?"

Dati, an excellent judge of people decided to explain to this man the complete truth of his visit. "There are three reasons I visit and hope to offer you financial support. We sometimes work together, but the City-States are really rivals. The twenty-one families of Florence are joined, but even within such a group we have rivalries. The Florence soldiers are mostly from a family that hates my Leader, the Medici Family. If they do not return home we would not be upset."

Rolf nodded he understood.

"Two - the men of Venice are led by a knight Count Magglie." This is his family crest. He placed a small painting of a Eagle with a red banner behind him on the table.

"Magglie will be wearing yellow, his standards will always be with him. We do not want him to return to Venice. We are willing to pay you 10,000 Florins today and another 10,000 Florins if you are successful in killing him. Of course, we trust your discretion in this matter."

Rolf did not care about the reason, but he was concerned about the logistics.

"How can I be sure I'll find him, the Duke has a big army?"

"He will be with the center, we are sure he will be very close to the Duke."

Rolf smiled again, they think we can find one man in a big army and kill him, our reputation is gaining strength.

"What if we only wound him, or he runs away?"

Dati was prepared for such a question.

"If he returns home wounded we are honorable businessmen, we would assume you have fulfilled your contract. But if he runs away and is not hurt, or returns home not hurt we would not pay the second 10,000 Florins."

He left unsaid the Duke might win and Magglie survive.

Rolf extended his hand and Dati told his servant to bring in the money.

After Rolf had the money taken away he said. "What is your third reason?"

"The Swiss are gaining the esteem of Europe. Someday we might need your services. We suggest a monthly payment to be agreed on and a contract to be written up if you are prepared to come to fight for us if we are ever in danger."

This was what Rolf expected the visit was about and he quickly agreed. The two men had several more glasses of wine and Rolf questioned.

"How big is the Dukes Army?"

Dati. "Five thousand knights and ten thousand Infantry about twice the size of last time. The knights are good, the Infantry mixed. For example the men of Florence could not stop you for ten minutes."

This was consistent with what Rolf's spies told him.

Rolf did not ask why Dati wanted Magglie killed, but he did ask, "This Count, is he a brave knight?"

"He is a drunk and cruel to his servants. The world would be better off without him."

Dati decided to confide in the man he someday expected to employ.

"The competition among our cities is fierce. Questions of honor, ability to invest wisely and above all to be successful in war, business and politics are critical. My patron the Medici Family is rapidly gaining power but it is a never ending quest. If Magglie does not return to Venice it will hurt the honor of his cousin, the Doge of Venice."

Rolf asked. "Have you met the Duke?"

"Yes, once, it was after his unfortunate meeting with you ten years ago."

Rolf. "He was fortunate, if he was unfortunate we would have killed him."

Dati laughed.

Rolf serious. "We fight for our land, and our homes, what does the Duke fight for?"

"Money, his prestige, honor, and he dare not lose to you again."

"So he can't run away?"

"No, you will have to kill him this time."

Rolf. "We intend to."

#

After he left, Dati thought. He is a smart man, they fight for honor and freedom now. In the future they will be offered such large sums of money they will become mercenaries. They have a quiet confidence, the Swiss approach war like a business. My Leader Giovanni Medici is not a man to gamble, he has studied the Swiss, his spy with the Austrians informs him of their plans. The spy will help Rolf.

Giovanni Medici of Florence sent Dati to the Swiss because he thought the death of Magglie would embarrass and weaken Venice. His anger over losing the opportunity to head the Syndicate that made the loan to the Duke was made greater by the memory of his father, Vieri Medici the historic Banker of Florence.

The two cities always rivals with an unforeseen event swinging the power to Venice. Shortly after Vieri died a plague hit

Florence reducing its population to less than 40,000 whereas Venice was in the neighborhood of 100,000. This made Venice one of the largest cities in Europe and gave Gillani the stature to lead the Syndicate.

The political cross currents in the city of Florence demanded that Giovanni not fall behind Venice in financial and political influence. Giovanni remembered the morning he received the votes of the other cities making Venice the head of the Syndicate.

He forced himself to walk from his palace to the cathedral. Then to his place of business, to maintain his daily regimen, with five senior officials meeting him, and expressing concern about losing the leadership of the Syndicate. His friends were sympathetic, his enemies joyful. The last of his enemies was Signorie, the fat landowner who aspired to replace the Medici Family as leader of the city. Signorie met him outside the cathedral, a move calculated to embarrass and hurt Giovanni. Signorie whose family built the palace of Signorie, the seat of the government did not disguise his joy at Giovanni's defeat despite the fact it would cost him money.

Twice that day Giovanni showed his anger by yelling at subordinates and hitting a slow waiter at the café during dinner. When he returned, a plan formed in his mind to help the Swiss defeat the Duke.

First he laid off the city's share of the loan to other rich landowners in Florence and the surrounding areas. None suspected other investors were given this great opportunity, so he sent Dati with a proposal to the Swiss with an offer they could not refuse. Secondly Dati was head of the Secret Police, created when the workers revolted in 1378. Dati's police work told him one of the Dukes strongest military units, the Germans, were uneasy about the project. In addition, the most respected knight in the great host, William Thomas of England, hearing of the Dukes plans for revenges against the poor and the weak expressed his concern about the venture. Dati also recruited an important spy in the territory the Duke was about to invade.

Medici spies told him despite the size of the Duke's Army, the Swiss would acquit themselves well and if they did he intended to broker the Swiss as mercenaries. He even considered the Swiss might represent a police force if another lower class revolt occurred in his city. One other reason to see the Duke fail, was that Signorie was the strongest member of the Council voting to loan the Duke the money.

#

Medici's chief spy against the Duke was a Dwarf who worked as an entertainer at the various pubs and drinking taverns on the Austrian Swiss border. An important consideration for using the Dwarf was, he also was in the pay of Rolf the Swiss Leader.

Dati told the Dwarf the make up of Dukes Army and a breakdown of the strongest and weakest units. Medici finding out about a possible ambush of the Swiss by the Duke, had Dati tell the Dwarf to pass it on to Rolf.

Dati returned and described his meeting with Rolf.

"The Swiss accepted the commission to kill Magglie and I believe they were enthusiastic about future ties with us."

The next issue was delicate. "You gave the Dwarf the make up of the Dukes Army?" Said Medici.

"Yes, and he will give it to the Swiss."

Dati was puzzled why he could not give this information directly to Rolf.

Giovanni explained. "Rolf will understand we have political duels with the city of Venice and cooperate, but if he sees we undermine an ally like the Duke, he will maybe suspect that in the future he cannot trust us. No, let him believe we killed someone from a local City-State, but to an outsider like the Duke we remain loyal."

Dati marveled at Giovanni and waited for the second phase of his plan.

"If the Swiss are victors you are to plant a story that Signorie gave the information about the Duke's Army to the Swiss."

Giovanni saw the fear in Dati's eyes. If caught, it meant this death and every member of his family too.

Giovanni. "Speed if the Duke loses, you spread the story of Signorie's treachery and then kill Signorie quickly and we blame the Dukes family. I give you a third of Signorie's estates."

Dati blinked. "He would be rich beyond his wildest dreams, but the business of the plan also stunned him.

"And if the Duke wins?"

Giovanni stood up and walked to the window, his rich red robe extended to the floor. Slowly he poured two wines.

"We make a profit and send word to Gillani of Venice that Signorie is plotting against him, and that Signorie wants a war with Venice. Gillani will then dispose of our problem"

CHAPTER 5

The Leaders of the Swiss met in the Central Hall. Rolf the Senior Captain described the coming war against the Austrians. With the meeting completed Rolf, a big man at six feet two inches sat at a thick wood table across from his best friend, Urst, one of his Captains. Rolf felt small. Urst at six feet six inches rawboned, large hands and never defeated in any combat, towered over everyone.

Urst led the halberdiers, the light Infantry of the Swiss Army. The halberd was eight feet with a hook to pull a knight off his horse, and a sharp point and a blade to slash. The pikes and cross-bows were the remainder of the Army.

Rolf intended to give details and an important assignment to Urst.

"Urst, if our information is correct, the Austrians are negotiating to buy horses and food from the towns south of us. They should attack in four weeks. I expect their forces will be twice as big as the group that attacked us ten years ago."

Urst's mustache curled as a smile dominated his face. "So, we kill twice as many Austrians this time. I look forward to pulling knights out of the saddle."

The long arms of Urst and the length of the halberd extended beyond the reach of any knight no matter how long the length of the sword he carried.

Rolf said, "I have a job for you. We need more money this time and the town of Berne will contribute the most. The good Burgers of Berne hearing that the Austrians are bringing such a large Army want to negotiate with them."

Urst let out a loud laugh.

"Negotiate!? ……Negotiate….. with the Austrians? Have they lost their minds?" He banged his halberd on the floor.

"This is the only negotiations the Duke understands."

Rolf expected such a reaction. "Urst, Berne will contribute almost fifty percent of our pay and supplies, I could decline, but why argue with them? With the Duke spending his money already, the Austrians don't intend to make any deal with us except surrender. You will act as body guard to Renders the Mayor from

Berne. He meets the Austrians at the river south of Berne at the Ale House. You know it?"

The Austrians will bring twenty men, you bring ten. Let them talk for awhile, then start a fight, kill a few, let some escape. The Duke should hear our answer. Try not to let Renders get killed."

"No prisoners?" asked Urst.

"No prisoners," was the response.

#

The Duke shifted uncomfortably in his saddle. The damp skies overcast, were not unusual in the late summer in the mountains of Switzerland. He motioned to the scribe at his side.

"Record the date we hung four peasants next to the Laupen Lake." The Duke was determined to conduct a campaign of terror. This would not frighten the Swiss, but fill his troops with resolve. Some of his Infantry knowing the terror campaign, would expect no mercy from the enemy and fight harder.

The first raindrops began to fall. The youngest a boy of about ten began to cry.

"Shut him up," shouted the Duke.

A big man hit the boy and pulled a rope around his neck.

Count Magglie sitting on a horse to the Duke's right was drunk. He was drunk ever since they entered the lands of the Swiss. The Duke thought, he needs liquid courage, he won't last. The Duke did not approve of this sign of weakness. If he was one of the Duke's men he would be punished.

Magglie nudged his horse next to the Duke. Magglie spoke to the Duke.

"Stupid peasants, their fit only to hang. The brat cries but the rope will silence him."

Magglie's head dropped and he almost fell off his horse.

The Duke was annoyed for a knight to behave like this in front of peasants. "Disgraceful"

He said to one of his attendants. "Take the Count back to the Inn and put him to bed."

Count Magglie's head snapped up. "I heard that. You think I'm drunk, when we met the Swiss I'll show you. I'm here to watch our money but I'll fight."

It was the third time he told the Duke he wanted to fight the Swiss. The Duke recognized a man who was trying to convince himself he was looking forward to a battle. The Duke decided when he sent his men to talk to the Mayor of Berne a negotiation, but the real reason was to obtain a map from the Swiss Traitor, he would send Magglie along. The man would surely get into a fight with the Swiss and we would be rid of him. A man pulled from a horse by a halberd and stabbed might live to tell about it, but he might never be effective again.

Now the young boy was strung up, his legs kicking violently. The other three looked away, no sign of fear and expecting no mercy from the Duke. The Duke shifted again in his saddle. The Swiss did have courage and he was glad most of his Infantry were miles away and did not see the stoic bravery of the peasants.

A knight on a white charger rode next to the tree where the dead boy hung limply. It was William Thomas, the most famous knight from England. He just returned from the Holy Land and was joining his brother and one hundred other English knights in the adventure.

"Why are these people being punished?" he yelled.

The Duke's second-in-command, Gamilla, answered, "They are traitors and spies, we found the crest of the Canton in the wine cellar."

The Duke knew this was trouble. John Thomas the brother warned the Duke that the killing at Carssene greatly upset William Thomas who had taken a vow that he would make no war against civilians.

Seeing the Duke, William Thomas confronted him.

"Duke, did not my brother tell you I vowed to protect the poor and weak. I return from the Holy Land and pledged to our Lord my knightly vows?"

The Duke never spoken to like this was silent. He did not want to fight with William Thomas. Word would ripple through the Army and devastate the morale. When Thomas joined the expedition many had joined just to fight along side him.

Thomas seeing one of the Dukes men about to put a rope around a woman's neck pointed at him. "You take one more step and you'll meet your maker."

Gamilla aware the Duke did not want a fight with Thomas said.

"Sir Knight you joined us, you pledged to support the Duke."

Thomas turned with fury on Gamilla.

"My pledge is to my Lord, he is a higher being than the Duke."

Now Gamilla grew angry. "You are one we are twenty, stand aside Sir Knight."

William Thomas drew his sword. "Be you one hundred my word to my Lord stands. The first man to touch those people dies by my hand."

He snapped down the visor on his helmet, a sign he was ready.

The Duke was stunned. He did not want to fight or kill Thomas, but he could not back down in front of his men.

Now William Thomas's brother John rode up and instantly recognized what was happening. He said in a low whisper, "William, please do not do this."

William responded, "You know my vow."

John. "William if you start this I will have to join you, we both will be killed. The hundred I brought with me will be without leadership, I beg you let me talk to the Duke."

William nodded.

John rode over to the Duke." Sir, let us have a parley. My brother will not yield. Kill us both and you lose my hundred all good and true knights."

The Duke held up his hand. "Stay this event. I will parley with these knights."

The three men rode one hundred yards away. The Duke spoke first.

"I respect your vow, but you cannot interfere with my justice."

William. "I have said all I'm going to. Kill them and you face me."

The Duke continued to hold his temper, he could not start his war with the Swiss this way.

"I'll spare them until we face the Swiss. At that time they must take an oath of loyalty to me or they hang."

Before William could say no, John spoke up. "William you gave an oath, but I also gave an oath to the Duke. If we fight, I am your brother and our father will learn we both died because you would not compromise with the Duke."

"I beg you agree with the Dukes reasonable offer if this

campaign distresses you return home I will tell our knights you are ill."

William Thomas loved his brother, he was the only reason he joined the campaign at all. Never had he backed down where his honor or his vows were at stake, but he said.

"Duke, I leave. I accept your offer, but if you kill these people, I will return."

And so the truest knight left the campaign against the Swiss. Rumors spread through the Army, but most accepted the story he was ill.

#

The Banker Gillani returned to his beloved Venice and not even the sight of this great city of 117 islands, 150 canals and over 300 bridges excited him. His great enemy Padua a major threat to Venice, years ago was defeated.

With the loan to the Duke he should have felt triumph. The great mercantile marine expanding Venice, moving to be the great power in Italy.

He needed to keep importing foods and exporting finished products, to be strong against his long-term danger, the Turks. However, what troubled him today was a message from Signorie in Florence. For years he ignored Florence. The plague hurt the population and the size of the city was less than half of Venice. He was wary of Giovanni Medici a dangerous man, one of the smaller families of Florence, but his control of the city was startling. Only a series of bribes gained Gillani control of the Syndicate over Medici.

Now word from Signorie that Medici had sent a representative to the Swiss. At first he guessed Medici would pay the Swiss to kill Magglie. Gillani didn't care, Magglie was a drunk, not worth caring about and his death would not hurt the City or Gillani.

Than he realized, if the Swiss defeated the Duke, the Syndicate would turn against Venice. A chill passed through his body. His greatest move could turn to ashes, and worse, if Medici thought the Swiss could beat the Duke, it could probably happen. He looked out at the beautiful flowing promenade of the Grand Canal. His city and the Grand Canal were the most beautiful street in the world. Medici, gambling on a group of farmers and Gillani backing the famous Duke. War was not predictable and beauty and education could go under because of the slash of a halberd. Farmers could destroy his City, but how could they defeat the Duke? Gillani studied the war. Simple farmers against royalty it should not be in doubt. What made the Swiss so good? He did not understand because his underclass was not like the Swiss.

What none of the Military experts understood, the great discipline of the Swiss was voluntary. These were men fighting for their homes not pay. The rank and file understood that outnumbered, and on paper, the underdog, the shock attack, the speed was a byproduct of hours of training, and would strike terror in the hearts of their enemy. On many battlefields not just against the Austrians the Swiss with eighteen foot pikes and halberds represented a morale answer to aristocracy and knighthood.

Royalty might rule in some lands, but the answer was the Cantons. Barons and knights would fall when brawny peasants swung pikes against breastplates. It was like cutting wheat on their farms.

Like Medici, Gillani began to think of lying off part of the loan, and reducing the risk to Venice. Gillani heard William Thomas, the great English knight left the venture. The story was that Thomas was ill, but one of Magglie's men sent word that Thomas almost fought with the Duke. Medici was appalled. You couldn't lose a man like Thomas. The Duke might have new plans, but his unwillingness to lead such a man was an ancient weakness, and the pride and haughtiness of royalty. Gillani decided he would sell off part of the loan. His father would support him.

CHAPTER 6

The knight on the white horse traveled alone. Not since the voyage to the Holy Land did he feel so despondent. Then leaving his home and children the voyage to the Holy Land, long overland marches, his horse dead, fighting on foot. His epiphany, his dream where God told him to go home and his pledge to God to help the weak and the poor. Finally, word his brother was with the Duke and his failure to save the boy.

He had seen much death and pain. Why did the boy's death hurt him so much? Because he had failed God weeks after his promise to help. Barely sleeping and with heavy heart he traveled a country lane and saw an old man lying in the road.

The man more dead then alive was covered with blood, bones stuck out of his legs and arms, compound fractures, eyes blackened, he had been beaten with sticks. Thomas gave him water.

"Who did this to you old man?"

"Brigands, a man with a red beard."

Thomas could see he was close to death.

"Our men, they take fish to Rolf, our village is on the river, we stretch nets to catch fish, the Brigand killed two old men yesterday, me today. They will kill the children and the women next."

He passed out and died. Thomas stood up. Was this a sign from God? He spurred his horse on and within an hour found the village, a river ran at the end of the road. Near the dock the villagers had built a barricade. Several women, four or five young boys, and some old men. They had bow and arrows and farming implements as weapons. Perhaps twenty villagers manned the barricade. The rest were hiding. There were perhaps twenty-five huts and a small tavern to serve travelers who crossed the river.

He heard smashing and yelling inside the tavern. One of the four men descended from the tavern was the Leader, his shirt a grape color from wine spills.

"Sir Knight, you are with the Duke?"

Thomas didn't answer but continued to look at the barricade.

The Leader pointed to the barricade. "They are Swiss, loyal to Rolf, we will kill them, there is nothing of value in this town, not worth your time Sir Knight."

Thomas looked at the Leader.

"Is there any wine left?"

"Yes Sir Knight, two full caskets in the cellar. How many knights are behind you?"

The Leader immediately stepped back. The question made it appear he was trying to judge if the knight was alone. The horse and the armor were worth a great deal of money, but if the knight was not alone and he was from the Duke, the Brigands wanted no part of him and they would melt away.

Thomas fixed a gaze on the man, who stepped back even further.

"Sir Knight, these people are enemies of the Duke, if you would allow us the honor, we planned to attack within the hour."

Thomas saw three other men come from his right, one with a red beard, and all had blood stains on their clothes and carried strong wooden staffs.

Thomas judged they could have many more by the noise inside the tavern. He had to even the odds.

"Open those two caskets, my men behind me will be thirsty."

This direct order activated the Leader. He yelled at two men to open the caskets. "knights would be arriving and they would be thirsty."

Thomas in a commanding voice said. "I will look at the barricade, he spurred his horse and drew even with the three men. The man with the red beard bowed his head taking his response from the Leader.

Thomas saw blood on the wooden staff. "That is a fine staff." Thomas unhooked the ball and chain from his saddle.

Red Beard surprised responded. "We kill the Dukes enemies. We destroyed a Traitor this morning."

With a flick of his wrist Thomas whipped the ball into Red Beards chest, killing him. The man next to him never moved and the ball hit him on the top of his head. The third man attempted to run but Thomas's horse cut him off and he joined his companions on the dusty street.

Thomas looked behind him. Men were piling out of the tavern and gathering around the Leader all yelling and in a great state of agitation.

He rode toward the barricade and stopped twenty yards away. He could see five or six young boys, several women, four old men and a Priest. He said a prayer thanking god for giving him another chance.

"Do not be afraid, God has sent me to you. This village is under my protection."

The villagers expecting to be killed shortly were stunned and didn't move.

"God has sent me I am his servant, he sent me to help you. You are under Gods protection."

He dismounted and knelt before the Priest. "Bless me Father, make my right arm strong.

This the Priest did.

Now Thomas looked back on the long street. The Brigands were still in the street. He counted twelve, they might run away, be he hoped they wouldn't. This filth would attack other helpless men and women. He was there to avenge the old man and protect the weak.

The Leader of the Brigands knew if they ran away he would not be the Leader for long. Who was this crazy knight and why in this forsaken village? If it was two or more knights they would run away, but with just one man who struck Red Beard and his two brothers, they were crazy with hate and wanted to attack immediately. Two hundred yards from the barricade the Leader was thinking, if he kills four or five of us we split up the proceeds, a lot more money than from the village.

He said, "Don't hurt the horse, we can sell the horse, try and get him off the horse as he rides by two parallel lines, get him off the horse!"

By the river, the Priest said, "They are not going away, what do we do Sir Knight?"

"Priest, pick out your five strongest people and I will tell you what to do."

Thomas mounted the horse and watched as two women and two young boys formed behind the Priest.

"Do not be afraid, God wants you to live. God has sent me to you."

Thomas waved his arm. "They are forming two lines, they will try and get me off the horse. I will ride to the end of the street. Priest, I will isolate one man."

He looked at the five, now spellbound, listening to him.

"If one man is alone attack him, if you get him down kill him and retreat behind the barricade. Be quick, God loves you, he has sent me to you, Gods enemies are your enemies, show no mercy."

Thomas looked up the street, the Brigands were forming two lines, a gauntlet.

The Priest grabbed Thomas's hand. "You are right God has sent you to us."

Thomas pulled down his helmet and slowly spurred the horse. "I will return, you are under my protection and Gods."

At fifty yards Thomas spurred the horse and rode directly at the first man on the left, circling he drove the man who ran towards the barricade. Immediately Thomas spurred his horse towards two men who gathered on the right. Catching one with the ball, the man went down. The Brigands were paralyzed. The lines widening, hugging the small huts staying away from the middle of the street.

Five attacked the Brigand near the barricade. Watching the Priest who was swinging a hoe, his sword caught a woman in the shoulder. A small boy on all hands and knees drove a knife into his ankle and the Brigand went down never to rise again.

Thomas rode down the open street, circled back and attacked the last two men, killing one, his horse reared up as three men, the wine giving them courage tried to tackle him off the horse. The horse narrowly missed, kicking one man who while ducking drove a knife into Thomas's leg, gaining the first victory for the Brigands. Thomas, feeling great pain and seeing two more men running towards him, turned and raced one hundred yards outside the town. He halted — he felt faint and it took all his strength to pull out the knife.

He looked up. There were eight Brigands gathered in the village street. Their Leader was in shock, one hour ago he had fifteen men, and was about to put the town to the sword. Now, a man ran from a hut, threw a spear at him, which fell short, and raced to the barricade. More people were descending from the steep hill and joining the barricade.

The Brigand looked to his left, the barricade more of a threat now, many more people gathered. Ahead of him the steep hill.

Could there be more village people on the hill? A possible ambush? Behind him thick woods, and he suspected to retreat that way they would reach the river and be trapped. To his right was the insane knight who had mounted his horse again.

Suddenly he heard singing. The town people behind the barricade were singing. No more cowered, they were turning to their faith and gaining strength. His men were afraid, the knight yelled, "Saint John," and began to ride towards them. The towns people began to cross the barricade and this broke the Brigands.

Two men turned and ran for the woods, the Leader yelled "stop," but running at full speed they disappeared into the trees. Looking about he pointed to the hill. He and four others ran toward the hill.

The younger brother of Red Beard ran towards the knight, but alone he had no chance, and Thomas dispatched him with a sword stroke. The towns people followed Thomas's horse who despite a severe ankle injury spurred and caught a Brigand who had thrown his weapon away.

The Leader of the Brigands was right, there were towns people on the hill and they began throwing rocks at the climbing Brigands. One tried to surrender, but it was not accepted. It was over quickly and the towns people gathered in the street and knelt in prayer. The Priest next to the knight asked him his name. "William Thomas."

The Priest looked at his flock. "I rename this town William Thomas for the man God sent us, and each year we will have a day of prayer on this date."

CHAPTER 7

The small Swiss Guard accompanied Mayor Renders of Berne to the Ale House south of the city by the river. Urst prudently ordered a second group of pikemen to trail the escort two miles behind. They were to act as rear guards and also provide a support group if needed.

The day was bright and cool. The Alps a beautiful background of green rolling meadows. Renders was nervous, rubbing his hands, twice he said to Urst.

"This is a parley, no fighting, we are here to talk."

The first time Urst did not reply. When he said it again. Urst said.

"The Austrians want peace, good to see it. I was concerned all the knights were coming to make war."

Renders winced. This was an answer he kept hearing from his fellow town Leaders. When they arrived the Austrian official party was just entering the Inn. Urst sent one of his men to walk Renders to the Inn. He looked at the Austrian knights, relaxing in an orchard just over one hundred yards away. Suddenly he was alert, one of the knights was wearing a yellow surcloth with an eagle on a red banner as his standard. It was Magglie. He called his second-in-command to his side.

"See the knight in yellow. That is Magglie, he doesn't leave here today, at least not alive."

The second man's stoic look said he understood.

Urst. "Let them talk until noon, then we break up Mayor Renders parley."

Urst's son Ulbrecht said. "Father, we can see about twenty Austrians in the orchard, why don't I ride around just to make sure there are no others."

"Go, but be back by noon!"

#

When Ulbrecht returned it was just before noon. Urst signaled his second-in command.

"Get ready, I'm going to visit the parley."

Urst walked slowly into the Inn. Renders was sitting at a table across from an Austrian knight wearing a beautiful dark blue cape drinking wine. Behind the blue cape was a knight with a deep scar down the side of his face and without a right ear. The mans hand went to his sword hilt. The Swiss Giant was intimidating!

Renders, who was nervous around Urst spoke up.

"Urst, the Duke is being very reasonable, he will tax us at half the rate of the previous years and if we pay early will consider we don't need to give them hostages."

Renders smiled at the knight with the blue cape who grunted, but did not answer. The knight sent to meet with Renders was talking to give his Agents time to meet the Swiss spy. He was to delay the parley and even to leave with a vague agreement, so that some of the Swiss would believe there was a chance of peace. However, his real mission was to bring back a map that showed the Swiss plan for assembling before the war. The knight considered all Swiss sub-human and intended to hang Renders when the war was over.

Urst, his halberd in a relaxed position smiled. "Very reasonable."

The knight in the blue cape put up his hand to signal his associate there would not be trouble. The Swiss were dumber then he expected. His mission was not to fight, but bring back the map.

Now Urst leaned forward and smiled at the knight in the blue cape.

"If there is peace, the only thing I'll miss is pulling Austrian knights off their horses."

He slammed his halberd on the table with such force it spilled the wine over the blue cape.

The man a dagger in his hand tried to attack, but Urst's halberd, the hook side was slammed into his back pinning him to the table. The dagger fell to the floor and he groaned a death sound.

Blood on the blue cape, the table overturned, Renders fell to the floor. The man with one ear reached for his sword, but Urst was too quick. His halberd point drove into the man's back and the blade ended his life.

Renders a look of terror and surprise on his face was helped to his feet by Urst.

Urst didn't let the Mayor question what happened.

"You saw him attack me? In fact I was worried he was going

to stab you, I saved your life."

Urst brushed wine off the jacket of the Mayor.

The Giant towered over the Mayor and his sympathetic but forceful comment, who started the fight influenced Renders.

"He had a knife?" Said Renders.

Urst confident, the Mayor would tell the good Burger of Berne that the blame belonged to the Austrians said. '"Let me get you out of here. Ride back to my rear guard, they will take you back to Berne, we can't trust these people"

He quickly put Renders on a horse and his ten men were at attention in front of the Inn.

The Austrians aware something had happened were stirring.

Urst ordered the five pikemen to form a frontline.

Urst yelled at the visitors. "Your men are dead, the parley is over, you may leave in peace."

His voice louder. "Magglie _ _ _ _ _Count Magglie you should run away. Magglie we don't want to kill you at a peace parley. Go run and hide behind the Duke."

Magglie was drunk, but heard his name and the last insult from Urst.

Mounting his horse he led three knights in a head-long charge against the Swiss. They were met by the pikemen who suffered no wounds, but killed Magglie and another man. One knight wounded returned to the watching knights and the last man trapped was pulled from his horse by a halberd.

The Austrian knights retreated one hundred yards to decide what to do. The Leader expected the Swiss to regroup, but Urst formed two lines — pikeman and halberdiers, and they advanced at a quick pace towards the knights. Three knights, followers of the blue cape charged and inflicted injuries on two of the Swiss before they died.

The Leader of the rest of the Austrians, with the precious map in his saddlebag, understood his duty. It was his responsibility to return to the Duke. He ordered the others to follow him and they left the field.

The men of the Canton relaxed, only two hurt, two of the young started to boast.

Urst. "We caught them off guard today, don't expect that

when the Duke brings his Army. Now lets make the sure we get Renders back to Berne. One asked Urst if they could stop at the Inn for a drink. Urst cuffed the man in the head and growled.

"One small action and you act like a veteran, we drink when we get to Berne."

#

The Dukes second-in-command Gamilla, returned to the Duke who fully agreed with him, it was more important to bring the map back then fight the Swiss. The Duke asked about Count Magglie.

Gamilla. "He was drunk, a huge Swiss called his name and insulted him. Magglie charged with the others, and the big man killed him."

The Duke stood up. Gamilla thought he was reacting to Magglie being drunk at the parley.

The Duke turned. "Are you sure the Swiss knew who he was? They were aware it was Magglie?"

"Yes, he said Count Magglie insulted him."

"He said Count Magglie?" The Duke a look of concern on his face sat down.

"He called Count Magglie, are you upset he's dead?" asked Gamilla.

The Duke. "No, I'm glad we got rid of him. In fact I told you not to fight the Swiss, to bring the map back half expecting Magglie would start a fight with the Swiss and get killed. Tell me exactly what happened."

"The big man went into the Inn, killed our envoy came out and shouted at Magglie. He shouted that Magglie should run away and hide behind the Duke."

"An insult that would surely provoke Magglie a man we didn't need. Said the Duke. He rubbed his chin.

"The Italian Banker." The Duke repeated again. "It had to be the Italian Bankers, only they were aware he was with us."

Gamilla. "The one from Venice?"

"No, if Gillani wanted him killed he would have paid me to do it. It was one of the others in the Syndicate, they are talking to the Swiss."

Gamilla. "Does that worry you?"

"No, they don't know our plans, they hate each other. This has nothing to do with the map, now tell me about the Traitor."

"He was young, nervous, said they were moving in two weeks,….. expected us to move to take the Swiss Plateau again….. agreed they would be strung out until just before the lake road….. He would meet us three days before…. The Swiss are to join up,….. just enough time for us to gain the ambush place."

The Duke said. "They killed Magglie that proves they don't realize there is a Traitor, they wouldn't risk killing him at the parley and making us more alert. No they killed Magglie because they were paid and the parley was just to keep the Mayor of Berne happy. The Traitor has much to gain with our victory."

The Duke was right, if Rolf suspected a Traitor he never would have killed Magglie at the parley, but hunt for the Traitor. But if the Swiss didn't care what the Duke thought they would kill a man that didn't matter.

The Duke was sure the Traitor to the Swiss had accepted his gold and would rule a Canton, a very generous bribe. Now he showed his plan to Gamilla.

"The road is narrow just before the Lake. We can set the ambush at that spot. They will be strung out. Our horses will ride them down before they form up. It will be like a falling tree. The more horsemen we push onto the road the harder it will be for them to extend their pikes and halberds.

The Duke looked at the map. "This is perfect, a patrol has just returned, they rode through this ground, it is firm. I intend you to lead. We blow them back you have five hundred horses. I follow with a thousand, but we must keep moving, the Infantry follows, no one can stop."

Gamilla asked. "How many Swiss do you expect."

"Three thousand."

He was silent. Three thousand Swiss were dangerous even if the Duke had fifteen thousand men.

The Duke responded. "The idea is to create a melee never let them form. Break through the first men you meet, keep riding, we will keep breaking through a wall of men like water rushing down stream, horses…. Infantry…. horses….. more Infantry. Let it be four or five of our men against one Swiss. The knights when the melee starts, to welcome the Infantry to help them individual combats. The knights were trained for individual combats, the rewards will be great, any man that fights and returns will bring all the wealth he can carry and the Swiss women and children will be beast of burden, they will carry the plunder."

"Is that not against our knightly vows," said Gamilla.

The Duke brushed aside his question.

"The Church agrees with me, the Swiss are not Christians, they deserve no protection especially the Cantons that have paid their soldiers. You saw no mercy at the Inn. Several Cantons will be spared, but the taxes will be higher than my Grandfather charged them."

The Duke was right, the Swiss leadership did not know there was a Traitor in their camp.

#

The Dwarf was Rolf's spy, but he was also in the pay of Giovanni Medici of Florence. Medici also had a spy at the Dukes castle. A week after the Duke saw the map, Medici understood the Duke planned an ambush at the Swiss Plateau. The Dwarf was told of the ambush and the details of the Dukes Army and even their marching schedule, Infantry and knights. The Dwarf was told Medici's name should not come up. He learned all this from the Austrian knights a plausible answer since he had gathered much information about the Duke's Army working at the Inn where the young boy was hung. When he asked if Medici understood who was the spy, he was told that gold was exchanged at the Ale House where Magglie was killed, but that they did not know who was the spy in the Swiss camp.

#

The Dwarf rode slowly into the Swiss camp. The sun was setting and he didn't want to alarm the guards who recognized him and his horse. He slid painfully off the horse and stood at less than four feet, smaller in the camp of the Giant. Quickly he entered Rolf's tent, his bandaged wrist hurting.

Rolf directed him to sit in his favorite chair. The Dwarf was Rolf's best spy and he accepted a glass of wine in his good left hand.

Rolf. "What happened to your wrist?"

"Austrians at the Inn, they were drunk, one picked me up, threw me against the bar. I think he broke my wrist."

Rolf was not surprised. Austrian knights were frequently cruel to helpless or smaller people.

"They hung the Innkeepers son and the Duke would have hung him and his wife if they didn't swear loyalty to the Duke. An English knight, William Thomas stopped them from hanging the Innkeeper that day."

The Dwarf continued.

"I have important news. The knights drinking were bragging the Duke has your schedule of march."

Rolf sat up. "When did you hear this, and how did they get it?"

"I heard two days ago and they said gold was given at the Inn the day Magglie was killed."

Rolf was a man that never showed emotion, his life was leading men in battle, hearing good and bad news and keeping an even keel. The Leader was not allowed to feel or show fear or joy especially a Swiss Leader. A Traitor in his camp, it shook him.

With great control Rolf asked. "They were talking about the Ale House at the Berne River? Gold was given to a Swiss?"

"That's what they said." The Dwarf was shaking, telling this man the news that someone in the Leadership of the Swiss was in the pay of the Duke.

"Could it be possible the knights were just bragging and it was not true?"

The Dwarf said, "I heard them say your halberdiers would lead the veteran pikemen, all from the Plateau region. The Army would continue to move in that fashion, crossbowmen after the young pikemen."

Rolf slumped in his chair. It was exactly the formation, he agreed to with Urst and his Captains.

The Dwarf had other news. "They kept saying you won't be able to form up. They said we won't face dense pikes, it will be a melee. Three or four against one, they were very happy when they said that."

Instantly Rolf understood what the Austrians planned. He thanked the Dwarf, told him he would double his pay and suggested the Dwarf stay with him. It was too dangerous to return to the Inn. The Dwarf agreed, and after the Dwarf left, Rolf called Urst to his tent.

Urst sat down and was stunned when Rolf said. "The Austrians have our plan of march. The Dwarf was just here, he told me exactly what we agreed to with the Captains."

Urst. "The Captains?"

Rolf. "No he said gold was exchanged the day Magglie was killed at the Ale House, and I know what they plan to do."

Urst didn't hear the last of the sentence. The day Magglie was killed, what did it mean, his men, who could have done this?

The Giant shook his head and looked at the floor speechless.

Rolf asked. "Did any of the Swiss leave the group before the fight? It had to happen before the fight?"

The Giant stood up. He held on to the table tightly so his legs did not buckle.

"My son Ulbrecht. He was gone for three hours."

"It can't be Ulbrecht," said Rolf.

"Yes, it could be." The Giant sat down, a look of pain on his face.

"My family, we have had trouble. When the high pasture was divided, I gave a larger section to Pooser, he is a much harder worker than Ulbrecht.   Ulbrecht's wife was very upset, she complained for weeks. I finally told her to keep quiet. Ulbrecht, at the Ale House was away for almost three hours, he said he was scouting to see if the Austrians had other men. He could have spoken to them."

They talked for an hour.

Rolf had a plan. "Go to your sons tell them we are marching sooner. If Ulbrecht is in the pay of the Duke, he will want to warn him. Tell them both we need someone to scout the Dukes Army. The one whose is guilty will want very badly to be the scout."

Both felt that the other son Pooser could have followed Urst to the meeting that day and both sons had seen the plans.

Urst returned two hours later. The man was destroyed. He confessed it was over the land and Ulbrecht gave the plans to an Austrian knight.

"Ulbrecht wanted to be the scout, when I suggested someone had to check the Duke." Rolf could see Urst's hands were bloody. This must hurt him greatly.

"Rolf, I'll leave the Army if you want."

"Urst we have been friends since boys, I can't understand how much this has hurt you. But you are the Leader of the halberdiers, I need you. I see you joking with our young boys and squad leaders, you love this Army as I do. We are the Leaders, but we owe this Army much. I have a plan."

Urst wiped tears from his eyes. "I'll do whatever you say."

"Send Pooser to the Duke, tell the Duke his brother has been sent to signal all the Cantons. We're marching sooner, not two weeks but ten days. Pooser wants an equal share of the gold since he came at great risk to the Duke. They probably have another deal with Ulbrecht, but Pooser wants gold. That Ubrecht, if he did not do as ordered to go to the Cantons would raise suspicion, but the deal still worked."

"Do you think he believes Pooser?"

Rolf. "The Duke believes the world is corrupt as he is. I think he will."

Pooser rode to the Dukes camp. Urst did not sleep that night. Next day he said to Rolf, "What was this about, why did they want the map? What is the marching plan to them?" Rolf paused. "The Austrians were at the Plain just before the Lake. A set of trees by the water, that's where they plan to ambush us. Four or five of them mounted were testing the ground, they wanted to see if it was firm enough for a Cavalry charge."

Urst. "What did they mean by a melee?"

Rolf. "They intend to attack our column on the march via Cavalry to disrupt and disorganize us so we can't form up. Thus it becomes a series of small hand-to-hand fighting, their numbers have the advantage. When Pooser comes back, if the Duke believes him, we move immediately and in the fog of the Swiss Plateau, attack him on the Lake road.

#

In a valley of hard men, Hans Gruber was considered a very hard man. At five foot ten inches, he was smaller than his neighbors, but in the war against the Duke ten years ago, he pulled three knights out of their saddles and dispatched them. He was the master of the Duck and Pulls, ducking under the knights' attack and hooking his halberd on the armor. His neighbors started the days work at six a.m. but the Gruber household began work at five a.m. All the barn floors in this area were clean enough to eat off, and the local joke was that the Grubers procreated on the barn floor to take some of the pleasure out of the act.

Yesterday when word came the schedule to march against the Austrians was moved up Hans reacted as his neighbors expected. If his farm and his family were his pride, the infantry and his church were his life blood. He accepted never questioned, always right never wrong. He voted for Rolf and was devoted to the man. With the change in schedule, he told his twelve year old daughter and wife that while he was gone they would have to work harder. He expected the farm to be in the same condition when he returned as when he left it. If that entailed longer hours and working Sundays the Lord would understand for they were fighting the inferiors, and he considered the Austrians thieves and inferiors.

Ten years ago he heard the Austrians were invading and meant to steal and plunder his farm. He reacted even more violently when told the Austrian peasants and the animals lived in the same house together, instead of in a neat barn where every animal had a stall. On the Gruber farm, the animals name's were on the stall. The barbarians lived with the pigs.

No wonder the Austrian inferior wanted to steal from the Swiss, the superior. This was a source of amusement for most of the people in the valley, but not to Hans. Thus his plan for the ritual of leaving for war was pushed ahead four days. Yesterday his son Edden who was three inches taller and a pikemen went to the Church with three other young men and had his pike blessed. Hans spoke to the women last night, and today he would emphasize to Edden what he expected of him.

Edden was a good son. When, at five years old, he fell off the barn and broke his arm and was in great pain, Hans asked him, "What are the two things the Swiss never do?" Holding back tears the small boy said. "The Swiss never run from a battle and never cry."

This elicited the answer *good* from Hans. There were not many goods from Hans.

Today a cool crisp autumn morning, Hans looked with pride at his farm, twice the size, with twice the animals from the land his father gave him. His family assembled at the front gate and stood at attention. Halberdiers, older pikemen and younger pikemen would be here in ten minutes— at nine o'clock. The Swiss Infantry was never late.

Katrina the daughter had tied Edden's cow to the fence as instructed.

"Edden, how old were you when I gave you your cow?"

"I was seven father."

"So you have taken care of that animal for nine years?"

"Yes father."

"I want you to remember that when we meet the inferiors and thieves, they are coming to take your cow and our home so what are we going to do?"

"We are going to kill them Father?"

"Good." Hans said.

He turned and hugged his daughter. "Watch Bessie, she has not been feeling well." He brushed her hair for he loved her very much and she was a sensitive child.

Next his kissed his wife. "Mother I want you to kiss your son only once. I don't want the neighbors to think we spoil our children. Swiss mothers do not spoil their children."

She answered, "Yes, Hans."

Now he did something he had never done before. He kissed his son on the cheek and said, "Make you family proud of you."

Make your family proud of you, not one man in the Duke's Army would fight harder for all the gold in the world, then make your family proud of you.

The drums and fife were louder, they would be here in a moment. Hans looked at his sixteen year old son and remembered at field practice two months ago the boy had held his pike over his head for two hours when no other boy in the valley could hold it for more than an hour and half. He remembered the day Rolf told the men in the valley, the Austrians may cross the border to Switzerland, but none will return home. Hans and several other men told the Priest he must end every sermon with Rolf's words. Hans felt a tightness in his throat. One last look at his farm and his family. He was glad when he took his place in the line.

His neighbor Johann patted him on the shoulder as a sign of welcome and Hans' said, "Good. Many goods today."

As the older pikemen passed, his mother kissed Edden and handed him the dough with the chocolate on it that he loved so much. She kissed him a second time and whispered in his ear. "I love you my son, come home to me."

Edden like his father was glad when the young pikemen arrived and he joined his best friend Maxim as the last in the squad of eight.

Maxim was two inches taller at six foot three inches and possessed a great sense of humor. These young men took their charges seriously but they were also young.

Maxim said. "My father told me I had to protect our barn from the Austrians."

Edden. "My father said I had to protect my cow."

Maxim. "The Austrians don't want our cows and barns, they want our women."

Both boys laughed, but quickly stopped as the twenty-one year old squad leader with the powerful right fist glared at them.

CHAPTER 8

Two hours march from Hans and Edden, in the City of Lausanne on Lake Geneva, the clock maker Livius polished his sons cross-bow. Awake since dawn the wood shined to a fine brown finish, the winch checked and oiled and each shot bolt checked. It was a better weapon than the one Livius used against the Duke ten years ago. He folded the note inside the case to remind his son that war required a discipline as well as courage to stay alive.

The note stressed three things.

If your equipment gets wet, dry and oil it quickly.

Never draw the string of a cross-bow with one hand, it could pull the string out of line.

Never shoot with a string frayed or damaged.

The clockmaker/teacher wished his son had more discipline. He was a bright boy, but lazy. Karl had something most Swiss boys did not have – he had imagination and Livius suspected he would make a good soldier. At the Junior School he was a Leader and given the right circumstances, Karl would prove to his father he could lead. So Livius spoke to the Swiss officer about making Karl a runner. The Swiss stressed speed and a runner was critical in a fluid battle.

Rolf was very good at exploiting the enemies weaknesses.

He limped from his work bench. It was time to awaken his son who had come in late from drinking at the local tavern last night.

He shook his head. Karl drank too much and chased the girls. Livius also taught math at the local University and when Karl was asked to leave because he neglected his studies Livius thought of asking him to leave the apartment and find a job. The boy redeemed himself when under Livius's prodding he started a running program.

"A good cross-bow-man must have good legs." His father said. As a skirmisher in front of the Army you must be able to move quickly, especially if the Army is advancing and the Duke sends his knights after you!"

Livius was crippled ten years ago when an Austrian knight put a lance through his leg.

Karl accepted his fathers advice after a fake war game on the village green. His father said. "Karl be careful of the pikemen, especially the young boys. Many are just off the farms and they get crazy at the end of a battle." This happened when a young pikeman got Karl down. Even with a cotton covered blunted pike and Karl yelling for him to stop, the young man about fifteen, kept hitting Karl in the chest. Finally he stopped and helped Karl up and apologized. It was after that Karl started running each day to build up his legs.

Karl sat up and rolled his legs onto the floor. The wine gave him a headache. His father handed him a glass of water and said. "Two hours, you have to be on the green in two hours I have packed sandwiches for you, Gruyere cheese and a fine French ham. They were close enough to France to get their hams. This was Karl's favorite and he appreciated his fathers consideration. Sitting at the table drinking coffee, he thought of last night. He bought the one girl drinks, but she went home with a halberdier who was tall. Why did they all love the tall pikemen and halberdiers?"

For days his father lectured him about the Austrians, but now Karl listened with more concern.

Karl heard his father talk of Rolf many times and listened to the evaluation on the Leader.

"Rolf will hold you back in wet weather, when the string gets wet the thick gut bowstring is a problem. He'll use you in close, the weapon can penetrate a knights armor. He will use bow-men to shield the advances of the pikes and pull you out just before the attack."

Karl a cross-bow-man for only two years was an accurate shot not like the long bow-men who needed five or more years experience.

"Did we always fight this way father?"

"No, Rolf is the first one to use combinations, its all speed, he stirs up a battlefield. When we fought the Austrians Rolf was always ahead of the Duke."

Livius paused, then he said, "The Captain asked me about using you as a runner."

A look of disappointment crossed Karl's face. He wanted to shoot bolts.

"Karl, a runner is very important to Rolf, he shifts units very quickly. The runners take the orders, that's important to our speed.

You can run, I told the Captain you worked on your speed, you can learn a lot, do what the Captain tells you to do."

Karl changed the subject.

"Where is our Unit going Father?"

Livius produced a map. "The Duke last time advanced between Berne and Zurich by the Swiss Plateau. Its foggy up there and Rolf will use the fog to cover his movements."

Karl asked, "Do we always attack, father?"

"Yes, unless we are outnumbered by more than five to one, then we form a square. I was with the pikemen ten years ago, we held off ten times our number. The oldest unit in the Army, very tough, led by a kindly old tavern owner Peter Hugger."

Karl on the eve of battle suddenly wanted to know all about the enemy.

"Why do the Austrians want to invade us?"

"The Duke, he wants to tax us and the man is stupid, he can't even read or write. Rolf spoke at the University last spring he is an educated man, but he beat the Duke last time and he'll beat him again. He understands how to use crossbowmen."

Karl drank more coffee "Are we richer than the Austrians?"

The Father replied. "No, we actually have less farmland because of our mountains but we work harder and are more prosperous and because we're free, our people are more productive. Our animals are fatter and worth more. The Duke is greedy, he would rather conqueror than work. His Grandfather was the same way, cruel to some degree, but we should thank them, they made us great soldiers."

He said great with the usual confidence. The Swiss had no illusion about their prowess in war. When the Cantons marched they expected to win and quickly. Fighting the Austrians was like spring planting or raising a barn.

CHAPTER 9

The oldest unit in the Swiss Army was a unit of pikemen called the *Old Reliables*. They were oldest from standpoint of service and average age, but they were also the least disciplined of the Army. On the marches, they were always last because the two hundred man unit were the slowest marchers and most likely to forage — stealing chickens and stopping to buy wine. They rarely cheered Rolf and were more likely to trade quips with him and act like he was a younger brother. This bizarre relationship began with Rolf first engagement as leader. The *Old Reliables* stood for five hours against the French Cavalry charges and at the end of the day only twenty-five men were still on their feet. The French never broke them.

They were the only unit that Rolf would dismount from his horse and walk along side, listening to their advice as they called him Rolfe. Some of the fifty year olds even called him young Rolfie. This was not a sign of disrespect, for they voted for him to a man, and would thrash any man that would question his judgment. Their Captain was Peter Hugger, a tavern owner located near Berne.

Captains in the Swiss Army observed strict protocol and total obedience, but Peter Hugger was the perfect Captain for the *Old Reliables* since he ran the unit like a committee not a strict military unit. Ambling along, smoking his pipe at the end of the march he would say. "I see good water over there, why don't we bed down there. What do you fellows think?" Several of the veterans would agree or argue, and Peter would smoke his pipe contentedly and listen. Almost all decisions were consensus and the rest of the Army called them a debating society. The *Old Reliables* had a nickname for everyone, and Leopold - was Leo, or Leo, the Loser.

Indeed, the Army would say the *Old Reliables* were not really part of the Swiss Army and also admit that in any Army of brave men they were the bravest of the brave. That was established ten years ago when the Duke advanced two thousand of his knights against the two hundred *Old Reliables*. Odds of five to one were not unusual, but even Rolf was concerned when he saw ten to one.

It was the day Hugger earned his nickname *A Long Day*. As

the Dukes knights with banners and trumpets lined up to charge, the good defensive position water one side, cliffs on the other, Hugger slowly walked in front. "Leo is going to make it a long day. Take some water boys you might not get a chance later. It's going to be hot and a long day."

Puffing his pipe it looked like Peter was back at his tavern loading large tankards of ale rather than facing the cream of the Austrian Army.

As he walked in front, he heard the call. "How about an ale Peter?"

"Can't we have an ale?"

Looking up and smiling, he answered, "Do your work and I'll buy you an ale but work comes first."

After defeating five charges and suffering fifty casualties, during a lull at noon, Rolf asked Peter, "Could he hold?"

"Yes, Leo, making it a long day, but we're going to get our ale at the end of the day and Leo won't break us."

Rolf remembered that and rode on to a group of halberdiers who were under heavy pressure. Watching the fierce fight he leaned over to the Captain. "You can't let them separate you from the *Old Reliables,* it will open a gap."

The Captain who did not approve of the loose leadership of the *Old Reliables* yelled at his men.

"Hold! Hold! Don't let those old men outdo us." Minutes later the Captain led a counter attack that killed the Dukes second-in-command.

The one man the *Old Reliables* respected was Urst, for he was the only soldier in the Army that could fight with them. Urst had not smiled in two days since the death of his son Ulbrecht, and this concerned Rolf. He was the head, but Urst was the heart of the Army.

Walking along side Peter and listening to the usual advice, Rolf knew Urst would ride up in a few minutes.

A veteran said. "Going up to the Swiss Plateau, is it going to be foggy up there? Rolf, make sure the crossbowmen don't shot us by mistake."

Rolf acknowledge he had to be careful.

"We're walking too fast Rolfie." The *Old Reliables,* many had leg wounds that would open up after long marches. Peter looked at

Rolf as if to say I can't do anything with them.

"Leo might not show this time Rolfe," said a man Rolf recognized.

Rolf looked at the man. "He'll show, I sent word you men would Lead and he found out how old you were."

This brought laughter from the front row.

Now Urst was with them and Rolf said in a loud voice. "I have to ask you men to do more, some of the halberdiers want to be friends with the Duke."

Seeing Urst with them, the first three rows started to laugh.

A man called out. "We heard the halberdiers started a fight at the Ale House and killed a Count."

Rolf quickly responded, "No, the halberdiers were peacemakers, the Austrians started the fight."

This was so absurd, the whole unit started to laugh, with men in the front relaying the jokes to men in the rear.

A man called out to Urst. "You a peacemaker Urst?"

Urst with a broad grin answered. "Yes, the Austrian wanted to buy our chocolate and we argued about the price."

Peter, Urst, Rolf and the whole unit broke down in gales of laughter.

The last man of the unit was Stankey, sixty years and the only pikeman who carried a pike, less than eighteen feet — his was sixteen. Next to Rolf he said, "Urst wants to be friends with the Austrians?"

Rolf said. "No that's a joke."

Stankey mumbled. "You can't trust them. Tell Urst not to trust them." He stumbled along but Stankey would stand just as he had for forty years.

Urst joined Rolf who watched the columns leave them.

Rolf. "There are the best."

Urst. "For pikemen, very good."

Rolf. "One said to me the Plateau will be foggy, he is right, but if we time it right we'll be on top of them before they see us."

Urst. "I saw Hans this morning. Old Duck and Pull almost smiled. He is serious even for a Swiss. He has a fine big boy with the pikemen, the boy marches well."

Rolf understood that Urst was sad only one of his boys was

with them.

"Urst all the Swiss are with us this day."

Urst was himself again.

The tradition of the Swiss Army on the march was, they would see their Leaders. Rolf quietly sitting on his horse, the Captain of the crossbowmen, and always the Giant Urst.

The veterans would cheer Rolf, but the young men who had not fought before were silent, not allowed to cheer until they had seen action. A man who was not quiet was Urst. He would slide off his horse, talk to the squad leaders and joke with the troops. His jokes always seemed to center on the Duke, and because he found Maxim a quick wit he would start with him.

"Maxim, we're sending you and your friend," Edden's face turned red, "in first. You two don't shave yet so the Duke won't run away so fast if he sees you." This brought a loud laugh from the squad and Urst continued.

"No, if he sees you polite boys, he may stand and fight, but I wouldn't guarantee it. More laughter.

Next day. "Maxim we heard the Duke used women's clothing to run away last time. Now you won't kill the Duke if you see him in women's clothes?"

Maxim reacted. "Don't bet on it."

This brought a great laugh from the squad but none louder than Urst himself.

Hans and the halberdiers were quiet as they walked, but Urst rode up and they knew the jokes would start. Hans had great respect for Urst. He once saw the Giant pull a knight off his horse with his hands and Urst loved to tease the serious Hans.

"Hans, I saw your boy, he can march you taught him well."

Hans was ready, a joke was coming.

"He asked me how Old Duck and Pull was doing?" Even Hans smiled for everyone was aware his boy would not talk like that. Hans visited the boy that night to check on his feet, to see if he had the proper sox but did not repeat the joke.

#

George the Crazy Hermit stood on a broken tree stump and cursed at the Swiss Army as they marched by.

"Murderers!" he yelled.

"Talk to the Duke, he is a reasonable man."

He shook his fist at Peter Hugger and the first line of the *Old Reliables*.

Several of the old men cursed back at him but none threatened him with harm.

There were two reasons why he could stand for an hour and yell at the pikemen and the halberdiers as they marched by.

One he was considered a good luck charm. Before every battle he was seen cursing at the Swiss and they never lost a battle when Crazy George harassed them. So Urst and Rolf declared he was not to be touched. He was their lucky charm.

Two, Urst told the soldiers, Switzerland was a free country, and this man had the right to free speech especially since he was crazy. If he spoke like that to the Duke, he would be dead, but Urst sitting on his horse made sure no one would touch the old man.

"The Duke is not a bad man he would listen to reason?" Crazy George yelled.

Two *Old Reliables* drifting close to the tree stump spit tobacco juice on him. One caught the hand that held his staff and the other dripped brown juice down his torn and dirty cloak.

"Did you see that! Did you see that!" He yelled at Urst, who looked disapprovingly at the two soldiers who kept marching.

"Your men are dirty, they spit at me." He shook his fist at Urst who ignored him.

Now he was in real danger, for Stankey always the last man, and the only pikemen in the army with a sixteen foot pike moved closer to the Hermit.

If the *Realiables* broke the rules Stankey observed no rules and with a underhand toss, threw chicken bones into the face of George. Most missed but one sharp bone struck him just under the eye and he winced with pain.

"Take that you shit," yelled Stankey.

George did not respond even with Urst there, Stankey might hit him with a pike.

Urst. "Stankey."

Stankey turned. "You big fool, Urst protecting him, why don't you do something constructive. Go chase the Duke, don't protect the Hermit."

George pulling the bone out of his face, was silent.

Urst did respond. "I'm going to tell Hugger and you'll get no ale tonight."

Stankey spit. "You big fool, you tell Hugger and I'll come looking for you. I'm not afraid of you, I've fought bigger men than you."

Stankey now stood in the road ignoring the marching column that was twenty-five yards ahead of him.

Urst trying not too laugh, said. "Stankey, your always the last man in camp, I won't have to speak to Hugger, you'll be so late you'll miss the ale."

Stankey looked over his shoulder at the disappearing last line of the *Reliables*.

"I'm going to get you George and if that big halberdier is with you I'm going to get him too. Once the Duke is finished I'm going to get you both." He turned and hurried away.

Urst leaned over. "Are you alright?"

George winced. "The old fool, he almost got my eye."

Rolf rode up, not aware of what happened and said in a low voice, "Where are they?"

The Hermit stood up straight. "They had patrols on the river road, the Army I estimate will march tomorrow."

Rolf. "Did they scout the Plateau?"

George. "Not really, its so foggy up there you can't see your hand in front of your face, but the sun broke out at noon as it always does."

Urst. "Will the front groups reach the end of the lake by noon tomorrow?"

George. "Yes, the middle of his Army will be just half way when the sun breaks out, it will be perfect."

Rolf spoke to Urst. "We camp at the beginning of the Plateau tonight, no campfires and double the guard. We move at dawn and we catch them on the road at noon."

Urst agreed and rode off to give the orders.

Rolf noticed George's face was bleeding.

"What happened?"

"Some of them spit at me, but Stankey threw chicken bones and almost put out my eye. I'm your cousin, but this is getting too much, I want to attack tomorrow."

Rolf in a serious tone. "No, I have work for you. If we hurt them tomorrow, the natural place for the Duke to retreat to is the Sempach Valley. The Dwarf is heading there tonight, you scout Sempach and report back when you can."

George grumbled and watched Rolf ride off. "One of these days I'm going to punch Stankey out." He said.

George did not mind he was not marching with the Army because what he did was important. Only Urst, his cousin and Peter Hugger knew he was a spy. Last year, late at night he sat in Huggers back room drinking ale.

"Peter, why are we so much better then the Austrians or the French?" Hugger puffed on his pipe.

"George the enemy pays his soldiers or forces helpless peasants to fight us. We all grew up together, brothers, friends, neighbors, I knew the first name of every man in my unit. A man no matter how afraid can't leave his friends or brothers on the battlefield. Besides, he voted for your cousin. A man can't blame someone else when he votes for him."

Georged nodded. "And what about the *Reliables?*"

Peter smiled. "Experience. Remember five years ago when the Austrians conducted a raid and we destroyed them at the River? For two hours they attacked, after the last attack, my boys were calling 'they are tired let's counter-attack'? We did and not many went home that day." My boys didn't need to be told what to do but when we finished them the two front rows were yelling 'Switzerland, men who fight for money can't stop that.'"

CHAPTER 10

Rolf judged the Duke correctly. The Duke wanted very much to believe Pooser when told the Swiss Army was on the river road and that the Swiss Plateau was clear of the Swiss. He sent a reconnaissance to the Plateau who in the heavy fog could find no Swiss. The Austrians moved as fast as they could along the road. The Dukes precaution was weak, speed was the watch word, not caution.

Looking up at the fog, the Duke cursed. They could be up there and not be seen. When word came the head of his column reached the end of the lake, he felt better. The tail end of his column was two hours back. When his Army reached the half way point, two miles from the spot he picked to begin his ambush, he heard big logs and boulders beginning to roll down the hills. This coincided with the noon hour and suddenly the sun burned the fog off. The Swiss knowing the sun usually appeared at noon waited to begin the attack, and now thousands of their Army were on top of the hills.

The logs and boulders sent hundreds of the Dukes followers into the Lake, many hurt.

Out of the fog from the Swiss Plateau, halberdiers were descending in a large group attacking his flank knights. The Swiss Army moving at lightening speed were upon the Austrians, many of whom were not even ready with weapons, most carrying them on their back.

The Duke rode forward yelling for his knights to attack, but the steep hills favored men on foot. With no room to maneuver the knights were driven into the Lake. Quickly crossbowmen appeared and protected by the halberdiers, fired at the knights who took many casualties.

Beyond the knights he could see other Swiss attacking the front of his column. The Duke was about to ride forward to rally his men when he realized another attack behind him would descend on his largest group of Infantry.

The Duke watched his Army try to gather itself, then he heard the music — drums and fifes, he looked up. The Swiss were moving down the hill toward him at a fast pace, pikes held horizontally in both hands above their heads. Three groups in echelon, flags waving, the group on the right, fifty yards ahead of the group in the center. The five hundred men on the left fifty yards behind the group in the center.

Rolf on a horse behind the lead group could see his brave men would be on the Austrians in minutes.

Some of the Austrians stood paralyzed. The Austrians driven into the water were trying to decide if they could swim the Lake. Rolf saw two riders, their horses ankle deep in the water racing away to his right. They would try and bring the head of the column back to the center. He had timed the attack to meet the middle of the Austrian Infantry, and he watched as a group of riders under the Dukes flag, raced to the rear of the column. They also would try and rally the rear of the column. He smiled his men would destroy them piecemeal. This was perfect.

He heard Urst's distinct yell and the four ranks of his lead group leveled their pikes forward. They barreled into the Austrian soldiers like farmers trimming a field of wheat. One moment the black clad Austrians Infantry was standing and moments later they were gone. The center group of the Swiss routed six hundred Austrians driving many into the Lake where they were speared like fish.

Minutes before on the foggy crest of a hill the young pikemen assembled on the Swiss Plateau. They could see the halberdiers attacking knights below near the Lake.

Suddenly Rolf was with them. As the unit moved down the hill they were halted. Rolf pointed a sword at a large group of the Dukes Infantry.

"They have crossed our border, what do we do with men who have crossed our border?"

The unit as one yelled. "We don't let them go home."

A horn sounded and the young pikemen moved at quick step down the hill. The eighteen foot pikes were held shoulder high with a downward slant so the front rank projected twelve inch points. Behind the front rows the pikes were held upright by warriors who were ready to step forward.

The halberdiers had cleared out the knights and fifty yards from the Austrian Infantry the Swiss let out a loud cheer. Many of the Dukes Infantry turned and ran into the Lake. Those that stood were run down and killed.

In this section several minutes ago the Duke had several hundred men, now none were upright and crossbowmen were shooting at unarmed men waist deep in the water. The Swiss took no prisoners and it was over quickly with two casualties on the Swiss side — one a man who tripped and sprained his ankle. Immediately the squad leaders re-formed the young pikemen. They executed a right turn and attacked the knights and Infantry from the front column of the Dukes Army. The Duke had his melee, but it was not four or five to one, instead pikemen and halberdiers routed the Austrians driving them back along the road, a confused frightened mass of fugitives trying to escape. The pikemen were halted and halberdiers kept the pressure on. Edden thought he saw his father in the front of the column.

The Austrian knights gathered with the Infantry on the road. The Lake was on their right, and the hills on the left. Once again the pikemen charged and shattered the formation. Halberdiers moved forward, and like a well oiled clock, the Swiss kept driving the Austrians towards the end of the Lake.

At the end of the Lake, the Swiss were attacking large companies of Austrians, just at the spot the Duke planned his ambush. The Swiss were outnumbered, but the speed and shock of the attack stunned the Austrians who could see men ahead and behind them, wielding pikes and halberds. Once again Rolf was mixing his Army. Instead of leading, the crossbowmen were on the slopes of the hill and a steady stream of bolts confused the Austrians especially the knights.

Rolf seeing this going well turned back towards the center of the column.

The Austrians knowing they must halt this rolling onslaught tried to re-form but the pikemen charged again.

Edden was out of breath, but he was ready to charge. Maxim was also out of breath, and too excited to make a joke. "Edden we go again."

The Squad Leader was yelling. With all the noise they couldn't hear him, so they followed his hand signals.

The Duke looked wildly about. It was a route, and most of his Infantry were throwing their weapons away and running for their life. Both the Infantry and knights were pushed into the Lake. The Swiss working with machine like precision broke any Austrian defense and small knots of men trying to resist were brushed aside and killed.

The Duke had to stop this, the Swiss might roll up much of his Army strung out behind him. He saw Peter Schaeffer, one of his best knights.

"Peter form a defense at this spot, I'll get help, we have to stop the Swiss."

Schaeffer. "Yes, this is the spot." It was twenty yards from the Lake to a rock ledge, a natural barrier for Mache and himself to stop or slow the pikemen.

The Duke rode off yelling for men to form up. He took his sword and hit a man on the head who was running away.

"Form up! Form up!" He yelled at four who stopped and turned to face the dreaded enemy.

The Duke, waving his sword was seen by two knights who began yelling. *"Form up! Form up!"* Slowly the knights and Infantry gathered one hundred yards behind Schaeffer and Mache, who were confronted by two Swiss. The older Swiss attacked Schaeffer with his halberd and Mache faced a confident young man who seeing the smaller knight expected to pull him out of his saddle easily. The halberdier thrust his weapon at Mache whose quick left hand grabbed the shaft and held on. The Swiss surprised, attempted to turn the weapon and use the blade to stab the knight.

Mache let go. The Swiss had leverage, while on the horse Mache could never control the halberd. Driving his left foot into the stirrup he swung his right leg over the rear of the horse. He did a three hundred and sixty degree turn, vaulted and landed on all fours next to his horse and at a right angle to the Swiss. Never had the halberdier faced a quicker opponent and slow to turn he went down as Mache's sword thrust tore at his knee. Mache scrambled to his feet and chopped at the man's neck killing him.

Mache stood up and looked for Peter Schaeffer who was down and being stabbed by the Lake. Mache knew he couldn't help. Now a column of Swiss were gathering to attack the Dukes rear guard. Mache mounted his horse and slowly rode back to the Dukes lines. He rode around the line who were bracing for the Swiss, moving quickly towards them.

Mache's mind was racing, this was the way to defeat them, grab the halberd, get off the horse and get underneath the halberd or pike. Attack from below. He could see the Duke fifty yards behind the rear guard and Mache rode over to tell him, when the Swiss column scattered the Dukes rear guard. The Duke quickly made a judgment.

Retreat! Retreat!" He yelled, and he and Mache rode away from the battle waving for all Austrians to retreat.

The Captain of the crossbowmen was using Karl as a runner. He knew the boys father a clock maker and teacher from Lausanne. The boy was quick and decisive in his command and could run fast.

As the rock slide engulfed the Austrians the Captain ordered Karl. "Go to my two Lieutenants, tell them pikemen and halberdiers will be attacking on the right. They are to proceed, each man fires two bolts then moves to the left quickly, protect the left flank of the attack. If the Austrians come up the hill, or if they see no Austrians, they are to harass the Dukes men either forming up or retreating, but move left, we need to keep driving the soldiers.

This order was obeyed by the crossbowmen. Two shots each man and then they formed on the left as the attack started.

The Captain watched the successful attack of the pikemen and turned to check his crossbowmen. They were standing still, no Austrians were coming up the hill. Then he could see why, the Lieutenant on the far left was down and hurt. The second group did not want to cross or entangle themselves with the first group.

The Captain spurred his horse, but before he got there he heard Karl yelling, *"Move left, fire on the Austrians!"*

The Duke's troops were preparing a counter attack, but Karl grabbing one of the Junior Officers began forcing the men to move down and fire. Now the second group were firing on the Duke's men.

The Duke's men were retreating, but with Karl yelling under the name of the Captain the crossbowmen kept contact and kept harassing the knights just as the orders were given.

The 2nd Lieutenant saw the Captain. "Is this what you want?"

"Yes, keep driving them."

The Lieutenant directed his men and the missile attack upset the Austrians.

Now a small group of the Austrian began to flank the crossbowmen, but Karl formed ten men at an angle and drove them away. The Captain decided this man would be an officer.

Now Rolf rode up. "Who was that young man waving his arms and yelling?"

The Captain. "That is Karl, son of the watchmaker and a teacher at Lausanne. My Lieutenant was hurt, but he obeyed orders and got the men moving."

Rolf. "Yes, he was very good. The men were stalled and they followed him and broke up a counter attack, excellent work. I know his father, I met him at the University."

Both men were pleased, an Army full of brave men but every Army needed men who could lead at a critical instant.

The Captain said, "I'm going to make him an officer."

Rolf's horse turned behind the Captain's horse, and he said, "Good idea, a plan is forming in my mind. Talk to him and you both come to my tent tonight."

#

The Dukes Army beat a quick retreat. Half were gone, but they would never cross the Swiss border again.

#

Karl was surprised when he was made an Acting Lieutenant and told to report to Rolf's tent. The Captain and Rolf were waiting for him.

Rolf. "Good work young man, now we have another job for you."

"After the beating the Duke took today, he has to fight again and quickly or his Army will fade away, desert."

The Captain. "You don't think he will leave with his Army and attack Berne?"

"No, he has to beat us here."

Rolf turned to Karl. "The Captain and I have a plan. He will pick fifty men, quick firing men and you will lead them and train them for two days. I expect to meet the Austrians here in three days."

He circled the map. "This is the formation I expect."

Karl looked at the Captain.

"If this happens and they line up this way the Captain will show you your position, your five lines of ten men each. He will order your attack, it will be close, ten yards at the most. Your first lines fires, the next line ready. Speed, move quickly like you did at the Lake today. If a man is killed or wounded pull him out of your line. It is not important that you keep ten men in a line, if one line has five men keep going, we want a volley every ten seconds."

"Push, pull do it anyway you want, but keep moving. First make a crack, when the Captain sees the break in the Austrian line he will order you to move left or right. The center of our line will be a wagon fort, so if you turn left it will be towards the wagon fort and they roll up the Austrian line."

"No matter how many men you have push hard, speed. When you formed an angle today that was a good judgment, you didn't let the Austrians flank you, but this move is all about attacking. Don't worry about your flank. pikemen will follow you into the crack, they will support you and if the opportunity presents they will turn opposite from the way you turn, and attack the Austrians from the other direction. However, some pikemen will follow you, but you must lead, we must have a missile attack."

Karl listening thought about today, and how when the Lieutenant was injured the first group did not move."

He asked a question. "And if the Captain is hurt or I can't hear him, which side do I turn?"

It was an excellent question, Rolf understood he picked the right man.

"If Austrians are facing you, they are forming a defense, turn to the side where the enemy is facing our troops so you are shooting at their blind side."

The Captain. "Karl instruct each of your men they must keep moving. No one must stop if a cross-bow is damaged get the man out of the line. Wounded, pushed aside, but push the enemy."

Karl understood his orders.

#

The war had gone so well, the Duke was beaten. The Gods of War changed the dynamics on the second day against the Swiss.

In a light drizzle Rolf sent one hundred crossbowmen and four hundred pikemen to probe the Dukes left flank. He believed the fog enshrouding the Swiss Plateau would give them cover if they ran into trouble.

In the fog the two groups missed each other and now the crossbowmen descended in a valley without fog, their strings wet, and alone without the support so necessary to be moving in enemy country.

The head of the crossbowmen was Tona Parklet, a man that hated the Austrians who humiliated him and his village when he was a young boy. The Austrian head of the village had placed his family crest on a pole, and forced the people of the town to bow to the pole. As a young boy, he saw his father beaten one day when he didn't. He vowed to destroy the Austrians.

When Parklet missed the pikemen he should have retreated, but his hatred for the Austrians drove him on. The Dukes scouts saw the unescorted Swiss and within an hour five hundred knights cut off the crossbowmen from the safety of the fog shrouded plateau.

The Swiss formed a square but with wet strings the outcome was never in doubt. Fighting with knifes and swords only two Swiss escaped, and reported back to Rolf.

Of Rolf's six Captains, two reacted with great pain to the defeat, one understandably was the Leader of the crossbowmen. Rolf was disturbed when the man in charge of the supply was so distraught, he almost collapsed. Rolf spoke to him.

"Gillen, you must pull yourself together, we fight a great battle this week, we mourn the loss of our friends, but many other Swiss depend on us."

Gillen. "They took no prisoners."

Rolf said. "Neither do we, this is to the finish."

Gillen still looked sad.

Rolf. "We have no time for this, except we fight the Duke in two days and this is what you will do. Bring your wagon to the end of the Lake. Strip the covers off them and I'll place crossbowmen in the wagons. I expect to meet the Duke in the Sempach Valley.

"You bring your wagons to the center of that plain and tie them together. Your men will be in reserve of the crossbowmen."

Gillen. "So, it's a wagon fort for defense?"

Rolf drew circles. "I expect all of the Duke's knights on the wings. You will face dismounted knights and some Infantry."

Rolf dismissed Gillen and spoke to Urst. "The Duke will dismount his knights and form a long line with spears. They intend to face us man to man. The Dwarf went behind their lines two days ago. They have wagons of spears and he saw them practicing. He'll meet us on the Plain."

Urst. "What will you do?"

Rolf. "At some point we have to break that line. Most of your halberdiers will be on the wing to keep them from circling and attacking our rear. I want you with fifty halberdiers to open a hole. Young Karl follows with crossbowmen and I bring the pikemen in. If we break the line we will win the battle."

#

The day before the final battle both sides sent out reconnaissance. Mache Rouchmelle led out a group of three and Urst with two others. Both groups met in a wooded glen. The Austrians, attacking from an ambush, killed the two Swiss, but lost three. Urst faced Mache.

Mache had never met a man as tall as the Giant. He stood quietly trying to decide how to attack. Urst was surprised the man did not run away and started to laugh. Mache faked and skipped away when the Giant leveled his halberd. Urst recognized a very quick opponent, his footwork dazzling. Usually Urst would attack a man alone, but he thrust his halberd and watched as Mache quickly parried.

Urst said in French. "Fast hands?"

Mache understood the Giant. "Fast enough to kill you Swiss shit."

Urst stepped back. "French you understand?" Normally Urst would taunt such an opponent resting his halberd on the ground, but being older, he would not underestimate this opponent. They circled with Urst probing his long reach easily dominating the encounter. Mache faked left and with broad sword, slashed at Urst falling far short.

Urst noticed he was quicker to the left, a fake or some wound.

Now they circled to the right. Mache trying moves, but if he gained a small advantage the Giant displayed excellent footwork. His long reach not only with the halberds but his long arms. For three minutes they circled, Urst breathing hard gave Mache confidence. He parried, and going to his knees, slashed at Urst's legs. Urst jumped to one side, made his first real thrust, the sharp point of the halberds passed over Mache's shoulder. Suddenly, Urst twisted the weapon and the hook caught the smaller man under his armor and Urst yanked him off his feet. Mache twisted in mid air, landed on his back, dropped his sword but rolled away and picked up a ball and chain from a dead man. Urst was astonished the man got away, never had he faced an opponent so quick and maneuverable. "This one is a killer." He muttered.

Now Mache swung the ball over his head. Urst recognized the man might throw it and stepped back to decide what to do.

Mache undaunted, moved forward not realizing he was bleeding from the shoulder. Mache rapidly loosing his temper faked left and sprung right to swing the ball. Urst understood this was a man who always attacked and was stronger to his left. He did not parry, but thrust his sharp point into the knights right foot. Urst decided his great speed to the left came from the right foot being planted, so he stabbed the foot and hit it. Mache screamed in pain, his right knee on the ground, but before he could use the ball and chain the Giant slashed the sharp edge of the blade and tore it out of his hand. Urst had used the hook, the blade and the point, and had scored three telling blows to Mache, who was wounded in the foot, hand and shoulder.

Like a wounded animal Mache on one knee drew a knife. Still treating his opponent as dangerous Urst stepped back to catch his breath.

Mache in French said, "If you were more a knight, you would let me get a weapon."

Slowly Urst circled, seeing if Mache could turn. Mache slowly used his hands to turn his body but was painfully slow.

Urst. "Like a tournament?"

Urst stepped back a good ten feet and rested on his halberd still trying to catch his breath. Urst was about to relax when he realized this was a man skilled in all weapons, he was probably good at throwing a knife. Instantly he was alert and assumed his stance.

"You fight for pay, I fight for my friends."

Mache cursed at him. "You know what the Duke thinks of you? He calls you sub-humans."

Urst circled again watching if Mache could turn the other way.

"It doesn't matter what the Duke thinks, he'll be dead by tomorrow night."

Mache frothing at the mouth said. "He has new tactics, your women and children will be dead next week."

Both men were taunting each other trying to gain an advantage. Urst marveled at the crippled knight, down but not conceding. Clearly not afraid of death, a man who had sent many others to the beyond.

"Tell about the new tactics and I'll let you live."

Mache faked throwing the knife. Urst ducked.

Mache. "I'll put down the knife, you put down the halberd. We will see who is the better man."

Urst still alert. "I know who is the better man, its just a question how long you live."

Mache faked throwing the knife and Urst noted he was off balance. The throw would not be strong.

Quickly Urst rejected that thought. This was the most dangerous man he ever faced, never, never, underestimate him.

Urst circled again, skipped and was behind Mache who he stabbed in the back. Mache fell forward and was breathing hard, his knife lying on the ground. Urst using his point pushed the knife away. Mache with super human quickness turned and almost pulled the halberd out of Urst's hands. The Giant held on to the halberd and Mache once more tried to pull it away from him.

Mache cursed at the Giant Urst in French. "You don't go easy Sir Knight," said Urst.

Mache, dying took no comfort in the fact that with every juncture the older man would not relax and consider him beaten. It was not Urst's weapon, but the attitude that won the battle. This was not a tournament or a game. He realized the knight would never explain the Dukes new tactics, and Rolf understood, anyhow. He must return to Rolf. He yanked the halberd out of Mache's hands and ended the contest with his point.

#

George the Hermit crept through the Swiss lines and entered Rolf's tent just as the sun was dying. He drank a coffee and explained what he had seen.

"They intend to fight just as you thought. They're dismounted. I was with a camp follower, she told me they are drinking heavily. The knights want to fight but what Infantry he has left is scared."

Rolf continued to listen as George said, "They'll line up across the Sempach. They outnumbered us three to one."

Rolf stood up. "When they were on horseback we could funnel them, the odds don't matter today only who ever breaks the line first wins!"

George. "Its strange the whole Army keeps talking about the Germans, they think the Germans are as good as we are."

"Where will the Germans be?" asked Rolf.

"In the center, the Duke plans to break us and the Germans will exploit the break through and circle behind us."

Rolf walked across the tent. "That is what I would do, use the Germans to exploit a breakthrough and use his Infantry at the end when we are tired."

George asked, "What do you plan to do?"

"We have to break them first, I want you to tell me where the Germans are. We gamble, all just before they are about to deliver the final blow."

George had never seen him so serious." Your worried?"

"No, we win tomorrow or we kill so many of them they can't take Switzerland. Old men, young boys and reserves will protect our country, but the Duke and what's left of his Army will have to go home, even if we all die he still can't win."

Rolf handed George a pike. "All Swiss fight tomorrow. Switzerland needs every man."

George had never realized until that moment how much his cousin loved his country.

"I always wanted to fight, but can I help in any other way?"

"Yes, you stay with me, tell me where the Germans are. I guess the Duke will use them against our center, the wagon fort is our weakest position. I have a picked group to break their line. Urst with halberdiers, you and I with pikemen and the son of the watch maker from Lausanne with the crossbowmen."

"He's a boy, I know his father," Said George.

Rolf smiled. "He has drive, you should have seen him two days ago on the Lake, pulling men, driving them. We have an Army of brave men, but every Army needs a spark, men who will lead other men. Urst is that kind of man, and I believe this boy is that kind of man."

George. "I think the wagon fort is your weakest position, it looks strong.

"You have no reserves, no depth, its looks strong but its not." Rolf. "The Germans are important, and he'll use them at the end, but they fight for profit, if we start to win they'll leave."

CHAPTER 11

The third day after the battle at the Lake, the Austrians and the Swiss met at the Sempach Valley. Rolf expected the Austrians to be dismounted and watched as the Duke's men - five thousand knights and his best Infantry lined up across the Valley floor. Behind them he could see another two thousand men in reserve and some knights on horseback planning to attack his wings. Rolf moved his wagons to the Austrian center. With the wagons loaded with crossbowmen he was outnumbered in men at the center, but not fire power. The Swiss Army had a total of twenty-five hundred men.

The Duke, with a picked group of knights took a position to the left of the center. As they closed with the Swiss he raised his arm, retainers holding the knights' horses sent them racing away. The Black flag of Habsburgs some twenty yards behind the advancing knights who were holding spears. The symbolic gesture of the Duke announced the knights would not leave the battle. It was a fight to the finish.

Urst was caustic, "The Duke is not going to run this time."

Rolf. "The overlap is not a problem, we will refuse the wings. They won't get around us, but the spears could delay our breaking that line and the longer we fight, the more their numbers are an advantage. If it goes past three hours our men will be tired and their reserves may commit and the melee they desperately want may happen."

Rolf's horse moved closer to Urst.

Rolf. "At some point you and your halberdiers must break the line followed by Karl and his crossbowmen and pikemen."

Urst. "Where?"

"The Duke is on our right, I think he is covering up his weakest men. We attack on the right. Lets probe one hundred yards to the right of the Black flag.

The Battle began with great shouts and pikemen and Spearmen against each other. On the wings, knights tried to circle the Swiss Army, but halberdiers held them off. Neither side had ever been in a more fierce fight.

The Austrian spears were as long as the Swiss pikes. The

battle in the center, missile against shield and sword. The shields allowing the Austrians to get close to the fort. On either side the Swiss with their long pikes and great discipline fought off the greater numbers, but the knights with more armor and inspired by the Duke held their own.

After thirty minutes, both sides fell back exhausted. A pause and they clashed again. Now it was more parry and thrust, small groups and individuals ignoring the dead and wounded on the ground.

The Duke was wounded, with a cut on his face stood with twenty knights at the center of the battle. His Black flag twenty yards behind him, the symbol of the Habsburgs.

He was gaining confidence, they had withstood the Swiss charge, he had some reserves. The battle was exhausting, but if he could hold another hour against the Swiss, then they could win. His number decisive.

To his left the Duke seeing Rolf had halberdiers behind the line set up a reserve of two hundred of his Infantry.

The halberdiers twice tried to break the Austrians line. The pikemen would part and Urst led his men on a rush to break the Austrian knights, but it didn't work. The crossbowmen waiting were pushed aside by the pikemen who resumed the front line.

Rolf, riding behind the line could see Swiss by the wagon fort pushed back. They made a might effort and gained the original line, but looked tired. Many halberdiers were down at the end of the right line. Hans was on his knees as a knight with a ball and chain hit his leg and he couldn't stand. Most of the halberdiers were down, they couldn't hold more than a few minutes.

Edden was exhausted, Maxim went down a half hour ago and Edden lost sight of him as the two lines surged back and forth.

Now Rolf heard the Austrian Infantry cheering. They were seeing the Swiss tiring and expected to be brought into the battle quickly. Rolf for a moment, almost dismounted to lead the halberdiers. He knew he had little time left. He must break the line quickly or lose the battle.

Urst bleeding from wounds grabbed Rolf's saddle.

"Get the crossbowmen ready I'm going to break them."

Rolf started to ask if the Giant intended to lead another charge. He could see the Giants eyes, he waved to Karl and yelled. "Get your men ready."

He grabbed Urst's hand, shook it and Urst turned away. Now Rolf signaled the pikemen. "After the crossbowmen we charge, no one stops, keep them away from the crossbowmen."

Urst pushed two Swiss to their knees took a running start, vaulted off the men's back, over his pikemen and crashed into the surprised Austrians holding spears. He pulled the spear out of one mans hand and with his free arm clubbed another. A small crack, but Urst made it larger he speared a man, dropped his spear, and tackled two more rolling into another man, knocking him down, and now a gap. Urst had five Austrians down.

Rolf yelled. "*OPEN.*"

The pikemen stepped aside for the bow-men.

"Now Karl."

Five lines of crossbowmen advanced, ten men to a line. Karl yelled, "*FIRE!*" The front line of crossbowmen fired, several Austrians were hit.

"*ADVANCE!*" Karl's second line fired driving a pocket into the Austrians. They tried to fill in the pocket but the third line of arrows drove them back.

Rolf saw Urst go down, but he was too far away to help. Urst on hands and knees continued to drag more Austrians to the ground. A knight drove a spear into his back, but the Giant grabbed the mans leg and pulled him down. The pocket was twenty yards wide with Urst at the apex a swirling stabbing mass.

The fourth and fifth line of bolts drove the pocket deeper. One side of the wall was collapsing and the knights with their backs to the Swiss were trying to escape.

"*LEFT!*" Yelled Rolf.

Karl pulling three men to his left held his first line. The others trailing fired, destroyed all cohesion of the enemies defense. Now a deep salient was driven into the Austrians.

The crossbowmen losing their lines moved forward and sent the Austrians back, and were shooting at men ten feet way who did not see them until it was too late, began rolling up the Austrian defense.

Rolf waved. "pikemen."

The pikemen overwhelmed the Austrian reserves and more

and more Austrians were dropping their weapons and running to the rear.

Karl took this pause to reform. He had four lines of crossbowmen, several of his men were down but now with precision they moved towards the center and the wagon fort. pikemen secured their flank.

The Duke dropped out of the line bleeding from his cheek. The Swiss and his knights were tiring. Now to send in his Infantry, his knights were about to break on top of the wagon fort the hub of the Swiss defense. Mounting his horse he could see on the far left many of his knights dismounted and attacking a small knot of Swiss. One man fighting on his knees.

Suddenly he was aware of Swiss crossbowmen moving towards the center fifty yards away, firing bolts at point blank range, destroying his line. The pikemen behind them had created a bulge and some Austrians were running. He had to stop this. He should have gone back and gotten Infantry to plug the hole, but if the line kept collapsing it would reach the German knights on his right and they might bolt. The Duke believed the Germans were his best if they were winning, but worried the Germans didn't believe in his crusade.

The Duke jumped off the horse, motioning the men carrying the flag to follow and charged towards the advancing Swiss. Karl's crossbowmen were mixed, half were dead, or injured, stepping over bodies, the remainder were not a line but a group again trying to remain on their feet. Some were down to two bolts. Karl was hoarse from yelling. Then he saw the Black flag advancing.

He tapped one of his men on the shoulder who put a bolt through the flag carriers neck. The Duke felt the staff brush his shoulder as it fell. He leaned over to pick it up. One of the pikemen stabbed him, pinning the Duke to the ground. A veteran pikeman came up recognized the Duke and killed him. He yelled. *"The Duke is dead! The Duke is dead!"*

Four Austrians behind the Duke seeing the Duke on the ground and the pikemen yelling, turned and started to run.

More Swiss were yelling, *"The Duke is dead!"*

#

The German knights battling hard were attacking. Tired they drove the Swiss line back behind the wagon fort and the Austrians to their right were mounting the wagon fort. They were winning.

Suddenly the German Leader saw the Habsburg Flag go down. He paused, Austrians on his left were being attacked by pikemen and some crossbowmen. He heard a yell, and he stopped.

"The Duke is dead! The Duke is dead!"

It was louder, men yelling, the Swiss attacking from the side. Several of his men were watching him, he yelled. *"RETREAT!"*

Edden was fighting just to the right of the wagon fort. Suddenly the Germans stopped and began to run away. His Captain saw Swiss to his right and the Austrians mounting the wagons. He formed a line and swept the Austrians forming to climb into the wagons. This left some on the wagon, but a group dropped their spears and began to run.

The yells, *"The Duke is dead!"* were louder. Rolf couldn't hear the yells, all he could see on his left were, Austrians running or retreating.

But to his right both lines were still fighting. He jumped off his horse, grabbed a pike and was next to Peter Hugger and a group of *Old Reliables.* They formed up and Rolf yelled. *"SWITZERLAND."* The men began driving Austrians from the side to the cry of *SWITZERLAND"* that was growing stronger, and now the Austrians were melting away. If the Duke was alive he would have rallied the Infantry, but seeing the knights all along the line fleeing, the Infantry reserves started running.

Rolf, yelling, *"SWITZERLAND!"* kept rolling the Austrian line up. Peter Hugger drove his pike into a knight, who fell down. Peter, right behind Rolf, yelled *"SWITZERLAND!"*

Both men saw a halberdier on his knees fighting knights and both men drove pikes into the Austrian.

Suddenly there were no more Austrians. Rolf turned to look back to the center and as far as he could see Austrians were running, being pursued by halberdiers and pikemen. He saw Swiss crossbowmen on horses pursuing the enemy.

He looked down, Old Duck and Pull was trying to get up. Peter Hugger helped him up. "Hans you alright?"

Hans was exhausted, but surprised to be alive and seeing Rolf couldn't speak. Rolf patted him on the back and turned to find Urst.

#

The only men in the Dukes Army who knew where their horses were, were the German knights. They left ten men to hold the horses and they also defended the animals from men who tried to steal them. By leaving early almost two hundred Germans of the two fifty escaped.

The Germans did not feel they abandoned the Army, but with the Duke dead, their obligations were fulfilled and like a business decision it was time to leave.

The English knights tried to form a rearguard and were all killed.

The Swiss capturing horses started a pursuit. Many battles of this time saw the greatest killing when one Army tried to leave the field and by night fall less than two thousand of the Dukes Army were still fleeing. The final number to reach the border at the end of the pursuit was less than a thousand.

#

They found Urst, with six Austrians around him, all dead. Rolf knelt down and whispered, "You kept your word….." He spoke. "I'm going to miss you friend, the jokes, our walks. With the Army we promised each other we would finish the Duke. We did."

He started to choke. "I'm not going to cry, but tonight I'll visit our friends around the fires, the Swiss Army is quiet tonight, but when we walk home, you go with us. I'm going to tell the story of Urst to the young men in the future…….." He choked. He couldn't go on. A tear ran down his cheek.

"The Swiss don't cry!" He said. He wiped the tear from his cheek.

"On the way home pikemen, halberdiers, crossbowmen, the new man Karl, who was good today Urst, very good. He'll be with your wagon."

He stood up. "I go to tell our friends, the *Old Reliables,* they will be with you. I promise the *Old Reliables* will be with you…..the two old ones who always teased you and, the one with the white beard who called me young Rolfie, and the one who always said you were to tall to be a good halberdier man. I saw Hans, he was fighting them on his knees."

Rolf walked away, he couldn't go on.

That night Rolf moved from camp fire to camp fire many, of the old veterans were missing. The men exhausted asked him if the rumors were true about Urst. He touched men, and shook hands.

"The Army has lost its heart."

He explained how Urst broke the Austrian lines. The usually stoic Swiss Army shed tears, several men not able to face Rolf.

Rolf repeated a line he was to use all night.

"Friends we know this man, if he was here he would have said we saved our homes. He would tell jokes. You remember his jokes? I asked him to break the Austrian line, he did that, I asked you to stand against the knights and for the last three days you did that. When you go home tell the story of Urst. Let your children and your grand-children understand what we have is paid for in full. If they ever come back again, we will tell our new men about the men we lost. Freedom is not free."

At the campfires of the *Old Reliables,* Peter Hugger lifted an ale. "To Urst."

Many responded. "To Urst."

After a long night Rolf returned to his tent. He felt empty, but not alone. The Giant would always be with him. Most Swiss would be buried at Sempach, but Urst would go home with them.

\#

They found a horse for Hans to ride since he couldn't walk. Edden helped bury Maxim and led the horse with his farther riding. Neither spoke as they left Sempach the last battleground against the Austrians. No one buried the Duke or the other visitors.

Rolf on his horse was the last one to leave Sempach, his most difficult battle. He had lost Urst and his cousin and many others, but it would be a long time, if ever that a foreign Army would invade again. He rode along side his Army calling out names and patting men on the back.

"Well done Fritz."

"Cross-bow-men a good stand."

"Young pikemen you earned our respect."

There were no jokes about the Duke and Rolf never mentioned his name again. The Austrians who returned home and the foreign knights still alive felt fortunate and most vowed never to fight the Swiss again.

\#

With the Swiss Army returning home the group about to drop

off always marched at the end of the column. When it came time for Hans and Edden to leave, Rolf approached them. Hans tried to dismount to show his respect.

Rolf's strong hand held him on the horse. "You look good up there Hans, maybe I'll make you a knight next time." All three laughed.

Now Rolf turned serious. "Hans we lost a great man in Urst, we all need to do more. I want you to take more responsibility when you return to the Valley. I want you to teach the young men your famous Duck and Pull, will you do that?"

Hans in a whisper said, "I will."

Now Rolf turned to Edden. "You're a fine pikemen, if I need you again I know you won't fail me."

Rolf's people skills were never better. A great soldier, but a better motivator.

Finally he shook Hans's hand. "I plan to visit the Valley in two months. I'll send you a letter and we will have dinner."

Hans was quiet for an hour, then he said to his son. "We will have to clean just before he visits."

Edden spoke up. "Father our house is always clean, we will just have to have mother's famous beef pie."

Edden leading the horse looked back at his father. This was not the boy of two weeks ago. This man was a Swiss pikemen.

Hans understood. "Your right and I think we should start our day at six like everyone else does, five is too early, your mother works hard enough."

Edden looked straight ahead and smiled. "Good!"

#

The Italian City-States found out about the defeat and in several, the bells tolled for the loss. Gillani and Medici met and agreed their political and economic feud was over. Great events were to over take them.

CHAPTER 12

The Christian Military and economic powers of the Mediterranean were shocked when in 1389 the Turks destroyed the Serbs on the Battlefield of Kossovo. The Serbs a highly respected Military power was destroyed completely and this spread terror to Leaders in the Balkans and surrounding lands.

The Pope called for a Holy War and German and French knights prepared to drive the invaders from Europe.

The Italian City-States not wanting to participate called a meeting to discuss what they would do. Not interested in increasing pressure on themselves to support the Pope, they said the meeting was to complete the evaluation of the Dukes defeat at Sempach.

The large Italian City-States had fared far better than expected financially. They divided the Dukes collateral and both Venice and Florence expecting the venture was risky laid off large parts of the loans to smaller cities. Gillani of Venice and Giovanni Medici of Florence met to complete the final study and they summoned Gamilla who was second-in-command to the Duke to report. With a greater threat the City-States completely forgot their rivalry.

Gamilla was surprised when he was told that the two Bankers wanted an in depth report. Both of the Bankers agreed that a study of the Habsburg past would help them decline future courses of action in regards to that part of the world.

Gamilla took his charge seriously and explained his Grandfather was the first of his family to serve the Habsburgs.

In 1308, the Leader of the Habsburg was Albert, who was described as kindly, intelligent and loved, but was murdered by forces that wanted control of the family and to rule the country. After Albert was killed the Dukes Grandfather began to destroy the conspirators who had grievance over the land. The revenge including killing the innocent members of the opponents family.

Thus it was the Dukes Grandfather who ruled, and was very cruel indeed. He would sit on his throne and watch his enemies beheaded. Hundreds died this way and his wrath grew greater as the power of the Swiss grew and he became old and frustrated. It was widely assumed he had the Dukes father and older brother killed so that the Duke would rule as ruthless as the Grandfather.

Medici grew impatient. "Tell us about the war?"

Gamilla sat quietly for a moment.

"Rolf the Swiss Leader clearly was better than the Duke. We started with an ambush at the Lake. We were supposed to destroy them, but instead they came out of the fog of the Swiss Plateau. We lost almost half of our troops mostly Infantry, but also an excellent knight, Peter Schaeffer. I was riding up and Schaeffer and another knight Rouchmelle tried to hold the Swiss. Rouchmelle was French and he performed the most amazing feat of the whole war. I saw him face a Swiss Halberdier. He grabbed the weapon, held it for a moment vaulted off his horse, did a full turn and landed on all fours. He came up under the Swiss soldier and stabbed him. I have never seen anything like that."

Gillani was amused. "You don't see many knights jump off their horses, where did he come from?"

"Just before the war started Schaeffer hired him and he rode with Peter, There was talk he was very fast and a bit crazy."

Gillani. "What happened to him?"

"Just before the last battle he disappeared. I think the Swiss must have killed him."

Now Gamilla resumed his narrative.

"Before I talk about the final battle I believe the Duke made several mistakes. I contacted a Swiss spy and got their marching plans. It was the day Magglie was killed."

Giovanni and Medici did not react to the death of Magglie.

"The Duke should not have sent Magglie to the meeting, and next he made an even greater mistake. We destroyed towns and hung peasants and this cost us the services of a great knight, William Thomas. Thomas was the most respected man in our Army, and when he left morale sagged.

Giovanni. "Could one man make a difference?"

"Thomas took religious vows and when he refused to follow the Duke, many knights were concerned and I think began to have second thoughts about the venture. This was especially true of the German knights, who always seemed to have reservations about the Duke. The Germans were important, very professional, great soldiers. The Duke placed them close to the Swiss middle, the plan was once the wagon fort was taken they were to storm past the middle and attack the Swiss from the rear. Instead, when the battle turned, they left. Perhaps they heard the Duke was dead."

Giovanni. "I would never hire the Germans. Instead I would hire the Swiss."

Medici. "The Germans were excellent in the Holy Land, they even sent someone to talk to the Duke before they joined. Could it be the ambush at the Lake convinced them the Duke could not beat the Swiss?"

Gamilla responded. "The Germans were at the rear of the column they didn't even see the Swiss that day."

Medici asked. "If the Germans were so good why were they at the rear, wouldn't you want them up front when the ambush started?"

Gamilla. "I spoke to the Duke about that, he liked to save his best for last when the enemy was tired, bring in your best.

"This was the plan at Sempach, they were to end the battle."

"What happened at Sempach?" Asked Giovanni.

Gamilla. "The original plan was to ambush the Swiss near the Lake, but if the Swiss didn't lose there or we couldn't find them, the final battle we would be dismounted, fight them on the ground. Use our numbers more effectively. Rolf must have suspected we didn't think we could beat him on horseback. His decision to set up the wagon forts in the middle was very clever. It occupied a lot of ground, made for a wide center and our numbers were not as effective at the forts."

"The Duke fought in the front line, that was good, but his weakest troops were with him on our left and that is where Rolf attacked all day. I am told they broke our line with a man who vaulted into the line and was quickly followed with crossbowmen. Of course once the Duke was killed the battle was over. I was on the right and from where I was I could see we were winning in the center, and suddenly men were running back and the Swiss were yelling "the Duke is dead." We all retreated and for two days they charged us, the Swiss do not take prisoners. I had two horses killed but I walked out. I don't intend to fight the Swiss again."

After he left Giovani said to Medici. "Gamilla is a good soldier, and he is right, the Swiss are the best soldiers in Europe. We talked to Rolf, they don't want to be mercenaries, but the Cantons will make the rewards so great they won't be able to refuse."

Medici. "The Turks winning at Kossova shows they are a great danger to us. They will try and expand into our side of the Mediterranean. We must use the Swiss to stop them."

Giovanni. "The Swiss are our best, but they are a small country. The numbers will never be large enough to halt the Turks. The Pope begins with the French and Germans, but I think in the long run it is Spain that must stop the Turks."

Medici. "The Swiss will be dominant until science overcomes them. The Turks and Spanish are working on gun powder. Guns will eventually overcome even the courage of the Swiss.

Medici was correct. The Swiss would be the greatest Army in Europe until gun powder would eclipse them.

The Austrians never understood that free men demonstrating speed, courage and endurance created a free Switzerland. The Austrian house like a weed sprouted again and did not die until after World War I, but they did not outlive free Switzerland.

THE END

Author Biography

Arthur Rhodes, a former bond syndication manager and thirty year senior executive in Wall Street, continues his life-long interest in military history with a series of books about World War II and the Cold War. Not content to mirror history, he tries to keep alive the warriors of the greatest generation. We have fictional heroes with real battlefields, Guadalcanal, Midway, Lexington and modern jets with World War II weapons. It is a blend of nostalgia and what-if history.

Currently, Arthur Rhodes is working on a book about the attack of the Spanish Armada on England.

Books by Arthur Rhodes

On the INTERNET at
http://3mpub.com/rhodes/

𝕿𝖍𝖊 𝕷𝖆𝖘𝖙 𝕽𝖊𝖎𝖈𝖍

America 1960: After nearly ten years under the control of the Nazi regime, the United States is suffering through a period of severe economic depression and spiritual despair. However, as the oppressed citizens plod through their grim lives, there is a whisper of hope. The underground movement — a dauntless network of American patriots working tirelessly against the German forces that occupy the country — is preparing to make another major strike against the hated Blackshirts. The weapons are different at the second Battle of Lexington, but the courage is the same as two hundred years ago.

The Last Reich is a riveting thriller that imagines a stark dystopia created by Hitler's success inn his campaign to dominate the world. In this ingeniously conceived post-World War II fantasy, the balance of power is about to shift again. While insurgence escalates to open warfare in the United States, Germany is also contending with internal conflicts and civil war. As a ravening Reich Chancellor desperately grasps to maintain Germany's authority, the American Army, the legacy of the land of the free, strikes with unprecedented speed and power in the climactic battle.

The Return of the Rising Sun

Endless War

The year is 1964. The Second Battle of Guadalcanal rages in the South Pacific as the United States makes a bold attempt to free ten thousand Allied prisoners who have been languishing in Japanese prisoner-of-war camps since the disastrous defeat of 1950. Surely a modern navy, equipped with giant aircraft carriers and flying the latest jets, will prove more than a match for the undefeated Japanese Imperial Fleet.

It is a time of change. Germany has finally been defeated after decades of war. The Russians are expanding into Eastern Europe while the Japanese Secret Police wage a relentless unconventional war against America from the Pacific to Central America. Drug dealers are among their most lethal weapons ...

Return of the Rising Sun is the second book in Arthur Rhodes' Alternative History of the Second World War. Come read how things might have gone differently.

Invasion England 1917

A timeless mystery. The home fleet destroyed at Scapa Flow, Scotland.

The Germans poised to invade England, and evidence points to one of the five most important men in England as a Traitor.

The King asks an American Naval Officer Gibbon Stillwell to find the Traitor. There is conflict on the German side. Prince Rupprecht who defeats the French is the architect of the Scapa victory. The Kaisers jealous aides plot to eliminate Rupprecht. The Battles rage from the Atlantic to the trenches of France. Will the Kaiser win World War I?

The Swiss Pikemen

The Swiss Pikemen is the alternate history of the actual invasion of Switzerland by the Austrians in the year 1386. Will the Swiss prove they are the greatest soldiers in Europe and defeat the much larger Army of Austrian Knights? The men of Switzerland defending their homes have a military moral weapon......Freedom.

The Red Menace

Against the backdrop of the Korean War, the FBI pursues the Nazi underground in America. There is a mighty fight in the Politburo for control of Russia. The FBI closes in on Nazi and Russian fugitives.

The third book in Arthur Rhodes's alternate history of World War II continues where its action-packed predecessors left off.

The Derby Day Murder Mystery

The murder of the most famous child in America triggers an official response. The President sends the FBI's most famous team to investigate. Unique in style, they are as ruthless as the criminals they pursue.